An Unfinished Marriage

An Unfinished Marriage

A NOVEL

CINDY BONNER

DECK NIGHT PRESS

© 2024 by Cindy Bonner

All rights reserved. No part of this book may be reproduced or transmitted in any form or by any means, electronic of mechanical, including photocopying, recording, or by any information storage and retrieval system, without permission in writing from the copyright owner.

Design by Betty Martinez

Author Photograph by Lisa Richard

With thanks to Lauren Humphries-Brooks and Duncan Murrell for your careful editing.

This is a work of fiction. All names, characters, places, and incidents are either products of the author's imagination or are used fictitiously. No reference to any real person is intended or should be inferred.

Library of Congress Control Number: 2024912491

ISBN 979-8-9859225-7-8 (Hardcover)

ISBN 979-8-9859225-9-2 (Paperback)

ISBN 979-8-9859225-8-5 (ePub)

First Edition, October 2024

Also by Cindy Bonner

LILY
LOOKING AFTER LILY
THE PASSION OF DELLIE O'BARR
RIGHT FROM WRONG
FOR LOVE AND GLORY

Prologue

OCTOBER 26, 1988

When Adam comes home, I'm downstairs in my nightgown. For the past four hours, I have paced from window to window, watching the driveway. He called at six, said he had to take a client to the airport. Said he'd be home in a couple of hours. A couple equals two, right? It's now half past midnight.

When the headlights on his Jeep flicker through the bathroom window, I dash through the kitchen and upstairs for bed. I dive beneath the covers and shut my eyes. Silently, I plead with my lungs to regulate and not give me away. I don't want him to know I've waited up. He'll say I'm hovering too much, smothering him. He'll say he doesn't need another mother, that the one he has is quite enough.

I've left his supper in the oven on low. Probably he'll see the oven light and eat before he comes upstairs. By then, if I try hard enough, I might be able to will myself to sleep. I wedge my arm beneath my pillow and tell my body to relax.

The back door opens and closes. I hear it clearly and feel the slight shudder through our old house. In another moment his feet hit the stairs, each step creaking as he climbs. Either he missed the oven light or ate somewhere else. God, let him be sober I pray, then tell myself it doesn't matter. He's home. That's the important thing.

He comes straight into the bedroom as if he senses me pretending to be asleep. He touches my hip, his hand warm through the quilt. "Sarah?" He gives me an easy shake. I lift my head. His figure is a silhouette in the light from the hallway. "Are you awake? Please get up."

I rise from the pillow. Something in his tone makes me forget to act sleepy. It's that word *please.* It sounds so formal, so foreign, so un-Adam-like. "What is it?"

"Can we talk?"

"Talk? What time is it?" I ask, as if I don't know, as if I haven't been watching the clock for the past four hours.

"Come downstairs, please."

There it is again. That *please.* My stomach tightens.

I follow him out of the dark bedroom and into the hall. The doors to both boys' rooms are closed. They've been asleep for hours. School day tomorrow.

We descend the stairs in a line, me behind Adam, matching my steps to his. I feel like Marie Antoinette being led to the guillotine. My brain scans through possibilities: The client's flight was delayed, or maybe the plane crashed. Ridiculous—that would have made the news. He's been in an accident. No, he's home and unscathed, walking right in front of me. Light from the window on the landing catches the blond whirl at the back of his head. Could it be something's happened to his parents? Mine are still on vacation in Europe, so it would have to be his. Adam's dad, Oliver, has a bad heart.

Once we're down in the den, Adam switches on the lamp beside the couch. The room smells like the new varnish and wallpaper paste from the recent remodel, all mixed together with the complicated, musty, hundred-year-old-house smell.

He waves me over to the couch, then begins to pace in front of me, the same steps I've taken for several hours. His stride is uneven, listing to one side and then the other. So he *has* been drinking. His tie is missing, his collar open and wrinkled. His hair looks wet.

The leather couch against my back feels cold. It causes an involuntary shiver. "Why is your hair wet?" I ask, breaking the silence. "Where have you been? Adam?" I soften my tone. I don't want to sound confrontational.

He stops pacing, gives me a strange, piercing look. "With Carolyn."

"Carolyn?" My voice is thick. Carolyn Jeffrey is my best friend. She lives in west Austin, in a new apartment complex halfway between Adam's office and the airport. But until this second I didn't realize he even knew that. "You were at her place?" Why hadn't she called me? "What's going on, Adam? What do you want to talk to me about?"

He puts his hands on his hips. His face is tight, mouth pale at the edges. He keeps his eyes on the floor, the rug under his feet. I look where he's staring and see nothing but his brown tasseled loafers.

"I don't think I love you anymore, Sarah . . . I mean, I just don't feel like I love you—"

"What do you mean you don't *feel* like it?"

"I don't want to sound cold, I really don't. But I don't know how else to say it. I'm not in love with you anymore. I'm just not. I feel like we're friends, or . . . I don't know . . . roommates."

"You do too love me, you know you do." I move to the edge of the couch. I feel hollowed out suddenly.

He hurries to sit down beside me, takes my hand. His thumb presses my knuckles. "That's not how I meant to say it. I do love you, I'm just not *in* love with you anymore. I feel like we've lost that . . . like we're just living together. Like brother and sister. Or like—"

"Roommates. I heard you." I pull my hand away from his. "I think we've just hit a lull. We've talked about this, remember? We both said it's normal for good marriages to have hills and valleys.

We said that. *You* said that. Well, I think we're just in a valley. That's all."

His eyes are Paul Newman blue. I've always loved the color of his eyes. They waver away from me. A single tear slips down his cheek. I resent that tear. I'm the one who gets to cry right now. I haven't just told him I don't love him. But I sit there dry-eyed, numb.

"This is more than just a lull," he says finally. "I don't want to argue, Sarah. Please, let's don't argue. Carolyn said I should come tell you before I left."

My mouth goes dry. "What do you mean before you left?"

"I wasn't planning to do this tonight. I thought I would just check into a hotel and call you tomorrow. But Carolyn said—"

"Carolyn said what? She told you to leave me?"

"No, you're not listening to me. You never listen. *She* made me come home and tell you before I just walked out."

"She *made* you?"

"Christ, Sarah, I'm trying to do this the right way, OK?"

"You mean you're leaving now? This minute?"

"I just came home to get some of my things." He stands up. I grab hold of his arm. I want to pull him back down on the couch beside me. I only manage to make him bend a little sideways.

"Don't go, Adam. Not tonight. It's late and you've been drin—" I stop myself, quickly course correct. "You're tired. We're both tired."

"Drinking? You were about to say *drinking*." He flicks my hand away. "You think I'm drunk and don't know what I'm saying?"

"No—listen, Adam . . ." I stand, too. I don't want to make him angry. Not right now. "It's late. We're both tired. Let's talk about this in the morning."

"Nothing will be any different in the morning. This isn't going away."

"You can't leave like this. Not so abruptly like this. Let's talk tomorrow. I want to understand, I really do, Adam. Please. Think about the boys. What will they think if they wake up in the morning, and you're gone? Just like that. Without a word."

I hold my eyes wide and unblinking, until the air stings them, and finally, *finally*—they start to water. Two tears drip off my bottom lashes and slide down my cheeks. Adam has never been able to withstand tears. He's softhearted that way. When he sees my tears his own eyes well up again. I reach my arms around him, press my cheek against his chest. I hear the familiar thud of his heartbeat. His hand ventures up to pat my shoulder.

HE DOESN'T LEAVE. In fact, he doesn't go anywhere for four days—not to work, not outside. Neither of us do. We sit in the den or at the dining table, while the boys are at school, and we talk—and talk and talk—until we both feel crazy.

He has needs, he says, needs I'm not providing. I want to throw up. *Needs?* I've given him children, a home, a life. What more could he possibly *need* from me? But I don't say any of it out loud. I'm afraid to provoke him into leaving—not just me but two children and fifteen years of an unfinished marriage. I don't think I could make it on my own. I wouldn't know where to start living without him.

At one point I ask, "Is this about Carolyn? Are you having an affair?"

He gives me a disgusted look. "Jesus, Sarah."

I sit quiet; try to listen. He feels trapped. I don't understand him. I pay more attention to the boys than I do to him. He wishes I'd put on a dress once in a while, wear heels, comb my hair a different way, get a manicure, be somebody who isn't me. At the end of those four days, when school lets out for the weekend and the boys are home all day, we stop talking. I feel drained, stripped to bare bone, ugly and undesirable. At times during these long, too long, conversations, and during those first days afterward, I wish I had just let him go.

Gradually, without any resolutions, promises, or apologies, we drift back into our old routines, except maybe there's more politeness, more caution. There's definitely a new distance. I work hard at smoothing things over, like spackling a hole in a wall. But we aren't newlyweds anymore, and quietly I wonder if marriage is supposed to be this difficult. And if this is just another lull, a valley, can we drag it back up the hill again?

Sarah

One

For the first time in recent memory, we're having Thanksgiving dinner alone, just the four of us. Adam's parents, Maureen and Oliver, are in Kansas City with Adam's younger brother and his family. My parents are in Europe for four months, celebrating Dad's retirement. It's nice to plan my own Thanksgiving menu for a change, bake my own pies, baste my own turkey. Cody, our youngest, helps me cook. He's eight and can finally read my handwriting on the recipe cards. He likes punching down the bread dough after it has risen, and now I watch his little boy hands squeeze the lump of dough that will eventually become molasses bread.

I'm grateful for the two ovens in our newly renovated kitchen. Our house is a Queen Anne Victorian, circa 1892. We've been here four years and it's still a work in progress. We haven't gone into debt for it. Adam waits until we have enough to pay in full for the work that's done. The next project is the upper balcony. The floor needs to be replaced and the porch columns need repair, upstairs and down. After that, Adam has plans for a swimming pool—by next summer, he promises.

Joel, our oldest, is upstairs, most likely with his stereo headphones wrapped around his ears. He's fourteen and deep in the throes of adolescent moodiness. Adam's in the den on the phone with his partner, Marty Dean, planning tomorrow's hunting trip. They're also talking business. I hear snippets of their conversation—something about McCabe and Company—some big deal they're putting together.

"Bradley Harper's parents are getting their Christmas tree this weekend." Cody continues to knead the bread dough, gritting his teeth. "They're going to a place where they grow wild, chop one down and bring it home to decorate."

I crumble cornbread into a bowl for the stuffing. "A Christmas tree farm?"

"I guess so. He wants me to go with them if it's OK with you."

A Christmas tree farm is not exactly growing wild but I don't correct him. "It's OK with me. But maybe you should ask your dad."

"He'll just say to come ask you."

That's probably true. I move behind Cody and take the bread dough from him before he kneads the life out of it. "We need to divide this into two pieces, now, so we'll have two loaves of bread. Once they're in the pans, you can brush them with butter." I reach into a cabinet for two loaf pans.

He stands back, rubbing his doughy hands together. "I could chop down our Christmas tree, too, while I'm there. If you want me to."

"Do that over the sink, Cody, you're making a mess." I guide him to the sink where he continues to rub dough balls off his hands. I flip up the lever on the faucet. "Here. Try a little soap and water." I fuzzle the blond hair on his head. "You know we usually buy our tree from the Boys Optimist. That way the money goes to a good cause. To boys who aren't as lucky as you and Joel." I poke at his nose. He swipes my hand away.

"Well, this year couldn't we chop one down anyway? Just this once?" He rolls the soap in his hands under the faucet. "Mister Harper said he's gonna show me and Bradley how to swing an axe. He said every boy ought to learn how to swing an axe because you just never know."

"Never know what?"

Cody shakes water off his hands, shrugs. "How to chop stuff down like Christmas trees."

"That's something you think you'll be doing a lot of in life?" I turn off the faucet and hand him a cup towel to dry his hands, then steer him back to the cook island. A bowl of melted butter sits ready to brush onto the two soon-to-be loaves of molasses bread.

"I don't know. Maybe," he says, as he picks up the butter brush.

I watch him drip butter all over the counter. "Brush it on evenly, honey."

I hear Adam's footsteps come from the den, and in a second he appears in the kitchen doorway. He stops to take us in, then goes to the window on the back door and moves the curtain aside. A norther has blown in and the windowpane shakes. The windows in this house operate with weights and pulleys so they're gappy and rattle like maracas.

"If it's all the same to you," Adam says, without turning toward me, "Marty and I thought we'd go on up to the deer lease today instead of tomorrow."

"Dad?" Cody keeps brushing butter on the bread dough. "Can I chop down our Christmas tree this year?"

Outside the window the pecan tree whips around in the wind, flinging brown leaves and nuts like bullets against the house. Adam doesn't answer Cody. He continues to stare out the window. "With this front blowing in, the deer will move early tomorrow."

"Can I go with you?" Cody drops the basting brush in the bowl of melted butter. "I want to target shoot again. Can I go?"

"Not this time, son." Adam lets the curtain fall back over the window.

To Cody I say, "I thought you wanted to chop down Christmas trees." I laugh and give his shoulder a little shake.

Adam gives me a pointed look. "You're avoiding me."

"No, I'm not. How could I? You're standing right there."

"I asked you a question."

The smile leaves my face. "You didn't. You said this norther will make hunting better, or something like that."

"Something like that," he repeats, his voice condescending. He folds his arms. "So? Is it OK with you if I go early?" He sounds exasperated, like he's asking permission and resenting it.

"Now? Before dinner?"

"I'll wait till after."

"Will you drive, or will Marty?" I don't know what this has to do with anything. I'm stalling. It's Thanksgiving and I want Adam to stay home today—maybe play board games with the boys later, or all of us watch a football game together. Be a family.

"I thought I would drive. Why?" he says. "Do you need the Jeep for something?"

I shrug, pick up the basting brush to finish the job Cody has abandoned. "Carolyn mentioned going to an antique auction tomorrow. I haven't seen her in ages—" My car's small, the Jeep has more hauling room in the back. Adam knows what I'm getting at. "I just won't buy anything."

Cody cuts in, "Why can't I go with you, Dad."

Adam eyes me as he moves from the window. We're circling each other again, lions after the same prey. We've been doing a lot of that lately. "I guess I could ride with Marty if you need the Jeep."

"I don't know if I'll need it or not. I might not find anything anyway."

"*Dad*," Cody complains. "You haven't taken me hunting this whole year—"

"You can't go," Adam snaps. "Now shut up and let me talk to your mother."

Cody clamps his lips together and looks hurt. I give him a pat on his back. "Why don't you go upstairs and find something to do, sweetie. We've got to let this bread bake for a while anyway. I'll call you when it's ready."

Cody sulks out of the kitchen and pounds up the stairs. He likes to be in the middle of everything, unlike Joel, who lately avoids the rest of the family as if we're contagious. I go back to brushing butter on the unbaked loaves of bread.

"He needs to learn not to interrupt." Adam leans against the counter with his arms still folded. It's such a defensive poster and it irritates me. "Just say if you don't want me to go, Sarah."

I slide the two loaves into the bottom oven, then check the top oven where the turkey roasts. "I thought it would be nice for us to have this day together. The four of us. Since we're alone without the grandparents this year."

"So you *do* mind if I go."

I close the oven, set the timer, reach to adjust the apron around my neck. I haven't even bathed yet this morning, or combed my hair. I've been too busy in the kitchen. I imagine what Adam sees—a harried, thirty-six-year-old housewife without makeup, hair wadded in a scrunchie. "I didn't say I minded."

"You didn't *say* anything. That's why I'm asking you, one more time: do you mind if I go to the lease today instead of tomorrow A simple answer, yes or no, is all that's required."

It isn't as easy as that. And anyway, I don't understand why he can't read between the lines. If he were at all tuned in to me, he would know what *it would be nice to have this day together* means. If he were at all tuned into our family he would want to be here with us on Thanksgiving, and the question would never come up.

I go back to mixing cornbread stuffing, giving him one sideways glance. "Do whatever makes you happy."

He breaks an edge of crust off the pecan pie cooling on the counter, puts it into his mouth. He doesn't speak, just chews softly, staring at me. I can feel his eyes. After a few moments of this silence, he exits the kitchen. I keep mixing, adding sage, thyme, savory leaves. I hear him on the phone again:

"Yeah? Marty? Yeah . . . can we take your car? Sarah needs the Jeep. Yeah, she's got a shopping date with a friend. OK . . . I'll be ready by five."

I'M NOT USED to a clutch and shifting gears, and there's a lot of it involved getting the Jeep through the steep hills on the way to Redbridge. Carolyn reads the brochure about the antique auction, running her finger down the list of items.

"Oh, there's a mermaid lamp." She says this with eagerness. She reads, "*Metal mermaid holding a nautilus lamp.* Oh my god, I wish they had a picture of it."

"I'm suspicious when they don't publish a picture. It probably needs rewiring or something." I steer into the parking lot of a convenience store and park in front of the pay phone on the outside wall. "I want to check on the boys real quick."

Joel's old enough to be left in charge of Cody for a couple of hours, or at least that's what I tell myself, but I'm still adjusting to the idea. As soon as I park Carolyn hops down from the passenger's seat.

"I'll go get us something to drink." She heads into the store.

It's cold and we're wearing nearly identical velour jogging suits, hair pulled back in similar jaw clips, but that's where the resemblance ends. Carolyn is four years younger than me, single, gorgeous, confident. She has long, thick hair the most peculiar combination of brown and natural platinum. I've been racking my brain for eight years trying to think of some single man good enough for her. I haven't seen her in a few weeks and I wonder if she's dating.

Through the store windows, I watch her smile and flirt with the clerk behind the counter, and realize I've missed her company. The store clerk is more of a boy than a man, but Carolyn has his full attention. I pick up the pay phone on the wall outside. The quarter I drop in falls with a chink. Wind blows into the earpiece. Joel answers on the third ring.

"Yes, Mom." He sounds bored—and a little too cute, guessing right away who's calling.

"Is everything all right there?"

"You haven't been gone twenty minutes. Give me some credit." His voice is changing. It cracks halfway through his words.

"OK. Sorry I called. We'll be home in a couple of hours. There's leftover turkey for sandwiches. Mayo's in the fridge, and mustard, cheese. You know where the bread is."

"I know where everything is. I live here, remember?"

"Well, pardon me," I say, with a frown. "I'll be home soon. Love you."

He mumbles something barely discernible—a choked "Love you, too," I think. Anyway, it's what I want to believe he said.

I hang up as Carolyn comes out of the store with two glass bottles of fruit juice. I had hoped for hot coffee or cocoa, but Carolyn recently converted to a healthier diet, and says coffee has *ugly bad* caffeine so I should have known better.

We met when we worked at Balcor Electronics together. That was right after Cody was born. I had just come back to work again after maternity leave, and there she was, a newbie in the computer room. Sometimes people just click, and that was us. We laughed at the same jokes, liked the same music, and had the same opinions about a few of the others who worked at Balcor.

Adam and Marty had just teamed up and left Waterton-Pierce Financial to strike out on their own. Glasser Dean Investments took a few years to provide a living, so I stayed on with Balcor until we bought our Queen Anne. I wanted to get the boys out of Austin, and Adam wanted me to quit work to be a full-time wife and mom. He said he always hated how his mother worked full time. He felt like he'd missed something because of it. He said he wanted an old-fashioned family—who knows what he wants now. Anyway, even though I left work, and even though we moved to this bedroom community thirty minutes from Austin, Carolyn has remained my closest friend.

We find the auction by following the other cars. The only

reason anybody goes to Redbridge is for antiques. The auction is in an old warehouse building with benches lined up in the center of the room. Along the walls are the items up for auction: barrister cases, tables and chairs, pitchers and bowls, crystal, and a hall tree with an etched-glass mirror that I immediately covet.

"That would look gorgeous in your house," Carolyn says, as we both admire the hall tree. She reads the attached tag. "It says it's *carved English Walnut with fluted columns and Corinthian capitals.* Whatever that means."

"It means exquisite." I laugh. "But will it fit in the Jeep?"

"Adam won't like this?" She turns the starting bid price tag toward me: *$1,800.*

I lift my eyebrows. "Let's keep looking."

We find the mermaid lamp, which Carolyn says she absolutely must have. "Look, her tail wraps around this piece of—what do you think this is supposed to be?" She touches the stem of the lamp that has been handled so much it's grooved and shiny in the middle. "Is that driftwood?"

I laugh, shake my head. She laughs, too. "Whatever it's supposed to be, it looks kind of nasty."

"I want it." She hugs the lamp to her body, but puts it back on the table when she catches the dirty look from one of the women workers.

By the time we finish admiring all the items, the only two seats left together are in the back row. A woman with a lace collar on her dress hands us a list of suggested opening bids.

"They take plastic." Carolyn points to the Visa/Mastercard logo at the bottom of the sheet.

The auctioneer steps up to the podium. The buzz in the room stops. He's solemn and stiff in his black tie and Stetson, as he explains that the items on the block come from a large estate and are valued at twice what's listed on our sheets.

Carolyn lifts her eyebrows at me and gives me a look. "Wonder if he's single?" I remember she has a thing for cowboy types.

When the program starts, the auctioneer's chant comes all of a sudden at a breakneck, tongue-twisting speed. It gives me the giggles. I try to suppress it but I can't. When the bidding starts, the auctioneer's cadence gets even faster and more chaotic. I burst out in open laughter. Carolyn looks at me, confused, but she catches on and starts to laugh, too. Before long we're both covering our mouths, tears running. It's uncalled-for yet uncontrollable, and it's the sort of thing that has endeared us to each other. Since we're thankfully on the last row, we sneak out of the auction barn without causing too much commotion—empty-handed, of course. Outside on the walkway, we catch our breath. Laugh a little more. Catch our breath again.

"What was *that* all about?" I say, when I can speak.

"You started it." Her mascara has run circles around her eyes. She looks like a raccoon.

"I couldn't help it." I swipe my eyes. "And I really wanted that hall tree."

"I wanted that nasty lamp," she says, still smiling. "And I planned to go up to that cute auctioneer when it was over, see if he was worth some attention."

When we get in the Jeep and she paws through her purse for tissue. She flips down the visor mirror, starts rubbing at the mascara smudged under her eyes.

"Can you just imagine him in bed." She changes her voice to resemble the auctioneer's cadence. "One little rub, now two, two, will you give me two? Now can I get three—"

I burst into a new fit of laughter. "Stop!"

WHEN WE PULL into the driveway, Cody's in the yard wrestling with Snowball, the big Persian cat who lives with us periodically during the year. He disappears sometimes for so long we think he must cheat on us with another family in the neighborhood. We had him fixed so we know he's not tomcatting. Anyway, he has been missing for several days but I'm not surprised to see him now. He always comes with the first norther because we let him sleep inside.

Cody has brown leaves stuck on his sweatshirt and in his blond hair. An angry red cat-scratch runs down the side of his cheek. He's grinning and out of breath.

"Who won?" Carolyn calls out as we exit the Jeep.

"Snowball always wins," Cody answers. "He has switchblades!"

I inspect the scratch on his face. "We better put something on that."

Snowball beats us all to the back door. He purrs so loud, we hear him over the television in the den. As we step inside the kitchen, Carolyn looks up at the tongue-and-groove ceiling twelve feet overhead. "I can't get over how good it looks in here. Like it was always supposed to be just this way. When do you start on the outside?"

"Adam's got someone coming next week to give us a bid."

I take Cody into the bathroom to wash the scratch. While we're in there, Joel comes from the den with Snowball in his arms. Joel's dark hair is rumpled and unkempt. He has Adam's sleepy blue eyes. He's tall for fourteen. When Carolyn hugs him, the cat leaps down. Joel has a big crush on Carolyn so he hugs her back. There's nobody else Joel willingly hugs, not even his grandparents.

"How many girls have you got following you around school?" Carolyn says.

"None." He gives an embarrassed smile, adds, "At the moment."

"At the moment, huh?" Carolyn gives me a look. "He sounds like Adam."

Joel almost blushes, then with the usual bored tone he uses with me, "Dad called. He shot a ten-point." Joel stands there, letting Carolyn's arm rest on his shoulder. He keeps his arm around her waist, clearly enjoying himself. "He said he would call back later."

"Ugh!" Carolyn grimaces. "How can you let him shoot Bambi, Sarah?"

Cody squirms out of my grasp and takes off running past his brother like he thinks I'll try to chase him and doctor him again.

"You smell good," Joel tells Carolyn, then he turns to head back to the den and the television.

"Such a charmer," she says, making a comical face.

"I'm starved. Are you?" When Carolyn nods, I take leftover turkey out of the fridge. There's an avocado, too, for sandwiches on homemade bread. That should pass Carolyn's health food test.

"How's it going these days?" Her voice takes on a more serious tone. It's subtle but I hear it. I give her a glance.

She's fingering Granny Mabrey's teapot, an heirloom passed down to me on my dad's side of the family. It sits on a shelf inside my antique bread-safe. But I know the teapot isn't what she's referring to. We haven't mentioned the night Adam went to her apartment, not even in passing. The subject is too sensitive, and since she doesn't make eye contact, I think she must know how I feel.

I slice the turkey sandwiches diagonally in half on two salad plates, and slide hers across the cook island. "Are you asking about me? Or Adam?"

She gives a tentative shrug. "You can say it's none of my business."

"But he made it your business, didn't he?"

"I thought you might want to talk about it." The seed falls out of the avocado and she starts slicing.

"I don't need to talk. Maybe Adam does. Ask him." As soon as I've said it I realize how catty my voice sounds. "I'm sorry, I just—"

"I should have called you," she says, quickly.

"Yes, you should have. Why didn't you?"

"I didn't know what to do. It was so late." She searches my face. "He just showed up, Sarah. I mean I literally looked through the peephole and there he was. I was like—my God, Adam? Here? I didn't even know he knew where I lived."

"Neither did I."

"He'd been drinking. A lot. And he just passed right out on my couch—"

"It's fine," I interrupt. I don't want to hear anymore. I screw the caps back on the mustard and mayo and return them to the fridge.

"I'm so relieved you're not angry with me, Sarah." She picks up her sandwich. I close the fridge and watch her bite into her sandwich.

I force another smile; each one a little harder to fake. "How long was he there?"

She puts her hand over her mouth, finishes chewing. "Maybe an hour. I don't know, a tad longer. He said he needed to talk to somebody. I told him that should be you. I really did, Sarah. He was pretty wasted."

"So he didn't actually *just* pass right out on your couch." I push my sandwich plate away. My appetite is gone. "About once every other year we have one of these big dramas." I try to sound nonchalant. "It clears the air, I guess. Sorry you got dragged into it."

"You're my friend, Sarah, you know I love you. But Adam's my friend, too. I don't want to take sides."

"Of course not, and I don't want you to."

Despite the cold creeping into the house, my neck feels sweaty. I watch her eat and try to think of something else to talk about, something lighter, something not about Adam and that night. I wipe off the countertop, even though it doesn't need wiping.

"That's all that happened?" I ask, and hate myself for it. "The two of you just talked—before he fell asleep on your couch?"

"Passed out," she corrects. The sandwich in her hand stops halfway to her mouth as she realizes what I'm asking. She lays it down on the plate. "Sarah, are you serious? You think I would—"

"Forget it. I'm sorry. You know how I dwell on things. If you say nothing happened then I believe nothing did. Adam said the same thing." I feel my eyes well up. I hate this so much, having somebody, even Carolyn, know something so personal about my marriage, about me, that I don't trust my husband, or my best friend.

She moves around the end of the island and reaches for me. "Oh honey . . ." She puts both arms around me and squeezes me tight. I squeeze her back, but I'm uncomfortable with her pity or whatever this hug means. I sway out of her grasp.

"What we need is a glass of wine." I reach for the fridge. "There's a bottle we didn't open from yesterday. Adam left without drinking a drop, can you believe it? He says he never drinks and handles guns."

"Well, thank God for small favors." She takes the cold bottle from my hand.

I fetch two wine glasses from the cupboard, find the corkscrew in the gadget drawer. I struggle with the cork. She takes over and struggles, too. We laugh at each other again and it feels better when we're laughing. The cork breaks apart and half of it falls back into the bottle.

"No matter," I say.

She pours for both of us and we hold out our glasses for a toast. A speck of cork floats in hers.

"To friendship," she says.

"And auctioneers," I add, "who save us money."

We clink glasses and take a drink.

Two

In my dream someone is hammering. Intermittent, distant hammering like when the subfloor in the kitchen was being replaced. I dream I'm in my overalls, stripping the old varnish off the carved wainscot in the dining room. My knees ache from kneeling for so long, and I remember I meant to put on the knee pads I found in the bottom of Cody's closet. The hammering continues. It's relentless. It comes right out of my dream and wakes me up. I find myself in the middle of the bed, balled up under the covers.

When the sleep fog clears, I realize the hammering is real—it comes from downstairs—someone is knocking on the front door. I unfold my aching knees. I slept too long in the fetal position. I squint at the clock on the bedside table. Seven-thirty. Saturdays are mine to sleep late. No school lunches to pack, no bus to be on time for, no reason at all to get up early. Except someone is knocking. And they don't sound likely to go away.

I roll out of bed. Recirculating blood needles through my legs as I fumble for my robe and fuzzy booties. The house is frigid. I turn up the thermostat as I pass through the hallway, push at my hair as I tramp down the stairs two at a time. I try to comb out the tangles with my fingers. The knocking continues. The boys both seem able to sleep through it.

"I'm coming," I mutter, wiping my eyes. *Coffee*. I long for a cup of hot coffee.

Snowball paces on the lower landing, mewing at me to do something about the noise. Through the beveled glass on the front door, I spot a tall man with a ball cap on his head. The caps says ACE REBAR across the front. He smiles at me through the glass, waves. I can't be friendly, not at seven-thirty on a Saturday morning. I open the door. The cat darts out between my feet, dodges around the man standing there.

"Sorry, did I wake you?" the man says.

I'm standing here in my nightgown and robe with bedhead and crusty eyes. "No, this is how I always look. Magnificent, isn't it?

He gives me a straight-in-the-eye look; then a slight smile bends his mouth. "Sorry," he repeats. "Mister Glasser told me to come by early." He says "Glasser" like it has two *z's* in the middle. I can't place his accent but he's obviously not from around here. "He wanted me to take a look at the upper gallery and those columns." He pivots to look at the porch columns behind him. "I rang the doorbell but I'm guessing it doesn't work."

"No, it doesn't." It dawns on me finally. The carpenter. Here for the balcony, or gallery, or whatever you want to call it upstairs. "No, oh no, that's next week. You're supposed to come by next week. Adam's not here. Mister Glasser . . ." I say it with purpose so he'll hear the correct pronunciation.

The carpenter reaches into the back pocket of his jeans and pulls out a small spiral notepad. "I'm pretty sure he said . . ." He starts scrolling through pages. "Yeah. See here." He shows me a page in his notebook. "Four-oh-two East Main. Seven or seven-thirty. Adam Glasser." He still says *Glazzer*.

I look over his arm at the notepad. "It says Friday, doesn't it? Next week." I take the pad and turn it around for a closer look. Scribbled there is today's date, Saturday November 26.

"Shit." I breathe the word more than say it out loud but he hears. He gives a light chuckle and takes his notepad.

"I can come back if your husband's not here." When I don't take his handshake, he flips pages in the notepad again. A nervous tick maybe? "Let's see. . . . I've got another estimate next Saturday. It's in Austin so I couldn't get back here in time . . . and . . . nope . . ." The notebook pages flip. ". . . nope . . . not free the following two Saturdays either . . ."

"Does it have to be a Saturday?"

"I work during the week. Saturdays are when I look at new jobs. Your husband said Saturday would work for him." He folds up the pad and stuffs it in his back jeans pocket and at the same time, sticks out his hand. "Troy Middleton. Sorry for the miss-up."

Still groggy, I hang onto the doorknob. *Miss-up? Did he just say miss-up?* I remember my manners and finally reach out my hand for a shake. "Adam must've forgotten. I'm afraid you'll have to deal with me. I'm Sarah."

"What does he want included in the estimate, do you know? He said something about doing the work in phases."

Here come questions I can't answer. I shake my head. This is already taking more attention from me than I want to give it right now. "Can you wait a second? While I go get dressed?"

"Oh yeah. Yeah sure." He rocks backward. "I'll just take a look around out here if that's OK."

I close the door and rush to get the coffee pot going before I sprint upstairs to throw on jeans, the top to the jogging suit from yesterday. I step into a pair of clogs and grab my brush off the dresser. I run it through my hair on the way back downstairs. It was probably rude of me not to ask him inside. I get angry at Adam for leaving this task to me. He knows dealing with carpenters and painters and repairmen of any kind makes me feel inadequate. It's up to him to handle these things. And he hadn't said one word about a carpenter coming today. But then he seems to lose track of everything lately: me, the boys, this house.

Troy Middleton is out in the yard. He seems to be taking a visual assessment of the front porch columns, scribbling with a stubby pencil on his trusty notepad. There are five columns, three downstairs, and two up, all in need of repair. As soon as I step outside I realize I should have put on a jacket. It's chilly. The wind blows right through me. Dead leaves from the pecan trees crunch underfoot as I join him in the yard. I look in the same direction he's looking—at the corners and angles and bay windows of our stately old house.

"We want it painted," I say after a while, feeling the need to interrupt the silence. As soon as I say it, I feel ignorant. The man is a carpenter not a painter. *Dammit, Adam.* "And uhm . . . any rotten boards you see . . . we want all that replaced."

"Your husband said something about the fascia and soffits."

What is a fascia? A soffit? I sigh.

Troy Middleton scratches in his tiny spiral notepad. He points with his pencil at the warped boards under the eaves. "Those things up there that look like they've been chewed by Godzilla," he says, as if he has read my mind. "Those are your soffits."

I laugh at the Godzilla line. "Oh, yes. Definitely those. And the upstairs gallery is completely rotten." I say gallery because he did. We normally used the word balcony, but *gallery* does have a fancier ring. "You'll have to come inside to look at that. I think my kids are still asleep."

I say this so he won't tromp up the stairs. I glance as his scuffed work boots. The boys are as grumpy as their mom when they're awakened too early on a Saturday. He writes something else on his notepad.

"How old are your kids?"

"Eight and fourteen." I stretch to peek at what he's writing. Not my kids' ages, I hope. No, just a lot of numbers and straight lines. I realize he was only making small talk.

He gives me a polite smile. "What color paint?"

"Oh. I was thinking tan, with white. Maybe green trim."

He nods. "Contrast is always good." He takes a step back,

looks up at the house. It soars forty feet straight up, not counting the little turret on top the boys call a witch's hat. Count that and you've got fifty. "You could even do one floor one color and the second floor another."

"Really?" I step back, too, shade my eyes, visualizing the house painted that way, multicolored.

"Or maybe just contrast the attic level so the fish scale stands out." He points with his pencil at the scalloped siding above the two main floors. The way the shingles overlap does make them look like the scales on a fish.

"Ah, yes, the fish scale." I nod, just now realizing that's what it's called. In the last five minutes I've learned more than I ever knew about my own house.

"It's going to take a lot of scaffolding," Troy Middleton says.

"So you *are* a painter?" I say. "I thought maybe you were strictly a carpenter."

He lets out a laugh, like I've made some kind of funny joke. "I'm anything you need me to be."

He follows me inside. I take him up the stairs. It's my clogs that do most of the clomping. The smell of brewing coffee fills the house, makes my mouth water. We turn the corner on the second landing, a few more steps and the upper landing opens onto a wide octagonal sitting room, except we don't use it for sitting. There's an antique bench there that has become a catch-all mostly. The boys have piled their schoolbooks on it, along with a soccer ball, and Joel's zippered sweatshirt. I apologize for the mess as we go through the master bedroom. The bed is unmade, and probably still warm from my body.

"This is a grand old house," he says, glancing at the rounded bedroom walls, the picture-hang molding, as we pass through.

"Adam calls it a money sink. The gallery's out here." I'm getting used to the word, even though saying it makes me feel like a character in a Tennessee Williams play. I unlock the door. I keep it locked because the gallery is in the worst condition of any other part of the house. I have a fear of someone stepping out there and falling through. It'll be a relief to finally have it fixed. "Can I interest you in a cup of coffee?"

"That sounds great," he says, as he goes out the door.

Once I'm down in the kitchen, I realize I've forgotten to ask how he takes his coffee, so to avoid the stairs, I go out front and step into the yard. He's catwalking along the edge beams. He sees me below.

"You've got a real mess up here," he says.

"I know. Do you take cream and sugar?"

"I'm coming down. I've seen enough."

For a second, I think he means he's going to leap from the upper floor to the ground. Somehow it wouldn't surprise me. He moves around like a monkey up there. I would expect a forward gainer. The thought makes me laugh silently to myself.

I go back inside the house. He comes down the stairs and takes the "L" at the lower landing into the kitchen where I stand at the cook island with our cups of coffee freshly poured.

"Do you think you can fix that mess up there?" I say, repeating his words. I slide one of the cups across the counter in his direction.

"Oh sure." He takes the cup by the handle. "Just take out the rot and install new wood." He makes it sound like it will be nothing. He glances at the tongue-and-groove ceiling. "You've done a nice job in here. You used shellac up there?"

"How did you know that?" What a stupid question. He's a *carpenter.*

He shrugs, moves the cup to his lips, sips. "You can't get that amber tone with polyurethane."

"You should've seen this place before we moved in. The city wanted to condemn it."

He shakes his head. "They don't build them like this anymore. Did you choose these colors in here?"

"I did." Three shades of gray, the lightest to the darkest on the door and window trim.

"You've got a good eye."

I blush even though I know the flattery is meant to help get him the job. "However I hadn't thought of painting the stories two different colors. You've given me some ideas."

"No charge for that." He smiles, then drinks down the cup in one gulp. It must scald his throat but if so he doesn't show it. He sets the empty cup on the island, closes his spiral notebook, tucks it into his shirt pocket this time. "I'll get this bid put together," he says. "Tell your husband I'll have it ready Monday morning."

I walk him to the front door. This wasn't so bad after all. I actually feel a little pride in how I was able to handle everything. The man seems pleasant enough. Better than the carpenter we hired for the kitchen remodel. That one was either grousing or whining about something.

I close the door and turn to see Cody coming down the stairs in his Superman pajamas. They're too small for him and his navel pokes out from under the top.

"Who was that?" he says, rubbing his eyes. He looks cranky.

"The carpenter. He's going to fix our house." I go over and give him a good morning hug. He hugs me back.

"Make pancakes," he says in my ear. He thinks he has caught me in a good mood. And it's true. I'm excited the exterior work on the house is about to start. I'm already imagining white willow furniture with tufted cushions for the balcony—*gallery*. My good mood lasts all day. It feels nice, and it's rare lately, so I don't question it.

After breakfast, we get down in the floor, all three of us, and play with Snowball. Joel has discovered the cat will chase and bat small balls of aluminum foil. He's frisky and brings them back to us, again and again, like a Golden Retriever.

It's good to laugh and enjoy my boys. I'm more relaxed without Adam here. I don't have to worry over dividing my time. And as soon as that thought comes to me, I feel guilty for having it. But it's true. Maybe I could manage on my own.

SUNDAY MORNING, Adam comes home with his ten-point buck all cut up and packaged like beef from a meat market. It fills most of the freezer. Marty helps carry in the meat and stays to drink a beer, which turns into several beers. They watch a football game in the den. I worry about Marty driving all the way back to Austin after so much beer, but I don't say anything.

They both shout and cuss the players and the refs on television. Adam rarely watches football, and to my knowledge doesn't follow any team, so the enthusiasm is all for show—for Marty. That's one thing that has always bothered me about Adam: the fakery, putting on airs. He tries to act like we're rich, like he enjoys watching football, like we're happily married. Sometimes I can't tell where the phony Adam leaves off and the real one begins.

Bradley Harper's parents come to take Cody with them to cut down their Christmas tree. Joel retires to his bedroom, his stereo, his headphones. I go into the living room away from the men, their beer drinking and hollering, to sit down and work on the needlepoint seat covers I'm making for the dining room chairs.

We never use this living room—or parlor, as my dad likes to call it. Dad would approve of calling the upstairs balcony a gallery, too, I feel sure of it. The big, elegant picture window is framed with jewel-toned squares of stained glass, two etched sidelights and an etched arch above. The walls of the room are octagonal. As I sew I visualize the levels of the house outside painted different colors. I glance at the picture window, thinking the exterior colors should complement the ones in the stained glass. Tomorrow I'll drive to the paint store and pick up color chips.

From the den comes a burst of unintelligible shouting. The quiet solitude of the living room, just the thwick of the needle in and out of the fabric, calms me. I daydream about the renovated exterior of my lovely old house.

Three

Monday morning, while I'm fixing school lunches, the telephone rings. School mornings are planned down to the last second so I don't appreciate unexpected interruptions. However, Adam's in the shower so I stop what I'm doing to answer it. I recognize the accent immediately.

"I hope I didn't wake you again."

"God, no. I've already put in a full day's work." I listen for the shower. The plumbing hums through the walls. "While I've got you, what do you think about painting each of the stories outside a different color, plus another color for the attic? Or should we just use one color for the house, and another for the attic? I can't make up my mind."

"Whatever you decide, your house will look great with new paint. We can look at some sample pictures," he says, then adds, "If I get the job that is."

"You have pictures? That sounds like fun." I hear the shower shut down. "Just a second, I'll get Adam."

I lay down the phone and go to the landing to holler up "Telephone!" Then I go back to my end of the line, listening for Adam to come on. When he does, despite my curiosity, I hang up my end and go back to packing lunches. It's something I don't do anymore, listen in on his telephone calls.

The school bus pulls up outside and I run to stop the driver. Cody and Joel race after me. I barely have time to relay their lunch boxes into their hands. A quick toothpaste kiss from Cody. Joel says, "See ya!" and waves goodbye. He no longer gives goodbye kisses.

Out of breath, back inside, I'm wiping the counter when Adam comes down. He's toweling his hair, shirtless. He's gone a little soft and pudgy around his middle. I notice but would never mention it. Mostly he hides his vanity, but it's there, lurking behind his nonchalance. I have a sudden desire to wrap my arms around him, and I'm not sure why I don't.

"Helluva nice guy," he says, as he opens the fridge and grabs the milk off the top shelf. He drinks directly from the jug, a habit of his I hate. He wipes milk off his upper lip, re-caps the jug, and sets it back inside the refrigerator, germs and all. "He's really into this old house thing. Use as much of the original materials and all that crap. He says he can salvage some of the lumber on the balcony." He turns to me and I hand him a cup of coffee. He takes it without a word, blows on it and sips. "I think I'm going to give him a shot. What do you think? He says he can start Wednesday." He grabs the uneaten half of Joel's Pop-Tart off the plate, takes a bite.

"As long as he can finish by Christmas." I pour myself a cup of coffee.

"It'll be cutting it close. But you want the work done, right?" He takes his cup and the rest of the Pop-Tart upstairs to finish getting dressed for work.

I take my coffee into the dining room and sit at the table. Three long bay windows look out onto the side street. A massive built-in breakfront china cabinet takes up one entire wall. I've filled it with Adam's grandmother's Haviland china and silver pieces, gifts from our wedding. Carved wainscot plackets the other walls. The heartwood floors gleam. Two massive pocket doors can close off this room from the rest of the house if we want, but we never do that. I like the wide-open space between this room and the den. I love to imagine the people who lived here before us, what they were like, who they were, and the stories surrounding their lives. Did they have a lot of children? Did they entertain company in these rooms? I imagine bustles and wide floppy hats.

The first minute I laid eyes on this house, I fell in love with it, even though it was a shambles. It had been neglected for at least a generation. Peeling wallpaper. Blackened floors. Joel called it the Amityville House. Adam's parents thought we were fools to buy something so old and drafty. My mother said my antique collecting had gone too far. But we practically stole the place. It was slated for demolition and the vacant lot sold to offset taxes gone unpaid for years. We went before the city council with our plans and a pledge to renovate. Adam had recently done financial work for one of the councilmen, so he had strings to pull and he pulled them.

We've already put more into renovations than we paid for the entire house. But oh, the mysteries we've uncovered in the process. The biggest was the butler's pantry we found hidden behind a brick wall in the kitchen. A small window on the outside of the house clued us into the pantry. When it was unearthed all we found inside was an empty floor safe and a lot of old newspaper. We turned the pantry into a powder room, and gave the safe to the local museum.

Adam comes up behind where I sit daydreaming. He's dressed in shirt, slacks, a tie. He bends to kiss me under my ear, just behind my jaw. It surprises me; he hasn't done that in a while. I think he must feel excited to begin the exterior work like I am. He smells like Polo. His lips feel warm. I reach backward to hook my hands around his neck.

"Hey—" He laughs but shrugs away from me. "You'll wrinkle my collar." He straightens, adjusts his tie. "Listen—call Mom for me today. Make sure they got back from Kansas all right."

I'm wounded by the rebuff but try not to show it. "We would have heard by now if they had problems."

"True." He rubs my cheek with the back of his cool clean hand. "But check in with them anyway, would you?"

I follow him to the back door. He looks nice dressed for work, blond hair smoothed and sprayed, blue tie that matches his eyes. Why do men age better than women? Adam will turn forty-one this coming March, and he's more handsome now than he's ever been.

"I love you," I call to him as he takes the outside steps. He waves his hand at me without looking back, goes to the Jeep parked under the porte cochere.

I try to remember if he's said he loves me since the episode in October. I can't recall a single time.

Two days a week, I volunteer at Cody's school library reshelving books and reading to the younger grades. Since the episode, I've started wearing my old Balcor dresses when I work at the library. Slacks and a blouse would be more suitable, but I put on a dress for Adam, even though he rarely sees me in them. If Cody happens to spot me in the library, he acts embarrassed and ignores me, but the first and second graders adore me. They rush in at story time and hug me around my hips. Immediately, they start to make story requests. A few of them go straight to the shelves searching for a favorite. It semi-satisfies the latent librarian inside me. It's the closest I've ever come to using my Library Science degree.

When school lets out Cody rides home with me. It's the part of my volunteer work he likes—not having to ride the school bus.

"I want a new bike for Christmas," he announces, as soon as he's inside the car. "One with hand brakes this time, and wire-spoke wheels."

"Wow, you're getting fancy," I tease. "Maybe Santa will bring that for you. Do you think you've been good enough?"

"Come on, Mom. I don't believe in that stuff anymore."

I smile but it makes me sad to hear him say it.

Today, we're not stopping for Joel. He has band practice. When we get home, I see the red light flashing on the answering machine. I hit playback. It's Adam. "Yeah . . . Sarah? Don't wait supper for me. Looks like we're in for a long one up here tonight. I'll grab a burger somewhere."

I rewind the tape and play it again. There's background noise, people talking, or *someone* talking. I can hear it during the pause. I sit there staring through the lace panels over the kitchen windows at the branches of the pecan tree. There's always something more important he has to do than come home. It makes me wonder if he's having an affair. The idea of it sits heavy on me, like something rotten in my stomach. It would explain a lot about the episode in October and how distant and on edge he's been since. I wonder who it is. One of his clients again? Someone from downtown?

I pick up the phone and call my mother-in-law. For half an hour Maureen rattles on about their trip to Kansas to spend Thanksgiving with Adam's brother, Brent, who has a second wife and two toddlers. The first wife lives in Michigan somewhere with his other two kids. None of them, Brent's first family, are ever mentioned. I wonder sometimes if Adam and I were to split, would Joel and Cody—would I—be as easily forgotten?

JOEL WAITS outside the band hall at school as I pull up to the curb. He has his saxophone case in one hand, his homework in the other. I'm surprised to see him bring home the sax. It means he plans to practice instead of locking himself up with his headphones.

"Make him sit in the back seat," Cody says as Joel strides toward the car.

"His legs are too long, honey. You get in back."

"Oh man!" Cody blows air out of his mouth. "Someday I'm

going to have long legs, too, and then what? We can't both sit in front." He groans but crawls between the bucket seats and into the back. "I want a Big Mac and a chocolate shake," he says, petulance in his voice as if I owe him for making him take the backseat.

Joel opens the car door and gets in. "We're giving a Christmas concert at one of the malls in Austin," he says before I can ask about the saxophone. He wedges the instrument case between his knees. He doesn't sound excited about the concert. Lately, nothing excites him. It worries me. Do all fourteen-year-old boys find life so taxing?

We stop at McDonald's on the way home. The boys want to eat inside. There's already a crowd so we grab the first empty table. It's strewn with crumbs from the last occupants. I sweep them off with a paper napkin. As the boys eat their hamburgers they grouse about things happening at school, homework, and mean teachers. Absently, I watch people rotate in and out of the doors. My mind wanders to the McDonald's we frequented, Adam and I, near the UT campus, the smell of cheap hamburgers, the chatter of dead-broke students, just like we were, counting our change. Sometimes there was just enough for a Coke and a regular cheeseburger which we would split

When we first met Adam was already a grad student. I had just started my junior year. A mutual friend introduced him to me as some other girl's boyfriend, some girl named Brenda Penrod. Aside from his good looks, I didn't pay much attention to him. He was taken, or so I thought. Besides I was struggling for good grades, focused on my studies, not searching for a date. Except, apparently, he wasn't taken after all because he called me that same night and asked me out. When I said I couldn't, he called again the next night, and the night after that. And then he started chasing me everywhere. He chased me all over campus, like I was a butterfly he couldn't catch. I felt like a butterfly, too, the way he romanced me with flowers, poems, love songs on the radio, long drives in the country. He would rush across campus just to be there waiting after my classes. A lab mate called him my stalker. I couldn't imagine what I had done to get his attention. But before I knew it, I was caught in his butterfly net, deeply flattered, and wildly in love.

In love. What does that phrase even mean? How is it different from just *plain* love? Is there a difference? If you care about someone, even if you know their weaknesses and flaws, if you understand their perceptions and opinions, if they occupy too much of your thoughts, the things you do, plan, or decide—if you respect them, and take them into account in every facet of your shared lives, if you feel as strongly for them as you do for yourself, is that *plain* love, or are you *in* love? It seems like hair-splitting to me. Loving someone, and being in love, aren't they one and the same? I probably should have kept my class notes from Philosophy 101.

Before the episode, I never got distracted like this when I was with my boys. But now I second-guess everything Adam does or says. I wonder if he still feels he's not *in love* with me anymore. We haven't mentioned it again. It's too recent, too raw. But more than anything I wish I could quit this endless obsessing.

As I pull into our driveway, I see right away the back door standing open several inches. The light I left on in the kitchen glares like a golden slit in the twilight.

"Didn't you lock it, Mom?" Joel says, accusing me, even though he knows the slightest north breeze will blow that door open, even when you think it's locked.

"I'm sure I did," I say, getting out of the car. "Maybe I didn't push on it hard enough."

I slam the car door in case there *is* someone inside. I don't want to sneak up on an intruder. I would rather they have plenty of time to run away.

"Let me go in first, Mom," Joel says in his most manly voice. He tries to beat me to the back steps. I grab his shoulder and push him behind me.

"Maybe we should go somewhere and call the cops." Cody sounds scared.

I stick my hand inside the door, feel for the button lock on the doorknob. It's depressed just as I thought. "I just didn't slam it hard enough," I say, as I ease inside.

The boys come right behind me. The furnace is blowing full-blast, but the kitchen is frigid from exposure to the outside air. Nothing seems out of place.

"I'll get the gun," Cody says.

"No, you will not," I say and grab for him, but he bolts by me toward the den. He's already in Adam's desk drawer before I can stop him from taking out the pistol Adam keeps there. "Cody Glasser," I say, sharply. "You put that gun away." I have begged Adam to have the desk lock fixed.

"It's not loaded, Mom," Joel says, behind me.

"It doesn't matter. Put it up, Cody." I stand there with my hands on my hips until the gun goes back into the drawer.

I hate that we have guns of any kind in this house, but I especially hate that pistol. Marty gave it to Adam last year as a Christmas joke. "In case the business goes south," Marty said. "We can just blow our brains out like they did back in twenty-nine." I hadn't thought it was funny then, and I still don't think so.

I go upstairs and check all the rooms anyway, just so the boys will feel easier. Nothing is missing except Snowball, who most likely will return as soon as he sees we've come home. By the time I go back downstairs, the boys have the television on and they're piled up on the floor sharing the afghan I spent all last winter crocheting, the possibility of a burglar already forgotten. After a while, the house begins to warm.

ADAM COMES HOME AT ELEVEN. I'm already in my flannel nightgown and robe; the boys are both in bed. He takes off his jacket and throws it over the back of the easy chair, then slumps down beside me on the couch. He smells like cigarettes and he's not a smoker. He also reeks of Jack Daniels.

"We lost the McCabe account," he says, and lays his head back against the cushions. I turn down the volume on the television.

"How?" I want to sympathize with him but I'm caught in my web of suspicions. I look at him and try to imagine him in bed with another woman. Would he do that to me? To us? *Again.* He's certainly been somewhere besides the office.

"It's getting harder to compete," he says. "Money's tight. And we can't afford those slick TV ads like the big boys. I don't know . . . we probably blew it somehow." He puts his hand on my thigh. "How was your day?"

I study him to see if he's really interested, or if it's a perfunctory question. His eyes are bloodshot, glazed. He stares blankly at the TV.

"I called your mom. She said they had a wonderful time at Brent's."

"Thanks for doing that." He doesn't sound interested. His hand moves under my gown and up my thigh. He rubs just under the edge of my panties with the tip of his thumb—a not-too-subtle signal.

"Let's go to bed," he says. "I'm beat."

I turn off the lamp and follow him up the stairs. He strips off his clothes and falls on the bed. I hang my robe on the brass hook behind the door. I bend to pick up his clothes from the floor.

He makes a face at my flannel nightgown. "You're not wearing that, are you?"

I pull it off over my head, step out of my panties, turn out the light, and crawl naked under the quilt. He spoons me against him. I feel his erection at the small of my back, whiskey breath on my neck. He gives me a nibble just below my earlobe.

I roll over for him. He moves on top of me. No foreplay. And since he's been drinking, he takes a long time. I start to ache. When it's over, I sigh and turn away with my face toward the wall.

I hope he'll think I'm so satisfied I need instant sleep. I don't want him to keep trying to get something out of me—not when he smells so strongly of booze and cigarettes, not while I'm still wondering where he's been.

In a moment, his hand pats my hip. "I needed that," he mutters. And in another moment, he's snoring.

Four

Troy Middleton arrives on Wednesday as promised, with his extension ladder, his toolbox, and a helper named Lee. They arrive at seven, and Adam stays home long enough to watch them get started before he leaves for work. They begin on the upper gallery, tearing out rotten boards and chucking the lumber down into the yard. They sound like a swarm of giant termites. I think of the Godzilla reference and laugh. I have no desire to witness the chomping of my house. I'm glad today is my day at the library.

At eleven-thirty, just as I leave for the school, a truck backs into my front yard and dumps a load of yellow, Womanized wood onto my grass. By that afternoon, when I come home with Cody, there's a new floor on the gallery. The boards are too long and jut out at different lengths over the edge of the house. I go through our bedroom to the outside door and walk onto the gallery for the first time since we moved in. Cody comes behind me, but with the railing gone, I keep him away from the edge.

Down in the yard, Troy takes slats off three long pieces of railing, one slat at a time. Lee, the helper, loads the pickup with the old, torn-out, jagged lumber.

"Do you always work this fast?" I call down.

The ACE REBAR cap shades Troy's face. "Those long pieces up there aren't nailed down yet. Be careful where you step."

I shoo Cody back inside with instructions to get busy on homework. I stay to inspect the handiwork on the gallery floor.

The gallery makes a curved angle as it wraps around the east side of the house. There is now an elliptical pattern in the floor, like a sunburst fanning the curved corner. It's artistic and mimics the sunburst design in the transom above the gallery door. I look down at Troy bent over two sawhorses. I realize now he's pulling out the old nails from the railing and tossing them into a tin coffee can. Lee retrieves another armful of lumber from the discard heap on the lawn, and as he does, he smiles up at me. He's short and dark and wears a goatee. The smile feels lecherous, so I back closer to the house and then sideslip through the bedroom door.

When Adam comes home, he has Joel and Joel's sax case. He gives me a perfunctory kiss on the temple as he heads through the house, no doubt on his way to supervise the construction out front. I'm surprised and pleased that he thought to pick up Joel and save me the trip.

Joel goes up the stairs without even a hello. I call after him, "Hey, can I borrow your Walkman tomorrow? I need something to drown out all this racket." He doesn't answer. In a minute, the off-key wail of his saxophone mingles with the sound of the saw and hammer. I cover my ears and go back to the kitchen.

Just as I get our supper in the oven Carolyn calls. "You will never guess who I just talked to," she says, as soon as I answer.

I can barely hear her over all the noise. It's as if the walls of this house don't exist. I stretch the phone cord into the bathroom and sit on the closed toilet seat. I plug my free ear with one finger. "Tell me, I can't guess."

"Denver Carson," she answers, and I can hear the sneer in her voice. "Remember him? The saddle-and-hat guy?"

I do remember. Denver Carson, her most recent fling, a traveling western wear salesman. He took her with him in his showcase van to Amarillo where they checked into a motel and didn't emerge for an entire weekend, ordering in food and hardly getting dressed. When they got back to Austin, he gave her a passionate goodbye kiss and that was the last she heard from him—until now.

"He had the nerve to tell me he'd be in Fredericksburg at the Best Western if I cared to join him this weekend. Can you believe that? After two months of silence?" She acts like she doesn't care but I know better. Carolyn wants a family, mainly kids, and for kids there has to be a man.

"Did you ask why he hadn't called sooner?"

"I wouldn't give him the pleasure. What are you doing?"

I try to think of something interesting to tell her. Compared to her life mine must seem boring. "The carpenters are here. The noise is driving me batty. Listen?" I hold the phone to the window, but I'm on the opposite side of the house from all the work. "I can barely hear myself think. Adam came home early—to watch them saw, I guess."

"Must be a man thing." She laughs. "Any of them single?"

"There's just two. I don't know about single, but they're carpenters, Carolyn. Not your type."

"Carpenters can make pretty good money." She laughs.

The sawing stops. Only the blare of Joel's saxophone fills the silence. Her voice increases. A television chatters in the background at her apartment. I hear Adam bang through the back door, rummage in the fridge.

"There's an auction over in Taylor Saturday," she says. "Want to go?"

"Maybe so. Listen, I've got to—"

"I know, get back to your supper and your family. You don't have to rub it in," she teases, but it suddenly dawns on me that Carolyn and I should trade places for a while. It would no doubt stop the envy.

THE MEN STAND in a circle in the front yard, each with a beer in his hand. The moment I walk up, Adam sends me back inside for another round. Troy and Lee are still nursing theirs, so I go for just one—Adam's. When I go back outside with his beer, he takes the can from me and pats me on the rump, like I'm his prized horse. I want to coldcock him for doing it in front of the others. I feel my face get hot.

Lee stands off to one side and eyes me with what seems like a smirk. I don't like his looks. He's nowhere near a possibility for Carolyn. On the other hand, Troy Middleton could be, if he was a little less scruffy. He towers over Lee and is even taller than Adam by a couple of inches. That's a plus—Carolyn likes tall men. He needs a shave. I don't think that five o'clock shadow is there on purpose. Carolyn goes for stylish men with baby-smooth faces and groomed hair, who have office jobs and clean hands. I glance at Adam's immaculate fingers.

I listen as Troy talks to Adam about shoring up the foundation and repairing the columns on both porches. I notice he's not wearing a ring, but that doesn't really mean anything. Adam rarely wears his wedding ring. He says it gives his finger a rash, which seems doubtful since it's gold. It's always bothered me he doesn't wear it like he'd rather people not know his marital status. *Everybody knows I'm married,* he tells me. But do they really? I look down at the ring on my finger, then fold my arms and try to listen.

The screech of Joel's saxophone filters outside. It reaches us down on the lawn. I'm almost embarrassed at how bad he is, but at least he's practicing. One of the antique roses planted near the front of the house is smashed on top. And there's an extension ladder propped right in the middle of the tansy asters. By the time this job is done, I probably won't have a yard left. I leave the men alone and go inside to finish supper.

Half an hour later, Adam comes in and heads straight for the fridge. The spew of another beer can opening sends chills up my spine. It's visceral. I can't help it.

"That sonofabitch," he says, and somehow I know he means Troy Middleton. "He's already tacking more work onto the original bid. That's the way it is with these guys. They come in looking around for ways to stretch the job. He probably took one look at this old mausoleum and started salivating. Think we can trust him?" He takes a swig of beer. I see his agitation and recognize he's already in the tipsy stage. Next comes catatonia.

Plates and silverware clatter. The boys are in the dining room setting the table. I hear them argue in hushed tones.

"He did a nice job on the gallery," I say. "He seems to be a pretty good carpenter."

"When I got here he was ripping boards freehand with a circular saw. Cuts straight as an arrow. *Freehand.*"

I pretend to be impressed, although I don't know anything about it. However, I love that sunburst pattern on the gallery floor.

I take dinner out of the oven and carry the casserole dish to the dining room. The boys are bickering over how to fold the napkins. Joel says, "Who cares?" just before I enter the room.

Cody sends a pleading look at me. "Joel isn't doing the napkins right, Mom."

Joel says. "Nana's not here. She's the only one who cares about that stuff."

"I care about that stuff, too," I say, defending my mother.

Back in the kitchen, I can see Adam's still stewing. He can't stand to feel bested. He upends the can of beer into his mouth. I grab the salad from the fridge.

"Did you say no to the add-on work," I ask him. "You could have, you know."

"I should've gotten more references. He's only been in town eighteen months. Came from some damned place in Maine. *Maine?* That already seems shady."

"He's from Maine?" No wonder he sounds funny. I take a bottle of ranch dressing out. Ranch is all Cody will eat. "Why shady?"

"I don't know. Who the hell's from Maine?"

I shake my head at him. "Come eat."

When I go back into the dining room, the argument between the boys has devolved into swinging punches. Cody slugs Joel in the arm and Joel shoves Cody against the wall. The whole house shakes.

"That is enough!" I set the bowl of salad on the table. Adam shuffles in, oblivious to the ruckus. He takes his seat and sets a fresh frosty can of beer to the left of his plate. I wish he would have at least poured it into a glass.

Later, once the kitchen is clean and the boys are up in their rooms getting ready for bed, and after Adam is snoring on the couch, I put on a sweater and go outside to hunt for Snowball. He disappeared the minute the construction work began and I haven't seen him all day. It's past time for his supper.

"Kitty, kitty," I call softly, but he doesn't appear.

Moonlight filters through the bare branches of the pecan trees and burr oaks that canopy our house. A ring of mist encircles the streetlamp. Beer cans lie in the yard where the men stood earlier. I pick them up and spot another one sitting on the edge of the porch, just behind where Troy had been standing. It's nearly full. I pour the contents on my flattened rose bush.

So, he's not a drinker. As far as I'm concerned that's one strike in his column, although I'm sure Adam wouldn't agree. He doesn't trust a man who doesn't love a beer the same way he does.

I look up at the rounded edge of the upstairs gallery. The long boards that jutted out earlier are now neatly trimmed to conform to the curve of the house. The air smells of sawdust and the oily scent of new lumber. Below my knees, I feel Snowball weave a figure-eight through my legs. His eyes shine iridescent in the night.

"Where have you been?" I say, and scoop him up. His loud purr throbs against my chest.

Five

On Thursday, the construction noise starts at seven-thirty. At breakfast, Adam groans and the boys complain, but they get to go off to work and school, and I'm left with the racket. I'm sure our neighbors hate us by now. I almost hate us myself.

I find busy work, anything to keep my mind off the incessant cacophony. I climb into the attic and pull down Christmas boxes. We plan to get our tree this weekend, so I decide to have everything ready. The strings of lights are tangled into impossible knots. They take an hour to unravel. So do the strands of garland. There are broken ornaments to either retire or repair. I try to concentrate on my task and not the noise outside but it's nearly impossible. When they quit for lunch, it's as if nirvana descends. I pull myself out from the mass of Christmas decorations spread all over the floor and lie down on the couch in the den. My fingers massage my splitting headache. Without meaning to, I fall asleep, and the next thing I know, a voice startles me awake.

"Miz Glazzer?" I sit up. I recognize those z's. Troy stands in the doorway, his cap in his hand. "OK to use your phone?"

I push at my hair, feel my falling-down ponytail. Seems he's always waking me. He must think all I do is sleep. "Of course." I go open the door and point toward Adam's desk. "You have to start calling me Sarah, though. Missus Glasser is my mother-in-law."

He gives me a quick smile on his way to the phone. "Sorry to keep bothering you. Tear-out is noisy. Hopefully, it'll be worth it once we're done."

I watch him dial the phone. It's possible he's about Carolyn's age. It's hard to tell. He acts older. He speaks to the person on the other end of the line and orders several things using some secret carpenter code. I don't want it to seem as if I'm eavesdropping so I start stacking Christmas boxes against the wall in the dining room.

"Are you a reader?" His voice makes me jump. I chalk it up to being shell-shocked, like a soldier in battle—all the noise and now I can't take the silence. "I ask because we're about to knock out those old columns." He nods at the shelves lining the den wall. "You might want to take a book or something outside while we do that."

I glance at the bookcase, too. "Will the house fall in on me if I stay inside?"

"It might sound like it's going to." He laughs. He has a nice laugh. It lights up his face.

"Adam says you're from Maine?" I ask, out of nowhere. I'm still thinking about Carolyn, but I'm curious, too.

"I worked up there for a few years before I came down here."

When he doesn't elaborate I say. "I've never been to Maine. I hear it's cold."

"I'm originally from Illinois, cold doesn't bother me."

"Where in Illinois? Chicago?"

"Peoria."

"I've never been there either. What's in Peoria?"

"Nothing much." He laughs, shrugs. "Illinois River runs through the middle." He shrugs again. "I've been gone a while. Left right out of high school and never looked back." He eases toward the door. "We'll be getting started here in just a—"

"I wanted to tell you how much I like what you did on the gallery floor. Was that as difficult as it looks?"

"Nah." He waves his hand, but I can see he's pleased to have me mention it. "Basic geometry."

I follow as he steps toward the door. "So, when did you get out of high school? Ten years ago? Twelve?"

"Huh?" He turns to give me a questioning look.

"You said you left your hometown when you got out of high school."

"Oh." He cocks his head a little. "More like fifteen years ago. Why?"

Quickly, I do the math—that makes him at least thirty-three. So he *is* Carolyn's age, maybe a year older. I almost say, *I have a friend,* then realize I don't even know if he's married or not. "Are you married?" I hear myself ask.

When he smiles this time it's clear he's suspicious of all my questions. "Nope, no wife. No kids. No extensions of any kind. And besides Illinois and Maine I've spent time in Indiana and Colorado, California, Montana." He counts them off on his fingers. "Right now, I live in a house on Church Street. I'm remodeling it for the owner in exchange for rent. Doyle McIntire? I'll be glad to give you his number if you want to call him. He'll give me a good reference."

Oops! I've gone too far with my snooping. "Oh no—gosh no, I wasn't . . ." He's not handsome but he does have an interesting face, and a nice smile that saves him. I laugh, embarrassed. I'm certain I'm blushing. "I think all the noise has fried my brain." I walk with him toward the front door.

"We'll start knocking out those columns here pretty soon."

"OK. I'll find a book to read." I laugh. He laughs. I follow him outside onto the porch. "So you're thirty-three?"

"Thirty-four in April. Does that matter?"

"Of course not. What day in April?"

He shakes his head but his smile lines deepen. "The twenty-fourth. Should I expect a card?"

We both laugh at that. A wise-ass, too. I think he might be too sharp for Carolyn. "So . . . Taurus."

"OK. If you believe in that stuff."

"I'm Cancer. June twenty-eighth."

He has a perplexed look. "Well. Glad we got all that out of the way."

The roar of a truck engine comes up the street. The lumber yard logo is on the door. The truck takes Troy's attention. He goes down the porch steps and strides across the yard. I watch him wave the lumber truck to the curb and motion for it to stop there.

I don't usually pry so brazenly but I did learn some things about him—mainly that he's not Carolyn's type. She's more into white-collar guys who come off rich even when they're pretending. She would never go for a guy who doesn't drive a late model car, or own his own house, or who doesn't believe in the magic of sun signs. Carolyn has a regular psychic who does her cards and reads her palm when she needs help with life decisions. I think Troy Middleton may have his feet too firmly planted in reality for Carolyn.

All afternoon, I sit outside while they work. I take a book with me and open it but it's just for optics. I never read a word. I'm too busy watching as they jack up the roof with temporary posts, slip out one old round column after another, and carry it to the sawhorses where Troy cuts off the rotten bottoms and replaces them with new wood. It takes a lot of muscle and direction from Troy, but clearly he has done this kind of work before. The house creaks and pops and does sound like it might tumble down. I'm happy to stay outside. When they're finished, it takes both of them to load the heavy old round column bottoms into the back of Troy's pickup truck.

THAT NIGHT AFTER DINNER, after the boys are upstairs with homework, as Adam mixes himself a drink, I tell him, "I want to invite Carolyn over tomorrow night to help trim the tree. I want to invite Troy, too. I want them to meet each other."

"You're kidding?" He stirs a little water in with the bourbon, takes a sip, and starts for the den. I follow.

"No, I thought I would invite Lee, too. Make it a little party. The tree goes up faster when there are more people to help."

"I thought you didn't like Lee."

"That's before I found out he's only nineteen. A local boy. Troy rents his uncle's house over on Church Street."

"My, my. You have been a little busybody, haven't you?" He turns on the TV and sits in the center of the couch with his cocktail. He takes a couple of hefty swallows, pushes his loafers off one by one, and props his feet on the coffee table. "Invite the whole damned neighborhood. I don't care."

"Bad day?" I ask.

He looks at me like I'm a space alien, and seems about to say something, but takes another drink instead and turns his attention to the television. *Moonlighting* is on. "Yeah, invite your friends over," he says, absently. "That'll be fun for a change."

He holds out his arm to me and I sit beside him, snuggle against him. We haven't done this in a while. I watch the images flicker by on the TV screen. Maddie, the show's star, is having a baby shower. I'm enjoying the warmth of Adam's body.

"Why are they *my* friends?" I say.

He stares at the screen for a moment. "What?' He glances down at me.

"You called them *my* friends. I just wondered why they aren't *our* friends?"

"Whatever, Sarah. Does it really matter what I call them? Jesus." He takes his arm from around me, kind of pushes away.

"No." I get up from the couch. "No, it doesn't. I just wondered."

I go into the kitchen, finish straightening up, start the dishwasher, screw the cap back on the bourbon, and shove it behind the coffee canister. No, it doesn't matter that he calls them *my* friends, but it's the condescension. Am I being too critical? Couldn't I just sit beside him and enjoy having his arm around me? I don't know what's wrong with me, why I can't let things go. Now, here I am stuck in the kitchen, worrying over something I caused myself. I hang up the dish towel and consider going back to the den and apologizing, but the nice moment on the couch is already ruined. So I go upstairs to check on the boys and their homework.

The three of us—Joel, Cody, and I—carry in the Christmas tree and center it between the three bay windows in the dining room. The boys accuse their dad of nailing the tree crooked in the stand, which I don't doubt since he overslept and was in a hurry. So we wrestle with the tree for a while until it's as straight in the stand as we can make it. The needles prick us and it takes a sink of warm water and a bar of Lava to remove the sticky sap. Then I start fixing hors d'oeuvres.

Carolyn said she would be here at about seven. Troy never really committed. Lee turned me down flat. It's Friday night and he had other plans. While I work on the table, the boys start with their roughhousing. I have to send them both to their rooms for time-out to stop the ruckus. I hope this phase they're in—all this bickering and fighting—will end soon. Adam says it's what brothers do. I was an only child so I don't really understand sibling rivalry.

Before I finish with the table, Carolyn arrives. She has a bottle of Beaujolais. I get down four wine glasses. She doesn't ask about the extra glass but starts helping me arrange cheese and crostini on a platter. She's wearing a pair of sexy jeans tucked into high-heeled boots, a frothy silk blouse, and big dangle gypsy earrings. I don't see how Troy will be able to resist her—if he comes.

"Looks like there's been big progress on the house." Carolyn arranges *Merry Christmas* napkins beside the cheese tray.

I take the plastic wrap off the matching paper plates. "Good thing it's dark so you can't see the mess they've made of the yard."

Joel brings down his boom box and the Perry Como Christmas tape. It's the only Christmas music we have. Maureen, my mother-in-law, gave us that tape years ago. We have to play it whenever they spend Christmas here.

Carolyn gets a huge laugh out of it. "Perry Como? Is that supposed to be campy?"

I shake my head. "Joel, go pick out something else."

A broad smile hits his face. He takes the stairs two at a time, and comes down a minute later with an armload of pop music, with Cody trailing behind. The first song Joel picks out is "Take Me On." He turns the volume up too loud, but Carolyn starts dancing with him, so I leave it alone. I watch them for a moment, surprised at some of Joel's moves. He must have been upstairs practicing when I thought he was doing homework.

"I want to hang the first ornament this year." Cody kneels on the floor beside the tree and starts digging through the ornament boxes. "Where's Santa on a bicycle?"

Joel and Carolyn keep dancing. I notice Joel is taller than Carolyn, now. That happened overnight! I can't get over how well he dances. I could watch him for hours. I haven't adapted to him being a teenager yet. Seems only yesterday I was teaching him to tie his shoes.

The wood floor reflects the fire glowing in the fireplace. I've become expert at building fires since Adam can't be counted on to be home anymore. I open the screen and poke at the logs. Sparks flutter from the stack. I glance at the mantle clock and wonder where he is. When the phone rings, I jump for it, thinking it must be him, calling to explain why he's late and to say he's on his way.

"Turn down the music, Joel." I pick up the phone. It's Adam's mother instead.

Maureen's voice comes through the line, but I can barely hear her. "Hello, dear! Sounds like you're having a party."

"We're trimming the tree." I cover the mouthpiece. "Joel, please turn down the music!"

"I won't keep you. Oliver's dying to see the boys, so we thought we'd come get them tomorrow, if that won't interfere with your plans." Halfway through her sentence Joel finally cuts down the music so I hear most of what she says.

"Instead of after Christmas?" I ask, trying not to let disappointment creep into my voice. Traditionally, Maureen and Oliver take the boys for the entire week after Christmas, and I always look forward to that break.

"No, no. We still want to do that, too."

Someone knocks at the back door. "I'll get it," Cody yells.

"No, you don't!" Carolyn races him toward the kitchen and the back door. Maureen's voice drones in my ear. "They've decorated the Capitol building and we thought the boys might like to see it."

They see it every year, but I ask, "When should I have them ready?" I know I sound impatient. Voices come from the kitchen and I try to hear. I recognize Troy's accent. I wanted to be the one to introduce them.

"Ten-ish, if that works for you," Maureen says.

Joel comes over to where I sit at Adam's desk. "Mom," he whispers, frowning. "That builder guy is here."

I nod and wave. Cody and Carolyn walk into the dining room with Troy following right behind. He's dressed in jeans and a boxy dark blue shirt, hair neat and combed. Even from the den, I think I smell mothballs. It's kind of touching.

"Hand the phone to Adam, dear," Maureen says. "I want to ask him something."

"He's working late. Sorry, Maureen, I've got to run. My guests just arrived. See you tomorrow." I hang up before she can say anything else and rush to join the others in the dining room.

Joel is bent over the boom box, fiddling with the equalizer. The music is once again too loud: "Little Red Corvette." Troy and Carolyn stand at the table, staring at the food. Carolyn picks up a slice of cheese, skipping the crostini and pot of German mustard. Cody, bless him, Cody jabbers excitedly, showing them the ornament he plans to put on the tree first. He's found the bicycle Santa.

"Well . . ." I smile at Troy and Carolyn but the mood is awkward. I hope she's noticed his broad forehead and the way his smile brightens his face. And he's all smiles right now, uncomfortable, clumsy smiles. I rush to try to mend the situation. "You made it after all," I say to him. He nods, embarrassed. "I guess everybody's met?"

Carolyn's face is flushed. Her eyes shoot flames at me.

Troy has brought a bottle of wine, too—a screw-cap, grocery store, red blend. It's a brand I've never seen before. He holds it out to me.

"You didn't need to," I say, and take the bottle to the kitchen. Behind me, I hear Carolyn venture some small talk and I feel my shoulders relax. Charming men is her forte. She should be able to hold her own now, too.

I sneak upstairs to use the bedroom phone. Adam's answering service comes on but I don't leave a message. So he's not still at work. I wonder if he's on his way home. The drive from Austin takes half an hour, a little more if there's traffic.

Back downstairs, I announce, "Let's start trimming the tree."

"What about Dad?" Joel says.

"We're going to go ahead without him."

I see Carolyn's wine glass is empty, so I go to the kitchen to fetch the bottle of Beaujolais. Before I can do that, she comes behind me and steers me into the pantry.

"What do you think you're doing?" she whispers at me. "Your carpenter? Really, Sarah?"

You're the one who asked if he was single, I want to say, but instead: "He's a nice guy. Polite and gentlemanly. And he's a Taurus. Didn't you tell me you loved Taurus men?"

"I love all men. You know that," she says, then laughs and

covers her mouth. She leans to glance out the pantry door. "I hope he didn't hear me."

I take her arm. "Listen, he doesn't have any family here. I thought he might enjoy doing this tonight. If you don't like him it's no big deal. You never have to see him again."

I turn her around, give her a little nudge back into the kitchen.

"Well anyway . . ." She glances back at me. "At least he's tall."

"And has a nice smile." I laugh at her and we rejoin the party around the tree.

After the talk in the pantry she seems to loosen up. The wine helps. Once we start decorating the tree, everybody gets in a more festive mood. Cody puts on the first ornament. Troy and Carolyn thread garland through the branches. I add tinsel. It takes an hour to finish but once we're done, we all stand back and admire our handiwork.

Then Carolyn suggests we walk outside and look at the tree through the bay windows. After that, we decide we should drive by to see the lit tree from the street. All of us pack into Troy's pickup: me and the boys in the truck bed with two extension ladders and several lengths of rope. Carolyn rides in the cab with Troy. I notice them talking, finally, and wish I could hear what they say.

"Mom?" Joel says as we round the block. "Where's Dad?"

"I don't know, honey. Working, I guess."

"He should be here doing this with us."

"Yeah," Cody chimes in. "He's really missing it."

"He's always missing it," Joel says.

I sigh and shrug. I'm tired of covering for him. I put my arms around both of them, and *ooh* and *ahh* at the Christmas tree in our window as we ride by the house.

BY THE TIME Adam comes home it's ten-thirty, the boys have gone up to their bedrooms, and the wine bottles are both empty.

The back door opens and closes, and I hear Adam bump into the bi-fold doors that partition off the laundry room. Conversation stops as we wait for him. As soon as he appears, anger wells in me. He's obviously plastered. He reeks of alcohol and steadies himself against the big pocket door. My first thought is he shouldn't have been driving in this condition but that has never stopped him.

He smiles blearily at the three of us. "Y'all still here? I figured I'd missed everything." So he hadn't forgotten, simply chose to stay away.

"You have," I say, ice in my voice.

Adam doesn't acknowledge me. He points at Troy. "Glad you could come meet Carolyn here. Isn't she a goddess?" His voice is slurry.

Carolyn laughs and waves at Adam with the back of her hand. "Sit down before you embarrass yourself."

"You'll have to excuse me," he says and falls on the couch right between the two of them. He has a ridiculous grin on his face. I want to slug him. "I have had me a little whiskey to drink tonight."

Carolyn pats his hand. I want to smack her, too. He gives her a big, sloppy kiss on the cheek, and nuzzles behind her ear.

I gather up our empty wine glasses and take them to the kitchen. I have to get as far away from Adam as possible before my head explodes. I set the wine glasses in the sink, squirt Dawn into one, fill it with water, swish it around, and relay the soapy water into the next glass, and the next. I don't hear Troy come into the kitchen until he speaks.

"It was really nice of you to invite me over," he says.

I pivot. He's halfway to the back door. "You're leaving?"

"Yeah. Thanks. I really enjoyed it."

I doubt he means it. This whole night was a bad idea.

He stops before he reaches the door, glances back toward the sounds of Adam's loud chortle from the den. "Do you need help with anything?"

"No, no. But thanks for asking."

He glances again at the sounds from the other room. "OK, well . . . see you Monday then."

Once he leaves, I go back into the den. Adam hasn't moved from the couch. He's sitting right next to Carolyn even though Troy left the other end of the couch wide open. They're laughing about something. I have no idea what and don't really care.

"Troy's gone." I don't try to keep the accusation out of my tone. Not even for Carolyn. She knows all about us anyway. She looks at me and sees I'm angry. She stops laughing.

"Well, I guess I should be going, too." She stands and hangs her purse on her shoulder. I walk with her to the back door. "Are we still on for Taylor tomorrow?" she asks.

I had forgotten about the antique auction. "Why not?"

She pats my shoulder. "I'll pick you up around noon. We'll go in my car this time." She gives me a sisterly smooch on the cheek. "Don't be too hard on him. He's having a bad time right now."

"He's not the only one," I say, coldly. I resent her taking his side and giving me advice about my marriage. I lock the door behind her.

In the den, Adam sits gazing at the embers in the fireplace. He doesn't lift his eyes to me when I come into the room. "Don't even start with me. I'm in no mood."

"Don't tell me you were at the office because I called and got your service."

"We took some clients out for drinks. It was business. You know, as in M-O-N-E-Y!" He spells the word and waves his hand indicating the entire room, the house. "The stuff you use to buy all this crap!"

I bristle at that. It's an accusation he's never made before. "You could have called. You knew we were doing this tonight."

"I got tied up, OK."

We glare at each other. Tension runs between us like a hot cord. Joel's room sits directly over the den and I can hear him moving around up there. Adam hears it too and somehow it breaks the tension. He rises from the couch, goes to the stairs, plants his foot on the bottom step, and grips the newel post.

"Going to bed," he mumbles.

I follow him to the first landing. "Is she pretty?" I say behind him. "Whoever she is."

He stops, turns to look back at me. He's three steps above me so he looks down, and I can't remember ever seeing such contempt on his face. "Stop it, Sarah," he says. "Just stop it."

I don't respond. He stands there a moment gaining his balance, before he continues up the stairs, taking them carefully, one at a time. I watch until he turns at the middle landing, and then I take a deep breath to stop the angry tears burning my eyes. I go back to the kitchen to finish cleaning up. I fill the sink and rewash the wine glasses, the hors d'oeuvre plates and saucers. Black despair swamps me.

It's the disrespect that's so appalling, and the disappointment and disillusionment that follow. I reach for the cup towel. Absently, dry my hands. It isn't like there's no cause for my suspicion, like there's no history of other women, like I haven't had this bleak punchy feeling in my gut before. Forgiving doesn't mean forgetting. It means not quitting on the future, on parenthood, on home and family. It means weathering life together. Doesn't it? I don't even know anymore.

I hang the cup towel on the ring beside the window, and give an inspecting glance around the kitchen, making sure all is done, everything in its place. I turn off the overhead lights and trudge upstairs to bed.

Troy

Six

"Troy Middleton? Is this Troy?" The high-pitched voice that comes through the phone is completely unfamiliar. Full sun dazzles through the blinds—the culprit that awakened me seconds before the phone rang. I glance at the alarm clock: *8:04*. It's Sunday. For me, Sunday is sleeping-in day. I sink back into the warm pillows with the phone to my ear.

"Who's this?" My voice comes out like gravel.

"I woke you. Oh my god, I am *so* sorry."

"No, you didn't. Who's calling?" My first thought is that it might be someone I've given a bid to, and I don't want to make a bad impression.

"It's Carolyn. Carolyn Jeffrey? Remember? Friday night at Sarah's house?"

"Oh—yeah, sure. Hi, how you doing?" I can't think of anything else to say. I don't remember such a shriek in her voice. It's like nails in my eardrum. I hold the phone half a foot away.

"I wanted to catch you early. I had no idea . . ."

"It's OK. What's up?"

"Well, long story really, but . . . so I've come by two tickets to a concert tonight. Tom Petty and the Heartbreakers? I thought of you right away since you had that tape playing in your truck—remember?" She starts singing in my ear, "*You know you don't have to live like a refugee—*" I grimace, and pinch my forehead. It's a little too early for karaoke. She laughs. "Remember it was playing when we rode around the block to look at Sarah's Christmas tree. Well anyway, I thought . . . well, I thought you might be interested."

"Maybe. How much you want for them?"

"Oh God no!" She barks another laugh. "I really want to go, just not alone. Sarah thought maybe I should call you. She gave me your number. I realize you don't know me really, so I thought if you want to, we could just meet there rather than make it like, you know, a date or anything."

She talks fast. The meaning of it sinks in slowly. She's asking me for a date but doesn't want to call it a date. "Meet where?" I ask.

"Oh? So . . . it's at the Erwin. Eight o'clock. I don't know, where do you want to meet?"

"How about the west entrance?"

"So you've been there. Great! That sounds great. See you at eight."

We hang up. I fold my arms under the pillow, stare up at the brown stain on the ceiling, and wonder why that call is such a surprise. I knew the minute I walked into the Glasser's house Friday night there was some kind of hook-up underway. Carolyn Jeffrey—I didn't even know her last name until a couple of seconds ago. She smells like a woman on the prowl.

I roll out of bed and walk down the cold hall to the john. There's half of a cigarette in an ashtray on the sink. I light it with the pack of matches on the tank lid. Smoke fills my lungs and I cough. I've been trying for six months now to quit but I can't seem to go cold turkey. But after the second puff I feel lightheaded. Good sign. Body clearing out the nicotine. When I'm done with this pack, that's it. I've been psyching myself for a week now.

In the kitchen, I mix a spoonful of instant coffee into a cup of hot tap water. The granules don't dissolve completely. They form a bumpy flotilla on the top. I drink it down in one slug. So? A date. Haven't had one of those in a while. With Carolyn Jeffrey. I'm not sure I want to get caught in that trap. Been there. But Petty . . . Tom Petty's worth one night.

SHE'S WEARING BOOTS AGAIN—THE woman has a serious boot fetish. I imagine a closet stuffed full of boots. This pair is suede with silver conchos and feathers on the uppers. Her hair is moussed into a funky sideways ponytail. Around her neck, tiny gold binoculars are jumbled together with beads and chains and pendants. She's dripping with jewelry: huge gold hoop earrings and rings on every finger. She looks like she's going for a cross between Cyndi Lauper and Stevie Nicks. I smile when I walk up to her, but make it a friendly smile so she won't realize I think she's trying way too hard to be hip.

"Oh hi," she says, like she hadn't seen me coming. I bet she hated beating me here. Her eyes give a quick slide over my flannel shirt and faded blue jeans. A flash of disappointment comes and goes on her face, and she doesn't even make it all the way down to my new dark chukkas. The suede isn't even gone off the toes yet.

"Sorry I'm late. Traffic." I take her elbow and start guiding her toward the building.

As we approach the gate, she hands me the two tickets. So it's not a *real* date but she wants it to look like one, wants me to hand the tickets to the dreadlocks sitting behind the ticket booth. The guy slips two stubs beneath the metal bars. I hand one to her, tuck the other one into my shirt pocket.

A line of security guards herds us forward. One of them searches inside Carolyn's fringed handbag for a camera or tape recorder. No bootlegging allowed. Our seats are in the balcony, so far from the stage the drum-kit looks like a toy. I want to people-watch, but she starts in chattering about how she got the tickets from some friend at work who came down with the flu. The friend had won the tickets through a radio contest. Yada, yada, yada . . . I get the picture.

My attention wanders to the crowd around us. Three rows in front of us sits an old jerk who resembles my mother's fifth, and last—so far as I know—husband, Salvador. Old asshole Sal. Acts like him, too, hugging on three teenyboppers, sometimes all at once. His bald head reflects the overhead lights.

I catch a few of Carolyn words as she chatters: *Balcor Electronics. . . . Computer room . . .* until Sarah's name snags my attention. I turn to her. She's smiling.

"And that's how we met," she says.

"So you worked together?"

"Yes, at Balcor. Weren't you listening? Of course, that was back before she became a lady of leisure." There's a bit of derision in her voice. I find it odd.

"She doesn't seem leisurely to me," I say. "She's always busy."

Carolyn elbows me in my side—not my favorite thing, that elbow. "I was kidding. Figure of speech. I know she works hard, but I'd take what she's got in a second." She laughs, but I know I'm right about her. She's on the marriage prowl. For a moment, I feel kind of sorry for her. I go back to people watching.

THE CONCERT IS a good one but not like when I saw The Heartbreakers a few years ago in LA. They played for two hours, nonstop. This one is over in less than an hour. We step outside and I walk her to her car. It's not safe for a woman alone downtown after midnight. Hustlers linger around all over the place. One of them tries to sell us space in a taxi. I hold up my hand to him and he backs off.

We get to her car. She offers to drive me to the spot where my pickup is parked on the other side of the Erwin. Once we find it, she invites me to follow her home. "We can have a nightcap," she says.

I've got to get up early tomorrow but I follow her anyway. I'm not sure why. On the way there, I smoke my last cigarette, crumple the pack, and toss it to the floorboard. That's it. No more. I'm done.

She lives in a row of one-story apartments, third from the end. There's a little plant-filled patio we go through first. Once inside, her place is fixed like Alice in Wonderland—dolls, lace, sculptured mirrors, colored scarves thrown over lampshades. I smell leftover incense or scented candles. Like she reads my mind she lights a stick of patchouli. I knew another woman who burned patchouli incense so I recognize it.

"Obviously, I'm not a minimalist," she says, gesturing at the room; then she blows on the incense stick. "I'll go fix us a drink. Get comfortable." She balances the incense on an old brown snuff jar atop a bookcase, and leaves it burning there where it forms a licorice stick of ash.

When she comes back with two Irish coffees, I've already parked myself on the overstuffed couch. She settles an arm's length away, one bare foot tucked beneath her. There's a red box on the coffee table with gold Chinese writing on the lid. She opens the box, takes out a joint already rolled, and gives me a questioning look. I don't blink. She lights it with a crystal table lighter, then hands me the joint. It's been a long time since I smoked weed, not since my Rocky Mountain days and that was years ago. I take a hit and hand it back to her.

"Have you ever been married?" she asks, getting right to the point. Why has this become the first question from a woman? I remember Sarah Glasser asking me the same thing, and now I think I understand why. Should have known she was matchmaking. Sometimes I have trouble with *no*.

"So far I've managed to escape." I hit the joint she offers and hand it back.

She frowns. "That's cynical." She faces me. Smoke drifts around her head. "You don't get lonely?"

"Everybody's lonely. Even married people are lonely. Especially married people."

"Wow, you *are* cynical. What about kids? Don't you want kids?" She hands me the joint again.

"Last I heard marriage isn't required for that." I hold in the smoke; pass back to her.

"Well, it's preferred, but I've actually been thinking the same thing lately." She twirls the end of her ponytail. "I want kids and I'm not getting any younger. Maybe I should just place an ad." She laughs.

"You'd find some takers. No doubt."

She raises one eyebrow at me and offers the joint again, but I wave it away. My head is already spinning. She continues to smoke. I sip the Irish coffee. It's heavy on the Irish.

"I saw a movie about that once," she says. "I can't remember what happens in the end, just that the main character wanted a baby and not the man. She got what she wanted."

So she's baby hunting. Somehow that doesn't seem as threatening. Her eyes are enormous. Big eyes have always been a turn-on. We stare at each other. I wonder if she can tell I'm stoned. I wonder if she is, too. She's got a fetching smile on her face, twisting the end of her ponytail around and around her index finger. Her hair gets snagged on the big turquoise ring on that finger. "Ouch," she says, slipping out her finger. The ring hangs knotted in a strand of hair near her jaw. I almost laugh at the sight of it but don't think she would see the humor, so I sit down my cup and help her untangle the ring. When I work it free, she holds out her hand and I drop the ring onto her palm.

"Thanks. You saved my life," she says.

"Bit of an overstatement."

"So, do you have someone you're seeing?" Her voice has lowered.

I shake my head.

She leans closer. "It was so obvious the other night at Sarah's, wasn't it? How she was trying to pair us up. She's always doing that to me."

She moves her ponytail off her neck. I take her hand to test the strength of those lavender nails. She doesn't pull back. I think she's been waiting all night for me to touch her. "How can you run a computer with these things?"

"I don't do much computer work anymore. Not since they promoted me into management."

I think I'm supposed to be impressed by that. I punch at her fingernail for a couple more seconds, contemplating. I can tell by the way she's looking straight at me she wants a kiss. I can't decide whether or not to oblige. She's a pretty lady, would be even prettier if she'd tone down the jewelry and the artwork on her face. If I kiss her, I don't want her to make too much of it, but I'm afraid she's the kind that will. I shouldn't have smoked that weed.

When I move for her lips, she clutches onto me like a suction pump. The kiss heats up quick, with lots of tongue and rubbing hands. It feels like she's hungry and I'm steak. For a second I tense up, but then she wraps her arms around my ribcage and we sink down on the couch. One thing leads to another and the next thing I know, I'm tugging off her concho boots and she's got my flannel shirt unbuttoned, and we're both in a fired-up hurry.

Maybe it's because it's been a while—one brief encounter with Amy Landover from the lumber yard several months ago—but I get kind of carried away when Carolyn straddles me right there on the couch like a lap-dancer and pushes her hand down the front of my jeans. When she leads me into her bedroom, I follow. Our clothes end up strewn on the floor in a track that leads all the way to her four-poster bed. Afterward, when she starts asking me to stay the night, I know I've made a big mistake. At least I remembered the mashed condom in my wallet.

"You can shower here in the morning," she says, as I gather up my clothes, putting on each thing I come to along the track. "Sarah won't mind if you get there a little late. She might even appreciate it." Her voice keeps going up a notch. "We could go out for an early breakfast in the morning. There's a great place around the corner."

"Thanks, but I've got to go. It's been fun." I've already stayed way too long.

"Fun?"

I zip my jeans, stick my arms into my sleeves, shrug into the collar. "I had fun. You didn't?"

"Not exactly the word I'd use."

I know what she's thinking—one-night stand—and that's all it should be. But I cannot abide a woman who believes she's got me figured. Her ponytail is long gone but the mousse she used has her hair sticking out wild. She follows me, tying on a flowered robe. She pouts like a ten-year-old.

"Are you into TV?" I say, buttoning my shirt. The ticket stub from the concert is still in my pocket. I thumb it out and lay it on a table.

"What do you mean?"

"Television. Boob tube. Monday night football?"

She shrugs but her expression lifts. "I'm not crazy about football."

"Me neither, but they've got great pizza at Sharpe's. A big screen. Dollar pitchers, if you're into that."

She perks up. "Are you asking me for a date? A real date, oh my." She puts the back of her hand to her forehead like she's Scarlet O'Hara.

I laugh, think *Frankly, my dear, I don't give a damn.* Next, I look around for my chukkas, spot them under the coffee table. I step into them one at a time, fingering on the heels. "Kick-off's at eight."

She goes with me to the door. "Do you want to meet there, or what?" I hear an unmistakable sparkle in her voice. *Uh-oh.* Now she probably thinks I want to get serious.

I lean against the wall. "Do you know where the Glassers live?"

"Quit teasing me."

"That's where I'll be working." I chuck her under her chin. "Come when you get off work. We'll leave from there and go early."

She pulls my face down and kisses me hard on the mouth.

Seven

I'm getting too old to do an all-nighter and then work all day. By the time I get home, take a shower, and change into work clothes, it's already six o'clock. At six-thirty, I pick up Lee. By seven, we're up on scaffolding scraping old peeling paint off the Glasser's house. It's going to be a long day.

Soon after we start, Sarah comes out on the porch in her robe with a pair of fuzzy slippers on her feet. Her hair is still sleep-tangled. In the morning sunlight, she looks sexy. Mainly because it's effortless and she's oblivious to it. Or maybe because I've just spent the night with a woman and sex is on my brain now. Maybe it's the robe, or the slippers, or even the coffee mug she holds in both her hands. Whatever it is, she looks soft and touchable and I have to stop thinking about it before she recognizes desire on my face. I think I've done a pretty good job so far of hiding it.

From the beginning she attracted my attention. The way she fumbled through our first meeting, pretending she knew what she was talking about when she didn't, and how embarrassed she got about it. Then there was the day she played Twenty Questions with me, and I thought maybe she was flirting. Turned out not to be the case, and I have seen no other indication she shares my attraction. But even if she did, I can't let myself get mixed up with another married woman. Anyway, not *this* married woman. I need the work and the Glasser job is too lucrative to muck it up over some lustful overload.

It's a hazard of the job, though. You're stuck with somebody day in and day out, a lot of times it's the woman of the house, and you're both interested in the same outcome, which is supposed to be the work you're doing. But if she's young and pretty it can get dicey. It takes focus and determination to avoid problems. *Professionalism, Troy-boy. You can't let a woman be your downfall.* That was something my stepdad used to say to me.

"Good morning," I call down at Sarah.

She covers her ears, gestures toward Lee chipping away at the peeling paint, then shades her eyes up at me. "How long is this part going to last?"

"Couple of days. Maybe three. We'll blast what we can't scrape off with high-pressure water."

"Lovely." She grimaces. "What other inventive forms of torture do you have in store for me?"

I climb down the side of the scaffolding and drop to the ground. "New paint won't stick over all this old stuff. Is there someplace you could go for a couple of days? Hide out while we finish scraping?"

She waves that idea away, clutches the lapels of her robe to keep it from gapping open. Too late. I caught the top edge of her lacy nightgown underneath. Her skin is the color of figs. She gives me a wry smile. Perfect white teeth. "How was the concert?"

The question doesn't surprise me; I expected it. "Oh, we had a ball." It's all I can do to keep a straight face, but she doesn't get the double meaning anyway. That innocence is a turn-on, too.

"I knew you two would hit it off. Carolyn's fun, isn't she?"

Before I can clean up my answer, one of her kids calls her inside. I latch onto the scaffolding and haul myself back up to the top with Lee. I pick up the scraper and start going again. I don't like the noise either. Fingernails on a blackboard.

A little later, Sarah's kids run out to catch the bus, and then

Adam comes out—styled hair, pleated trousers, floral suspenders over a white dress shirt, tassel loafers. *Big money man. The man with the plan.* He carries his sports jacket over his arm. He waves to me. As I lift my hand he sinks into his Jeep.

The sun gets hot and white paint flecks stick on my sweaty arms and clothes. It's boring work and gives me too much time to think. I don't see Sarah again, but I keep half watching for her to take out the garbage, or maybe step onto the porch to shake out a rug. Usually, she makes a few appearances during the day. Each one gives me a little lift. She's got striking long hair the color of maple wood that's just been cut, bright clear eyes and high cheeks. But more than her good looks, when she talks to me she treats me like I'm somebody, like my opinions matter, like the work I do matters, and I take notice. I've been ignored an awful lot in my life.

AFTER LUNCH, we split up. We'll make better time on our own. So I leave Lee on the scaffolding and take the extension ladder around to the other side of the house. Up on the ladder, I can still hear Lee's scraper. He's a maniac with that thing and I wish I could afford to pay another worker just like him. Scraping old paint is a pain. My back and shoulders already ache. I would rather do almost anything else, something that makes a bigger impact, that's more of a challenge, like rebuilding those columns.

From the outset I knew I would have to cut the bottom of each column off to get rid of the rot. But since they're load-bearing, I couldn't just stick in a filler block and call it good. For days I mulled over the best way to do it, so the columns were strong enough to withstand the weight of the house. The solution I came up with was to lock miter the old wood to the new with a dovetailed, half-lap joint, a trick I learned from my stepdad. We worked on a lot of old houses together in Maine. I'm happy with how the columns turned out. They should last another hundred years.

Suddenly, my scraper hits a bee hole in the siding. Before I realize what's happened, they've swarmed out and popped me several times. I nearly topple off the extension ladder before I can hurry down to the ground. Lee hears me holler and darts around from the other side of the house. With his work gloves, he beats bees off my back, and we duck out of reach of the swarm.

"Hot damn!" he says. "What'll we do about that?"

I inspect the welts rising on my wrists and arms. I fingernail off a few of the stingers. "Guess the noise stirred them up."

Lee stares at my hand. "My old man always says chewed-up tobacco draws out the venom."

I give him a look. "Brilliant. Where do we get tobacco?"

"You don't any have smokes in your truck?"

"I quit again." And I realize I could use a cigarette right about then.

Lee nods at the kitchen window above us. "Ask the lady. She's got kids. She'll have something."

I rap on the kitchen door. It takes a while for Sarah to answer. When she does, she's got a towel wrapped turban-style around her head. She smells like soap and has obviously just stepped out of a shower. She's wearing a dress but she's barefoot. I glance past her at the ceiling. I can't look at her straight on when she's this close.

"Noticed any bees flying around inside your house?" I say. "We hit a hive."

"I found some dead ones in the pantry the other day." She winces at my wrist and forearm. The welts are starting to throb now.

"They're in your wall outside. They like to occupy old houses when nobody's looking."

"The stingers are still in there," she says, as I try to scratch one out with my fingernail. "No, don't do that. Let me get some tweezers."

I watch her run up the stairs. The dress shows a lot of smooth, shapely leg. When she comes back down, she's taken off the towel turban. Her hair is wet and uncombed, hanging over her shoulder. She disappears into the pantry and comes out with a small jar.

"Meat tenderizer," she says. "I've heard it's the best thing for bee stings."

As she uses the tweezers to pluck stingers from my wrist and arm, I notice a small birthmark on her collarbone, just below her neck. If I kissed her there, I imagine the way her wet hair would feel on my cheek. It's just a daydream. I've never been able to come on that strong, especially not when the woman is married. And this one doesn't seem like the type to cheat. Although it would serve him right if she did. It's clear he neglects her.

"Are you feeling OK?" She looks at me with concern. I nod. *Stay focused, Troy-boy.* She shakes some of the meat tenderizer onto my wrist. "Just like seasoning steak," she says with a laugh. "I'm pretending I know what I'm doing, I really have no idea."

I laugh, too. "Looks about right to me."

She uses her index finger to rub in the tenderizer, working in a circle, going from my wrist to the back of my hand and partway up my forearm, mixing it in with the paint flecks and sweat already on my skin. It causes an involuntary arousal I hope she doesn't notice.

"There. That should do it." She wipes her fingers on a paper towel, then uses it to dab away some of the excess from my arm. "Today's my day at the school library. I was just getting ready."

"Sorry to interrupt."

"I'm sorry you got stung by my bees."

We laugh again. And then there's an awkward moment where our eyes meet just long enough to make me wonder if maybe there is some attraction there. It's a far-fetched idea. Women like Sarah Glasser don't look twice at a working stiff like me. I don't even own a set of suspenders, let alone floral ones.

I clear my throat. "Do you want me to just spray some insecticide? Or do you want to find a beekeeper to come capture the queen?"

"Capture the queen," she repeats. "Sounds like a chess move. Will it work?"

"When somebody knows what they're doing. You might call the city and see if they can recommend anybody. Or we can just spray them out. Either way, we'll have to open the wall to clean out the honeycomb."

She pats her forehead with her palm. "Oh gosh." She searches my face. I can almost feel her thinking. Meanwhile, though she doesn't know it, her eyes have seized me. Sea green, smoky flecks of gold, a fringe of long lashes. I let out my breath.

"Would it be terrible to just kill them all?" she says. "Will I be able to sleep at night if I say to do that?"

"You want *me* to call the city?"

"Oh, would you? Thank you so much."

Could be she's just naturally friendly. Maybe she doesn't realize the effect she has on me. Just the way she says my name with her gentle drawl is intoxicating. I turn toward the door. I need to get back to work. This is crazy and it has to stop.

The air is crisp, not cold, but Lee, being a thin-blooded Texan, is bundled up in a sweatshirt, a down jacket, and his work gloves. He looks at me like he's about to laugh.

"She fix you up?" He's got a smirk on. "You were sure gone awhile."

I ignore his smirk. I think Lee knows what's going on with me but I haven't said anything. I made that mistake last summer when I took out Amy Landover from the lumber yard. Lee teased and heckled me about it so much I wanted to fire him. I might have if he wasn't such a tireless worker, and if he wasn't Mr. McIntire's nephew.

"Knock it off," I say, before he can make any more remarks. I glance up at the bee hole. "They're still swarming. We're going to have to take that whole wall down to get them out of there."

"How *do* we get them out of there, Boss?" he asks, still smiling that devilish smile. Or maybe I'm paranoid.

It's dark when Carolyn drives up in her compact car. Lee left hours ago, and I'm sitting in the truck, not wanting to intrude on the Glassers. It's given me a few minutes to doze. When she pulls up, I roll down my window. She keeps her car running and leans across the passenger's side to speak to me.

"Why are you sitting out here?" She's smiling and she's got on red lipstick.

"I was waiting for you. This wasn't such a great idea. I need to get a shower before I can go anywhere. And besides that, I'm bushed."

"You're not canceling on me, are you? Not after I've driven all the way from Austin." She parks her little car, and jumps into my pickup. The smell of musk fills the cab. "I'll wait while you take a shower."

I notice a curtain at one of the house windows pulls back for a second. I can't see Sarah, but I'd make a bet it was her.

We get to my place. The house is messy, but I don't want Carolyn going all domestic on me, to start straightening up or doing dishes. That's when they think they own you. I direct her to the green Naugahyde couch Mr. McIntire furnished for me. "Sit here. Don't move till I come back," I say.

"Can't I even snoop around?"

"No! This is no place for a woman." I laugh. Paint flecks fall off my cap and land in her lap. She brushes at them.

"Yuk! Go take a shower."

Once I'm in the washroom, I start thinking again the same thoughts I was having while I waited in the pickup for Carolyn. I'm not really into her, or this date. I can't even remember what possessed me to arrange it. Had to be the weed. I half-hoped she wouldn't show up. But it was fun sitting there spying on Sarah, watching her walk back and forth through her house, wondering what she was doing that took so many steps. As far as I could tell, Adam hadn't come home when we left. Some men can be unbelievably stupid about their women.

The pressure in the shower decreases and I figure Carolyn is in the kitchen, running water, probably cleaning up just like I asked her not to do. Women like her are predictable. Now, she'll act like she's done me a big favor washing my dishes, and I don't want to feel obligated.

Quickly, I turn off the shower, grab a towel and step out, wrapping the towel around my waist. I find her, as I suspected, scrubbing an egg pan from Saturday morning, humming "Dancing in the Dark," except in nowhere near the same key as Springsteen.

"Nope, nope." I reach over her and take away the pan and the rag. I dip my hand into the sink water and pull the plug.

"I just thought I'd make myself useful while I waited—" she says.

I shake my head. "Nice thought, but I like the lived-in look." I dry her hands on the towel wrapped around my waist. "Haven't you heard about dirty dishwater hands? You'll ruin these beautiful fingernails," I tease.

She looks me right in the eye and slips one hand inside the fold of my towel. She takes hold of my prick. The firmness of her grip surprises me. I stand still for a second or two, then lean my forehead against hers.

"You're soaking wet," she whispers.

Her hand keeps moving. Her mouth starts at my neck and slides down my chest. She takes my left nipple between her teeth. The towel drops off my waist. She's a horny little thing, and we don't make it to Sharpe's.

Afterward, because I'm exhausted, I fall asleep and I don't wake up until morning when I roll against her. It's like sticking my finger into 220 volts. I come out of bed, angry at myself for letting her stay, angry I forgot to set the alarm. It's already seven-fifteen.

"Get up." I push at her hip. I pick up the telephone. She rolls over and smiles. It's the last thing I want to see, that smile. "Get up," I say again, dialing Lee's number. "I gotta get going."

"My god," she says, when she spots the clock.

Lee's mom answers. She tells me Lee found another ride to work this morning. I don't think she realizes who I am. I hang up and start pulling on clothes—the first things I come to in my drawers.

Carolyn sits up in bed, holding the blanket over her breasts. She looks confused. Her clothes are still in the kitchen and I realize she doesn't want to walk in there naked to get them. Her sudden modesty strikes me as comical. I toss her one of my flannel shirts.

"I'm going to be late for work." She tucks her arms into the shirt, pulls the front closed and holds it there.

"There's the phone." I point to the bedside table and rush to the washroom to brush my teeth.

When I come back out, she's on the phone. I'm ready to go but she's standing there still in my shirt, gabbing to somebody on the other line like they're on holiday. Her car is still at the Glasser's and so I have to wait on her. And I'm not happy remembering her car sitting all night in front of Sarah's house, where she could, and certainly did, see it. Now, she'll think Carolyn and I are together. Dating for real. Like a couple.

"Can you hurry it up?" I say.

She turns to glare at me and ends her conversation. You would think I slapped her the way her eyes fling darts at me. She pushes past me to the kitchen. I see her gathering her clothes off the floor. When she comes back, she tosses her head.

"OK if I use your precious bathroom?"

"What's that supposed to mean?"

"I need to pee. Do I have your permission, or will it take too long? God, you really are Taurus, aren't you?"

"I don't have time for this." I fish my keys out of yesterday's jeans.

"You had time last night, though, didn't you?" She flounces passed me and slams the washroom door in my face.

That makes me angry—her acting like a spoiled brat. I turn the knob and shove in after her. She's already perched on the toilet. Her hands fly up to warn me away. Feeling like an idiot, I back out into the hallway. In a moment the toilet flushes, then water runs in the sink. I ease further down the hall, shame washing over me.

When she comes out, she's completely dressed. Splotches of red dot her forehead and chin. She gives me the once over and puts her fists on her hips.

"You know what Sarah said about you that first night at her house? She said, 'He's really polite and gentlemanly, Carolyn. I think you'll like him.' I was pissed off that she'd invited you without telling me and then she said that, and I thought, well maybe she's right. Maybe her taste in men is better than mine, because God knows, I have sure been striking out. So score one strikeout for her, too."

"Look." I sigh. I really wish she hadn't brought up Sarah. "I'm sorry I walked in like that. It was raunchy, I admit it."

"Raunchy? You could say that again."

"*You* slammed the door in *my* face." *Polite and gentlemanly?* Sarah said that? Maybe I should try harder. "But hey, I apologize."

"Don't bother."

She goes for her purse. It's lying on the couch. I follow her out the door and across the lawn to my pickup. She doesn't wait for me to open her side but flounces in and slams the door shut. In a storm she combs her hair and adjusts herself using a compact mirror since there's no mirror on the visor. The silence continues all the way to the Glasser's house. I pull up behind her car. Lee is already up on the scaffolding, scraping paint. Carolyn doesn't make a move to get out.

"I can be a bitch." It sounds like an apology.

"It's OK." I reach around her for the door latch on her side, pop it open.

"You're not going to call me again, are you? Ever."

"I don't have your number."

She takes a pen out of her purse and grabs scrap paper off the dash. It has measurements and figures on it. She turns the paper over and scribbles. "Now you do." She hands me the scrap of paper and gets out of the pickup.

Nobody seems to notice her car as she drives off, or that I've finally arrived. No upstairs curtains part. The noise of Lee's scraper drowns out everything. The spot under the carport where Adam Glasser parks his Jeep is empty. I wonder if he came home last night.

I stand near the scaffolding and watch Lee. Some guys his age are lazy but Lee's not afraid of work. That's why I like him. I want this job to get me more jobs. I want my business to grow. It's what I was focused on before and I need to get focused on it again, quit staying out all night and oversleeping—and chasing damned women. I can almost hear my stepdad scolding me. *Take care of business. Work first. Women second.*

Lee finally sees me and climbs down from the scaffolding like a kid on a jungle gym. "I was starting to think maybe we weren't supposed to work today."

"I'm sorry, man. I overslept."

He glances at the house. "The lady came out asking for you. She says her back door won't stay locked. She wondered if you could fix it."

I give him one pat on his shoulder and take the scraper out of his hand. "You go do it. You'll probably have to move the striker plate. Get a screwdriver from my truck."

"Are you sure, Boss? You don't want to do it?"

"I'm positive." I take hold of the first rung on the scaffolding and swing myself up.

Eight

Ever since I was a little kid, I've watched people who were supposedly in love do things to hurt each other. My ma has been married five times at last count, so she's an expert on how to make romance into mortal combat. I once saw her break a wooden chair over the head of husband number three. He left in an ambulance and never stepped foot in our house again.

When I turned seventeen, I had my first sexual experience. The woman's name was Marilyn Emory, a bowling buddy of my ma's. She was twenty-three years older than me, so it shocked me when, during the summer between my junior and senior year of high school, she made a pass at me, a pass that confused me until she made it clear what she wanted. Her husband owned a garage in South Peoria and worked long hours. We carried on a *Graduate*-style affair for nearly a year before Ma caught us. She broke off her friendship with Marilyn and kicked me out of the house. Only recently have I looked at that whole thing from a different angle. If the situation had been reversed, if Marilyn had been an older man and me a seventeen-year-old girl, and if that man had done the things Marilyn did to me, that man would be in jail for child molestation. Instead, it was me who left home filled with guilt and shame.

I drove my rusted-out '62 Dodge Rambler down to Terra Haute and enrolled at Ivy Tech. I thought I could work full time and go to school full time, too. I wanted a degree in engineering. I really wish I had done that, but I got mixed up with Claire Warren, another older, married, woman. She owned the boarding house where I rented a crappy, sink-and-hot-plate room. Her old man was a long-haul truck driver and Claire got lonely, just like Marilyn I guess. There are lots of lonely women out there. I stayed at Claire's boarding house for eight months and she only charged me rent twice. That fling ended when her husband busted up his Kenworthy and had to give up trucking. Anyway, by then I realized my caddy job at the golf course wouldn't pay tuition. I left Ivy Tech and Terra Haute midsemester.

The first ten years on my own were rough. I moved around a lot, tried all kinds of jobs, ran out of money, went hungry a few times. There were women along the way, some married, some not. One of the unmarried ones, a girl named Leann Hale from Great Falls, Montana, accused me of being a womanizer. She said all I cared about was the conquest and that commitment scared me shitless. At the time I blew it off, figured she was just mad because I said no to her proposal of marriage. But when somebody tells you something that keeps ringing in your ears, it's usually a sign you need to reevaluate. Leann's words have been ringing for quite some time, now.

In the spring of 1984, right after my twenty-seventh birthday, I finally realized I was going nowhere. Out of work, out of luck, out of money, out of confidence, I sold my Rambler, bought an Army jacket with big pockets, stuffed them full of gas station sandwiches, and hitchhiked to Rockland, Maine where my stepdad, Harvey Makin, lived. Harvey was Ma's fourth husband and the only one who ever gave a damn about me. I thought if I could just hang out with Harvey for a while, I would do whatever it took to find my feet.

As it turned out, I ended up staying with Harvey for five years, living in the back room of his yellow saltbox three blocks off Union Street. By trade, Harvey was a building contractor—a man of hammers and saws, spirit levels and plumb bobs—and tough as nails. Years in the sun had lined his face and neck and darkened his calloused hands and wiry arms. I always wondered what drew him to my moody, hot-tempered mother. He rarely spoke of her and never asked me why she and I had fallen out, but he seemed pleased to have me with him. He was the closest thing to a real dad I ever had.

He put me to work, remodeling all the old houses in and around that pretty harbor town. In return, I absorbed everything he could teach me. Before long he made me his foreman. I found I liked working with wood, and bringing old houses back to life, watching an idea come together. There's real accomplishment involved in that so the personal payoff is high. You finish a job, you've got something tangible in front of you. It's a little about perseverance and a lot about self-respect.

When Harvey got sick, I took over his responsibilities: hiring, firing, resourcing materials, tracking the money. When he died he left me his tools and his pickup, which caused a rift with his blood son, Jack, who lived up in Bangor, so I left for Austin. I'd heard it was a boomtown, and the weather sure was better.

One of Harvey's old squadron buddies lives down here with a rental house he lets me have for free—provided I do the work it needs. It gives me a way to meet ends until I can establish myself, which is what I'm hoping for with the Glasser job. I need to get a yard sign made so when I'm working people don't have to stop and ask who I am. Harvey had contractor signs like that. Once I get paid for this job, I'm going to set aside some of the money and have a sign made: *MIDDLETON CONSTRUCTION. Free Estimates, No Job Too Small.* I've been working on that sign in my mind for a while. I've got a picture of it I've drawn on my desk back at the house.

Wednesday morning, when Lee and I arrive at the Glasser house, the beekeeper's van is waiting at the curb. We help him unload his smoker, his generator and shop vac, his queen trap, and all the ice chests he brought for the honeycomb.

"I'm glad there's shade," he says, looking up at the big oak tree as he hands me a white bee suit.

"What's this for?" I take the suit from him.

"I'm going to need you to open up that wall." He puts on his hat and zips the veil to the chest of his bee suit. "You'll need the protection when the bees swarm out."

I breathe a big, anxious sigh, but I don the bee suit and send Lee to fetch a crowbar and hammer from the pickup. I stick my hands into the gloves the beekeeper gives me but I'm not happy about them. Most of the time, gloves inhibit my hands so I'd rather take the calluses. I hope I can pull down that wall wearing these gloves. Lee brings me the tools and I motion for him to haul the keeper's ice chests up closer to the house.

"Think I'll sit this one out, Boss," Lee says, snickering at me in the bee suit.

"Fine. You get to clean up the mess once we're done."

I follow the beekeeper up to the south wall where a few bees float in and out of the hole they've made. He lights his smoker to calm the bees while I crowbar the siding off the house. Bees swarm out just like he said they would. I dodge back but the suit keeps me safe, and it's just as I figured: the wall is loaded with layers and layers of honeycomb as well as hundreds, maybe thousands of bees. The sound of them vibrates the air around us.

The beekeeper puts me in charge of the shop vac. I vacuum bees while he slices out the honeycomb and keeps using the smoker. He knows what he's doing. The deeper into the layers we go, the thicker and drippier the honey. It's eerie working with bees swirling around me but my confidence in the suit and the smoker grows. When the queen falls out of the combs, the keeper scoops her into his trap.

"Looky there," he says, holding it up so I can see her. "Ain't she a beaut."

It takes two hours and three ice chests of honeycomb to finish. The keeper transfers the vacuumed bees into a bee box. There's a big mess left behind and a few loose bees still hover in the air. When I take off the bee suit I feel lightheaded and realize I've been shallow breathing the whole time.

Lee carries the ice chests to the white van, and Sarah comes onto the front porch. I haven't seen her all morning but she looks as sunny and fine as ever.

"What an adventure!" she says, clapping her hands together as she comes down the sidewalk toward the van. "I've been watching from the window. I want to see the honeycomb."

The beekeeper takes her to the back of the van for a look. I try not to stare at her but it's not easy. Her hair is a yellow braid down her back, blue jeans showing off her curves. My eyes are just drawn and I can't seem to help it.

"Did you get stung?" she asks, and it takes a second for me to realize she's speaking to me. "Do I need to go get my tweezers?"

"Nope." I glance at Lee, who has another suspicious smile on his face. "Lee here's going to need a lot of soapy water, though, to clean up that mess in the wall."

"Of course. Come on." She takes Lee's arm for a second. The smile leaves his face. She leads him to the side of the house. I watch as they stop to inspect the open wall.

"Tell the lady," the beekeeper says, interrupting my gaze, "I'll bring her some of this honey once we get it extracted." He looks out where I've been looking. "Nice ass," he says in a lowered voice.

I grunt and nod in agreement. *That's what I was thinking*, I nearly say it but stop myself.

On Friday, after I finish work for the week, Mr. McIntire comes by the house. We chat about what all he wants done inside and how much he wants to spend. He says he'll leave the choice of fixtures and paint colors to me as long as I stay within his budget. I'm honored by his trust in me.

He likes to sit a while and visit. Sometimes we talk about Harvey. Tonight, I show him the plans I've been drawing for my own house, the one I want to build someday. It's a bungalow style with a big porch and some half-timbering. Mr. McIntire seems interested in hearing about it and stays till nearly ten. After he leaves, I put a TV dinner in the microwave and take a quick shower. As soon as I step out the phone rings. I dry off as I go to answer it.

Carolyn's shrill voice comes over the line. "Wow!" she says. "I guess you must've lost my number."

She's right. It hits me—that scrap of paper. It's probably still in the pickup somewhere. "I planned to call you," I stammer.

"Yeah, when?" She pauses. I don't say anything either. "So? What were you going to call me for?"

Think. Why would I call her? I can't come up with a good reason. Finally, I say, "What you been up to?"

"I knew it! You're a terrible liar." A shrieky laugh stings my ear. "I've been Christmas shopping all week. Going straight from work, but I still have some left. You can go with me tomorrow. I need help carrying everything."

I glance at the ceiling and that brown water stain from before the new roof. I need to treat the mold and put on a coat of white ceiling paint, and there's a job I need to bid. But mostly, I don't want to go Christmas shopping with Carolyn. I can't think of a worse way to spend a Saturday.

"Troy? Are you still there?"

I gather my attention. "Yeah."

"I'll meet you at eleven. Center fountain at the mall. We can grab lunch."

"OK," I say, lamely. It seems the word *no* has exited my vocabulary altogether.

AT A QUARTER TO ELEVEN, I find a bench near the center fountain and sit down to watch mall custodians set up choir risers and music stands in the center court. Farther down, a line of kids, some of them clinging to their parents, wait to have pictures taken with a man in a Santa suit. Poinsettias fill planters attached to the upper-level railing. Fifty-foot lengths of tinsel and glittery snowflakes dangle from the skylights. It's noisy and crowded. I can't remember the last time I hung out in a mall.

When I spot Carolyn walking toward me, I almost don't recognize her. She's wearing plain Levi's, a tailored pinstriped blouse, brown corduroy jacket, canvas gym shoes, hair loose on her shoulders. She looks almost normal—except for the fist-sized bangles at her ears, three necklaces around her neck, and rings on every finger. When I stand up she hugs me. I'm surprised by the hug. It's like she wants the people around us to notice, to think we're a couple. I have to stop this; it's already getting out of hand.

"Let's eat lunch first," she says. "Before we get bogged down with packages."

"We're going to get bogged down with packages?"

She laughs, grabs my hand, and leads me through the melee. She knows her way around because we end up smoothly at the entrance to a cafeteria. As we go through the serving line I realize I'm hungry and pile food onto my tray. She gets a salad, mineral water, and a strawberry shortcake with a huge dollop of whipped cream. "Can't resist deserts," she says.

We find a table and as soon as we're seated, she starts picking apart my food choices. "That's loaded with fat." Her fork points at the steak and gravy on my plate. "That will put you way over your thirty percent limit."

"I don't think I have a limit." I cut into the steak and stick a bite into my mouth.

Her eyes widen like I'm a moron. "Being a man automatically puts you in a higher risk group for heart disease. Don't you know?"

"Oh, that." I laugh and point with my knife at her strawberry shortcake. "What about your thirty percent?"

"I'm not a man." She gives me a too-cute smile. "Lucky for you."

My eyes narrow on her. Perfect time for me to tell her I'm not looking for what she's offering. Leann Hale's words come back to mind to confuse me. *Womanizer. Conquest. Commitment.* I turn back to my steak, and saw off another bite.

"Tell me about these packages we're going to get bogged down with," I say before I put another bite into my mouth.

Change the subject. Keep it light and simple. The tactic works. She starts in listing off what she already has for people I don't know. I am not interested in hearing about her relatives, but she tells me about each and every one of them, how they're related to her and where they live. I pretend to listen and just keep shoveling in food. She tells me about a set of cloisonné hairclips she bought for Sarah. I have no idea what cloisonné is but as usual, I perk up when I hear Sarah's name.

Carolyn wrinkles her forehead. "I was hoping you could help me with Adam. Men are so hard to shop for. In fact . . ." She smiles. "You, for instance. What do you want for Christmas?"

"Don't get me anything."

She grins. "Oh, I knew you'd say that. People always do."

"But I'm serious. Let's don't start with that."

She studies me, then says, "OK—no gifts. Provided you come with me to Nacogdoches. I'm leaving Friday and I'll be back a day or so after Christmas."

"No." I shake my head, use my napkin. "Thanks, but no."

"Oh come on, Troy. Don't be such a hard ass. You already said you don't have any Christmas plans. You'll feel right at home, I promise. I can't let you be alone at Christmas."

"Who said I was going to be alone?" She looks like I slapped her. Her entire face turns as pink as her blush-powdered cheeks. She stares at me, clearly hurt. Now, I feel bad, and I'm not sure what made me say it since it's not true. "Look, you don't really know me. I could be out on murder charges for all you know."

"Are you? Out on murder charges?"

"No, but why would you want to rush me off to meet your family?"

She blinks. "Do you even like me? At all? I can't really tell."

It's a question I'd rather avoid. Either way I answer, I'm screwed. No, and she'll have Sarah hating me, too. Yes, and I'll be labeled her boyfriend or new lover or something equally inaccurate. I cuss myself for letting things get to this point.

"Would I be sitting here right now?"

"I have no idea. Maybe you think I've got money or something."

I spit out a humorless laugh and snatch the ticket off the table. She follows meekly to the register. I pay for both meals so she won't think I'm a cheapskate. Right away I see it backfires. She gets this adoring look on her face and I think she's going to kiss me right there—just because I paid for her meal.

Back out in the mall, she links her arm through mine. She says, "I shouldn't have said that back there. I'm sorry."

I look down at her, realize I'm going to have to shake her off, if not today then pretty soon, but I can't think of how I'm going to do it without endangering the Glasser job. I should have stayed home and painted the ceiling.

We head to a toy store for gifts for nieces and nephews. She goes wild with her credit cards, then yammers about how she doesn't know how she's going to pay the bills when they come. So, she's in debt like every other red-blooded yuppie. I'm no help to her when it comes to choosing a gift for Adam Glasser. When I suggest a flask or a beer stein, she accuses me of being tacky. We end up in the tie department of a men's store off the center court. Adam is a tie kind of guy. She buys one with maroon paisleys.

"He'll look great in this," she says, holding the tie under her chin. "Of course, he'd look great in anything. To tell the truth, I've always had a little crush on him." She laughs when she says it but it strikes me as weird, and the laugh seems phony. I search her face. She shrugs. "All us girls at Balcor did. He's just so damned gorgeous."

"He is?" I frown. "All I see is a drunk. Who doesn't appreciate what he's got."

"If you mean Sarah, I'll let you in on a little secret—he wants to leave her. They nearly split up about six weeks ago." She flicks through a rack of men's pullovers.

Suddenly, I'm interested. "Does she know you keep secrets with her husband?"

She doesn't seem savvy to what I'm asking. She keeps flipping through the shirts, takes out one, and holds it up. "It's a bad situation. I think they're both miserable." She looks at the price tag. "I think I'll get this one for Daddy."

She lays the shirt over her arm and moves away. I watch after her for a second, digesting this new bit of information. But I also question the easy gossipy tone she used while telling me. Are we both hung up on the Glassers? Wouldn't *that* be classic irony?

IN THE CENTER concourse of the mall, near where I waited an hour or so ago, a school band is rustling around behind the music stands, some of them warming up. Horns blow, off pitch. A drummer does a roll and a rim shot. The band director gets up on a platform and taps his baton on the side of his music stand. He wants attention. Silence drowns out the mall noise. Then "Deck the Halls" powers out. We stop walking, both of us loaded down with Carolyn's packages.

"Let's listen for a minute," she says near my ear. I'm about to suggest we make a trip to her car first, when she screeches and twirls away. When I turn she's gone ten feet, grabbing Sarah in a bear hug. Sarah catches my eye over Carolyn's shoulder. She shakes a wave at me. Carolyn bends to give Cody a hug, too.

"Joel's playing," Sarah shouts at us and points toward the band. I can barely hear her over the music but I nod. I recall the saxophone that's been bellowing for the past few weeks. Over the sea of players dressed in navy pants and white shirts, I spot Joel on the third riser, just behind the oboes, blowing sternly on his horn. He looks scarecrow skinny up there with all the other skinny teenage scarecrows behind the music stands.

Carolyn pulls the paisley tie out of a sack and shows it to Sarah. From where I stand I can't hear what they say to each other, but with their heads bent together, standing side-by-side, I can't help but compare them. Even in jeans, Carolyn is flashier with her jewelry and makeup, while Sarah's face looks scrubbed clean, eyes bright. Wispy strands of hair uncaught by her ponytail feather her face. The only jewelry I can see on her is the gold band on her hand and two pearl studs in her ears. She's all soft, warm, California-girl colors. I can't stop staring at her, but that's nothing new.

The longing sickness starts in my gut again. I have to sit down and find a cold bench where I pile Carolyn's packages around my feet. Cody comes to sit next to me. He draws his right shoe under him to tie his laces. He says something I can't hear, so I bend down, cup my ear. He leans in.

"Do you like arcades?" he asks. "Video games?"

I peel my eyes off his mother and look down at him. He's a younger, male version of her. "Are you bored?"

He nods, swings his foot. "Mom says I can't go off alone, and she won't leave here because of Joel." He grimaces at the school band.

I glance again at the two women. Sarah's face beams toward where Joel sits blowing on his saxophone. "Are you asking if I'll take you to the arcade?"

He points behind us with his thumb. "It's just around the corner."

I pivot. I see the sign now. I consider Carolyn, then Sarah. I can't take being with both of them together right now anyway. I start gathering up the packages. "OK. Let's go."

"Cool." He leaps up from the chair. "I'll go tell Mom. Don't leave."

He shoves through the crowd gathered for the band concert and tugs at Sarah's jacket. She bends toward him, her head turned slightly. She straightens and shoots a questioning look my way. I nod and give a thumbs-up. And Cody comes rushing back in my direction.

AT THE ARCADE, I leave Carolyn's packages with the girl at the change counter and buy a handful of tokens. Cody swears he'll pay me back. I find that cute and funny. The kid is a demon with a joystick. He beats me at every game I try. The clanging, ringing, buzzing, and computer blips work on my nerves worse than the school band back out in the mall. I feel ancient all of a sudden.

"Point me to a pinball machine," I shout. "I bet I can beat you at that."

Cody wrinkles his nose at me. He probably doesn't even know what a pinball machine is. He keeps shooting down enemy aircraft on the video screen.

Just before I reach total brain meltdown, Sarah and Carolyn come into the arcade, with Joel toting his saxophone case. Carolyn comes up behind Cody, and while he's on his nineteenth game of Sky Soldiers, she pinches his ear.

"Hey, you. You stole my date," she says.

I don't approve of her loose use of the word date. I give Sarah a quick glance. She's handing money to Joel. The lanky boy towers over her by a few inches.

Carolyn rubs the back of my arm. "Sarah wants us to come to her house. She wants to feed us dinner."

"Adam's gone to the deer lease," Sarah chimes in. "I could use the company."

My brutalized ears buzz. It's just the three of us standing there, Sarah, Carolyn, and me. The boys are off playing. Carolyn grips my elbow. "Look! Pinball machines in the corner." I'm surprised to see a row of machines back there with nobody playing on them. "I challenge you both," Carolyn says and takes off in that direction.

Sarah hangs back. "*Will* you come to dinner?" she asks me. "It's just a casserole I've thrown together."

For a second I lose myself watching her mouth and eyes. I nod lamely. We head toward the pinball tables against the wall where Carolyn waits. I don't mean to but I cream both of them three games in a row. I don't mention the endless hours I spent as a kid playing at the pizza joint down the street from our house, mostly to escape family craziness, but all that practice comes in handy today.

"Show off," Carolyn says, and *frogs* my arm.

AFTER DINNER, I stay in the kitchen to help Sarah clean up. Carolyn has gone upstairs with the boys on some secretive errand. I can hear them trooping around up there. Sarah loads the dishwasher while I wipe down the counters.

"Carolyn told me she asked you to go home with her for Christmas. She said you turned her down." She glances at me. I shrug. She goes back to stacking dishes. "I know she's over-eager, but she means well." More banging and stomping come from overhead. The ceiling shakes. Sarah scrubs at the casserole dish. "I'm supposed to find out who you're going to be with while she's gone."

"Give me a break," I breathe the words, then hope I haven't shown her my impolite, ungentlemanly side. But I'm already sick of this discussion. I feel her eyes on me.

"Conniving women, huh?" She turns back to scrubbing. "But I can tell she really likes you."

"Well, she's not too particular." *Any old prick in a storm*, I want to say.

Sarah laughs, almost like she reads my mind. "Are you slamming yourself?"

"No." I buff hard at the edge of the counter. "But I *am* particular. You want the truth?" She waits for me to go on. "I'll be alone at Christmas. But when she asks, I'd rather you just tell her I wouldn't say."

"Is something going on with the two of you?"

"Not nearly as much as you think." I watch her pour detergent into the dishwasher cup. "Maybe if she was more like you—" The words are out before I can stop them. At least, I put in the *more like* instead of saying flat-out what I mean.

She raises away from the dishwasher, leaves the door open. "More like me how?" Her voice sounds kind of mocking, like she already knows what I mean, and I think she probably does.

"Easygoing. Honest. She takes everything too serious. Herself, for one."

"I take a lot of things seriously, too. Almost everything. Too seriously. And if you feel that way, you should stop seeing her. She might think she's being led on."

"She doesn't need to be led on. She clings."

"That's because she wants a relationship." I can tell she feels the need to defend Carolyn. I think she's a better friend than Carolyn is.

I drop the dishrag on the edge of the sink. "She's not my type."

"That is such a cop-out, Troy." A smile teases her face.

I step in closer and she doesn't move away. "OK then . . ." I'm also smiling, can't help it. "She doesn't do it for me."

"Oh, you guys, always talking about *it*. What is this mysterious *it* anyway?"

"I know *it* when I see *it*." I hit both "its" hard, the same way she did, keeping it light, jovial. I laugh. So does she. I'm so deep into her space I can smell her perfume, something floral yet spicy. "And don't lump me with other guys."

"Oh?" She leans backward against the counter. "You're different, huh?"

"I think so."

"Of course you do." She looks right into my eyes. "Not looking for a girl who's sexy and maybe a little too over-eager. You want someone honest, who doesn't take things so seriously?"

I smile. "There you go."

"Someone who's more like me?" She says it with humor.

"Exactly."

"Except I'm not available."

"That's too bad." The humor leaves my voice. I try to keep it there, but it won't stay.

She notices. She straightens and blinks. I keep eye contact with her. I wonder what would happen if I kissed her. Just took hold of her and kissed her. Would she stop me? Something in how she's looking at me says maybe not. I'm on the verge of it when Carolyn and the boys clomp down the stairs.

At the sound, Sarah jumps away just as they burst into the kitchen, giggling and noisy. Their arms are full of gift-wrapped packages.

"I told them they owe me their allowances for life," Carolyn says as they pass through to the dining room, headed for the Christmas tree.

"What's all this?" Sarah follows after them. I have the distinct feeling she's not as interested in the packages as in running away from me.

"Presents for you and Dad." It's Cody's voice.

I stand there in the kitchen for a minute, gathering myself, feeling foiled—probably a good thing. I cough, clear my throat to stall and focus, before I lean to close the dishwasher and join them in the other room.

Sarah

Nine

I stand at the three long windows in the den and watch Troy Middleton out in the yard. He's having some kind of trouble with the paint sprayer. He kneels on the brown grass and studies the nozzle. I situate myself behind a section of wall between the windows so he can't see me. He has on an old pair of jeans and a plaid jacket. Lee walks up from the direction of the porte cochere to help with something that takes three hands. I peek through the lace panels.

School has let out for the holidays. The boys are upstairs cleaning their rooms. Joel's music travels down to the den, too loud. They have only been home for two days and they're already on my nerves. Christmas is this Sunday and not only have I not finished shopping, but I also haven't done my usual baking either. I don't even have all the groceries bought for Christmas dinner. I haven't sent out a single Christmas card, not even to Adam's clients. I have no interest in any of that. It all seems tedious and trite. The only energy I have for anything is what I'm doing right now, hiding behind the den wall watching Troy through the window.

For some reason, he isn't wearing his cap today. The sun glints coppery highlights I never noticed before in his hair. His shoulders fill out the chambray shirt he wears rolled carelessly to his elbows. He moves with an agility unusual in a man so tall and lean—like a swimmer. The day I tweezed bee stingers out of him I noticed his long hands and chiseled forearms. I would have had to be blind not to notice, but the sight didn't cause the deep thrum inside me it causes now.

It started last Saturday, after Joel's concert when we were alone in the kitchen. I didn't expect him to flirt with me. It came out of nowhere. It felt fantastic to have a man make eyes at me like that, to flirt and flatter me, a married woman. A mom. And I thought I had forgotten how to flirt, it's been so long. But now it's left me unsettled, off-balanced enough to hide behind a wall and moon out the window at a man who isn't my husband. A man who has been dating my best friend.

When I think about it, if I'm honest with myself, I've been drawn to him for a while, watching for his truck to arrive, rushing out to say hello, or finding some other excuse to go out to talk to him. It hasn't been entirely because of the work on the house either. I've looked forward to his pleasant smile and easy conversation, dreaded the long drab weekends before he was back again. I just never suspected he was drawn to me, too—not until Saturday night in the kitchen—and that makes everything different, slightly dangerous. When we were standing there in front of the kitchen sink, for just a moment I thought he was about to kiss me. His eyes absorbed me in a way that seemed much more than just friendly.

When he got here this morning he told me they would be finished by Friday—before Christmas as promised. It will be a good thing to have him gone. The right thing. With him gone, these twitchy, giddy, overstimulated feelings will fade and life can get back to normal. But I think I might miss him. I can already feel the coming loss. My days have been brighter with Troy working here, even as the arguments and fights with Adam have escalated each night.

It's as if our marriage has a terminal disease, one that goes into remission for a day or maybe a few hours, then returns with more virulence. Last night the fight was over the bicycle I want to give Cody from Santa. It will be Cody's third bike, and Adam doesn't think he deserves another. But the first bike he outgrew, and the second was stolen out from under our porte cochere. Someone cut the chain and took it during the night late last summer. Neither loss was Cody's fault.

"You spoil him rotten," Adam said. "How will he ever learn the value of anything if you give him everything he wants? Anyway, he's too old for a goddammed bicycle."

"He's eight. I rode my bike until I was fifteen."

"Of course you did. You were an adolescent when I met you."

That isn't true, I was twenty, and the only reason he said it was to insult me. I grabbed my pillow and slept in the guest room. I've done that a lot lately. I'm mystified by wives who manage to make their husbands sleep on the couch. Adam would never budge from our bed. It's always me who makes the sacrifice.

Out on the lawn, Troy doesn't seem to be getting anywhere with the paint sprayer. When he finally stands and glances toward the house, I know he's coming inside. I rush to the kitchen and glance around for some busy work. I grab a scrubber from the sink, but before I can even pretend to have been doing something other than staring out the window, two taps sound on the back door. I take a deep breath to quiet the rush inside me.

As has become his habit, he pokes in his head and calls out. "Anybody home?" then spots me at the sink. "Hey, there." He eases inside. "OK to use the phone?"

I nod, drop the scrubber, and even though he knows where the phone is, I take him into the den. I watch him pick up the receiver from Adam's desk. I notice the smatter of dark hair on the back of his hands. He gives me a smile and I look away.

"That's what I get for using rental crap," he says, with the phone pressed to his ear. "Spray head's completely clogged."

I keep my eyes averted and listen while he talks to someone on the other end of the line. What he says doesn't register, but I like to hear him talk—the elongated vowels and dropped last consonants, the rounded Rs that pop up in places where they don't belong. When he hangs up I'm still there, milling around the bookcase, rearranging Christmas candles, acting as if I haven't been listening.

"They say they've got another one," he tells me as if I'm as concerned about the paint sprayer as he is. "I'll go get it so we can finish and be out of your hair."

"You're not in my hair."

He lets out a laugh. "You've got to be ready for some peace and quiet."

He starts for the dining room. I shadow him. "Actually . . ." I say, "I was thinking there might be some other things I'd like you to do, later on. After the holidays."

At the cook island, he stops so suddenly I nearly run into him. I dance backward a few steps. He pivots around. Up close his eyes aren't as dark as they seem from a distance. They lean toward hazel and they look right into mine. "Oh yeah?" There's a deep hollow in his throat. "Like what things?"

"Well . . ." I step back, and bump into the door while facing him. I look around for something, then point at the glass pane over the dining room doorway. "This transom. It won't open. None of them do. Would be nice for air circulation. I guess they're just so old and . . ."

He reaches up. He's so tall he can touch the bottom of the frame. He pushes and there comes a crackling sound. "I'm pretty sure it's just painted shut. We can fix that before we leave."

"Oh—really. That's all?" I'm sure he hears the disappointment in my voice because I do. My eyes land on the bread-safe with my granny's teapot sitting on the open shelf. "You don't happen to refinish furniture, do you? I've been wanting this bread-safe worked on . . . ."

"I don't have much experience with that. It's a whole other ballgame." His attention stays on the safe. "Isn't this what they call a primitive? I wouldn't do anything to it if I were you."

"You wouldn't?"

He shakes his head. "No. It's rustic. And look how rounded the edges of the board are, all the hands smoothing it down through the years. It's solid." He continue to inspect the safe, and so do I, with new appreciation. He leans to rub at a spot just under the overhang of the kneading board, goes down to one knee to peer under the safe. "This is interesting." I watch him feel around. "Somebody started to put in a drawer down here."

"Really?" I bend to look, too. He pulls a penlight from his pocket. The beam of light flashes down two short parallel boards.

"These are runners. Or they were going to be runners." He pockets the penlight, with his fingernail scrapes out a bit of wood putty from under the overhang. "Right here on the front. They made these two cuts. Probably planned to pop out this piece and use it for a drawer front. For some reason they changed their mind and puttied it."

"I have never noticed that before." Our eyes meet under the bread-safe. I'm first to break away.

"That's what's so cool about antiques. The history." He stands and dusts his hands on his jeans. "I might be willing to try to put that drawer in for you."

A thrill rushes through me. "You would?"

"Yeah, it won't take much. Cut out that puttied piece. Box in the sides, maybe add a turned-wood knob if you want that."

I almost clap my hands together but somehow refrain. We both smile, me backed against the cook island, Troy leaning beside the dining room doorway. We stay that way for a moment. I think he knows why I brought this up—it's just to keep him here longer.

"Would you come over on Christmas Eve?" It comes out of nowhere. I didn't even realize it was rolling around in my mind until I say it. "We're having a little party," I add. "Well, not a *real* party. Just Adam's business partner and his wife. They always stop by."

"This wouldn't be another setup, would it?"

I shake my head and laugh. "No, I promise I won't do that again. But I'd really like it if you would come. You can bring anybody you want to."

He presses his finger to the corner of his eye like he's making up his mind. He dips his head and gives me an elfin smile. It's absolutely the most charming thing I think I've ever seen. "If I do come it'll just be me."

I SLOG through the next days, and finish my shopping. I buy Joel a CD player to add to his stereo system, and despite knowing it will make Adam angry, I find a bicycle for Cody with spoke wheels and handbrakes. For Marty and his wife, Laura, I find a Black Forest cuckoo clock at an antique shop in Taylor, forgotten in a dusty corner. It's key-wound, and when the hour strikes, a troupe of polka dancers spin out to dance a few turns.

For Adam, I draw a blank. I feel so much bitterness towards him lately, I can't seem to get passed it enough to come up with something thoughtful. I wander into the sporting goods department thinking of some kind of hunting gear, but I'm lost in there, and anyway, he already has everything. I end up with an Angora sweater the same color blue as his eyes.

I want to get Troy something in case he comes Christmas Eve, but nothing in any of the stores seems suitable. I wander in and out of men's departments, bump into other last-minute shoppers. Cologne seems too impersonal—or maybe too personal—anyway not appropriate. Clothes are impossible and also inappropriate. I have no idea what kind of music he likes apart from Tom Petty and the Heartbreakers. Tools, of course, are not an option. A gift certificate seems lazy. I end up buying him a pair of kid-lined work gloves since I've never seen him wear any, and at the same store, I also buy a sock hat to keep his ears warm. Neither gift is inventive, both are probably too motherly, but it's the best I can do.

On Thursday, just before she's due to leave for Nacogdoches,

Carolyn comes over and we exchange gifts. She seems to love the Bill Blass bathrobe I picked out for her. Adam detests his tie, I can tell from his forced laughter, but he's gracious. She gives the boys books, which they toss aside almost immediately. For me, she has a lovely set of cloisonne hairclips. She takes me upstairs and makes me sit in front of the mirror while she arranges them in my hair.

"I went by to see Troy before I came here," she says, as she brushes my hair up off my neck. "He told me you invited him here for Christmas Eve. That was brilliant, Sarah, thanks. You can keep an eye on him for me."

I maintain my expression. It never occurred to me to consult with her. I feel a sudden pang of guilt. "Oh Carolyn, what if you're getting ahead yourself with him?"

"What do you mean?" She runs the brush through my hair. "Do you know something?"

I breathe a sigh and shake my head. "I just worry about you is all."

"Well, don't. This time I'm handling it right. I'm going to let him call me next time instead of me always being the one. I made sure he knows the day I'll be back."

I focus on my reflection in the mirror and not hers. *Change the subject.* What kind of person fixates on her best friend's boyfriend?

She takes a step back from me. "There. I knew these would look gorgeous in your hair."

She gives me the hand mirror so I can see how she's swept my hair up off my neck. It's elegant, too fancy, and not at all my style. She sprays me down with loads of hairspray. After she leaves, I keep the hairclips in until Adam finally notices. He takes one look at me and shakes his head.

"It's not you, honey. You don't have the swan neck to wear your hair piled up like that."

He buzzes me on the cheek as he heads to the den for the TV and the couch. I frown at his back. As soon as he's gone, I remove the clips and brush out the hairspray with my fingers.

Troy and Lee finish painting early on Friday. By noon, when I go outside to look, they're already clearing up their mess.

"I'm afraid we crushed your shrubbery," Troy says.

"It'll grow back." I shade my eyes and admire the house.

It gleams in the bright sunshine. We went with dark tan for both stories, white trim, and sea green on the attic level, both the fish scales and the turret. The house looks fantastic, like it might have when it was first built. Stately white columns you can't even tell have been rebuilt, silver-gray porch floor, sky blue on the porch ceilings to keep away mud daubers. I can hardly wait to put up all the outside Christmas decorations. I have them piled in a corner of the dining room.

"I love it," I say.

Troy admires the house, too. "It did turn out pretty good. We should have taken before and after pictures." He moves his attention to me. "About tomorrow night . . ."

"You're coming, aren't you?" I can't let him back out.

He shifts from one foot to the other. "I don't know, you have your friends coming."

"Adam's friends. And I *want* you to come. You're *my* friend. Please, come."

He looks away out toward where Lee walks back and forth, to and from the truck, loading up. "OK," Troy says at last. "What should I bring?"

"Nothing. I have everything. See you tomorrow night." I wave as they drive off. I rush

inside, calling the boys down from their rooms. I yell up the stairs. "Come on outside. Let's decorate the house."

I rummage in the sideboard for the camera, find it. I grab the Christmas wreath that has been waiting for a freshly painted front door. Cody hurries down the stairs. Joel comes more slowly.

"Grab the boxes of pine garland and the lights." I point at the boxes waiting in a corner of the dining room.

We hustle outside with our arms full. We wrap the garland around the new porch railings and the columns. We do the upstairs gallery, too. Joel strings lights. Cody finds extension cords. We do it all in record time, before it gets too dark for pictures. I hang the wreath, then take the camera and back a few steps down the front walk. I tell them where to stand, then I back up a few more steps—back, back, back until the entire front of the house is in the frame. Even Snowball makes it in, curled on the Santa doormat beside the boys' feet.

Ten

I haven't seen Laura Dean since last Christmas. Having the Deans over on Christmas Eve has become a sort of tradition, but there's too much difference in our ages for Laura and me to be close friends. She's nearer to my mother's age than mine. When she gives me a hug in the kitchen, I smell *Joy* behind her ears. Exact same perfume Mother wears.

"Merry Christmas, Sarah," Laura says. "Your home looks lovely, as usual. You've done so much work on it."

Over Laura's shoulder, I see Adam eyeing my jeans with disapproval. He wanted me to wear a low-cut, slinky cocktail dress that had been hanging in my closet for years. He even laid it out on the bed for me. I didn't mention it, just hung the dress back in the closet and put on these jeans and an olive-green blouse. I look at Laura's slacks and poinsettia sweater and I'm glad I kept it casual.

"Why don't you give Laura the ten-dollar tour, honey," Adam says to me. He's holding a glass with my pink punch in it, punch I saw him spike earlier with vodka. We'll have to keep the boys away from it.

"She doesn't want to see the house again," I say.

"Oh, yes I do. Show me what all you've done since last year." She hooks my arm in hers.

We go up the stairs. She makes over the carved newel post, the smooth mahogany banister, the same way she did the last time she was here. She likes the dove gray paint I chose for Cody's room, and comments on the crown molding around the ceiling.

"I do so admire you and Adam taking on a project like this house," she says, as we pass through the master bedroom. "I believe it would drive me bananas being under construction all the time."

"Well, hopefully, we're through for a while." I flip on the outside light and lead Laura out the door onto the gallery. The exterior paint still smells fresh. I glance down the street. No headlights. I told Troy to be here about seven-thirty. By my watch, it's nearly eight.

Laura looks at the sunburst design on the floorboard as it rounds the curve of the gallery. "Who's your carpenter? What a nice job he did here."

"He might be stopping by later," I say, but I don't think she hears me. She's too busy telling me about a set of porch rockers she saw on sale somewhere.

"They would be perfect out here." She puts her hands together. "I can just see you and Adam sitting here, listening to the birds, growing old together." She laughs.

Back in the den, Adam and Marty stand around the dining room table, holding glasses of pink punch. There's a big difference in their ages too, but it has never seemed to matter as much with them. They laugh and mumble jokes to each other under their breath. Off-color ones they don't want the rest of us to hear. Adam has always loved a dirty joke. And Marty seems to have a repertoire of them. Better than shop talk, which they long ago promised not to do on Christmas Eve.

The tradition of getting together with the Deans began the first Christmas after Glasser Dean Investments was formed. "We should do it as a gesture of appreciation," Adam told me. "For all the money Marty's poured into it." True, it was Marty who provided the seed capital since we were young marrieds raising kids and didn't have a nest egg built yet. Adam wanted me to ask my parents to invest, but it felt too risky to me. Marty still likes to brag, "I'm the one with the deep pockets. Adam's got the smile." I know Adam sometimes feels pressured because of that attitude as if the success or failure of the business rests mostly on him. It's probably the reason for the pretension when the Deans are here. But understanding that doesn't make it easier to tolerate. I watch Adam chug back at least four cups of punch when he thinks nobody's looking.

On Christmas Eve we eat hors d'oeuvres and finger food, dips, chips, peanuts, cold shrimp and cocktail sauce, all set out on the dining table. And Laura has brought a veggie tray with a spicy white clam dip. Joel and Cody sit at the table with all the rich food in front of them and gobble down plates of it like two little pigs. After I hear Adam brag about their appetites, so I don't reprimand them over their manners.

The adults settle down in the den for small talk. This is the part that bores me most. It seems so surface-y and banal. Marty and Laura start telling us about the European trip they have planned for the summer. They're always going off someplace and they think everybody wants to hear about it.

"Seven countries in thirteen days." Marty swirls punch around his glass. That's when I notice the men have dispensed with the dainty punch cups and gone straight for the highball glasses.

"Sarah's parents are in Europe right now," Adam tells them as if this information is of any importance. I find the bragging tone curious "Spending Christmas in Portugal, isn't that right, honey?"

"It is, yes." I pull back the curtains and look down the street. Still no headlights.

Cody comes over to me. He whispers, "Can we open their present now?"

"Of course," I say at the same time Adam says, "It can wait until tomorrow."Cody looks surprised and disappointed his dad heard him. He clasps his hand over his mouth. His eyes plead with me.

Laura chimes in, "Oh, Adam, let them open ours at least. We're not Santa and we want to watch them."

"What the hell." Adam nods at Cody and then gathers glasses to refresh everyone's punch. I wonder how many he's had. He isn't noticeably drunk yet but his volume has begun to increase. First sign.

The gift to the boys is a miniature pool table with marble-sized balls and tiny cue sticks. It's too babyish for Joel but Cody is delighted with it. Marty and Adam get down on the floor with Cody and it doesn't take long before the men dominate the game. Joel, as I expected, creeps unnoticed by everyone but me, upstairs to his music and headphones.

Laura gives us a set of carving knives in a wooden block. She opens the cuckoo clock. I can't tell if she likes it or not. She seems more interested in telling me where she got the knives, that they were made in Scotland. "As soon as I saw that cook island you put in, I knew these would be perfect," she tells me. I think we need to swap gifts. I already have a nice set of knives. I bet she doesn't have a cuckoo clock.

Time crawls. Marty and Adam continue to play miniature pool. Occasionally they let Cody shoot a ball or two. After a while, Laura and I grope for conversation and are reduced to watching the childish pool game. Adam says I don't try hard enough with Laura but I'm trying, there's just not much we have in common. At nine-thirty, I realize Troy isn't going to show. It's probably for the best. Now that the evening is here, I can't picture him fitting in with this crowd anyway.

I pour myself a cup of punch. My first. It's stout, and I realize why the mini-pool game has gotten so loud. I pour a cup for Laura—her second. She already seems groggy. I take empty cups to the kitchen sink. I'm already thinking about tomorrow's Christmas dinner. I check on the ham in the fridge and that's when a familiar tap comes on the back door. My heart skips. I go to move aside the curtain. Troy smiles at me through the glass pane.

"I didn't think you were coming," I say as I let him in. He has a bottle of wine in his hand, the same grocery store brand he brought before. He holds it out for me to take. "This is just what we don't need," I say.

"I couldn't come empty-handed."

"Oh, but you could have. We're soused already." I grab him by his arm. "Come meet everybody." I pull him through the dining room and into the den.

"Hey-hey! The man of the hour," Adam says when he sees Troy. "Should we give you applause for your super good work on the house?" Adam stands to shake hands as if he and Troy are the best of friends. I remember how he blew up earlier when I told him I invited Troy. *This one night! You can't give me this one night!* Now, though, Adam drags Troy over to introduce him to Marty and Laura. Despite it all, Adam is always congenial in front of people. He cares too much about appearances to be rude. He ladles a cup of punch and hands it to Troy.

Under the Christmas tree, on his hands and knees, Cody digs busily through the gifts. He finds Troy's two and looks eagerly at me for permission. I nod *yes* and smile. I think he must have the entire landscape under the tree memorized. He hands the two gifts to Troy. "These are for you," he announces.

Adam and Marty resume their game of mini-pool. They're betting money now and don't even bother to include Cody. Laura slumps on the couch, slack-jawed. I think she might fall asleep at any moment. Cody waits expectantly for Troy to open his gifts.

"Thanks," Troy says to him; to me he says, "This was nice of you." But seeing the sock hat and gloves in his hands now, they both seem trivial, like something he'll stick in his closet and never look at again.

"I've got something for you, too." Adam looks up from a bank shot. "You're going to like mine better." He rises on one knee, digs out his wallet, thumbs through it, and then hands Troy a check. "Here. You did excellent work."

Troy takes the check and without looking at the amount mumbles, "Thanks," and folds it into his pocket. I didn't realize Adam had the check already made out, or that he intended to give it to Troy tonight, right in front of everybody. It makes clear the nature of the relationship. My instinct is to apologize for Adam's faux pas but I let it go.

The punch bowl is nearly empty. The food table is wrecked. I send Cody upstairs to get ready for bed. Another hour passes, and at Adam's insistence, Troy gets in on the pool game. They're all drinking wine now. Laura has passed out on the couch. One of the poinsettias on her sweater has a clam dip stain.

"Remember we've got a bicycle to put together," I whisper to Adam. He gives me a sour look. His eyes are swimming. I promise myself I will not say another word about it.

At a quarter to midnight, Marty finally notices Laura snoring on the couch. With some difficulty, he wakes her and they stumble out to their car. I worry about them driving in their condition back to Austin but they refuse the suggestion of a taxi. When I come back inside, Adam has talked Troy into another game of pool. Since the wine is gone, Adam opens an old bottle of Wild Turkey liqueur. He pours an inch into both of their wine glasses. I'm sorry I invited Troy. I don't think he's having fun. I wonder what he must think of us, all the boozing and mindless drivel, the pretension. I notice he doesn't touch the glass of liqueur.

I start clearing the dining table. Even the floor under the table is a mess. My arms are laden when Adam lurches passed me, almost running me down in his hurry to the bathroom. He doesn't even close the door before he vomits into the toilet. I peer in and see him hunched over, heaving. I leave the dirty plates on the cook island and go into the bathroom, shutting the door behind me.

"Oh Adam—the bicycle . . ." I wet a washcloth to wipe his forehead but he shoves me away.

"Your goddammed punch," he mutters before he retches again.

"You're the one who added the booze."

He waves at me to get out of the bathroom. I leave the washcloth on the tank lid for him. When I come out, Troy stands in the kitchen looking uncomfortable.

He says. "I guess the wine *was* a bad idea after all."

"He was loaded before you got here." I try to sound lighthearted. Troy gives an uneasy laugh. I hear the toilet flush and wait for Adam to come out. "He'll pay for it tomorrow," I say. I listen at the bathroom door. Silence comes from the other side. "Adam?" I call softly. When he doesn't answer, I ease open the door. Just as I thought, he is passed out on the floor with his head halfway between the toilet and the bathtub.

Troy helps me get Adam to his feet. We start up the stairs with him wedged between us. It's not easy, and Adam doesn't help much. I'm humiliated but also angry and disappointed. In the bedroom, Troy somehow keeps Adam upright while I turn back the covers. As soon as Troy lets go, Adam collapses on the bed. I yank off his shoes, then shoo Troy from the room. I go out, too, and shut the door. No light comes from under either of the boys' bedrooms. I hope they didn't hear anything.

"I should get going," Troy says.

"I hate to ask you this," I whisper. "But will you stay? I need help with Cody's bike. It's in a box." Troy searches my face, then checks his wristwatch. I sense his reluctance. "If you can't, it's OK."

"No, I can stay, if you need me to . . ." He glances at the door to the bedroom where we just deposited Adam. I see the concern on his face. He whispers, "Where's the bicycle?"

I point at the hatch door above our heads. "In the attic. There's a million pieces."

He glances up at the attic hatch, the cord dangling from it. "Can we get up there without waking the whole house?"

"I don't think we have to worry about Adam," I say, and suppress a laugh. I don't know why I laugh, it just comes out. The release of tension, maybe. Or the utter dismay and degradation of it all.

Troy gives me a questioning look, and then he laughs, too, or suppresses a laugh. And that does it for me. I get the full-on giggles, the same way I did at the Redbridge antique auction. There is not one thing funny about the present situation, but I can't stop laughing. I see right away when Troy catches the contagion. He puts his finger to his lips and tries to shush me, but I can't help it. I keep on laughing. And so does he, in a quieter, more subdued way.

I cover my mouth with both hands as he slowly pulls down the attic hatch. Every time there's a squeak, he mugs at me, which causes even more choked-back laughter. He finally gets the steps down and starts climbing.

"There's a light switch on the right," I manage to say.

He finds the light, and the bicycle box easily and backs down balancing the box in his arms. And of course, for some reason, I find it all hilarious.

Downstairs in the dining room, where we don't have to be so quiet, I let out a bigger laugh and so does he. It takes a moment before we can get ourselves together. He pulls out a pocketknife and unfolds the blade. He gives the box a long look. "Ready?"

That cracks me up even more. I clamp my hand over my mouth, shake my head. He cuts open the box. Inside is a sobering jumble of parts. He lets out a low whistle. We both stare into the abyss. The sight of it terminates the laughter once and for all.

"Hand brakes, huh?" he says, pulling out something that looks like a jumble of cords.

I take in a deep breath. "Sorry."

While he goes out to his truck, I poke around inside the box. I'm not even sure a sober Adam could assemble all this. I should have paid to have it done. In a moment Troy comes back with his wooden-handled toolbox—the same toolbox that set on my porch for the past few weeks. Until that moment I had never really looked at it. There's a faded red "TM" painted on the side in what looks like child's lettering. The toolbox has three sections inside and gabled ends. His tools stand neatly inside.

"Did you make this?" I ask, touching the initials on the side of the toolbox.

"First thing I ever built by myself." He starts shuffling around in the bicycle parts. "I modeled it after my stepdad's. I think I was maybe twelve."

The years have smoothed down the dowel-rod handle, and the wood has darkened to a deep brown. I try to imagine one of my boys building something like this at their age and can't fathom it. "So you always liked building things?"

"Mainly I liked hanging out with my stepdad." He gives me a paper with a list of parts. "Your job is to hand me pieces when I need them. Everything appears to be numbered."

I study the list in hopes it will come clearer as we go along. I can't really read the expression on his face as he selects two parts from the box and lays them out on the floor. "Thank you," I say. "You're saving me here."

I never realized how difficult assembling a bicycle could be, or that so many complicated parts would be involved. Mostly I don't recognize anything I hand to Troy until they're fitted onto the bicycle. Around one-fifteen in the morning it begins to resemble something familiar.

"I would have died for a bike like this," Troy says, as he aligns the wheels. He's been mostly quiet with concentration, so when he speaks, I perk up. "There was this one summer when I was a kid, our neighbor down the street hired me to clean up his garage. Said he'd pay me ten dollars, and that sounded like a lot of money, so I said yes. He should've paid me a hundred. His garage was stacked full of junk. Floor to ceiling. Decades of stuff." He chuckles as he uses a socket wrench on the wheel. "Way in the back of his garage, buried behind all that junk, I found this old, rusted bike. Had a busted-up saddle seat that had been taped together with black electric tape. You couldn't even tell what color the thing had been."

He turns Cody's bicycle upside-down and balances it on the seat and handlebars. He gives the wheel a spin. It's nearly soundless, just a faint ticking. "I told the man I'd take the bike instead of the ten bucks." He chuckles again and glances at me. I'm trying to picture him as a little boy. "I dragged that old thing home. I was determined to fix it up. So pretty soon, my stepdad started helping me. I guess he felt sorry for me."

"So you're saying you're an old hand at this sort of thing." I nod at the upside-down bicycle. We both laugh.

"No. Not hardly." He spins the wheel of Cody's bike again and makes yet another adjustment with the wrench. "So anyway, we repacked the hubs. He showed me how to patch the tires, grease up the chain. I went a little wild with the grease. First time I got on it, the chain fell off."

We both laugh again. I watch the wheel turn. It's hypnotic. "So you have a stepdad?"

"More than one. But this was the one who counted. He called me Troy-boy. Even as a kid, I knew it meant something when somebody gives you a nickname." He glances at me. "He died a couple of years ago. Cancer."

"Oh. I'm sorry."

"No, no, it was good. I was with him. Harvey. That was his name." He shoots a smile at me. "He lived in Maine."

"Oh." I nod, understanding. So that's what took him to Maine. For some reason, it pleases me to know this additional bit of information. I think about Adam judging it as a shady thing to come from Maine.

I watch Troy adjust the wheel again. None of the adjustments make any difference to my eye, but he peers critically at the spinning wheel. It looks perfect to me, but I already know he's a perfectionist about certain things. My gallery sunburst is exhibit one.

"I wanted a Schwinn Stingray." He makes another adjustment to the wheel bolt. "Man, that banana seat. Those high-rise handlebars."

"Did you get one?" At this point, I settle back on the floor. It's been a long day. I'm exhausted and have a little headache, the effects of the pink punch.

"No, I never did." He laughs. The wheel of the bicycle spins on its own, perfectly in balance. "This looks pretty good."

"I don't know how I can thank you."

He glances at me. "Are you kidding? This was a blast."

"But if you weren't here, well, I don't know what I would've done. Adam's been so—I don't know . . . unreliable." I release an unbidden sigh.

Troy spins the wheel again, absently now. I think he finds it hypnotic, too. "My ma's an alcoholic," he says, calmly, without looking up. "Most of her husbands were, too. It's not an easy thing to tolerate."

"I don't think he's a . . . Adam, he's not an alcoholic." My vocal cords sound stretched taut.

I turn my gaze toward the Christmas tree. The strings of white lights flash rhythmically. I think about Adam lying on the bathroom floor, nearly incoherent as we hauled him up the stairs. I try another laugh. It comes out abbreviated and false. Troy doesn't say anything. I keep staring at the tree, the ornaments, the tinsel, the lights. The bicycle wheel is slowing to a stop.

"We had this big crisis a couple of months ago." I give Troy a glance. He's not looking at me. "He wanted to move out. I wouldn't let him." I pause, feeling his eyes on me now. "It's humiliating to try to hold onto someone who doesn't want to be here. It takes two, you know?" My heart thuds in my ears. He watches me through the spokes of the wheels. A tear starts and I swipe at it. "I think he's seeing someone." I stare at the flashing tree lights. Another false laugh comes out of me. I look down at my hands. "It wouldn't be the first time."

I can't believe I just said that. It's not something I have ever confessed to anyone. It's too raw and degrading, too personal. My skin feels prickly. "I probably shouldn't be telling you this."

"Probably not." His voice is just above a whisper. "But I like talking to you, Sarah." I hear his toolbox scoot over the floor, and when I look he's reaching for me. Instinct causes me to back away, but he catches me and swallows me in a hug. The way he does it I realize it's meant to comfort me, like a friend, or a brother. I never had a brother; I don't know the way that kind of hug would feel like. "You shouldn't be sad on Christmas Eve," he says.

I lay my cheek on his shoulder. He smells like laundry detergent, and something smoky but sweet, like ripe fruit maybe—so different from the cologne and whiskey scent of Adam. I feel the spread of his warm hands on my back, one at my waist, the other near my neck. His knee touches mine. He doesn't say anything else. And I stay there encased inside his arms until it begins to feel awkward. I don't know how to break it off.

My mind leaps back to Saturday night, after Joel's Christmas concert, after I fed them all dinner. There was nothing brotherly about the way he came on to me, I'm certain of that. I thought he would kiss me, and if he had I don't know how I would have reacted. I don't have experience with that sort of thing, just like I don't know how to extract myself right now from this embrace.

Finally, I decide to just be friendly about it, like I would act if it were Carolyn instead of Troy. I lift my head off his shoulder, rise a few inches on my knees, and take his face in my hands. "Thank you," I whisper and plant a light kiss on his lips.

It surprises him, and it doesn't come about at all the way I intend it. I'm suddenly engulfed in his arms again, but it's different now. Not brotherly, or comforting. Mortified, I push back, but "*Oh*" is all I get out before he resurrects the kiss, except his mouth feels feverish on mine, intense and persuasive.

Suddenly, my struggle dissolves. At first, I think if I don't respond it will end on its own. But after a second, I realize I don't want it to end; I want the rush of desire that comes with it, have been wanting it since Saturday. I breathe it in, along with his essence. My arms circle his ribcage. I feel his bones, the solidness of him beneath his clothes. The kiss becomes dark and intoxicating. It intensifies, grows hungrier and more dangerous. Our tongues probe. I feel his heart pounding, or maybe it's mine. Somehow, before it's too late, I find the willpower to pull away from him, unlocking the spell. I sit back, my wrist pressed to my mouth.

"My kids are upstairs." My voice sounds breathy and unfamiliar.

He nods and looks shaken, too. "I should be going."

Quickly he gets to his feet, turns the bike over, and puts down the kickstand. The front wheel settles at a deep angle. I stand, too. I touch his arm, then pull my hand back like he's hyper-charged. For a moment I think he might grab me again.

"Thank you." My voice still comes small and weak.

"For what? The bike? Or for leaving?"

"Both." I let out a nervous, stupid laugh. "And for the kiss."

He smiles at that but it's a different smile, looks pressurized. He keeps his eyes on me as he bends for his toolbox. "Any time."

I laugh, too, even though I believe he means it. He's so direct. Best to laugh it off, laugh off the kiss, too, as if it's something that happens to me every day, a kiss from a man who isn't my husband. I'm still rubber-kneed, but I don't want to act offended or like anything is different from ten minutes ago. So I decide to walk with him to his truck, as normal.

As soon as we step out the back door, I think it's a bad idea to walk him out. The sky is clear and salted with stars. A big moon shines over the neighbor's house. "Beautiful night," I say, a lame attempt to lessen the awkwardness. It doesn't work. The kiss lingers between us. I keep my distance.

His truck is parked at the curb. He sets his toolbox over in the bed, then he leans back against the wheel well, crosses his arms, and gazes down at me. The Christmas lights from our house, the streetlight, and the moon cast soft shadows on his face. He looks beautiful, desirable. I can't believe I once thought he was homely.

He seems to want to say something but he doesn't. He smiles. "Well, thanks for having me over."

"Thanks for playing Santa Claus. You're a nice man, Troy."

He lets out a wry laugh, looks off down the street, then back at me. "What I want right now, more than anything, is to steal you away, take you home with me, and make love to you all night. How's that for nice?"

His arm circles my waist. He pulls me against him. Before I can react, he gives me another kiss on the lips, a gentle, lingering, teaser of a kiss this time. I push against his chest, and thankfully he lets me go. I don't know what would happen if he decided not to. It feels risky out here in the moonlight—like I might lose my mind or something. I want to either run for the house or fling myself back in his arms.

"Night, Sarah," he says and opens the truck door. He slides in. "Merry Christmas."

I'm still reeling from that light and gentle second kiss. Before I can recover enough to return the goodbye, his truck is already headed down the street. I stand there, frozen, and watch the taillights till they disappear from my view.

Eleven

The boys creep down the stairs. They try not to make noise but they wake me anyway. At the lower landing, they stop, surprised to see me stretched out on the couch, swaddled in an afghan and still wearing my clothes from last night. Gray dawn colors the three windows in the den.

I rub my eyes and pull myself from fitful sleep. I must've finally dozed off. I don't remember it—only staring wide-eyed into the smoldering embers inside the fireplace, trying to turn off my high-velocity mind. Too much happened. Too many thoughts, too much emotion. The last I heard from the mantle clock was four chimes.

"What're you doing down here, Mom?" Cody says.

"Waiting for Santa," I answer, sitting up. "He must've sent the Sandman ahead to knock me out."

Joel rolls his eyes. "Cute, Mom."

"Oh wow!" Cody spots the bicycle parked beside the Christmas tree—thanks to Troy's magic. For a second, I stare off in space, recalling last night. My hand touches my lips. Somehow, in some unclear way, I feel like a different person this morning.

I drag myself up from the couch, woozy from lack of sleep. I turn on the Christmas tree and plop down on a chair at the dining table. I find I'm still keyed up.

"Oh man, I love this thing," Cody says and throws his leg over the center bar of the bike. The seat needs adjusting. His feet barely reach the pedals.

Joel tears into the package that contains his CD player. He tosses the wrapping paper onto the floor. I'm too bleary and disconnected to scold him.

"Maybe Dad should be down here for this," I say to them. Neither of them pays any attention to me.

The ugly part of last night comes back to me—Adam vomiting and passing out in the bathroom, hauling him up the stairs. *An alcoholic. . . .* I'm not ready to accept that as truth, but his drinking has gotten out of control. I watch Joel rip the CD player from the clam wrap and Styrofoam.

"Stop," I say. "Everybody just stop. Cody, run wake up Daddy. He needs to be here."

Reluctantly, Cody steps off the bike and heads up the stairs. Joel raises the CD player as if to show me. He grins. "Cool," he says. "Thanks, Mom."

In a few minutes, Adam plods down the stairs with Cody leading the way. "Dad slept in his clothes, too," Cody tells us like it's a coincidence and a magnificent joke.

Adam is rumpled. Red sheet wrinkles crisscross his face. His eyes are cloudy and bloodshot. His skin has a bluish tone. I take in the sight of him.

"Looks like Dad got hit by the Sandman, too," I say.

He rubs his eyes and squints at the presents under the Christmas tree. "You're hilarious," he mumbles without looking my way.

You deserve it, I want to say, but from his deathly color, I imagine he feels as bad as he looks. He slumps in the dining chair to my left and stares at the bicycle as if he's trying to recall assembling it last night. I decide to let him wonder.

I dig out the camera from the sideboard and snap some

pictures: Joel holding up his CD player; Cody astride the bike; hungover Adam gripping his bedhead in one hand—to remind him one day when I need leverage. As I'm framing a shot of the boys digging more presents from under the tree, I spot the two opened boxes off to one side. Laying on a bed of red tissue paper are the gray sock hat and the pair of kid-lined work gloves.

ALL MORNING, as I cook Christmas dinner, I make one absentminded mistake after another: setting out the ham with a big spoon instead of a carving knife; and pouring a scoop of sugar into the sink instead of the tea pitcher. Just before noon, Maureen and Oliver arrive. We sit around the dining room table passing bowls. I have trouble following the conversation, and then after a while, I stop trying. It's as if my hearing has gone out overnight.

. . . Steal you away. What does that even mean, steal you away? It sounds like a cheesy line from some pop song. And what made him think it was OK to say something like that to me? Did he want to kidnap me? Was that what he meant? It was the damned kiss. I should have never let that happen. It was an idiotic thing to allow. I should have pushed him away the instant it started. I *did* push him away. I'm sure I did . . . one hundred percent positive I did.

Across the table from me I watch Cody's mouth move, but whatever he says doesn't register. With my fork, I chase a green bean around on my plate and laugh absently when I hear the others laugh.

. . . Take you home and make love to you all night . . . He had to be kidding with that one, surely. Just the thought of him saying those words makes me cringe with embarrassment. I bet he's used that one a million times. Does he think I'm stupid and don't recognize a pickup line when I hear it?

I stare at my plate and remember the feel of his body pressed against mine, slightly damp from his own heat, firm under his clothes. The spread of his hands on my back, like we were dancing, him leading and me—

"Sarah?" Adam's voice cuts into my thoughts. I straighten. He gives me a curious look and snaps his fingers in front of my face like he's testing my brain. "Pass the gravy down to Dad—will you, please?"

"Oh." I scoop up the bowl of potatoes and pass it to Joel beside me.

"He wants the gravy, Mom." Joel grins, but gives me a confused look.

"Of course." I correct my mistake, laugh, and peer around the table at the others. Nobody's paying attention.

Joel passes the gravy boat down to Oliver. The conversation continues—meaningless conversation. Football playoffs. The hunting lease. Cody's bike. Joel's band concert. *Hate we missed that. Did you go, Adam? Can't believe it's almost 1989. Can you believe it? Where does time go?*

Suddenly, Christmas feels endless. What I wish is that I could just race upstairs, wrap myself in my afghan and sit on my new gallery, alone, in wonderful, luxurious solitude. I need to hear myself think. Troy's kisses—those two daring kisses—have completely possessed me.

After dinner, Cody wants to open the rest of the Christmas presents so Maureen and I put away the dishes, wipe down the table, and the boys start passing gifts around. When Adam unwraps the box with the Angora sweater, he gives my cheek a smooch. "You spent too much money." The sweater does match his eyes, exactly. Even Maureen comments on it.

Joel sets a gift in front of me, a square box, with store gift wrapping. The tag reads: *To Sarah From Adam.* It's not even his handwriting. There was a time when the card would have said something like *To Sarah From Santa,* or *To Honey from Santa.* I take my time opening it. They all watch as the paper comes off. The box has a picture of an electric skillet on the outside.

"It's completely immersible," Adam tells me. "It'll even go in the dishwasher."

I sit there staring at the picture on the outside of the box. *Oh, joy. . . .*

AFTER ALL THE wrapping paper in the dining room is stuffed into garbage bags and set outside the back door, Mother calls from Lisbon.

"Merry Christmas, darling," she says, once the operator connects us. Her voice is clear as if she's speaking from the next room instead of thousands of miles across the world. "We haven't forgotten about you all. We've been buying up Europe. Just wait till you see what we got you for Christmas. We'll celebrate again when we get home, all right?"

"I hope you're having fun," I say, needlessly. I can hear in her voice she's having fun. I realize I miss her.

"Oh Sarah, guess what! I had my ears pierced in Madrid."

"Mother! You didn't." I pretend shock and scandal.

"You only live once," she says, then she puts Daddy on the line but I can still hear her in the background, both of them talking at once. Finally, I turn the phone over to Joel, who doesn't say two words, and then to Cody, who chatters on and on for several minutes about his bicycle. At the end of the call, Adam gets on for two seconds.

"Merry Christmas to you two gadabouts."

I smile at his words, but somehow they make me feel sad. We have so much history, Adam and I. So many things we've shared through the years starting with the birth of Joel, the graduation party for Adam's master's degree, Oliver's heart attack and how worried sick we all were, the miscarriage in between Joel and Cody, the only pregnancy we planned and the sadness that came with it, all the relocating around Austin, each place a little better than the last. Then we moved here—our forever home. We have been working toward something: raising these boys, seeing them off to college, their marriages, having grandkids, maybe someday taking long trips like Mother and Daddy. We were supposed to stay soulmates. How did this chasm between us get so wide?

Maureen and Oliver take the boys with them when they leave. They'll keep them, as they do every year, until New Year's Day. This time I see a hint of disappointment on Cody's face at the idea of leaving his brand-new bike behind. Joel takes his CD player. It's not fair, but one fits in the car, the other doesn't. I give them both kisses and tell them we will see them next Sunday.

Watching the car drive off, leaving the boys in someone else's care for a while, their grandparents who adore them, I feel the weight of motherhood lift suddenly. One entire week to do whatever I want, to sit in a bathtub with face creams on, or to do needlework until noon. I might finally paint the guest room.

Once they're gone, Adam helps me clean up the kitchen. It's unusual for him to do that so I'm wary. I think maybe he wants to talk about last night, to apologize for getting so drunk, or to ask how Cody's bike got assembled. He hasn't mentioned the bicycle all day. Despite his efforts not to show it, he still looks groggy and hungover. He finishes bringing all the dirty dishes in from the dining table and wipes down a couple of counters, but when he finally speaks, he doesn't say any of the things I expect.

"What are your plans for this week?" he asks.

I give him a hopeful look. "I was just thinking about that, too. I don't have any, do you?" In years past we've used this week for together time, maybe a day trip somewhere, or multiple nights out for movies or the theater. Once we flew to Las Vegas on a whim.

He shrugs. "I'm working all week. Then Friday I'm taking a client to the deer lease."

I nod. I'm certain my disappointment shows on my face. "Will you be back in time for us to pick up the boys?"

"If it's required."

I pause and let that word sink in. *Required.* Like some

dreaded chore. Calmly, I say, "It's not required, Adam. I can drive over there and get them by myself."

"That sounds good." He kisses me on the forehead, one perfunctory dry kiss between my brows. "If we're through here, I'm going up to bed. I feel like hammered shit."

As he leaves the kitchen, a mental picture conjures in my mind of a pile of shit, hammered flat. His footsteps on the staircase recede, and then come again as thuds overhead. And that is that—the end of our sixteenth Christmas together

I remember the first one: the little flocked Christmas tree we stood in the window of our garage apartment. We had no money for real decorations so we bought a bag of Styrofoam balls, mixed sequins, and straight pins, and we sat at the tiny table that came with the apartment and made our own Christmas ornaments. We laughed all the way through at each other's funny ideas—Adam's mildly obscene hula girl with red sequin nipples and broom straw for a dress; my little ball pinned to a bigger ball, with a gold sequin belly button intended to depict me, already pregnant with Joel.

Whatever happened to those silly Styrofoam ornaments? I don't recall throwing them out, I can't imagine I would ever do that. And yet they're gone. Lost in a move, or just gone.

Twelve

The day after Christmas the weather wakes up sunny and cloudless. After Adam leaves for work, I take my coffee out onto my new gallery. I lean on the railing and admire the view down on the lawn, down the street. I gaze at the sky-blue porch ceiling, the ferns growing along the limbs of our massive burr oak. I decide to spend my week hunting for furniture for this gallery. I need a place to sit now that it's usable space, for reading or stitching or just watching the birds in the treetops.

 I wander downstairs, out the front door. I run my hand along the new columns, the smooth fresh paint. I walk around the house, one minute lamenting the destruction of my rose bushes, the next backing up to admire my rejuvenated old Victorian. The fresh paint gleams in the sunshine. I stoop to pull a few weeds out of the flowerbeds along the sidewalk. The weather hasn't turned cold enough yet to nip back the spider lilies. They stand erect with their blazing yellow blooms bouncing in the morning breeze.

 Carolyn is due home tomorrow. I'll ask her to go with me to look for some willow furniture. I realize I've missed her and need someone to talk to. Lately, the places my mind takes me are frightening. Last night after Adam went to bed, I sat with the Sunday newspaper poring through the classifieds, curious if there might be any job that would pay enough for me to support myself. I don't know yet if that's an actual plan, I just want options so I don't feel so trapped. I'm not happy. Neither is he. This reconciliation isn't working for either of us.

Around lunchtime, I go inside and fix a sandwich from the leftover Christmas ham. No calls on the phone machine while I've been outside. On impulse, I lift the receiver and dial Troy. I have his number memorized even though I've never called him. Whenever we needed to get in touch about something with the house, Adam made the calls. But Troy left his Christmas gifts here and they're bothering me. I don't want to keep running into them. The only polite thing to do is to let him know he can stop by any time this week and fetch them. It's what I would have done before Christmas Eve, and there's no reason to let what happened change my behavior.

Anyway, I'm over it. I've dwelled on it, recognized it for the misunderstanding it was, and now it seems trivial. I even let out a dismissive laugh over how shaken up I was during Christmas dinner. I take things too seriously; always have. That's what Carolyn tells me. It's what my mother always said, too. It's going to be my New Year's resolution: slough off stress, bring on more lightheartedness, and try not to take everything so personally.

The phone rings three times on Troy's end before he answers. I don't expect his voice to jar me the way it does. Panic overtakes me and I hang up. I stare at the telephone like it's a snake, and immediately feel ridiculous. "Oh my God, Sarah," I say to myself. "Stop acting like you're in high school." But I don't call again.

Even so, I ramble around the house for a few more minutes. There's laundry to do but I don't feel like it. The furniture needs dusting but who cares? I need something to engross me. Something to take my mind away from those kisses, from what they mean if anything. I search for any way to gracefully excuse them away.

I turn on the television and sit down with my needlepoint. The volume on the TV is too loud. I turn it down and flip impatiently through the channels looking for something besides soaps. Daytime TV is mostly a waste of brain cells. I turn it off, abandon the needlepoint.

We had two dates, Adam and I, before he kissed me. I was startled by it then, too. I couldn't believe he was interested in me, and I didn't understand why. I was a boring Library Science major living my boring sheltered life. I never had dated much, and then Adam.

In the kitchen, I get down a glass, put in some ice, and pour in tea leftover from yesterday. And that's when I notice, sitting on top of the freezer, the two rolls of film from the holidays. Adam was supposed to drop them by the pharmacy on his way to work today, but obviously he forgot. I grab my purse and throw on my jacket. On my way out the door, I snatch up the film and shove both rolls into my pocket. An errand, that's what I need. I don't even pull a comb through my hair. I race out to the car and back out of the driveway.

At the pharmacy, the photo window is closed. A small sign says to drop film at the front cashier so I do. The cashier hands me an envelope to fill out, name, address, phone number. Ten minutes later, I'm back in my car. Now what? That didn't take long enough. My thoughts are still nagging at me, addling me. It's not usually so hard to get my mind off a thing.

I drive aimlessly around town, down Main Street, by the courthouse. The Christmas decorations on lawns look dull and tacky in the daylight. Most of the downtown stores are shut tight. I didn't realize that would be the case. I thought I might lose myself shopping or browsing. It's one of the downsides of living in this small town. Stores close on holidays, or for no reason, a sign hanging in a window: *Gone Until The First.* I'm not ready to go home. I'm too jumpy for alone. Suddenly I miss the boys, miss all their noise and the distractions they create.

As my car bumps over the railroad tracks, I spot the sign for Church Street. It's standing there like a beacon, luring me, and just as if someone besides me is driving the car, I make the left turn. Maybe this is where I've been headed all along. As soon as I aim my car up Church Street, I realize I haven't thought this through. Here I am back in high school again, stalking a boy I have a crush on, honking as I go by—only I don't plan to honk. I'm not even sure why I'm curious. I never was before now. This isn't some teenage crush. I'll simply knock on his door, and like an adult, tell him he left his packages at our house on Christmas Eve, and then I'll turn around and get back in my car.

The street is one long block. Halfway down, on the lefthand side, I see his truck parked in the driveway, looking exactly as it did in front of my house all those weeks. Automatically, I stop at the curb but I don't turn off the engine. An oldies station is on the radio. "Blue Christmas" plays. I turn down the volume and stare at the house, listening to Elvis.

A sycamore tree planted too close to the sidewalk has cracked the concrete and stands with a drift of tan leaves surrounding its base. Overgrown azaleas beneath the front windows scraggle out into the yard. A fake wishing well sits near the sidewalk, holding an empty blue flowerpot. Gingerbread hangs all over the eaves, a weathervane on the gable. It looks like the kind of house an old faded couple would live in with their toy-breed dog. But there's his truck in the driveway so this must be his house.

When the front door opens, my heart somersaults. I almost accelerate away, my foot is poised to, but he steps outside and I know he sees me. He must have heard the engine running, or maybe the radio, but he stands there as if I'm expected. I can't seem to make myself move, either to wave or push the gas pedal. Our eyes lock and he starts down the sidewalk. He's barefoot—in late December. That seems reckless. Everything about this is reckless. The hems of his jeans are walked-off and ragged, his shirt untucked. The bottom two buttons are unfastened and flap in the breeze as he walks toward me. I get a glimpse of his belly, a dark circle of fine hair around his navel. My head pulsates.

When he gets to the car, he gives me a tentative smile. Reluctantly, I roll down my window and reach to turn off the radio. He anchors his hands on the door and squats so he's at eye level. Sycamore leaves flutter down in the grass behind him. For a second, I search for something to say.

"You left your Christmas gifts."

He peers around me, looking for the cap and gloves on the passenger seat. Of course, they're not there. They're back at my house, still under the Christmas tree.

"I didn't bring them. I didn't know I was coming by—" My voice dies.

"So you just happened to be in the neighborhood?" He acts the same as ever: kind of clever, wisecracking. Of course, I didn't just happen to be in the neighborhood. He knows that.

"I've been thinking about the bread-safe." My throat is so dry I can barely swallow. I sound like I'm down in a well. I keep my gaze away from him. "I don't think I'm ready for you to—" My voice breaks again. "I'm too busy. I have a million things—"

"Why don't you come inside?"

"I just wanted to say . . ." My tongue feels thick. "About the bread-safe . . . don't worry with it . . . I mean . . . I'm not ready—it's not something . . . it's not important—" I don't know what's wrong with me. I can't talk straight. I gape at him.

"Just come inside, Sarah." He sounds patient, now, concerned. He takes hold of the door handle, opens it, and holds out his hand to me.

One final time I consider driving off, but if I did that now I would drag him down the street, so I yank the keys out of the ignition and let him pull me from the car. I follow him up the sidewalk. He keeps my hand inside his. My heart races and I feel woozy. He opens the door and steers me into a small foyer. I stop, unwilling to go a step further.

The living room is furnished simply: a couple of worn chairs, a green Naugahyde couch, a side table, rummage sale furniture, or giveaways. The television is turned low, a soap opera or something. I can't identify it before he uses the remote to turn off the TV. He moves a pile of magazines off the couch, stacks them on the side table, straightens a pillow, smooths at a shabby brown and black afghan thrown over the back of the couch.

"Sit down here," he says. "Can I get you something to drink? I have water, and . . . well, water's about it."

"Water would be good." I still feel like I'm choking. I clear my throat and watch him go off down a hall.

What am I doing here? This is a mistake. Now he'll think I'm obsessed with him. But I cannot continue like this, endlessly reconstructing Christmas Eve, that kiss, kisses plural, wondering what it all means, why it's making me crazy. God knows I have enough going on without thoughts of Troy deviling me. I'm compelled to get this settled right now. I try to plan what to say, but I'm still not thinking straight.

I perch on the edge of the couch hyperaware of how I must look: I'm wearing Adam's gray sweatshirt that shrunk in the wash and no longer fits him, but it's too big for me and hangs off my shoulders. It's tattered around the cuffs. My jeans have garden dirt ground into one knee. I scrape at the dirt with my fingernail. My hair needs brushing. I rake my hand through it a couple of times.

My eyes snoop around the room, imagining him living here, sleeping here. It's an old house, almost as old as mine, except more rundown and much less grand. The ceilings are ten feet high. A yellowed, dusty chandelier hangs in the center. I glance through the magazines stacked on the table. *American Woodworker, Fine Woodworking, Workbench.* There's a partly smoked cigarette in a dinted tin ashtray.

He comes back with a glass of water, no ice but it's cold like it came from a jug in the refrigerator. It has a bit of a refrigerator smell. Etched on the side of the glass are three brown ducks in flight over a cluster of cattails.

"You smoke?" I ask pleasantly as if we've just met. Small talk. Nothing talk, when there's so much to say.

"I'm trying to quit. I'm always trying." He sits in a faded blue easy chair two feet away. He needs a shave. Whiskers darken the lower half of his face. "Yesterday I broke down and bought a pack." He shrugs. "Christmas." He waves his hand as if to dismiss this discussion, leans forward, and rests his forearms on his knees. "I'm glad to see you," he says. "You've been on my mind."

"I have? Really? Why is that?" My question is disingenuous and he cuts right through it.

"Why do you think?"

The sight of his hands affects me deep in my stomach, slender thumb, watch on his wrist. One knee of his jeans is nearly worn through. It's all too intense. I look away and watch as the condensation rolls down my glass of water. It pools on the magazine. I've been on his mind for the same reason he's been on mine.

"Did Cody like his bike?" he asks, obviously willing to play my small talk game for a bit longer.

"Yes, he did. He liked it a lot." I allow my eyes to meet his for a second but jerk them away. They return to the water glass. "He's gone with his grandparents this week. He and Joel both are gone."

On the wall beside the foyer hangs a faded picture of a gristmill with a deer sipping from the millpond. There's a cobweb on the corner of the picture frame. Near the front window stands a small desk, paper and pencils scattered on the top. I reach for the glass of water. My hand shakes so much I decide to leave the glass where it sits. I tuck my fingers under my knee.

"Relax, Sarah," he says, softly. "It's just me."

I look up and his eyes are watching me. "I have never cheated on Adam." The words come from out of nowhere. I feel like an idiot for saying them.

"I know that."

"How would you know?"

"A hunch." He shrugs. "And you still haven't."

I try to meet his eyes but mine wander to the brick fireplace at the far end of the room, painted over and not in use anymore. An old gas space heater sits inside the firebox exhaling puffs of warm air.

"If you know that then why did you think it would be OK—" I can't make eye contact, but I glance at him. "—to kiss me?"

He plants one elbow on the arm of the chair and rests his chin on the heel of his hand. "You kissed me. Didn't you?"

"No." I shake my head. "No, I did not."

He squints. "That's how I remember it."

My mind spools backward. *Is* that how it happened? I held his face in my hands . . . so, yes, maybe I did start it but I didn't mean it like that. . . . "All right, but you didn't stop me."

"No." He lets out a chuckle. "I didn't want to."

"So you *would* have kissed me."

He leans back. "I doubt it. Look, I'm sorry it's upset you so much."

"I'm not upset. I just want to know why you kissed me. It's been nagging at me. Do I put off that kind of signal? That it's all right to . . . to just—just kiss me like that?"

A smile plays around his mouth. He squints. "You kissed me. Remember? We've gone over this."

I stare at him. I see now he's about to laugh. His eyes have a merry glint that maddens me for a second. But then I reassess and think it through. He's right, this is a ridiculous conversation. I let out a tentative laugh, which seems to give him permission to laugh more heartily.

I rest back against the couch. I let out my breath. I feel less lightheaded and uptight. "So . . . I guess we kissed each other."

"I guess we did." He keeps smiling. "You have to admit it was a pretty good kiss."

"So you've been thinking about it, too." Now, I sound like it's all a big joke, and somehow it suddenly feels that way. This was the right thing to do, talk it out, lessen the importance of it all.

"Yeah, a little bit, I have been." He nods. "More than a little bit."

"That second kiss, though. Out on the street. You definitely started that one."

"Well, I thought we needed an encore."

"You mean, you thought *I* needed an encore?"

"I think you need a lot more than that."

The kidding subsides, then dies completely. I look directly at him, now. He returns my look. I say, "Like a roll in the sack? Something like that?"

He's still got a grin, but it's subdued like he's holding back. "Geez, wonder why I didn't think of that?"

"But you did. You said you wanted to make love to me all night."

He taps a finger on the arm of the couch. "Sometimes I do get a good idea."

"I can't stay all night." It just comes out, without a thought, and it wipes the grin from his face completely. I realize what I have just said, the implications of it. Is that what I meant to say? I feel like I'm vibrating all over.

He stares at me, as if he's deciphering my meaning, too. He rises suddenly from his chair and I have a momentary urge to break for the door. I force myself to sit still and wait. I don't want to think too much. Or talk too much. I have to see what happens.

When he takes my hand and pulls me off the couch, I let him. He kisses me just like before, except this one feels heavier and even more intense, like two lovers who have been apart for a long while. When our lips finally break, he looks into my eyes, one and then the other, as if he's searching for—what? Permission? Capitulation? Certitude? Whatever he finds seems to satisfy him. He lifts me into his arms. I hang on to his neck.

"You're going to carry me?" I laugh.

"Like a caveman so you don't get away." He kisses me again as we go down the hall.

"Should I be grateful you're not dragging me by the hair, too?"

"I'll do anything you want me to."

He takes me into a bedroom—his bedroom, I assume. The curtains on the windows make it dark, but I'm not inspecting the surroundings. I can't take my attention off him. The bed is unmade. He lays me on the cool sheets. I slither up toward the two pillows.

"I've had children," I say, watching him unbutton his shirt. "My body is well-used."

He whips his shirt off his shoulders, and there's a tattoo, a small one on his pectoral. I don't have time to study it before he starts on my clothes, unbuttoning my jeans, which I help him slide off. I sit up for him to pull the sweatshirt over my head. He kneels above me, his knees on either side of my thighs.

"You're perfect," he says, sliding his arm behind my back.

He raises me against his chest, kissing me more passionately than I've ever been kissed. His hand runs down my ribs, over my belly, into the front of my panties, into me. I haven't an ounce of air left in my lungs. I take his tongue, his fingers. I moan and he rolls me onto my stomach, handling me like I'm one of those resuscitation dolls. I think I might need resuscitating. I'm already panting.

He dispatches my panties in one motion, my bra in another, and then he's kissing me, turning me over again, kissing me everywhere, my neck, my breasts, my stomach. He hasn't given me time to change my mind or feel embarrassed or reluctant. All I feel is wanton and lusty. I know I should be doing something for him, too, but I'm incapable of anything but taking from him, every bit of him, like I'm enraptured.

"I want you inside me." I barely recognize my voice.

Just as an orgasm quakes through me, he penetrates me deeply, thoroughly. I wrap around him, clinging, quivering. He thrusts three, maybe four more times, then comes a groan of release from him, too, and more kisses. His breath is hot on my neck. My hand slides up to gather his hair, fingers open, entwining, feeling the shape of his head, his skin. We stay like that a few moments, hearts pounding, gathering our wits.

And then he does almost the best thing of all. He rolls to his side, taking me against him, presses my face to his chest, kisses my forehead. And he holds me like that, in that close, silent embrace. I love the care of it, the tenderness. No moving away, no jumping up for the bathroom, no offhanded, crude remark like *I needed that*. In that moment, while he holds me, I feel valued, fulfilled in some more basic way than physically.

With my fingertip, I trace the tattoo halfway between his collarbone and his shoulder. Up close I see it's a picture of his toolbox, a replica of the one he built as a boy. The head of a hammer sticks out of the toolbox, a screwdriver, and a tiny "TM" drawn in red ink.

"This is your toolbox," I say.

He cups my hand, brings my fingertips to his lips. I'm enthralled with the dark hair on his body, the bone and muscle and sinew of him. He's longer, slimmer, in better physical shape than Adam. I touch the outline of his mouth.

"Tell me the truth." My voice sounds lazy, and a little alien to me. "You couldn't do that all night. Not really?"

His mouth fishes for mine, a guppy kiss. "Too bad you can't stay and find out."

I laugh, flop back against the pillow, and pull the sheet over me. "I had no idea you were such a comedian."

"All right, time for a good look at you." He tears back the sheet from my body. "My God, you're a pretty woman."

"Stop it! You're embarrassing me."

I tug the sheet back over me and roll away. I feel his breath on my shoulder, then his mouth. He reaches over me, tucks me against him. His whiskers tickle. I'm not used to whiskers. I laugh again. So does he. I expected guilt, not this laughter. It comes from the euphoria of lovemaking but also from relief that it's over, that I don't have to wonder anymore. I always thought Adam would be the only man I would ever give myself to, but here I am, languishing naked, laughing, in another man's bed.

"I start a new job on Monday," he says near my ear. The flat of his hand moves up the length of my arm. "Which means I have this down week. So I was thinking . . ." His lips flutter along my upper arm, following his hand. ". . . maybe you could bring my gifts by tomorrow. If you want to."

"Save you a trip? Is that it?" I'm smiling because I know that's not it.

"If you get here early enough I'll make you breakfast."

"You cook?"

"And we can listen to some music."

"There's music, too?"

I look around the room and spot an ancient smoked-top component stereo on a shelf beside an oscillating fan. A stack of record albums sits on the next shelf. I roll to my back to look at him, so close: mole to the right of his nose, dark eyebrows, golden eyes, a tiny hole pierced in his earlobe where an earring must have once been fastened. I imagine him as a wild child—there's signs of it—his background so different from mine. It excites me a little. I kiss his mouth. He kisses me back, more than once.

"So you're thinking this should become a habit?" I say, raising my chin for his lips to find my neck. Goosebumps erupt on my body.

"Well, we've got this free week." He kisses the tip of my nose. "How do you like your eggs? Scrambled or fried?" He starts to roll away, but I grab him.

"Kiss me again," I say, and he does.

Thirteen

When I get home, the Jeep is parked under the porte cochere. Snowball is curled up on the hood, enjoying the warmth from the engine, so I know Adam hasn't been home long. It's a little after four. I pull in beside the Jeep and shut off my car. I open the visor mirror. My hair is in tangles. I dig in my purse for my brush. That's when Adam comes from around the side of the house. He's in sweatpants and tennis shoes, camouflage cap on his head. He has a pair of pruning shears in his hand. I push up the visor and stow my brush before he spots me. My heart starts pounding. I take a deep breath and get out of the car.

"You're home early," I say as he comes toward me.

"Everybody else was off so there was no point in me being there either. I thought I would try to shape up all this mashed landscape. The roses will come back. All of it probably will. Where've you been?"

I don't have a ready answer. I suddenly want to just tell him the truth. Be done with it. Our marriage is already teetering from the weight of his lies. I'm not happy to add more. The glow from the afternoon in Troy's arms leaves me. I look at Adam and feel guilt rain down like hail stones.

"I was looking for some willow furniture for the balcony." My voice sounds choked. "All the stores are closed today."

He nods. He doesn't even notice how I'm dressed. Certainly not for furniture shopping. I could be standing there with a scarlet *A* pinned to my breast and he wouldn't notice.

"I'm going to finish out here," he says, already walking away. "I'll be in later. We can go somewhere and get dinner if you want to."

"Dinner? Out?" I call after him.

He doesn't stop moving away but raises his voice. "Maybe that seafood place Mom and Dad were talking about yesterday."

He disappears around the front of the house. I don't recall mention of a seafood restaurant yesterday, but then I was barely present. I wonder how the boys are doing. I realize I haven't thought of them for hours.

I rush inside and toss my purse on the counter. My tea glass sits there in a puddle. All the ice has melted and overflowed. I dump it into the sink, then hurry to the phone on Adam's desk. I dial Oliver and Maureen's number. Cody answers.

"How's it going, honey?" I say.

"Good. Pops got us a BB gun. He set up a target and we've been shooting. I got one bull's eye. Joel got more than me, but I did get one." I let him rattle on about their day. Sounds like he's having fun, which makes me feel better. I ask to speak to Joel. "Pops is letting him mow the yard. Grammy says he's doing doughnuts."

I envision Joel riding Oliver's lawnmower, driving it in circles. All seems well with the boys. After I hang up, I rush upstairs to shower before Adam comes in. Any vestige of my afternoon with Troy runs down the drain.

I think about tomorrow, what he said about breakfast and music—and reality hits me. I can't go back over there. I shouldn't have led him to believe I would. I'm not the kind of woman who has affairs. I can't talk to my kids on the phone after a day in bed with my lover, as if it never happened—as if I'm just the same as I was yesterday. It was something I had to do to regain my sanity, I guess, but now it's over and I can't go back there. Shame swarms me like the bees in the wall. As I step out of the shower, my stomach knots and I feel faint. I hold onto the sink and stare at myself in the mirror. I don't even know who I see there.

AT THE SEAFOOD RESTAURANT, Adam orders oysters on the half-shell, and both of us a Peroni. He doesn't ask if I would like a beer, he just tells the waiter, "Make that two."

The beer comes in frosted pilsner glasses. I take a quick gulp of mine. I don't relish the taste of beer but I need something to fortify my nerves. We eat our oysters, six apiece, careful not to encroach on each other's half dozen.

"Don't forget I'm taking Sam Willoby to the lease this weekend," he says, as he balances an oyster on a saltine. He dabs a bit of horseradish on top, a squirt of red sauce.

"Who is Sam Willoby again?"

"The client I told you I'm working on." He gives me an exasperated look and stuffs the cracker and oyster into his mouth with one big bite. He chews, talking around it. "We want his business. Willoby and Sons. Sam's the old man. He's the hunter. The son runs the business."

He waves at the waitress and holds up his empty glass, looks down at mine, which is still half full. He flashes two fingers at her.

"I don't mind telling you, babe, this deal could make the difference. I was starting to get worried I'd lost my touch, but I had old Sam eating out of my hand last week. Marty's beside himself over this hunting trip. He wanted to go, but I told him to leave old Sam to me." He starts on another cracker, another oyster, a squeeze of red sauce, a dollop of horseradish. "I don't need Marty cluttering up the deal with his super-realistic forecasts and opinions." Adam lets out a laugh. "Sometimes you can be too damned honest. But that's just Marty. He doesn't know the meaning of finesse. So I just said to him, let me handle this one, pal."

Most of the time when Adam talks business my mind wanders, but the last part, the part about being too damned honest, grabs my attention. I interrupt him mid-sentence. "Do you really believe that? What you just said . . . about being too honest?"

He seems happy to have me chime in. "When you're trying to close a deal, yes."

But that's not the point I was getting at. It's that question of honesty, or more correctly dishonesty that bothers me. How dishonest has Adam been with me through the years—or right now, for that matter? And what about me? How much dishonesty am I capable of? It's never been something I ever considered about myself. I've always said it's easier to tell the truth than to lie. Lies catch up to you. Yet here I sit, drinking beer in a restaurant with my husband after spending the entire afternoon in bed with another man. Is that how it's going to be now? Both of us taking lovers and not speaking of it, at all, like in some French movie? Both of us telling lies?

After a while, as Adam continues to babble on about work, what he's got going and how he plans to deal with this Willoby person, I do stop listening. It's not that I don't care but I'm too over-stimulated, and conflicted. On the one hand there's the self-loathing, the deceit and dishonesty. But on the other I can't stop rehashing the day with Troy, how it happened, *what* happened. There was no awkwardness, no fumbling. He took hold of me and controlled everything. I have never before felt so conquered. And by a man I barely know, but whose kisses and hands seem to understand everything about me. I feel changed and wondrous in my own skin.

"Drink up," Adam says, startling me from my thoughts. "We're celebrating."

All on its own, my hand takes my glass of beer. "What are we celebrating?"

"Babe?" He pats my hand. "Have you even been listening? This deal. The money I'll make. We'll get that pool put in so the boys can have swim parties this summer." He holds up his glass of beer. "Here's to Sam Willoby."

We clink our glasses. I take a long drink, watching Adam over the rim as he drains the last of his beer. Immediately he pivots to find the waitress, gestures for more. My heart hammers. All I'm really certain of is the thought of giving up Troy, of never having another day like today, makes me physically ill.

It's raining when the Jeep pulls under the porte cochere, Adam cuts off the engine. He gives me a look I recognize, a cross between salacious and hungry. When the boys are gone he gets frisky. He drags me across the seat for a kiss, but I can't do it. I won't. Not tonight. I can't be the kind of woman who makes love to two different men in the same 24 hours. I give him a short kiss without much animation. He doesn't seem to notice my lack of interest.

"Come on," he whispers. "How long has it been since we had car sex, huh? Let's give the neighbors something to talk about." He gropes at me. A rumble of thunder sounds in the distance.

"Adam—" I start moving his hands away, but he's like an octopus.

"Take off your panties." His hand goes under my dress and starts pulling at my underwear. He nuzzles my neck.

"What are you doing?" I push at him. He pulls me over the console. "Adam, quit."

"Oh come on, Sarah. Loosen up." He backs his seat and unzips his pants. "Remember how we used to do it in the car."

My leg is crushed between him and the console. I can barely move, but I manage to pop open my door. I scramble out, adjusting my skirt.

I hurry to the back door. I'm drenched by the time I get there. Snowball hunkers on the porch, waiting to be let in out of the rain. I open the door and he tiptoes in, tracking the floor, miserable and wet. I glance back at Adam, just as he pulls himself from the Jeep, adjusting his pants. All I want is to get away. I slam the door and hurry inside, up the stairs, and into the bathroom for my second shower of the day.

Fourteen

In the morning when I get up, the house is silent except for the sound of rain hitting the roof. I walk outside on the gallery in my gown and robe and look down at the ditches running full. Cars splash through standing water on the street. It must have rained all night. I shut my eyes and hold fast to the railing. The air feels soft and wet, but warmer than in recent days. I will away the thoughts that plagued my sleep.

I have always stayed in line, followed rules. I have prided myself on that. I don't think it's made me rigid—or frigid, as Adam contends. He was angry when we went to bed, deprived of what he wanted from me. Yet this morning, down in the kitchen, he left the coffee pot on for me. I pour a cup and wander into the dining room. The two gifts for Troy lie there unwrapped—the sock hat and work gloves. He'll probably never use either of them. I should just wrap them up and return them to the store. I certainly don't want them lying around reminding me of my one-day affair. *Sarah's Big Adventure*, like books I read to the kids at school—except this one is X-rated.

I can't have an affair. I'm no good at subterfuge. Yes, it was miraculous sex, felt like real lovemaking: generous and sincere. But I can't go back there today. If I do, I'll be lost forever. I'll drive over there and leave the cap and gloves on his front porch. I won't even knock. I'll leave them on the rusty glider I saw there. Eventually, he'll find them. And that will be a clear sign to him that this is over before it has even begun.

I get down a box of shredded wheat and a bowl, pour in milk. When the telephone rings I jump. I know it's him. It has to be, phoning this early. I give my head a shake, grip the spoon and listen to the rings blast the silence. On ring five the answering machine starts up. I hold my breath, expecting to hear his voice with his crazy accent, saying my name like it's one syllable.

"I'm home!" Carolyn's voice crackles out of the machine. I jump up and jostle the bowl of cereal. Milk sloshes out onto the countertop. I race for the phone in the den, jerk it up just before she finishes her message.

"I'm so glad you're back." I sound like I've been jogging "Let's go furniture shopping."

SHE PICKS me up just after noon in her little brown Mazda. We hug when I get in her car. She smells like White Linen. "Feels like it's been forever," she says. "This is my last day off, and I'm so happy to spend it with you." She kisses my cheek.

She says she's taking me to a place she knows about on the other side of Austin, a place where they sell nothing but outdoor furniture. On the long ride she tells me about her visit home, her sisters, all their babies, cute stories about things they did and said. I keep expecting her to mention Troy, dreading it, but instead she namedrops somebody called Paul, an old high school flame who lives in Fayetteville, Arkansas.

"He's a college professor, now. Geology." She watches the road but her smile is dimpling her cheek. "My mother actually invited him for Christmas dinner. She thought I might like to reconnect with him. That was how she put it. Reconnect."

"Well?" Is this relief I'm feeling? I think it is. Maybe she's through with Troy. But what does it matter if I am, too? "What was he like?"

"Same dork he was in high school. The kind that carried around a briefcase." She laughs. "We made out in his car."

"Carolyn!" I say as if I'm scandalized. But the truth is, I feel unreasonably hopeful. Maybe I can get away with my fling without anybody finding out about it. "You didn't?"

"I know, right? We drove out to this park where we used to go. There's a tree where we carved our initials years ago. We actually found it. He's going through a divorce and horny as hell. Nothing will come of it. It was just a moment, you know?" She glances across at me. "It made him happy. It made my mama happy."

"Maybe not if she knew what you two were doing," I say and we laugh at the same time, like always. The Balcor girls. Joined at the hip. I look across at her and feel a heave of love.

We are well into our shopping trip before Troy's name is uttered. Even though I knew it was bound to come, I'm not ready for it. We're in the furniture store and my attention is on the wicker sets. She asks about Christmas Eve. I give her a shrug and a vague answer. I should probably tell her I had sex with him. If I wasn't married—and if she hadn't just been dating him—I might. As we move among the furniture sets, I mention that the Deans were there on Christmas Eve as usual.

"What about Troy? Did he come, too?"

"He came late, but yeah, he was there. He didn't have anything in common with the Deans, of course." I laugh. She doesn't.

"Did he bring someone?"

"No. He came alone." I've been trying not to look at her, but I can't help it—I give her a glance. She's running her hand absently over the arm of a wicker chair.

"I've been thinking about it," she says, "and I really don't think he's into me. I mean, at all. I got back last night. He knew when I was coming back but he didn't call me. In fact, he has never called me—not a single time. It's always me getting in touch, me making the connection. I want someone who's really into me, you know? Am I too idealistic?"

"Of course not. If it doesn't feel right to you it probably isn't." The knot in my stomach hardens. I feel treacherous realizing I want to talk her out of him.

Quickly, I turn my attention to the floor salesmen who comes to help us. *James,* his name tag says. I tell him what I want, and he shows us some sets. There's one that's a loveseat and two chairs. One of the chairs is a rocker.

Carolyn looks disinterested and James goes off to find a table to match the set. I try to keep him from leaving me alone with Carolyn, now that Troy is all she wants to talk about. She meanders through the furniture, looking moody.

"What do you think of this fabric?" I say, loud enough for her to hear. "James called it aubergine." I laugh, she keeps wandering through the furniture sets. "Is it too purple?"

She smooths at a cushion. "So you don't think Troy's the one either?" She says it wistfully and I don't answer. She starts to mosey back toward me. "He's really not my type anyway. He's kind of a hippie, don't you think?"

"No, not really," I say, feeling the urge now to defend him. "Hippies don't usually hold down jobs." I picture the tattoo on his chest, his pierced ear . . . his bare foot cupping my instep under the blanket . . . *hands . . . lips. . . .*

James returns just then, thank God, and he's found a table to match the set. I decide right then to buy it, without asking Adam's permission. He won't care as long as it's no trouble for him. Delivery on Thursday. Perfect. It will give me something to focus on and I need that—something besides what to do about Troy. I've already missed breakfast with him, and whatever else he had in mind.

We stop for frozen yogurt. It seems to me we don't have much else to say to each other. She talks about a lot of nothing, back to things that happened when she was with her family, and I have a difficult time staying focused. I don't add anything of value to the conversation. We have more moments of silence than are usual for us. Has yesterday with Troy changed me? I was so eager to see her earlier but now I would rather our outing end so I can go home and daydream.

"What the matter, Sarah?" she asks. "You seem down."

I shrug, lie. "Missing the boys, I guess."

"Things are OK with Adam?" She lowers her voice as if we're sharing some deep secret. This isn't a subject I want to get into either.

"He's off to the deer lease this weekend," I say, lightly. "Some big shot he's wooing."

"Oh good. Let's plan to do something on New Year's Eve together." She brightens at the idea. "We can go to a club. How long since you went club crawling on New Year's Eve?"

"I was thinking of going on ahead to spend the night at Maureen and Oliver's, bring the boy home New Year's Day." It's an untruth, but a convincing one. And who knows, I might even do it.

As we're driving back to my house, just after we pass the courthouse square and the post office, once we rattle over the railroad tracks, she makes a sudden left onto Church Street. I panic. The move is nearly identical to the one I made in my car yesterday.

"Where are we going?" I say, even though I know exactly where.

"I'm just going to see if he's home." She glances across at me. "If he is, I'll invite him to club crawl with me on New Year's Eve. Since you're not interested."

"He's probably working," I sputter, even though I know he's not. *I have this down week.* As soon as we're on Church, I spot his truck parked in his driveway. "This is a mistake, Carolyn. You should let him make the first move, like you said."

"Well, that was an hour ago. I've already changed my mind." She laughs and pulls her Mazda to the curb. She sets the handbrake. "Come on, Sarah, you know I can't go three days without a man."

I stare at Troy's house. Everything is just the same as yesterday. Same fake wishing well, same drift of leaves in the yard. A wave of desperation tightens my throat. I don't want to see him right now, especially not with Carolyn. My heart is a battering ram against my chest.

"I'll wait here," I say, but she has already climbed out and started up the sidewalk. I prop my head in my right hand, elbow on the door on my side. I catch myself in the sideview mirror. I look like I've just witnessed a murder. She bangs on the driver's side window. I nearly jump through the roof.

"Come on," she shouts at me. I shake my head. She bangs again. I wave her away . . . and then . . . then . . . Troy steps out his front door and onto his porch. He's dressed in nicer jeans than yesterday, with a dark blue shirt.

"Shit." I turn my face away and feel my cheeks burn. I sink lower in the bucket seat. I want to evaporate into the floorboards. I hear Carolyn talking but her words are muffled, and then I can't resist, I glance just in time to see her hug Troy. He looks over her shoulder directly at me. It's as if a pulse of electricity passes between us.

She turns toward her car again, waves at me to follow them. She's all smiles. I would rather have my teeth pulled, but of course, Carolyn will not leave it alone. She comes to the car and opens the driver's side door. "He's invited us inside."

I peer around her. Troy has a question on his face. He bends sideways to look at me. Quickly, I divert my eyes, but I see no graceful way to avoid this. I tuck my purse underneath my seat and ease out of the car.

"I wanted to show Sarah where you live," Carolyn says to him. "We've been furniture shopping."

He turns to head up to the porch. I imagine he feels cornered, too. Carolyn takes my elbow to hurry me along. He holds the front door for us. Carolyn goes first, and as I pass his hand comes down to touch me on the shoulder. His fingers crawl over to my neck. I respond with a slight headshake. I feel like such a betrayer.

"Can I get everybody some water?" he asks.

Water again. This must be his go-to opening line. Carolyn is still smiling, glancing at the room around her, the same way as I did yesterday. But since I have the room memorized I keep my eyes on the floor.

"Do you have anything stronger?" Carolyn says to him. "Wine maybe."

"No. Sorry." He heads for the kitchen.

Carolyn follows right behind him. "We've been shopping for Sarah's balcony," she says and her voice trails off as they go into the kitchen.

The television is on, volume muted. The scattered magazines are stacked neatly on the side table, the afghan folded over one arm of the couch, ashtray empty and clean. I realize he straightened up—in anticipation of my missed morning breakfast? A confusion of emotions rushes through me. I'm failing everybody, myself included.

From the kitchen I hear Carolyn's loud whine, "Oh, Troy, why not?" So he's turning her down for New Year's Eve, too. More mumbling comes, the lower register of Troy's voice, Carolyn's higher pitch. I can't make out any of what they say. I stand where they left me, just inside the front door. I don't want to sit down, don't want to stay. I don't want to know what they're doing. I hear a cupboard door, a knocking sound. Water running. A glass on a counter.

I glance down the hallway, remember him carrying me to the bedroom. Today it feels sordid and wicked. I'm shaken to my bones and wish I could just leave. I ease closer to the front door, grip the knob.

"You are such a bastard!" Carolyn comes storming out of the kitchen. "Come on, Sarah. Let's go."

She grabs my arm and heads through the door I've already opened. At first, I go with her but curiosity hangs me back. Troy comes out of the kitchen, head bowed. His eyes find me. His are agitated. "I need to talk to you," he says, quietly, as he comes forward.

I shake my head, throw up my hands, and slip outside. Carolyn is nearly to the car. Behind me, Troy comes to the door.

"If you don't call me," he says, trying to keep it quiet. "I'm calling you."

"Don't." I hurry down the sidewalk.

"Sarah." His voice comes after me. I quicken my pace.

I barely get the car door closed before Carolyn peels away from the curb. Her tires squall. I turn to look back. Troy has stopped partway down his front sidewalk. I watch long enough to see him turn back toward the house.

"Asshole." Carolyn hits the steering wheel with the heel of her hand.

"What happened?"

"Nothing much," she says, her voice dripping with sarcasm. "Just that he never cares to see me again." She says it like she's repeating his exact words, with his accent, although it doesn't sound much like him. "He said it's over, as if it was ever anything to begin."

"I'm sorry," I say, and feel like a duplicitous traitor.

"I'll show him, that bastard. He had the nerve to say he hoped we could stay friends. Ha!" She takes her eyes off the road to look at me, and we hit a curb going round a corner. I grip the dashboard. "What *is* the matter with me? Why do men run away from me? My mother says I'm too picky. So, I've tried to not be. I mean, God—Troy Middleton? A carpenter? Talk about the bottom of the barrel. You saw where he lives."

"What's wrong with where he lives?" I ask, but she doesn't hear. She's too busy raving. And it's hardly the time to start an argument. I wonder why he said all that to her. Was it because I was there? Do I matter that much, or am I reading things into it that aren't there?

"At my age, the good ones are all taken. All that's left are carpenters. Or married men like Denver Carson."

"He's married? You never told me that."

"Or Paul Stokel."

I figure she must mean the professor. "You said he was divorced."

She ignores me. "I don't even care about being a wife, all I want is kids. Before my ovaries dry up and die. I just want kids." She glances at me. Her eyes are dewy. "You are so lucky, Sarah. You don't know how lucky you are. To have kids and a man like Adam."

"Who cheats on me," I say, quietly. I look down at my hands, at the ring on my finger. So I'm going to tell the whole world, now? Now, that I've cheated, too.

"What?" She nearly drives into a mailbox.

I say it louder. "He cheats. I've looked the other way for fifteen years."

She slows the car. "Sarah? You . . . you never . . . how do you know?"

"Because I've caught him before. And lately, he's been coming home late. A lot. He stays drunk half the time. Sometimes I think I smell other women on him." We are barely crawling down the road, now. I look at her. She's not watching the road. "Look out for the curb."

She centers the car. "Do you have proof any of that is true?"

"Good lord, Carolyn, Adam could get laid every night if he wanted to. You know that."

"Doesn't mean he's having an affair. Maybe it's just work-related, staying out and drinking too much. His field, it's just so stressful, finance. Especially right now with the stock market like it is."

Of course, she would defend him. I would expect nothing less. I shake my head. "I don't want to dwell on it. It's my problem not yours." So we don't say anymore. At all.

She drives the few blocks to my house, pulls into the driveway. She leaves the car running. I fish my purse out from under my seat. "Don't you want to come in for a while?"

"I can't, Sarah. I've still got to unpack, do laundry, all that back-to-work stuff. You know." She reaches for me. We hug. "Call me."

I go in through the back door and Snowball darts out from under my feet. He nearly trips me. "You good-for-nothing freeloader," I call after him. He pauses to stare at me, then heads on to whatever has him in such a hurry.

The answering machine on the desk is blinking. The first call is from Adam. He'll be late. Of course. The second message is from Troy. It's short. "I need to talk to you. Call me when you get this." I erase both messages. He took a big risk leaving that. Adam could have been the one to hear it.

I glance at Troy's gifts still sitting on the dining room table. They feel like an axe hanging over my head. I want them gone. I want Troy Middleton out of my brain. What an ugly mess I've made. I can't even look my best friend in the eye without guilt. And now he obviously feels some kind of possessiveness toward me.

I gather up the cap and gloves and take them outside to the garbage can. When I open the lid, the putrid smell of rotting food leftover from Christmas hits me. Garbage day is late because of the holiday. I can't bring myself to throw these brand-new things into that murky trashcan.

Back inside, I find a shopping bag to stuff them in, then go for my purse and my car keys. "Snowball," I call out, on the way to my car, but the cat has disappeared. He obviously does not want to get trapped inside the house again. I throw in the shopping bag first, then get in and back out of the driveway.

At Troy's house, I walk right up to his door thinking I will hand him the shopping bag, tell him it is not in me to continue whatever this is between us. I raise my fist to knock but before I can, he opens the door, grabs my hand, and pulls me inside.

"I saw you drive up," he says, as explanation.

"Troy, please . . . I can't stay."

His arms are already around me. "What happened today? Why were you with Carolyn?"

"I think you broke her heart."

He lets me go. "Ah, you know that's not true." I push the grocery bag at him. He takes it, peers into it without interest, drops it on the couch. "What did she tell you?"

"That you don't want to see her anymore."

"You already knew that."

"I think this is my fault. I felt horrible standing here today, like I was in the way of you and my best friend."

"That's horseshit." He tries to grab me again, but I back away. "Nothing's there. I told you that before Christmas."

"Nothing for you maybe. I don't think she feels that way." I motion toward the sack he tossed on the couch. "I just came to give you that. And to tell you I can't do this. Whatever it is." I gesture at him, and down the hall. My attention stays in that direction, remembering him carrying me like a prize. "It was great," I say. "Earthshaking, in fact. But I can't see you anymore. I just can't."

I take a deep breath, and look at him. He's so close I can smell the detergent in his shirt. He searches my eyes, moving from one to the other. I'm sure he sees my tears brimming. His mouth compresses into a line. He shakes his head.

"That's not the deal we made." He keeps looking deeply at me. "You promised me a week."

"Deal? What are you talking about?"

"Your kids are at granny's. I don't start work till Monday. That's a week."

"I didn't promise you anything like that."

"You meant to." He holds up a handful of fingers, plus one more. "So we still have six more days."

"We're negotiating?"

"Call it what you like. I want those six days."

I give him a quizzical look and something inside me shifts—lightens. I almost laugh. Is that a smile starting on his face? Is he proposing a one-week affair? One week and then we're done? *No strings. No regret. No guilt.* He's way too clever. I smile, too, finally.

"Five days," I say. "My boys come home on Sunday."

"All right . . . five days." I hear a note of triumph. "Pinky swear?"

I laugh. He laughs. "You're crazy," I say, but I lift my little finger. He hooks his around mine. And then he reels me in like a big catch.

He kisses me and I sink into it, willpower flying out the windows. My arms go around his neck. I hear a little hum come from him like my lips taste delicious. He lifts my left leg around his waist, and then the right. A laugh erupts from me as he carries me to the bedroom. *Again.*

He sits me down on the bed, kisses me with one of his deep probing kisses. Then he stands back to take every stitch of his clothes off—and he's glorious, already erect. He puts one knee on the bed and smiles at me.

"Earthshaking?" he says.

I reach for him and he lays me backward. I run both hands over his chest to his shoulders. Desire sweeps through me, surprises me. I crave him. He starts pulling off my clothes, tossing them—blouse, bra, jeans, panties—one by one, onto the bedroom floor.

Fifteen

Adam doesn't notice any change in me. He doesn't notice I hardly hear him when he speaks. He doesn't notice the floors don't shine, furniture isn't polished. He doesn't notice the breakfast dishes in the sink or the laundry piling up in the bathroom hamper. He doesn't even see the pewter-colored paint stuck on my hands—the color Troy chose to paint his bathroom. Mr. McIntire's washroom he calls it.

When I arrive Wednesday morning, Troy has two cans of paint ready, two brushes and a roller. A drop cloth is spread over everything in the bathroom except the walls. We paint all morning, make love at noon, then we eat corned beef sandwiches, the most delicious I ever tasted.

All day, as we paint, laughter fills the spaces, along with music blaring from the bedroom. Besides Tom Petty, he likes Bob Seger, Springsteen, Mellencamp, the Eagles. All I ever hear anymore is Joel's new-age stuff, so listening to this old music makes me happy. We sing, sometimes loudly, as we work together. He teaches me how to brush-paint freehand without painter's tape and I'm amazed when I don't make as many mistakes. He tells me tape makes people think they can slop it on and then they're surprised when it's not a clean line.

We talk—a lot: about me, about my girlhood, about my parents, about my grandmother, gone now, who taught me to sew and stitch and crochet, and how I think of her every time I start a new project. He tells me about spending one summer working maintenance at Buffalo Jump State Park in Montana. "I painted washrooms there, too." He laughs at that. I love how much we laugh—at ourselves, at our pasts, at our right now. An unspoken rule develops—we don't talk about awkward things. We're learning each other's history, without reference to Adam, my marriage, or Troy's apparently dismal childhood. Happy talk, like the song in *South Pacific;* it makes me feel younger, more captivating, and charmed by the whole idea of this one secret week together.

On Thursday, I have to wait for the wicker furniture to arrive. It comes just before noon. I don't bother to set it in place or even unwrap the plastic. That can wait until next week. This week, I don't have time to spare. I rush to Troy's house. I find him in the bathroom, already at work installing chair rail molding he's cut and painted since I was here yesterday.

"Not fair," I say. "You worked through the night."

He stops long enough to kiss me. There's a speck of gray paint on his chin. I smudge it with my thumb. He gives me a smile, nods at the molding. "What do you think?"

"It looks great. You painted it first?"

"Easier that way. We'll have to putty the holes and touch up."

I sweep dust off the new sink cabinet with my hand. The whole bathroom is transformed. It smells of new wood, paint, and caulking. "What about a mirror?"

"Yeah, I need to find one. I was thinking about crown molding around the ceiling."

I shake my head. "The room's too small. It'll look busy."

He stops with the tack hammer, glances around the ceiling. "You're right." He goes back to tapping in the chair rail. "We'd make a good team, Sarah." I watch him for a moment, how deliberately he concentrates on close work, hammering through a red rag to keep from marring the chair rail, then counter-sinking each nail as he goes. The mitered corners on the molding fit perfectly together. He feels me watching him, raises his eyes. "What?"

"Nothing." I shake my head. "Are you hungry? I'll make sandwiches."

"Give me five minutes to finish this." His tack hammer starts in again.

I go to the kitchen, take sandwich ingredients out of the fridge—the corned beef from yesterday, plus condiments, pickles, chips, all of it goes onto the table. It's a yellow 1950s dinette set with a metal band around the edge, white Formica top. I find paper plates, silverware. I'm starting to learn my way around. I finish setting the table just as he comes in the kitchen.

"The bathroom looks fantastic," I say. "It really does. How did you learn to do all that?"

He shrugs, turns on the sink faucet, and scrubs his hands. He smiles over his shoulder at me. "Oval mirror? Round mirror? Square?"

"I don't know. Oval?"

"You want to help me find one?" He dries his hands on a cup towel.

"This afternoon?"

"Maybe tomorrow." He reaches for me. He is such a good kisser; I can't get enough of it. He doesn't let me go. "I missed you this morning." He nods at the Lucite clock on the wall. It's glittery and turquoise, the 1950s again. It says twelve-thirty. "I got cheated out of half a day."

"I'll be late tomorrow, too. Adam leaves for deer lease after noon."

"And you have to be there for that? How are you going to make up all this time you owe me?"

I laugh. "He'll be gone until Sunday."

"All right, so bring your toothbrush. Spend the night with me." He kisses the tip of my nose. "Spend two nights." He nuzzles my neck. "You smell like flowers."

My lips search for his. "You want to eat lunch or . . ."

"Shake the earth?" It's become a joke already, just like the way he picks me up like I'm a feather. He carries me down the hall again. I laugh and kiss him all the way.

I HAVEN'T SMOKED a cigarette since high school when a girlfriend of mine and I bought a pack of Belair from a drug store vending machine. Whenever she spent the night, we smoked one in my bedroom with our heads hanging out the window so the smoke wouldn't float downstairs to my parents. I tell Troy this story as I fork the cigarette from his fingers.

He watches me puff on the filter. "I can see you're an old pro. Most rookies cough."

"That's because I'm not inhaling." I hand the cigarette back to him. He leans his head into the pillow and blows a couple of perfect smoke rings at the ceiling. "Now you're just showing off," I say. He chuckles.

My hand smooths over his bare chest. I love how solid and strong he feels, how the hair on his body is weirdly soft yet wiry at the same time. He's tawny and dark.

"I bet you started smoking when you were a toddler," I say.

"Nope, high school for me, too." He takes another drag. "I think we should build a house together." He lets out a long stream of blue smoke. "I'm already working on it but you've got a good eye."

My mind flits to the small table in the front room, strewn with draft paper, rulers, and sketches. But he isn't serious. A house would take a lot longer than a week. "A tree house maybe," I say, playing along. "Like Swiss Family Robinson."

He pauses, and seems to be thinking. "We'd have to keep an eye out for a big tree. On a big lot."

"Can we make it a log cabin treehouse?" I keep teasing.

So does he. "OK, so a really big tree."

"With stairs, not a ladder. I don't love ladders. I'm picturing a winding staircase."

A few more smoke rings rise over the bed. "Stained glass windows."

"Maybe." I take the cigarette from his hand and stub it out in the ashtray on the bedside table. "You're never going to give these up, are you? I think you like to smoke too much."

"That is my last pack."

I swing my legs off the bed, snatch up my panties and bra. "I bet you've said that a hundred times."

"More like two hundred." His hand rubs up my spine. It gives me a shiver. "I guess I'll have to prove it to you." He gets out of bed, too. I hear him rustling on his clothes. "When I make a promise, I keep it."

"How will I know you've kept it?" I struggle with my bra hooks. He comes to my aid. I notice he does it pretty easily. Lots of practice?

"I'll send you a telepathic message." He lifts my hair and kisses my neck.

"I'm starving. Let's go eat a sandwich before I leave."

"Leave? You just got here." He watches me pull on my sweatshirt. "So this means I'm getting no work out of you at all today?"

Our eyes meet. He's grinning. "It's nearly three already." I step into my jeans one leg at a time. "And soon it'll be four . . ." I zip my fly, ". . . and that's when I turn into a pumpkin."

"You've got that story wrong. It's the carriage that turns into the pumpkin, not Cinderella."

"Well, I'm no Cinderella."

"But you do look a lot like her."

"The cartoon? Or the storybook?"

"Both."

I watch him pull on his shirt and start on the buttons. I want to stop him, lay my face there against his warm chest, hear his heartbeat. "I dread going home." I say it with seriousness. He can tell. He looks at me.

"Then stay."

"Don't tempt me. Where's my shoes?" I scan the floor. My vision goes fuzzy all of a sudden. I feel shaky and I don't understand it. I lean against the bedpost, my feet on the floor, and stare at my bare toes. I feel cold. "What if I went home," I say, slowly. ". . . packed a bag . . . told him I'm leaving him . . .?"

I look up. My shoes dangle in his hands. His shirt is half-buttoned. He smiles. I smile back. The weird feeling from a moment before recedes. I reach to finish buttoning his shirt.

He drops my shoes and grabs me by my wrists. I shriek as we flop onto the bed, my black moment chased away with laughter and rolling over each other, wrestling like two kids for a few moments. When I try to scramble away he holds onto my foot and tickles one finger up my sole. I jiggle out of his grasp.

Then he stretches out on the bed, takes me with him, one arm folded behind his head, the other tucked around me. We lie there, mostly dressed, staring up at the ceiling. There's a water stain in a corner. We give a couple more breathy laughs, a few little squeezes, then silence. The furnace cuts on and blows musty air from the rusted vent overhead. It sounds like a whirlwind.

"What were you just saying?" His voice is soft. "Something about packing a bag?"

"I feel like I'm at a crossroads."

He rubs my arm. "You know my door's open."

"That would put you right in the middle of it."

"As if I'm not there already?"

"You're a symptom, Troy, not the cause." I sit up, swing my feet off the bed. "When he came home telling me he was leaving, he caught me by surprise. I didn't have time to make the right decision. I think I would choose differently now."

"Big decisions are hard for everybody." His hand rubs my back. I hear it fall on the bed behind me as I get up. "Only a symptom, huh?"

I slide my feet into my shoes and turn toward him. "I didn't mean it that way. I've had such fun this week. It's been, well—like a miracle almost. A surprise. You've been a big surprise."

A half-grin plays on his face. "You know that's all horseshit, right? That whole one-week thing."

The jitters start again—hearing him say it so clearly out loud. *Yes, yes, of course, I know. A one-week affair? How stupid am I?*

"You conned me." I frown at him.

"It got you to stay."

"I guess I wanted you to convince me to."

"I knew that. Somehow. . ." He reaches for my hand, pulls me back. I sit on the bed. "Life's a crapshoot, Sarah."

"What does that mean?" I feel weepy and I don't know why. I bite my lower lip to steady it.

"Almost nothing goes like you plan."

"That scares me," I whisper. "I don't like uncertainty. *You* scare me."

"Go home, get your toothbrush." He moves a strand of hair off my forehead, studies my face. "Come spend the weekend with me. Nothing has to happen besides that. No plans. No bad vibes. Just come be with me."

I let him pull me against him, and I circle my arms around his ribs.

Sixteen

Toothbrush, I can't forget that. Makeup bag, a packet of birth control pills, an extra pair of jeans, extra sweater, sweatshirt, two extra pairs of panties—make that three—comb, deodorant. What am I forgetting? Nightgown? Shouldn't need that. Flannel robe—that either. What else? I can barely zip the overnight bag as it is.

For the last hour and a half, Adam has been downstairs, walking back and forth, gathering up his hunting gear. He didn't even want to stop for lunch, said he would pick up something on the way to the lease. I go downstairs with my bag and my purse. Chances are he won't even notice I've packed. Most of the time he never sees me. I'm tired of being invisible, ignored, at the bottom of his list. And I'm anxious to get to Troy. As soon as Adam leaves, as soon as I'm sure he won't come back for something he forgot, I'm heading to Church Street.

When I get to the lower landing, I drop the bag and my purse on the top step of the kitchen staircase. Adam's rummaging in the cupboard above the chest freezer. He doesn't look at me but somehow he senses I'm there. "Hon, have you seen my hand warmers? There's a front coming in. Supposed to get down in the thirties tomorrow."

Coat—I'll need my coat. I go back up to the lower landing, then down into the den, to the coat closet by the front door. I pull my brown corduroy coat off the rod, go back and add it to my pile on the kitchen landing. He's still searching through cabinets.

"Did you look in the sideboard?" I say. "I thought I saw some hand warmers in there next to the camera."

"What the hell are they doing in there?" He heads for the dining room. "Camera!" he hollers. "Glad you reminded me. I want the camera in case old Sam shoots a big one." He laughs from the dining room, and walks back into the kitchen with the camera and two fuel-stick hand warmers. "I need to be up there before dark in case he has trouble finding it."

I glance at the clock on the microwave: *3:15.* "You should definitely get there before dark."

"Oh, and my duffel. Would you run upstairs and get it, hon?"

I climb the stairs like an automaton. I feel like one, or a ghost. This is my life. *This.* His duffel bag is on the floor of the bedroom closet. It stays packed with his hunting clothes, like the go-bag we packed when Joel was due, all those years ago. I haul the duffel downstairs. As expected, he has yet to notice my overnight bag, purse, and coat sitting in a pile on the top step.

He continues to rifle through kitchen drawers. "Now, where the hell's my skinning knife?"

"Drawer under the toaster."

I watch him scavenge through spatulas, wooden spoons, the pizza wheel. I remember what he said at the restaurant—was that just Monday? Feels like a lifetime ago—*sometimes a person can be too honest.* Maybe he's right. But I believe every person should be self-aware enough to acknowledge their own shortcomings, and here's mine: I'm no good at secrets.

"Adam—" My voice is a disembodied echo. I clear my throat. "When you get back—"

"Here it is." He fishes the skinning knife out of the drawer and holds it up for me to see like it's a prize he just found in a Cracker Jacks box. The knife is in its leather scabbard. He unsheathes it, checks the blade with his thumb, then slides it back into the scabbard. "This thing won't even cut paper." He turns to me. "Where's the whetstone?"

"Adam . . ." Say it. Just say it.

"I bet it's out in the Jeep. I probably left it there last time." He starts for the door. I can't let him leave this room. If I do, my courage will go with him.

"Adam—" I say it louder. He finally hears me. Before he reaches the door he turns, waiting. My mouth goes dry. I swallow. I feel like I'm shaking from my hair to my toes. "I won't be here when you get back." My voice chokes off.

I have his attention now but he looks puzzled. "OK. Where are you going?"

I clutch the banister. "I'm not happy . . . Adam. Neither one of us is happy."

"What?" A slant of sunlight falls across the room and lands on him. He squints, then grimaces. "Goddammit, Sarah, you bring this up right now? When I'm about to walk out the door? We'll talk when I get back."

"And I'm telling you I won't be here when you get back." I motion toward my bags. "That's been sitting here right in front of you all this time. And you didn't even notice."

His eyes jet to the kitchen steps. Finally, he sees the pile there, my coat, purse, and overnight bag. The confusion on his face tugs at me. I want to get this over with.

"You'll have to pick up the boys," I say. "I need time for myself."

"Time?" It sounds like a foreign word the way he says it.

"Yes, like you get all your time," I say, "running off to the deer lease. Coming home late—"

"Is this to keep me from going? Is that why you're bringing this up right now?"

"Adam. I'm suffocating." I feel tears start to burn. I fight them. *I will not cry.*

He spits out a laugh. "Hell, we're all suffocating." He stands there like he's taken root. "Do I get to know where you're going at least? Where you'll be while you're out there taking some time?" His last few words are laced with venom.

"I don't know why you'd care now. I've been gone all week and you've been too blind to notice, or too busy fooling around, or whatever it is you do—"

He takes another step toward me. He wags his finger. "Oh no . . . uh-uh. No. I'm not going to let you turn this around on me. Your jealousy, your suspicion, that's on you. And your paranoia."

"Paranoia?" I ease around the cook island. "Maybe I wouldn't be paranoid if you hadn't been cheating since we were married. Did I dream up Rosalie Baker? You were acting the exact same way then as you are now? And that stripper who lived upstairs in Austin—"

"What the hell are you talking about?" I hear his anger building. But he's not the only one who can get angry. I feel my face redden.

"And Jaydean what's-her-name? Remember her? Or is she just more of my paranoia?"

"Jesus, Sarah. That was ages ago." He gets this pseudo-innocent look on his face. He's about to change tactics, I hear it in his tone.

"There's no statute of limitations on lying," I say before he can speak.

His face transforms instantly. Oh, he's such a good actor. He comes toward me like he wants to take me in his arms, like he thinks he can sweet-talk me now. I dodge away.

"Come on, honey," he says. "What's got you so upset? I thought we straightened all this out. What's wrong? I took you out to dinner the other night, didn't I?"

I laugh. "Oh, thank you, Adam. Thank you so much for taking your pitiful wife out to dinner. That was so generous of you." I stop my mocking. "What's wrong is I'm done. I'm just done."

I bend to gather up my things, hook my purse over my shoulder, overnight bag gripped in my hand, coat over my arm. I feel him watching. I turn to head across the kitchen to the door. I try not to look at him, but when I pass he grabs my by the crook of my arm. My purse falls down my shoulder to my elbow.

"Tell me where you're going?"

I take in his face, his eyes—those deep blue eyes—scan his mouth, how tightly he's holding his lips and jaw. No lies. I refuse to follow his playbook. "I'll be at Troy's," I say. "I'm sure you have his number."

"Troy?" His eyebrow knits. It registers. I see it travel across his expression. "Middleton?" He lets go of my arm and his hand goes to his forehead, like he's shading his eyes. "Why there?"

I give him as forthright of a glare as I can and I watch the lightbulb turn on inside his brain.

"You've got to be kidding me." He sounds incredulous. "You're fucking Middleton? Jesus Christ! I don't believe it." He seems ready to laugh, as if I'm making it up, as if I'm incapable of being anything besides a housewife and mother. It's the laughter in his voice that insults me most. "Nice try, Sarah. I don't believe you for one second."

"Why not? Because I'm so boring? Too ordinary? Miss Goody Two-shoes? Or is it because I'm frigid and have this thick linebacker neck."

"You're not making any sense." He's still smirking and I want to slap him.

"I know that's how you see me. Or rather don't see me. You haven't noticed the house is a wreck. You haven't even taken a look at the new furniture upstairs, because if you had—" He tries to interrupt me, but I raise my hand to stop him. "—if you had, you would see it hasn't been unwrapped. Because I've been in his bed all week. And believe me, he doesn't think I'm frigid." I put my hand on his chest to shove past him, but he grabs me again, and this time he hurts my wrist he squeezes so hard.

He gets right in my face. "Are you really fucking that goddamned asshole? That goddamned carpenter?" He clutches me by my shoulders like he's going to shake me. "What the hell is wrong with you?"

"Let me go." I try to stay calm but this is escalating too quickly.

"Does he think he's some kind of stud? That he can just fuck all the women he wants to around here?" His face is distorted with anger now. It frightens me.

"Stop saying that word, Adam. Just get out of my way!"

I shove at him and he loses his balance along with his grip on me. He bounces back against the bifold doors on the laundry room with a loud racket "Fuck!" he says, straightening. Then he turns and kicks the door in front of the machines. It rattles and vibrates. "Fuck! Fuck! Fuck!!"

When he kicks the door again it pops off the track, swings outward, and whacks him on the forehead. That staggers him, but he immediately grabs the door with both hands and rips it from the jamb, hinges and all. He flings it out into the middle of the kitchen. It hits the cook island, careens off, and crashes to the floor lengthwise.

I stand there dumbfounded, mouth open, watching his rage. I stare at the broken door. There's a ragged splinter where it was hinged to the frame. The second door hangs lopsided on the bent track. I lift my eyes. His forehead is bleeding. He's snorting hard.

"Don't just stand there," he snarls. "Get the fuck out of here!"

I grab the back doorknob, dodging past the remaining bi-fold door. It dangles precariously on the track. On the back porch, I take in a deep breath but I don't pause. I run to my car, get in, turn the key. I'm shaking so hard I can barely engage the gear shift. The tires spin as I back out of the driveway.

WHEN I PULL in behind Troy's truck, I'm still shaken. I take my bag, my coat, my purse, and race across the yard. I bang at the front door. When he doesn't answer, I bang harder. I know he's here. His truck is in the driveway. I knock until it feels like my knuckles might crack. Panic rises and now is when my tears try to start.

What have I done? I have never seen Adam so enraged. I handled it all wrong, let emotion take control, and didn't rehearse what I would say. It was impulsive and careless. *Oh God, I don't know what I'm doing.*

The whir of a power saw reaches me and I remember the shop, a shop I've never even seen. It hits me how little I know about Troy. I pick my way around the side of the house. There's a gate, overgrown with vines. One ropes around my shoe and nearly trips me. To get the gate open I have to shove hard against the grass and weeds obstructing the bottom.

The shop is at the deep end of the property. It's made entirely out of corrugated tin, with two barn doors. Both stand wide open. There's a light on. The sound of the saw comes louder. I cross the yard and peer inside. He's running a length of quarter round through a table saw. He can't hear me for the noise, and from the way he's turned, he can't see me either. I stand there and watch him, a stranger. I'm not a high school girl, I understand infatuation; that's not this.

A jerry-rigged fluorescent light hangs overhead by two chains. He holds his mouth clamped as he feeds the saw blade. A strip of wood falls away. The saw idles down. He reaches for the cigarette balanced on the edge of the table.

I lean further into the doorway. "Troy?"

He sees me, cuts off the saw, thumps the cigarette onto the floor, and mashes it out with his foot. He smiles, spots my bag. "You made it."

He reaches to take the bag and I lean against him, burying my face in his chest. There's sawdust on his shirt. His arm comes around me. His warmth, the sawdust, all of it releases my tears. I can't speak. I struggle to gain control. He doesn't say anything, just holds me. I can hear the hum of the fluorescent lights.

"He broke down a door," I say, finally. "I had everything

packed to come over here. It was all right there in plain sight and he ignored me. I'm so sick and tired of being ignored."

He hugs his arm tighter around me, thumbs a tear off my cheek. "So . . . tell me what happened."

"I couldn't keep lying. I told him about you and me."

His eyes remain expressionless. "I bet that got his attention."

"That's when he broke down the door."

Troy reaches to pull the chain on the fluorescent light. It goes out and the hum stops. He puts his arm around my shoulders and guides me toward the house. My bag is still in his hand. We follow a path of steppingstones toward the back door and go inside. He lays my bag on the kitchen table. I add my purse and my coat. He opens a drawer by the sink.

"I've got something for you. After we talked I went and had this made." He holds up a key, then hands it to me. "I thought you might need it." A crooked smile comes on his face. "Maybe not this soon, but I thought maybe at some point."

I take the key, turn it over in my hand. "I'm not moving in with you."

"OK."

"Because I can't go from one man to the other just like that." I make a snapping motion with my fingers but no noise comes.

"I get that. But you've got to go somewhere, and you're here right now, so you might as well stay for a while until we come up with something else."

I notice the word *we*. I cherish it. I can't read his expression. He doesn't look angry or upset, but almost jolly, and like he knows he shouldn't be. A smile continues to play with his mouth.

"A whole door?" he says.

"One of the bifolds in the kitchen."

He nods, looks at the floor, then at me. "Those things are flimsy. And easy to put back up."

"The wood's splintered."

He gives a more solemn nod, but the smile comes back to his

face. "Boy, when you finally decide something you don't mess around, do you?"

"I don't know what I've decided. It got really ugly. I've never seen him like that."

"We're not going to worry about him, OK?" He opens his arms, and I go into them. He smells like fresh-cut wood and cigarettes. He kisses the top of my head. "You knocked me over for a second, but I'm glad you left him. He deserves to be left." He leans back against the sink counter, and studies me at arm's length. He must see my despair. He says, "Everything's going to be all right, Sarah."

I want to believe him, but panic like bile keeps rising in my throat, and I can't seem to swallow hard enough.

Adam

Seventeen

The drive into Austin normally takes thirty minutes, but Mom and Dad live on the far west side, so it's an hour and fifteen no matter which route you take. I deaden my nerves with Metallica on an FM station and kick the Jeep up to eighty.

My parents bought this place outside the city limits eight years ago when Dad retired. Mom had already retired from teaching three years before. Now, they have a modern house on a half-acre lot in a planned community, plenty of rolling hills and oak trees, and other retired couples nearby. Everybody gets together at the clubhouse for potluck suppers and games of Bunco. Mom and Dad seem content. Forty-nine years they have been married to each other. That alone seems like an awesome accomplishment, especially today as I pull the Jeep into their circular driveway.

Their Christmas tree stands in the front window. Today will be the last day the tree is lit up. Mom takes the tree down on January 2, without fail. Joel and Cody are in the sideyard playing croquet—an old people's game. They're resilient little guys. The sun shines bright, and the day has turned out warm, but they're both in heavy coats and earmuffs—compliments of Mom. She worries about ear infections, head colds, bronchitis. My brother,

Brent, and I couldn't take off our sweaters or go outside barefoot until the first of May, no matter what the temperature outside. By then, most of my friends were tanned and had been in shorts for a month.

"Happy New Year!" Cody calls out when he sees me.

He makes it to the Jeep first and hugs me around my waist as I step out. Joel and I don't hug anymore. I clamp him on the shoulder and give him a little shake. He acts embarrassed by the attention. I don't know how he turned out so tall and skinny. He takes after Brent more than me. I can feel his collarbone through his coat.

"Where's Mom?" Joel says, squinting at the Jeep.

I let go of him. "She didn't come."

"Why not?" Cody pipes in.

"She was busy. Let's go in and see if Grammy and Pops have survived your visit."

"Of course they have," Cody says, sounding insulted. "What's the matter with your head?"

I touch my finger to the knot above my eye. "I bumped it."

"Grammy's cooking dinner," Joel says, and I know that means I'll be expected to stay and eat.

Mom greets me at the door. She wears an apron. Her earrings are still on from church. She probably doesn't even realize they're there—some things never change. She kisses my cheek. She has on Sunday lipstick, too, and I figure some of it just came off on my face.

"What happened to your head?" She touches the knot. I wince. It's sore today and was dark red in the mirror. "That looks bad."

"I had a little run-in with a door." I move passed her.

"You always were my clumsy one," she says with a laugh.

The boys stay outside. I watch them through the window, out there with the croquet mallets. They seem into it. I wonder if anyone bothered to teach them the rules, or if they're just whacking balls around the yard. I hear the familiar crack of a wooden mallet against a wooden ball. They know, as well as I do, that with Grammy cooking dinner we won't be rushing off soon.

"Where's Sarah?" Mom says. "I was hoping you would both come."

The house smells like New Year's dinner, baked chicken and black-eyed peas. Mom takes my jacket off to one of the back bedrooms. Dad's in front of the TV in his recliner. An afghan I remember Sarah crocheted for him several Christmases ago stretches across his legs. He looks as if he's been napping. He sees me and reaches for the footrest lever.

"Stay where you are," I say. A football game is on. I nod at the screen. "Who's winning?"

"Vikings, I think. I lost track of the score."

He won't admit he's been asleep. In his mind naps are for lazy people. The score comes up on the corner of the TV screen. The 49ers are ahead by twenty-five points. It's been a long nap. He cranes to look behind me.

"Sarah's not with you?" he says.

I shake my head and sit down on the couch. Is that the only question anybody can ask? When did I become Sarah's sidekick?

Playoffs or not, I'm too restless to sit still for long, and anyway, Dad keeps nodding off. I wander back into the kitchen. Mom isn't there so I check all the pans on the stove, and pick at the crust on the apple pie. It's warm from the oven. She returns just as I taste a spoonful of black-eyed peas. She's still using bacon fat even though Dad's supposed to be on a low-cholesterol diet. I guess she's already forgotten the hospital scare we all had with his heart attack or the long—too long—bypass surgery.

"Now, you'll have good luck all year," she says, reminding me it's 1989, New Year's Day already. I can't remember if I ate peas last New Year's Day. If so, I don't wish to repeat the mistake. It's been a shitstorm of a year.

"Did you get down to the park last night for fireworks?" I ask, thinking about my own New Year's Eve—alone. Just me and good old Jack Daniels after an all-day attempt to fix the damned laundry room doors.

"We did, and it was lovely. The children enjoyed it. What about you? Did you shoot a deer?" She shakes flour and water in a jar for gravy. She's used the same gravy shaker for as long as I can remember.

"The client canceled." That's not exactly how it went. "Had a quiet night. Watched the ball drop at Times Square."

"You stayed up late?"

She pours the thickening into the pan of meat drippings and stirs quickly. I have the desire to reach over and pet her graying hair. I remember when she was blond and younger.

"I'm disappointed Sarah didn't come with you. I've fixed this big supper and I know how she likes my sweet potato casserole. Maybe you can take some to her. Is she feeling OK?"

"I wonder myself," I mumble.

"What's that, dear?" Mom concentrates on stirring the pan of gravy.

"She left me." I say it with a weak laugh but I didn't intend to blurt it out that way. I hadn't decided for sure if I would even tell anybody yet. It seems unreal and I'm not convinced it's permanent. For all I know, she might be back by the time I get home. But now I've blabbed it out and Mom looks stricken.

She stops stirring the gravy, taking a big chance on lumps. "That's not a funny joke, Adam. Not at all."

"She said she's suffocating."

Mom backs up to one of the kitchen chairs and sits down hard. "Oh honey. I didn't realize you two were having trouble. You seemed fine at Christmas."

"You never know, do you?" I intend it to sound rhetorical, but it comes out sarcastic and I can see right away she takes it personally. I move the pan of gravy off the fire and pick up the spoon to stir.

"I try to keep up with your lives," she says. "I do. Yours *and*

Brent's, but neither one of you has ever let me in on your personal troubles."

"I didn't mean it literally, Mom. Of course, you didn't know. Hell, I didn't know."

"It seems you'd notice if your wife couldn't breathe."

A ponder that for a moment. I don't think Mom means to sound like Edith Bunker, it just comes naturally to her. I shake my head and open the refrigerator. There's a bottle of wine shoved way in the back with the cork plugged crooked in the neck. It looks like it's been back there a while. I have to fumble through a dozen little plastic containers filled with dabs of leftovers to finally reach the bottle.

"What about the boys?" Mom says.

"They're staying with me."

"You?"

The sugar in the wine has sealed the cork fast to the neck of the bottle. I scan the shelves for something else. Nope. This wine is the only alcoholic beverage in the refrigerator.

"What's wrong with the boys staying with me?" I ask.

"Nothing at all. But children should be with their mother. Well, that's my opinion anyway. Where will you go?"

"Me?" It takes an effort to wrangle out the wine cork. I grab a juice glass from the cupboard, and pour. "She's the one who walked out."

"Oh, Adam." She turns to look at me. The gravy bubbles like a cauldron. "That's Sarah's house. I can't believe she would just move out of it."

"Well, she did." The wine has soured. I knock it back and pour another glassful.

"Why don't you stay here tonight, you and the boys? They don't have to be back at school until Tuesday. You should just stay the night and drive to work from here tomorrow." She watches me pour a third glass of the god-awful wine. "I have stemware in the cupboard, son," she says. "You don't have to use that jelly glass."

I laugh. I would drink straight from the bottle if I thought it wouldn't offend her. "I don't have any clothes here, Mom. Thanks, but we're going home right after supper."

Nothing else is said about the situation with Sarah. Mom will wait until we have gone to tell Dad, and that's good. I've talked about it all I want to. Now I've just got to figure out how I'm going to break it to the boys. The wine goes down easier with each swallow, and then it's all gone. I search in the bottom of the china cabinet where Dad used to hide a bottle of brandy. Nothing there now.

After we eat, Dad asks me to climb on the roof with his blower to clean out dead leaves from the gutters. He stands on the ground and directs me, even though I can plainly see, once I'm up there, where the leaves have clogged the downspouts. I let him wave his hands and tell me what to do, then ignore him and do it my way. The wine has relaxed me enough not to complain.

The chore takes my mind off Sarah and how I'm going to tell the boys she's gone. I can't decide if I should tell them in the car or wait until we get home. As it happens, they decide for me. It's dark when we leave and both of them are sound asleep by the time we get out of city traffic.

I go over the words I want to say. It has to be simple so they'll understand the situation without it devolving into my own outrage. I don't want them bitter toward her. I don't think she's responsible for her actions right now. I have to believe that. The woman I've been married to for fifteen years would not abandon her kids and her home and the life we've built together, not for some two-bit carpenter. She is definitely not in her right mind. But I can't say that to the boys. It's too abstract. They'll think she has literally gone insane, which in a way she has, but . . . anyway. . . . *crap!* I can't come up with anything. Sarah would know the right thing to say to them. She's always been the one to handle complicated explanations.

We pass a Dairy Queen, and I pull in for milkshakes. I think milkshakes might make everything go down a little easier. Besides, it's been an hour and a half since we finished Mom's dinner, and growing boys always have room for a shake. Truth is, I'm stalling.

The lights at the drive-through window wake them, and I order three chocolates. By the time the boys come alive enough to drink them, we've turned up our street. They both suck dregs through their straws. *Singing the soda fountain blues,* Dad used to say me and Brent, so I say it, too. The boys respond with a loud groan. I guess I might have said it before.

All the outside Christmas lights are on at our house. I see Sarah's car parked under the carport. I'm relieved I haven't told the boys yet. Also, I'm kicking myself for my bad judgment with Mom. I might have worked her up over nothing. Sarah's already home just like I expected.

I pull the Jeep in beside her BMW. Through the car windows I see her clothes piled up in the backseat, some of them still on hangers, so I guess she's not staying after all. And I know she's in a hurry to have thrown them in there in such a haphazard way. That isn't at all like neat-and-tidy, no-clutter Sarah. A couple of brown grocery bags sit on the front seat. I don't think the kids notice any of this. They're busy unloading their duffels and the plastic containers of food Mom sent home with us. They bound up the back steps as if nothing is unusual. Cody stops to inspect his Christmas bike. It's still chained to the water pipe on the side of the house. I need to adjust the seat so he can reach the pedals. I still don't remember putting the damned thing together, and these blackouts worry me. Seems I did an OK job of it though.

When I step in the back door, Sarah's there, next to the freezer, giving Joel a big hug. She looks over his shoulder and our eyes meet. Hers look vacant. Maybe she really has gone nuts.

Cody races up the back steps, shoves past me, and grabs Sarah around the waist. "Glad my bike's all right." He stops at the laundry room. "What's happened to the door?"

"Nothing. Take your things upstairs," she tells them as if everything is normal. As if they can't see with their own eyes that the laundry door is broken. I feel stupid about that, plus I did a crappy job of spackling.

After the boys go upstairs, we stand there staring at each other. For several moments we do that without speaking. She goes first: "I want to talk to them together." Her eyes travel to the place where the door whacked me, just above my left eyebrow. She doesn't mention it.

"Afraid of what I might tell them?" I say

"I was only afraid you might not let me come in."

I have to suppress the urge to take her in my arms. It comes over me out of nowhere and makes me angry at myself. "You're really going through with this?"

She nods. "Remember when you were the one having a crisis? Remember how you felt? Well, now it's me."

"I stayed."

She turns away from me. "I did some laundry while I was waiting. It's folded on the dryer."

"And I didn't fuck anybody."

She whirls around. "How would I know that?"

"Because I'm telling you."

"And you've never lied to me?"

"Not on purpose."

"On purpose . . ." she repeats with a bitter laugh. Even with her back to me, I can see the flush on her face. "I don't want to do this right now. Do you want me to call them down here, or should we go up?"

"I don't care, Sarah. I really don't."

She glances at me and starts up the stairs. I stay behind in the kitchen long enough to grab a beer out of the refrigerator. The wine has already worn off and given me a headache. The pop-top hisses open. I take two big swallows and head up to join them.

They're all in our bedroom. Sarah sits on the bed with Cody. Joel is in the bentwood rocking chair. The boys know something's up. Their faces are drawn and somber. They have no idea what though, and I wish I could warn them, somehow prepare them for the shock they're about to get.

Sarah watches me as I come into the room. I see her give the beer in my hand a judgmental look. At least I won't have to watch that look come on her face anymore. That's a relief. She lowers her eyes. I select my spot and lean against the bedroom door.

"Your dad and I have decided to separate for a while," she says, wasting no time. She's obviously rehearsed all of this. I want to correct her: I played no part in that decision. "Do you know what I mean when I say separate?"

Joel stops rocking. "Split up," he says, accusation taking his voice up a notch.

"That's right," she says. "It's just for a while. We have some differences we need to iron out and we can't live together while we do it." Her eyes come to me. It feels odd hearing her include me in all this—as if I chose to have my wife shack up with some random asshole.

"What differences?" Cody asks.

Yeah, what differences? I wait to hear how she'll answer that one.

"Don't ask me which one of you I want to go with," Joel butts in with a threatening tone.

"What differences, Mom?" Cody says again. But Joel has Sarah's attention, now. He's always the one she worries over most. Firstborn, and all that.

"It's me who's leaving," she says. "You're staying here with Dad. It's just for a while. Then when I get settled somewhere, you can decide." *You've already settled in at your boyfriend's house. Tell them that.*

Tears are building in her eyes—in Cody's too. "What differences?" he says for the third time.

"Adult differences," I say, and Sarah shoots me a look of gratitude.

"I don't want to hear any more of this crap." Joel leaps up from the rocker. "This whole thing sucks."

"Watch the attitude." I intercept him before he can storm by me. "This isn't easy for us either."

"Whatever..." Joel rolls his eyes.

"Why are *you* going, Mom?" I hear Cody ask. "Usually when parents get divorced it's the dad that lives someplace else."

"We're not getting divorced, honey." She looks at me, pleading for another save. I don't help this time, but I am interested to hear her say no to divorce. "It's just for a while," she tells Cody. That seems to have become her mantra.

When I let go of Joel's arm he rushes out of the room. The door to his room across the hall slams hard. The walls shake. Cody starts crying outright. It doesn't bother him for us to see his tears. Sarah takes him against her breast and looks in the direction of Joel's room. She rubs Cody's hair back from his forehead. Her expression is pained.

"All right," I say, sarcasm dripping. "That went really well." I turn my back on her and go down for another beer.

NEITHER ONE OF the boys walks her out to her car. Instead, it's me. They're both up in their rooms bawling. She sniffles a little, too.

"I hope he's worth it." I open her car door so she'll get on inside. I'm ready for this to be done. She doesn't get in. I know she's cold standing out here. Sarah has never been a fan of winter.

"Do you think they understood anything at all?" she says.

"Do you? Because I sure don't."

"At least *you're* talking to me. I was afraid you wouldn't."

"There's no point in acting uncivilized."

She smirks and I know she's thinking about the laundry door. I have the urge to laugh with embarrassment. I want to tell her what a bitch that door was to re-hang, but I restrain myself.

She glances up at the windows to the boys' rooms. "How was the deer lease?"

I lean on the car. "If you're going, let's don't drag it out with small talk, OK?"

"I'll call tomorrow. To check on the kids."

"Don't call. I'll let you know if we need you."

"How will you do that?"

"I have his number, remember?"

She hesitates for a moment, then gets in the car. She's sniffling again, and it's what I hoped to avoid. I try to ignore it and shut her door. She backs out of the driveway and I stand there watching and wondering where in the hell she found the courage to go. I hadn't been able to do it—and I really tried. Shouldn't I feel relieved? Be grateful to her? Funny how things change when you're the leavee and not the leaver.

Back inside, I head to my desk in the den to call Marty. His answering machine comes on. I leave a message that I won't be coming in to work tomorrow. I don't give him an explanation. After I hang up, I go to the light switch controlling the Christmas lights outside and turn them off. I step out the door and unplug all the strands. I yank down the ones around the front door and let them fall onto the porch. *Enough with the holiday bullshit.* I step over the light strand, go inside and upstairs. I do the same to the Christmas lights on the balcony, too. The new porch furniture sits there, just like she said, still in the plastic wrap. If I had a knife in my hand I think I might slash it to shreds.

Eighteen

I sleep late. It's unusual for me and I'm on my feet the instant I see the clock—*9:36*. I tie on my bathrobe and walk out into the hall. Joel's door is closed. I peek in as I pass. The hinges squeak but he doesn't stir. Let the kid sleep. I know he had a tough night, even though he tried to pretend indifference. He's always been close to his mom, adored her in fact, and used to show it before he became a truculent teenager. I make a mental note to use some WD-40 on his door later.

Cody's room is open and I hear the TV in the den downstairs. There isn't anything I can do about the squeaky steps. We have twenty-three steps in this staircase—twenty-eight counting the set that splits off into the kitchen. All of them pop and creak.

This damned old house. I've always considered it Sarah's house, more hers than mine. It wouldn't have been my choice, I had my eye on a split-level on the outskirts of Austin, but that wasn't far enough from town for her, and as soon as the real estate agent showed us this place, she fell madly in love. When I saw the glow on her face, what could I do but find a way to buy it? Now, here I am and she's gone. And the house is partly to blame. *Middleton, the sonofabitch* . . .

I promise myself not to dwell on it all day. Today, I spend with my boys. They need it and so do I. We might go see a movie, or go bowling or something. It's been a long time since we did anything like that, just us guys. And no booze, I tell myself.

In the den, Cody lies on the rug with two pillows from his bed rolled under his head. He's curled up in a ball inside the robe Sarah gave him for Christmas, using it like a blanket. It's always colder down here than upstairs.

"Why didn't you turn up the heat, hotshot?" I say, going to the thermostat. The house has two heating and air-conditioning units, one up and one down, and an electric bill to match. This old place is breaking me, has been breaking me almost from the day the movers brought in our things and we found out the bathroom plumbing didn't work.

"Mom says don't mess with that." Cody comes up behind me, and watches as I twist the dial. "So that's how you do it."

I explain to him how to set the thermostat up or down. "From now on, you have my permission to mess with it."

I wander into the kitchen and spot the coffee pot with yesterday's dregs in the carafe. I do a quick cleanup, wincing at the chill of the tap water. Cody has followed me again. "How long you been up, sport?" I ask.

"All the way through Scooby-Doo. Now Superman's on."

"Did you eat something?" I spoon coffee into a new filter.

He shrugs. "Cereal."

"How about some bacon and eggs? A real manly breakfast?"

"Are you going to do it?" He sounds doubtful.

"I can cook. What, you think I can't cook?" I open the refrigerator. No bacon and only one egg. I sigh. "Well, cereal sounds pretty good, too," I say, changing tactics.

The milk jug is nearly empty. If I eat a bowl of cereal there won't be enough milk for Joel. Sarah does the grocery shopping. The rest of us assume anything we need will magically appear in the pantry or the refrigerator—but I guess she's been too busy having her affair to do any shopping. "Screw it," I say, and fling the milk jug back on the shelf.

Cody starts laughing. He holds his stomach and laughs hard, sounding kind of like when he was a baby. I look at him in surprise, then I laugh, too, although I hadn't meant anything funny. I guess he likes hearing me swear. The coffee pot dribbles coffee into the carafe. At this rate, it will take half an hour to get one cup.

"Mom puts vinegar in it sometimes," Cody says. He's still half-laughing. "She says vinegar makes it run faster."

"Mom knows best." I don't think he gets my sarcasm.

Upstairs, I hear Joel's door squeak, then his footsteps thunder on the staircase. He comes into the kitchen squinty-eyed. He has on a pair of underwear—no pajamas. I guess he's too hip now for pajamas.

"You guys are making too much noise," he says, and finds the box of cereal I set out on the counter. Cody and I watch him pour himself a huge bowl. He uses every last drop of the milk.

Cody squeals with laughter again. "You took all Dad's milk."

"Whatever." Joel rolls his eyes at his brother. "Where's the bananas?"

"Gone." Cody keeps laughing.

"What do you mean, gone?" Joel growls. He's a bear in the morning. "Grammy sent home a big bunch with us."

"There were five. I ate them all." Cody sounds proud of himself.

"Da-*ad*." Joel makes the word into two syllables. He looks at me like I'm supposed to do something—beat the bananas out of Cody maybe.

"*Five* bananas, bud?" I say. "You ate five just this morning?" He sees I'm no longer laughing and gives me a guilty nod. I soften my tone. "Why'd you do that?"

"I dunno."

"Creep." Joel carries his bowl of cereal to the dining room table.

The coffee pot is nearly finished. I study Cody and wonder

what it means when a kid eats five bananas. "Do you have a bellyache?"

"Kind of." He bows his head. He's got his mom's hair color—same face, too.

I glance at the trashcan. The peelings to five bananas are stuffed on top. Now that I see them I can smell them as well—a sickly sweet smell. I laugh—carefully at first, then with more gusto when I catch Cody's relief.

MARTY CALLS RIGHT AFTER NOON. The boys and I are watching a pirate movie on television. It's a funny movie and I'm not anxious to answer the phone.

"Are you under the weather? What's going on?" Marty's voice comes loudly through the phone. I back the receiver away from my ear.

"I think I caught a virus." How does a man say his wife has left him without drawing pity? I've known Marty for eleven years and I still can't say it. "I'll be in tomorrow."

"Well, I don't want to make you feel worse, but the Willoby deal looks like it might fall through. The old man called this morning. He said you canceled the hunting trip."

I let out a deep sigh. "Screw the bastard. He just wants us kissing his ass. I couldn't go. I got sick."

"Well . . ." Marty sounds pensive. "He said he has some more checking around to do."

"Let's get into it tomorrow, Marty. My head's killing me."

"OK. Tomorrow then. Come with your guns loaded."

It's an old joke we use when business is looking shaky, which is pretty often lately. We're up to our asses in debt. On the first of December, Marty took out another signature loan to keep the business going for ninety more days. We now owe two loans to the bank, and unless something big falls from the sky we won't be able to even make the interest payment.

Everything is coming unraveled all at once.

For supper, we eat Mom's leftover chicken and black-eyed peas. Cody heats up a can of corn, and Joel makes Texas toast in the toaster oven. After a whole day together, I'm feeling better about the three of us. We can manage without Sarah. It isn't much different than if she had died. None of us mentions her. Not even Joel, who usually has no qualms about bringing up sensitive subjects. I notice he stays downstairs all evening for a change, watching TV with me and Cody instead of skulking around upstairs with his stereo equipment. It seems like a good first sign.

I try not to think about Sarah either, which I do fairly well until bedtime. Her pillow smells like her cologne. I pull it under my arm and lie there trying to fall asleep. Instead, I daydream back to the first time I saw her.

She was standing outside my economics class wearing a crushed velvet jacket—midnight blue. It made all that burnished hair over her collar look like spun gold. Marjorie Whitfield was standing there, too, beside Sarah. I knew Marjorie, and had even dated her once or twice. I walked over to them and said. "Introduce me to your friend." When Sarah smiled at me it felt like my heart tumbled out of my chest.

For three weeks, I chased her all over campus before she agreed to go out with me. We got a pizza and a six-pack of beer, took it back to my apartment, sat cross-legged on the floor, and talked until after her dorm curfew. She seemed so sweet, a little bit shy, as rare in those days as now. I drove her back to campus and her friend sneaked her into the dorm. The next morning, I asked her to move in with me. Her answer was no, of course. I asked her twenty more times before she finally said yes. I never was sure why the twentieth time worked. Did she think I had chased her enough by then? I know Sarah. She loves the chase.

I figure that must be what happened with Middleton. He must have given her a good chase, the bastard. There's no other reason she would find him attractive. To me he looks like a bum, a deadbeat. He's not educated, not by her standards anyway. No money, other than mine—I think about that fat check I gave him on Christmas Eve—a check I could hardly afford. But that has to be it—he chased her until she let him catch her. I feel like an idiot for not realizing it was happening right under my nose. I never suspected a thing, not even with her inviting him to parties—which should have been a clue. But she's always been like that, taking in strays. And she's never been disloyal.

Finally, I give up on sleep, can't turn off my brain. I trudge downstairs for the bottle of Jack Daniels I nearly killed on New Year's Eve. There's still an inch and a half in the bottom. I drink it straight without bothering to get a glass. Then I toss the empty into the trash on top of Cody's banana peels.

TUESDAY MORNING, I sit in my office, five blocks from the Capitol building, and stare out the window. A pile of indices and several telephone messages are stacked on my desk in front of me, but I can't find the energy to take care of any of it. Who cares what the NASDAQ Composite says, or that the Dow is off 23.93 points?

I got here late. Marty had already gone out on some appointment. All I've done so far is stare out the window, watching traffic go by on Congress Avenue. It's better than staring at the framed picture of Sarah on my desk—head thrown back, hair flowing, that smile, the pearl earrings I gave her for her thirtieth birthday—better times. I reach over and turn the picture face down.

The boys were back to normal this morning, fighting over a pair of underwear they both claimed. We missed the school bus—hell, I hadn't even finished packing their lunches when it came. Then they fought over who got to ride in the front seat of the Jeep as I drove them to their respective schools. By the time I got them both delivered, I was irritable and exhausted.

Now, here I sit, my mind on everything except work. I add vinegar to the grocery list I've written on a pink *While You Were Out* pad, along with milk, bacon, eggs, bread. *Bananas*—I double underline bananas. When the phone rings, I let the service answer. I'm in no mood to speak to anyone.

Earlier, just after I first arrived, I got a call from Sam Willoby telling me he'd decided to go with Waterton-Pierce. He sounded cold, and indifferent, not the same man Marty and I met for dinner last week. I explained to Willoby that I'd been contagious and apologized for canceling the deer hunt. My lie didn't seem to break through. Truth is, I don't give a damn. None of it seems worth the bother anymore. I could sell the house, pay off my half of the company debt, let Marty worry about his half.

I pick up the phone and call Balcor Electronics. I've still got the number in the speed dial from when Sarah worked there. The switchboard operator answers and I ask her to connect me with Carolyn Jeffrey. I'm not sure of the extension. Carolyn's been promoted twice since Sarah left. I reach over and set Sarah's picture back upright and stare at it.

Carolyn's voice comes on the phone, recognizable, high-pitched, emphatic. I try to sound nonchalant. "What's up?" I say.

"Adam? You must've heard me. I was just talking about you to a coworker. She inherited some money and I gave her your name. I bragged about how good you are at investing for people."

"Thanks," I say, because it's expected, then: "Sarah left me," which is not. And yet, it's amazing how easily it rolls off my tongue. I sound like a stranger, even to myself. "She moved out over the weekend."

After two beats: "God, Adam. I'm in shock. I don't know what to say." Another pause. I can almost hear, through the phone, the wheels of her brain turn. "Why hasn't she called me?"

"Yeah, well, I think I know the answer to that." I drum a pencil on a stack of papers. "Are you free for lunch?"

We arrange to meet at an Asian place around the corner from Balcor. I've been there a dozen times. They have outstanding Peking Duck.

Before I even park the car in their lot, the smell of food arrives. I don't see Carolyn, so I decide to sit in the courtyard and wait for her. She's one of those late people; I try not to get impatient. Calling her was an impulse, one I probably shouldn't have followed after the last time I sought her out, but I need to talk to someone—someone with skin in this Middleton business. Carolyn knows him, was seeing him before. At least I think it was before, I'm not even sure how long this crap has been going on or how it played out. I guess I should have seen it coming, but I didn't. I thought she was matchmaking Carolyn like she has before.

The day is bright and sunny, not a cloud in the sky, temperature eighty degrees according to the digital bank sign across the road. I wish I hadn't left my Wayfarers in the Jeep. My jacket feels heavy and hot. I take it off, lay it on the bench beside me, loosen the knot on my tie. I haven't seen Carolyn since before Christmas and I'm halfway wishing I'd worn the gaudy tie she gave me. It's hanging in the closet at home, along with the sweater from Sarah, who knows I don't wear sweaters. At the time, it seemed like a last-ditch gift to give me but now I understand. Her mind wasn't on me, or what I might really want, which would have been for her to scale back her Christmas spending.

Carolyn walks up on my left and bends down to hug me around the neck. I smell her perfume, musky and sensuous. She's wearing a three-piece business suit, a far cry from her usual boho wardrobe. I stand and hug her back. Her hugs are always especially tight. I think she enjoys playing the temptress.

She holds onto my shoulders and looks me in the face. "Are you all right?"

"Oh, hell yeah. I'm fine." I wonder if I sound at all convincing. "Blindsided me at first, but now I'm fine. The boys are fine." I take her by her arm. "Let's go inside before all the good tables are gone."

"She left the boys, too?"

"There's more. Just wait," I say, as a maître d' approaches. He shows us to a booth, gives us menus. I don't need mine. I know what I want—the Peking Duck. I order saké, too.

Carolyn shakes her head at me, and gives me a scolding tsk-tsk. "In the middle of the day. Bad boy."

"After the weekend I've had . . ." My ears start to ring.

"I can't believe she hasn't called me. I was just with her last week."

"That's the hell of it. She left Friday. Packed a bag and left. Just like that."

I watch a waiter come with the saké. He sets down two bamboo coasters, two white cups, pours, then leaves the carafe. I feel Carolyn staring at me. She hasn't even heard the best part. I pick up my saké cup and hold it for a toast. She taps her cup against mine.

"One sip," she says. "I've still got to work." She sips and pushes her cup away. "I must say, I'm glad you're taking it OK."

"Yeah—well . . ." I down my cup in one swoop—to hell with sipping. It tastes like gasoline. I tip more into my cup. "She's moved in with Middleton."

The bottom falls out of Carolyn's face. Her entire demeanor changes in an instant. She sags back against her seat. "*What?*" She's too loud. I look around us. Nobody's listening. I see she's as dumbfounded as I feel.

"Yeah." I nod.

"No! Adam, I cannot believe this. What a sleazy bastard." I watch the shock on her face disintegrate into outrage—the twist of a kaleidoscope. "When did this happen?"

"Like I said, she left Friday. I don't know how long it's been going on. She said she'd been in his bed all week." Repeating those words nauseates me.

"That prick." Her jaw moves like she's gritting her teeth. "Because we were just there last week. Tuesday after I got back. She acted so weird about it, told me I shouldn't go over there. Let him call me first, blah blah, blah. She didn't want to go inside. She was just acting so weird. I asked him to go out on New Year's Eve, and he stood right there and said he wasn't interested in seeing me anymore. Jesus, Adam."

"Wait. You and Sarah went to Middleton's house?"

"Yes. She was there with me. Waiting in the other room." Carolyn looks stricken, hurt, angry. All my same emotions. "I feel so . . ." The fingers on both her hands taps her forehead for a second.

"Betrayed?"

"Exactly!"

I nod. I thought she'd be the right person to talk to. At this moment, I feel closer to her than anybody else in the world.

The table next to us is full of laughing, chattering women. They're obviously on their lunch break. Probably work in some office where talking isn't allowed. They're making up for it now. Our waiter brings two bowls of seagrass soup and sets one in front of each of us. He sees my empty saké cup and pours in more.

I pick up my spoon and swizzle around in the bowl of soup. "Were you hung up on him?" I ask. "Because I have to say, I don't get it."

She shakes her head but I see the lie. She hasn't touched her soup. "I don't think he really liked me. I didn't force myself on him or anything."

"I don't understand the attraction. I mean, does he have a big dick, or what?" I let out a laugh like I'm doing a comedy schtick.

"Well . . ." She shrugs, gives me a look, shrugs again. ". . . since you mentioned it. . ."

I nearly choke on soup. *Ouch!* "I could've gone all day without hearing that."

"You asked." She dips her spoon into the soup. "And he's smarter than you think, too, so watch out. Now, I'm wondering if maybe he had eyes for Sarah all along. He was always defending her."

I suddenly feel clammy. All kinds of disgusting images have just poured into my head. I loosen my tie some more. "Defending her how?"

"I don't know, just . . ." She looks off; a thousand-mile stare. She seems really torn up over this despite her denial. "I couldn't say one negative thing about her. Not one. Not even kidding, and he jumps right in with all this praise. My God, Adam, do you think he was using me? Were they scheming this up?"

"That wouldn't make sense, Carolyn." I'm struggling to keep up with the conversation. I'm stuck back at penis size. I reach for the saké and drain it. It scalds my insides again.

"I just can't believe she'd leave the boys," she says. A spoonful of soup finally makes it to her mouth.

I refill my saké cup. My hands are shaky. "I don't want them around that bastard anyway."

"*Sleazy* bastard," she corrects. We both chuckle over that.

"Fucking bastard," I say, and she reaches to lay her hand on top of mine.

"Oh Adam, are you heartbroken? In a way, isn't this what you wanted?"

"Not like this. There's the boys . . . and that goddammed house." I blow out my breath and lean back against the chair. "So you're telling me he actually *is* a stud. . . ." *Jesus! Did I just say that out loud?*

"It hurts more when you're the one who's been dumped," she says. "Believe me, I've been there. But you sat on my couch and said you wished she would find somebody else. That it would make it easier for you."

"If I said that I was talking out my ass." I watch the steam rise from my bowl of soup. I can't eat any more of it. My appetite's gone. "I can't shake the feeling she's getting even. She brought up a bunch of old crap when she left. Ancient history. People can change. I have changed but she won't give me credit for it. It's been years since I strayed."

There's a silence. Just the cackling ladies at the next table. I feel Carolyn's eyes boring a hole in me. I look up.

"Define strayed," she says.

I put up my hand. "I fucked up, OK? But that was a long time ago."

"Really?" This doesn't sound like a real question so I don't respond. Her appetite seems to have kicked in. She's holding her soup bowl to her mouth like she's about to drink it. "Sarah asked me about that night . . . you know . . . when you came to my apartment. She asked how long you were there. She wanted to know what happened."

I look away from her. I'm jolted by this turn in conversation. The night in question is mostly a blur. I'd had too many Manhattans at the airport, then stopped for a few more at the Landing Strip before I found myself at her apartment. I really don't even remember how I got there. "I was smashed," I say.

"Yes, you certainly were. You passed out on my couch." She puts down her bowl and uses chopsticks to cut a bite of lemon chicken. She puts the bite into her mouth and stares at me as she chews.

The waiter comes with our entrées. I still have a full bowl of soup. The smell of the Peking Duck and the shining glaze on it turns my stomach. I think the saké has fried my taste buds anyway. "When was all this? When she asked those questions?"

"Around Thanksgiving." She sticks another bite into her mouth. My eyes focus on the grinding motion of her jaw. *Blue silk robe. Sky blue. A kimono maybe.* She continues, "Yeah, it was when we went antiquing. I told her I sent you home. I told her you were drunk."

"I bet she loved hearing that." I smooth at the corner of my placemat, look up at her. "Yeah, about that night . . . I remember you making a pot of strong coffee. What else?"

"Are you having blackouts, Adam?" She shakes her head at me like I am just too pitiful. "You don't remember taking a cold shower? Sorry you missed it."

"Missed what?"

She's smiling. "I couldn't send you home in your condition. You were a mess."

I sit back against the chair, sifting through dead brain cells—*a shower?* "Jesus, I took a shower? At your place? Why?"

"I just told you. I was trying to sober you up."

The woman at the next table bursts into loud laughter. It makes me jump. I glance toward their table without seeing any of them. I feel my eyelid twitch. *Tan tiles with tan grout. Power pulse massage head waterboarding my face.*

"Were you in the shower, too?" I sound more detached than I feel.

She laughs, wipes her mouth with her napkin and lays it beside her plate. "Are we going Dutch? I need to get back to work." She scoots her chair away from the table.

"I'm buying." I lean forward, lay my hand on the check. I lower my voice. "Don't be coy, Carolyn. Did we . . . you know . . ." I shake my head, make a hand gesture, nothing obscene just kind of turning them palm up, "*do* . . . anything?"

She barks a laugh and gathers her purse. "I can't tell you how insulting that is. To be so stinking drunk you don't remember anything. Try harder. I bet it will come to you." She stands, leans down and gives me a peck right on the lips. "Take care, Adam."

Once she's gone, I sit there and stare at the empty chair across the table. *A blue robe, tan tiles, grout, water in my face.* That's it. I think I would remember more. A joint. I do remember smoking a joint, something I haven't done since college. No wonder I was so out of it.

I down the rest of the saké in my cup. Then I reach for hers and drink it down, too. I pay the waiter for the two lunches and I don't go back to the office. What's the point? I'll call later and leave a message for Marty: *Took sick again. Had to go home. Sorry. I can't seem to shake this bug.*

ON THE WAY out of town, I stop at a liquor store for a bottle of Johnny Walker. I crack the seal in the car and take a sip. It burns going down. Just what I need to kill the bad taste the saké left in my mouth. I take a second, bigger swig from the bottle.

Thirty minutes later, when I hit the end of our street, I've got a nice buzz going. The house looks huge, pristine with the fresh paint—and lonely. I drive past. I don't even tap the brakes. Part of me wishes I could just keep going till I run out of gas. The whole damned house has been tainted by Middleton. I don't think I'll ever be able to look at that paint job again without thinking of him up on scaffolding, probably diddling my wife when he wasn't working. I wonder if they did it in my bed. God, I hate the thought of that.

His address is stamped at the top of his invoices. *905 Church.* Not that I had any reason to memorize it, numbers just stick with me. I turn the Jeep in the direction of Church Street. I want to see if her car is parked at his house. As far as I know she hasn't even called the kids and that's so unlike her. But all of this is unlike her. After all these years, I'm starting to realize there's a lot I don't understand about my own wife.

Her car is there all shiny and royal blue in his driveway. The title to that car is in my name. I should stop making the payments and let the bank repossess it. Or anyway, stop paying the sky-high insurance. What I really should do is go in there and drag her out, take her home, by force if necessary. She's got kids to think about. Not to mention the fifteen years we've spent together. Does she just want to flush that? Has she forgotten when she asked me that exact question and reminded me of how co-mingled we are? Not just our kids but our families, our friends, our finances, our futures.

Middleton's truck isn't there. Too bad. I had plans for it, for him, too. He's a big guy but I think I can take him. I pull the Jeep to the curb in front of his house. I pause for another pull on the scotch. What if I just went in there and dragged her out? I can picture it—holding her by her collar, her kicking and screaming. *That's enough of this shit,* I would say, taking charge, being the man. *I'm the head of this family. I'm the only who gets to decide who stays and who goes, and you don't get to go!*

"I'm heading in," I say out loud. I take another hit of the scotch, screw the cap back on the bottle, yank off my tie, and climb out of the Jeep. I march up to the front door and bang hard on the frame with my fist. Before I can bang a second time, the door opens and there's her face behind the screen.

"Adam?" She pushes open the screen door.

I step back. My resolve begins to crack. "Hi," I say, lamely.

"What are you doing here? Is something wrong?" She glances around me, as if she thinks I might have someone else coming behind me. "Are the boys all right?"

"Nothing's wrong. Where's Middleton?"

She steps out the door onto the concrete porch. "I hope you didn't come to make trouble."

"Trouble? Oh, that's rich." I laugh, and glance at the house next door. A gray-haired woman is staring at us through her window. The curtain drops when I make eye contact with her. "I feel like I'm sneaking around to see my own wife."

I toe a pile of leaves on the porch. I don't want to look at her. Looking at her makes me feel like I could do something stupid, weep for instance. I could easily turn into a big blubbering idiot right now.

"The other night," I say, and hear the tremble in my words, "when we were standing by your car, you seemed to want to talk. I brushed you off. I'm sorry for that. I'm sorry for a lot of things. I've been a real asshole, Sarah, I know I have been. That's all I wanted to say. And also—" I step backward and nearly stumble off the porch. She comes forward like she thinks she can catch me.

"Have you been drinking? Adam, are you drunk?"

"For chrissake, did you hear anything I just said?"

"Yes, I heard you. But it's two o'clock in the afternoon, and I smell liquor on you. How are you going to pick up the boys?"

"I'll take care of the goddammed boys. Don't you worry about it." I kick up a bunch of leaves. "That's not the point, Sarah."

"Yes, it is the point."

"No, it isn't." My mind wanders. I watch a jet way up in the sky. My eyes burn.

"Adam. Go home and—"

"I love you. That's the point. I mean I'm *in* love with you. Always—you know . . . have been. Talking out my ass . . . crazy crap that night." Suddenly my tongue feels thick and I'm having trouble forming words. It comes out like *crathy crath*. "That's all I want to say."

"Your drinking—it's gotten out of hand. You know it has. It's affecting everything. The boys, me, the way you act. Look at you right now."

"You want me to quit? Ish that what thish is all about? OK, I quit." I've been backing up, but now I turn for the Jeep at the curb. When I get there, I reach inside and grab Johnny Walker by the neck. I look back at her. She's followed me partway down the sidewalk. I hold up the bottle. "See this? I'm done wiss it."

I wind up my arm and throw the bottle as hard as I can. It does a high-flying, absolutely outstanding midair somersault, end over end. Centrifugal force keeps the scotch inside the bottle until it lands with a crash and a big splat in the middle of Church Street. Sounds like a bomb. Almost immediately I regret the wasted booze.

"Adam!" She rushes the rest of the way down the sidewalk.

"I'm giving it up," I say, triumphantly. I dust my hands together and hold out my arms. "See how much you mean to me?"

She takes hold of my arm, tries to lead me toward the Jeep. "You're making a scene."

The woman next door is back at the window. I flip her the bird. Sarah grabs at my hand.

"Stop it, Adam. Please! Go home!"

I pull her against me. "Come wiss me."

"You're in no condition to even be driving."

"Come on, baby." I don't let go of her. She's coming home. Whether she likes it or not.

"Stop it! Let go!" She struggles to get out of my grasp. "It's too soon."

"Why? Hasn't he fucked you enough?"

She shoves me away, then slaps me. Hard. It's an openhanded roundhouse, and it catches me off guard. The sound of it echoes against the house and down the street. My eyes water up, and then instinct takes over. I slap her back—harder than I mean to. She staggers and flops down flat on her bottom. Her mouth drops open, and tears cascade down her face. I have never—ever—not even once come close to hitting her. I drop to my knees next to her.

"God, Sarah. Oh honey . . . oh baby. I didn't mean to do that. I'm so sorry."

She shoves at my hands, her eyes bright with anger. "Get out of here, Adam! Just . . . just leave me alone." She pulls herself up off the ground, smooths down her shirt, turns her back on me, and starts toward the house.

I scramble up, wobble a little. "Don't walk away from me! Goddammit, Sarah! We're having a conversation! I mean it, you cannot walk away from this!"

"I'll pick up the boys from school," she hollers at me without looking back. The screen door slams.

"Fuck!" I pace back and forth, say it louder and louder, with each step. Then I lean down for a rock lying in the gutter. I hurl it at the house. It hits a window, and the pane of glass explodes with a crash. That feels so satisfying, I find a stick at my feet, and throw that, too. It bounces off the siding. I kick at a pile of leaves in the yard. I kick at the tire on Sarah's car. My car. *It's my goddammed car!* I kick the tire again. Again. And again until my foot starts to hurt. And that's what I'm doing when the police car turns down the street, lights flashing. No siren, just the red and blue alternating lights on the roof bar.

When the cruiser stops next to the Jeep, I glance at the house next door. The gray-haired lady stands at her window, hands on her hips, glaring in my direction. She flips me off.

"I was jiss leaving, officer," I say, as I stumble toward the Jeep.

The policeman climbs out of his patrol car. He points at the broken bottle in the middle of the street. "Is that your work?"

I shrug. I keep my hand on the car door handle and watch as he points at Troy Middleton's house. Sarah is out of sight. "And that window?" He indicates the broken glass pane on the front window.

I nod again, close my eyes. I squeeze my forehead, and raise my face to the hot January sun. "Fuck," I say under my breath.

Nineteen

Marty answers the phone on the first ring. We used to give it at least two rings so clients wouldn't think we were sitting there waiting for the phone to ring. Today, Marty doesn't even pretend to be busy. I'm relieved to hear his voice. I clear my throat.

"Hey," I say. "I need you to come get me."

"OK. Where are you?"

I press my middle finger into my temple. My head is pounding. "At the police station. Don't ask any questions. Just come get me out."

"You're in jail?"

"I said no questions. I'll tell you when you get here. I owe a fine so cash a check before you come."

"How're we going to write this one off, partner?" He says. Unbelievably, he sounds ready to laugh.

It takes him an hour and a half to get here. Thankfully, they don't lock me in a cell. "No room," one of the cops tells me. Another one shakes his head at me and says, "Ain't no broad worth it, bro."

Instead of a cell, they let me sit on a bench in the hall with a stack of old, curled magazines. I grab one, open it, and stare vacantly at a picture of two fat guys on the bow of a fiberglass boat, fishing rods bent double. I don't bother to read the caption. I wouldn't be able to concentrate anyway. This is the lowest I've sunk. Just what I need: a rap sheet, on top of everything else. They have my fingerprints now, and a mug shot.

By the time Marty comes in the door looking out of place in his jacket and tie, I've sobered up. He pays my fine and the cop behind the desk says I can go. "Five hundred dollars," Marty says as we walk to his Jaguar. "What were you doing?"

"Drunk and disorderly," I mumble, hoping he doesn't hear, but of course he does. I get in the car when he unlocks the doors.

"Hey, I thought you'd been sick," he says.

I slump in the luxe leather seat and wait until we've left the police station before I give him the quick version of what happened. I get a few sideways looks from him, especially when I tell him the part about Sarah walking out on me. God, I hate how desperate I sound. We sit in silence for a while. My head pounds.

"I think I might've slept with Carolyn," I say.

"Who's Carolyn?" Marty glances from me to the road and back.

"Sarah's friend. Suede boots. Big hair. Tight jeans."

"Oh yeah, that one." Marty focuses on the road. "You *think* you did? Or you know you did?"

"I have a feeling."

"Uh-oh, pal," Marty says, shaking his head. He lets out a low whistle. "No wonder you're in deep shit."

"Turn up here," I say, directing him to Church Street.

My Jeep is still parked crooked at the curb. Middleton's truck sits in the driveway, right next to the BMW. The thought of his worried face when he saw my Jeep there, wondering if I was hiding nearby, waiting to ambush him—the idea of that makes me smile. I'm sure Sarah watched me go off in the back of the police car. I notice there's a sheet of plywood nailed over the broken window.

I get out of Marty's car and sneak into the Jeep as quietly as possible. He follows me home, even though I didn't ask him to. He gets out at the same time as I do.

"Are you going to be all right?" he asks, standing inside the open door of his Jag.

"Yeah," I say, cutting him off with a wave. I aim myself toward the back door.

"Hey Adam," Marty calls out. "Don't come in tomorrow. Take some time. Get yourself sorted out."

I stop on the bottom step, turn around. "You want a drink?" I ask him. "I think there's gin left from Christmas. That's about it. I've drank up everything else, unless you're into cordials."

He cocks his head at me, questioning.

"Come on," I say. "I'm home now. I can't get into any more trouble."

He comes in and uses the phone to call Laura while I'm digging the gin out from behind bottles of amaretto, Grand Marnier, crème de menthe in the sideboard. I listen, and he doesn't say anything about Sarah to Laura. Marty's good with discretion.

I holler at the kids that I'm home. They don't answer, so I go up. They're both doing homework. I'm too embarrassed to say more than a quick hello. Cody asks where the Jeep broke down. I have to think quickly. Turns out Sarah is quite the liar. I'm realizing that more and more each day. So I embellish the lie, telling Cody I was halfway home from work, out on the highway, and had to be towed. What would he think if he knew his dad had just spent the last three hours in the pokey?

"Mom says to tell you she'll call later," Joel says without looking up from his books.

Back downstairs with Marty, I pour us both a hefty glass of gin. The bottle of tonic is flat so I toss it out. The gin tastes like medicine without something to cut it.

"Might be a little orange juice in the fridge," I say.

Marty shakes his head and swallows. "I don't need it."

"Me neither."

We stand there in the kitchen and drink in silence. We have three in a row, quickly. It's unceremonious, not even collegial. Marty needs fortification almost as much as I do. He's got a wife with Pierre Cardin taste, a wife he promised to take to Europe this summer. And she'll be needing a new wardrobe for that trip. Meanwhile, I've got this house. Sarah's house. He leaves before she calls.

She doesn't sound happy. She wants to know what happened, even though I'm certain she saw the police cruiser. When I tell her she doesn't seem surprised—or concerned. She's right about it being too soon for her to come home. I feel cheated, belittled, unimportant. But also guilty, ashamed, contrite. We can't make up on these terms. It might be too late to make up on any terms. I just wish I'd been the one to leave.

"I'm sorry I slapped you," I say. She doesn't acknowledge the apology.

"I'm picking up the boys from school tomorrow." It's a statement not a request. It sounds like argument is futile so I don't offer one. It's obvious I've failed as a single parent. "In fact," she continues, "I'll pick them up from now on. I don't like them going home to an empty house."

"You should've thought about that before you walked . . ." The dial tone sounds in my ear.

I want to yank the phone from the wall and throw it out the front door. Instead, I go into the kitchen and look around for something to eat. There isn't much. I didn't make it to the grocery store. I find a can of tuna in the back of the pantry, mix it up with mayonnaise. We're out of eggs. No pickles. There are six stale slices of bread, counting both heels. We can each have one sandwich apiece. I stick the bread in the toaster, then scrub my hands with Lava until the black ink stains come off my fingertips.

THE NEXT MORNING I wake up sick. It's more than just a hangover. I can't get out of bed. My throat is on fire, head throbs, chills, muscle cramps. When I stand up, everything gets fuzzy and white. It's like payback for using illness as an excuse these past few days. Probably picked up that jail-cell virus I've heard about—even though they never put me in a cell.

I tell Joel to get lunch money out of my wallet. He and Cody will have to eat in the cafeteria today. He grumbles about it, but I hear him rustling through my dresser before he leaves the bedroom. My eyes burn so I keep them closed and stay in bed. I have no idea what they find for breakfast, but they make it out to the bus on time. I hear the hiss of the airbrakes and distant voices, the sound of the engine as it grinds slowly away from the house. I roll over and turn the electric blanket on high.

Weird dreams interrupt my sleep. In one, my feet are covered with blisters and open sores. In another, I'm flying around the neighborhood—not like Superman, but vertical and upright so I keep crashing into obstacles like treetops and power lines. I'm not into dream interpretations but once I wake up both of these dreams linger.

When Mom calls around noon, her voice is the sweetest music on earth. "I called your office," she says. "Marty said you're home sick."

My head throbs. "I think I've got the flu."

"You sound terrible. I'm coming right over."

"No Mom, you don't have to do that," I say, but she's already hung up.

I'm asleep when she arrives. Undoubtedly the boys left the back door unlocked because she wakes me coming up the stairs. She enters the bedroom, and the first thing she does is feel my forehead, like I'm one of her first graders instead of her grown-up, forty-year-old son. Her hand is cool.

"Adam, you're burning up. I think we should get you to a doctor."

"I'll be OK. I'm sorry you drove all the way out here."

"Another thing, son, you shouldn't leave your doors

unlocked. Even if you are outside the city a burglar could still just come right in while you're sleeping."

She disappears. I hear her moving around downstairs. When she comes back, she has a hot towel rolled up in her hands. She makes me sit up and wraps the towel around my neck same as she did when I was a kid.

"Sarah doesn't keep any Vicks?" she says. "How can she raise two boys without a jar of Vicks in the house?"

She turns on the TV across the room. We never use it and the picture comes on slowly, rolls a few times before it settles on a game show in progress. She doesn't bother to hand me the remote but lowers the volume. Blearily, I watch the game show for a while. People are dressed in all kinds of stupid outfits, with face paint on, probably so they can't be recognized. I drift in and out while Mom busies herself downstairs. It seems like hours later when she comes back with aspirin, iced tea, and a bowl of chicken soup.

"I'm going to the store," she says. "Your cupboard is bare. Don't you dare get out of that bed."

"There's money in my wallet," I say, even though I know she won't use it. And for all I know, Joel took every cent I had anyway.

I sleep while she's gone. Once, for a second, I awake groggily. Game shows have been replaced by soap operas. They interfere with my dreams. My life is a soap opera. I don't need to see one on TV. I wish I had the remote but I don't wish for it enough to get out of bed.

Much later, when I awaken more fully I hear the boys off in the house somewhere, so I know they're home from school. Cooking smells drift up from the kitchen. In a little while, the boys bound up the stairs, both of them, and come into my room pink-cheeked and smiling. I soon see the reason for the smiles: Sarah comes right behind them. It aggravates me that the boys are so happy when their mom is here. She takes one look at me, wrinkles her brow, and comes to sit on the edge of the bed. She feels my forehead exactly the same way Mom did this morning. Sarah's hand is even cooler. I look for a mark on her face from yesterday. Nothing, or else she's covered it with makeup. I feel like a lout.

"You never get sick, Adam." She frowns like she doesn't believe me, but she sounds concerned. I decide right then to play it to the hilt. I mean, since I've got this flu and it's no joke, I sigh, moan a little, and try to look even more pitiful than I feel. "I'm going to call Doctor Teagler," she says. "See if he'll prescribe something."

When she rises from the bed, Cody plops down in her place. "It'll be OK, Dad," he says like an adult. He pats my hand. "Mom's here. She'll take care of you."

"Cody!" Sarah calls as she leaves the room. "Get away from that bed. I don't want you to catch the flu, too."

MOM BRINGS up a plate of food on a tray. Little meatballs rolled in ketchup like the ones I loved when I was about eight. They taste like sweet garbage to me now. I can't get more than a couple down, but I do manage to eat most of the mashed potatoes. Mom's always been a good cook, but she's lost a step since she retired. She stands there and watches me, as if she's a monitoring nurse. I'm surprised she isn't taking notes on my appetite.

"Is Sarah still here?" I ask.

"She's gone after the medication the doctor called in. I've let your dad know not to expect me home tonight."

"That's crazy, Mom. I don't need you to spend the night."

"You're ill, Adam."

"And I'm a big boy."

"I'm not leaving. No argument. Eat and rest. That's your only job. And drink all that tea. Fluids. Lots of fluids."

She leaves me with the tray of food. I lean over the edge of the bed and set it on the floor. I try to stand but almost pass out, so I crawl back under the covers.

At six o'clock, there's news on the television. I strain to hear it.

Nobody has bothered to turn up the volume or give me the remote. The weatherman points to another cold front on the way. During the sports report, also nearly silent but I can read scores, Sarah comes in the room with a green prescription bottle of pills and a glass of water. She steps square into the middle of the tray of food.

"Shit!" she says. "What is this doing on the floor?" She sets the bottle of pills on the nightstand, along with the glass of water.

"Help me get rid of Mom," I say, as she wipes her shoe with a Kleenex. "She's been here all day and she's driving me nuts."

I barely get the words out before Joel comes in. He sidesteps the bed and wrinkles his nose at me. "You look like crap," he says, his voice cracking with the words.

"Language," Sarah says to him, and I laugh at her hypocrisy. "Take this tray of food down to the kitchen and leave your dad alone." She leads him with her hand on his neck to the door. When he's gone, she glances back at me. "I'll see what I can do about Maureen, but no promises. You know how she is about her boys."

Yeah, about the same as you, I think, but then I remember she's left her boys to go live with her stud hoss on Church Street. My mom would've never done that to me and Brent.

THE NEXT TIME I see Sarah, she wakes me. The room is dark except for the glow from the television. She turns on the bedside lamp. "How do you feel?"

"Is Mom still here?"

"She says she'll be back tomorrow." She sits down on the bed. "How much did you tell her about what's going on?"

"The basics. That you moved out."

She nods, stares at the television. "She was kind to me. She told me I've always been like the daughter she never had."

"She loves you. They both do." I touch the button on her

sleeve. It's a fluttery green blouse I've always liked. "Sorry about yesterday."

"You've already said that, Adam." She looks at me, pulls her sleeve out of my reach. "I'm going to stay here tonight. I'll sleep in the guest room and get the kids off in the morning. You just rest."

"I miss you."

She stands. "It's just for tonight. I've already explained that to the boys." She frowns at me. "If I didn't know better I would swear you did this on purpose. You never get sick."

THAT NIGHT, after the lights are out and everyone is in their respective bedrooms, my eyes snap wide open. Maybe it's because of all the sleep I've had in the past thirty-six hours, or maybe it's because I know Sarah's in the room across the hall and we've got so much we need to hash-out. I have to work to tamp down the urge I have to go in there and get in bed with her, pull her up close, and hold her.

Overall, I suppose I have been a crappy husband, but we've had good times, too—when the boys were born with all the charged emotion and change they brought, when we moved into our first house. Not this mausoleum. That first place was a dollhouse by comparison. Three modest bedrooms, two equally modest bathrooms. How proud I was to be able to provide my family with our very own house. I carried Sarah over the threshold. She was pregnant with Joel. We fixed up one of the bedrooms as a nursery. She loved doing that. She got so wrapped up in it, decorating it with every baby thing she could find at garage sales and thrift shops. And after he was born, she got even more wrapped up in him, keeping charts and schedules, memorializing every milestone: first time he rolled over, first tooth, first day he crawled, the day he babbled something that sounded like "mama" and then "dada." Our life was all about Joel, whatever he needed, his least little desire. He always came first. . . .

The woman's name was Jaydean O'Donnell, not Jaydean

What's-her-name. Sarah hasn't forgotten she just wants to make sure I understand she's still hurt. Jaydean was an accountant at a firm Waterton-Pierce represented. She was my client; I was tasked with handling her. She had a reputation for being difficult. It was stupid of me to get involved with her, but it wasn't serious—not for me anyway. But it did get physical and way out of hand, and it turned lethal when Jaydean decided to call the house and let Sarah in on the secret. She knew I wouldn't be there yet; I had just left the motel and hadn't had time to get home. She didn't like that I wanted to break it off, and I guess she needed revenge.

Sarah was waiting for me. There was still hope on her tear-streaked face—hope that it wasn't true, that Jaydean was just some crazy woman making random prank calls. That unmistakable look of hope broke my heart. It took her a long time to forgive me—outwardly anyway. Inwardly I guess she still hasn't. But I truly do not know what she's talking about with some stripper who lived in an apartment above us. And as for Rosalie Baker, she was an old high school flame I ran into at our twelfth reunion. We had a drink. One drink and nothing else, but that's the trouble with infidelity. Once it happens trust evaporates. And once trust is gone everything else erodes, too.

I've spent a decade working to rebuild that trust, and that's why I find that backsliding night in October with Carolyn so disturbing. I have remembered a few more things about that night —things I wish had stayed hidden behind the blackout curtain, like a tile shower stall and a pair of pink nipples. But I have no memory of the actual deed. If it did happen, I blame it all on work pressure and Old Overholt. Me and rye whiskey have never been good mates.

It takes hours before I can shut down my brain and finally nod off. When I awaken, bright sunlight pours in through the lace curtains over the windows. I can tell before I lift my head from the pillow that I'm better. A putrid taste lingers in my mouth. I put on my robe and go to the bathroom to brush my teeth. While I'm there, I floss too. It's a delaying tactic. The longer I take to go downstairs, the longer Sarah will stay home.

I smell coffee and hear her downstairs vacuuming. The bed in the guest room is made up and so are both the boy's beds. It's after nine so they're already in their first classes at school. I dress in some sweatpants and stare out the windows onto the balcony until I hear the vacuum cleaner stop.

Decorations have been taken off the Christmas tree. All the boxes are neatly stacked on the dining room table, ready to be hauled back into the attic. The tree looks naked and depressing, silvery tinsel dangling like shiny earthworms on a few branches. Sarah's sitting on the couch working on the needlepoint covers for the dining room chairs. She's been working on them for almost a year. I start to ask her why, if she's not planning to live here anymore, she still wants to finish with those chair covers, but she looks up at me with her bright smile, and I don't say anything.

"You look like you're feeling better," she says. "Let me get you some coffee."

"Stay where you are. I can get it myself."

I go into the kitchen, pour a cup, and come back to sit on the other end of the couch. If she can forgive me for my past transgressions then surely I can forgive her, too. Maybe I'll tell her that, see if it will convince her to come home. I can't do without her.

"You've been busy," I say, glancing at the boxes on the table.

"I'll drag the tree to the curb, if you'll take it out of the stand."

"That sounds like a job for the boys."

We small talk for a while. She tells me about getting the kids off to school, about something she saw on *Today* about the ambassador to Hanoi visiting Washington. The Vietnam War was still going on when we met. Seems like so long ago. She looks especially beautiful to me today. She seems to grow more into herself the older she gets. I remember when she was more girl than woman, and I suddenly miss those days. I fight the desire to hold her in my arms. Maybe she reads it on my face, she looks away, up the stairwell.

"I was thinking this morning," she says, "about what a welcoming, homey old place this house is. And then I was remembering what a hard time we had stripping that ugly paint from the china cabinet. It's still hard for me to believe someone would paint over that beautiful wood."

"I'm glad there weren't two china cabinets."

She chuckles, pulling her needle through the fabric. "Well, I still love this house despite all its flaws."

"And this is where you should be." I blow on my coffee. "We've done this whole thing backward."

"I've wondered if you still feel the same way you did that night you came home so late . . ." She glances at me over the top of her needlework, ". . . from Carolyn's."

Mention of that night makes me squirm a little. "I don't want to leave you, if that's what you mean. I don't want you to leave me either. I want us to work things out." The hot coffee feels good on my raw throat.

"And you think that's still possible?"

"If we both try. Keep communicating." I add, "But, of course, you'd have to give up your boyfriend." I try to sound light and make a joke, but I see right away she doesn't take it that way. The needle in her hand stops. She frowns. I hold up my hand. "That's not what I intended—"

"Why do you have to do that? Call him my *boyfriend?*" Her tone has gone combative. "It sounds so—I don't know—childish. And condescending."

"OK. How about scumbag? Is that better?" I sip the coffee. "Or oh wait, the fucking bastard—that's the one." She still doesn't think I'm funny. She glares at me.

"It's not his fault, you know." She sets aside her needlework but she doesn't argue about which name befits him more, so I guess it's OK for me to call him either one. "The problem, Adam, is with you and me. With us. He doesn't have anything to do with that."

"Of course he does." I set my cup of coffee down on the table in front of me. "Let's look at this realistically, Sarah. What if you met somebody. And he's married but you're not. Suppose he has kids and all the responsibilities that go with that. Would you consider this married man to be a romantic possibility? Would you set out to break up his family?"

"That's not what happened."

"I think it is."

"Why? Because that's how it happened with you and all the women you've slept with—"

"Jesus, Sarah, there hasn't been other women."

"Jaydean—"

I wave her off. "We've covered that, haven't we? Haven't we really—covered it enough already? But since then . . . *since then*, I have been faithful to you. I have, baby." *Well . . . maybe.* "Not that there haven't been opportunities."

"You always have to keep on talking, don't you? Say just a little bit more. Turn the knife a little deeper."

"I know what you're doing. This thing with Middleton. That's just about making me crazy, isn't it? You want to teach me a lesson, even up old scores."

"How could we be married for fifteen years and you know so little about me?"

"If you're in love with him . . . if I could hear you say you're in love with him . . . *are* you in love with him, Sarah?"

"There's all different kinds of love, remember? There's the love you feel for a friend. Or a sister. Or, I don't know, maybe a roommate. . . ."

"Stop throwing that shit in my face. You sit there like a martyr, like you're the one whose so goddammed misunderstood. Maybe you were sending signals I didn't pick up. OK, I'll concede that. But it goes both ways. If I haven't been there for you, you haven't always been there for me either."

She rubs absently at a cracked place on the leather couch. "See?" she says calmly, and raises her cool green eyes. "We can't work this out. There's too much disappointment."

"I have never been disappointed in you."

"What's amazing is that we made it this long."

"You make it sound like a death sentence. Honey, please." My voice breaks. "I don't know what I'm going to do without you. I don't want to fight anymore. I just want you to come home."

The last time I sobbed, just sobbed outright and in the open, was when I saw Cody, pink and wrinkled, fresh from Sarah's womb. I cried over Joel, too, and the baby we lost in between the boys. But the pregnancy with Cody had been so rough, it seemed twice as long as it should have been. There were times when she was bent over the toilet puking her guts out, and I would get so scared I would lose her, and the baby. The tears on the day he was born, those were the opposite of the tears right now. Those were joy and relief; these are misery and guilt. I get up and head for the bathroom where I can lock the door, sit on the toilet, and bawl in peace. Before I get there she's following me.

"Adam—" she says behind me. "It's got nothing to do with teaching you a lesson. It's about being happy, and none of us are. You. Me. The boys either. We don't have a happy home."

"That isn't true." I feel my shoulders shake. "It's just not."

"Oh Adam . . ." She puts her head against my back, her arms circle me from behind, hands locking around my waist. We stand like that for several minutes until finally I get control. I swipe at my face and force a smile, turn around. Her face is washed with tears, too.

"This is only because I'm sick, you know," I say, pointing at my red eyes. "This whole thing is just a virus."

She laughs and hugs me again, from the front this time. We're standing there, in this messy embrace, when the phone rings. I feel her body stiffen.

"Do you want me to answer it?" she says.

"It's probably Mom. I'll head her off before she drives over here."

I go for the phone, figuring it's either Mom or Marty, checking on my health or sharing another doomsday report from the frontlines. As soon as I pick up the phone, though, I know it's neither one. There's a second of silence, faint breathing, and then Middleton's voice comes over the line, so Yankee-prissy.

"Is Sarah still there?"

"Yeah." I turn and see she's followed me to the den. My head pounds right between the eyes. "And by the way, it's Sare-rah. *Sare Rah!* Not Sare, you idi—"

She jerks the phone from my hand, shoots daggers. Maybe sabers. I make no move to step aside and give her privacy.

"Hello?" she chirps. Her lips aren't their usual rosy color. They seem dry and chapped. *Too much kissing.* She holds the phone with both hands and gives me a pleading look. She wants me to move away. I don't. I stay right in my spot and stare at her. "Yes, he's much better." She turns her back to me. "No, it's OK. I was just about to leave. . . . Yes, I'm fine . . . sure, I'll bring them. Give me twenty minutes." She hangs up, exhales, sets her shoulders. "He needs me to take some of his tools to him. He left them in his shop. He's doing a job over on Seventeenth."

"So you run his errands for him now? And he just *had* to call you here."

"Well, this *is* where I am."

"And he couldn't send Joe or Shmoe or whatever the hell his name is after his tools?"

"Lee. His name is Lee. And he's not working today. He didn't know you'd answer. He was embarrassed by it."

I snark. "Aw, what a sensitive guy."

I sit on the couch right where she sat earlier. Her needlework slides against my thigh and stabs me through my robe. I take up the whole bundle in my hand and chuck it on the coffee table.

"Here. You'd better take this with you. And there's a whole bunch of your clothes still upstairs. Perfume bottles, makeup, all kinds of crap. If you're leaving, I want all your shit out of here. Your books, your magazines. Take all of it."

"Adam."

"I'm serious. Either you leave completely or stay for good. I can't take this popping in and out."

"I came to help take care of you."

"I don't need you for that." I'm talking too loud and it hurts my throat. "And you only did it to soothe your guilt anyway."

"I did it because the boys asked me to." She stands there, one hand on her hip. Her eyes have welled again.

I turn away from her, stare out the window, not looking at anything, just staring. We don't say anything else. She clomps up the stairs, knocks around up there. A few minutes later, she comes down again, into the kitchen. The back door closes.

Distantly, out under the carport, her car starts up—that high idle, BMW cold-start. I stay where I am, staring out the front windows. I see she forgot to take down the Christmas wreath. It still circles the leaded glass window on the front door. Tomorrow I'll throw it out with the trash.

Something brushes against my foot. I look down just as Snowball jumps into my lap. He must've come in when Sarah went out. He rubs his head on my chin, purrs. "She's abandoned you, too, you scroungy cat." I scratch him between his ears.

Troy

Twenty

Sarah's car pulls up at the Judson's house where I'm working. She gets out and walks toward me. She has the recip saw I asked her to bring. She also has a sack full of food: ham and cheese sandwiches, a bag of Doritos, two cans of Fresca. I'm happy to see her and glad she's brought lunch.

"I thought you might be hungry," she says. Her eyes wander up and over the Judson's house.

"Nobody's home." I take the saw case from her and set it on the porch. She brings the sack of food. I'm hungry but hadn't realized it until this minute. I sit down on the top step. She sits down beside me and starts digging food from her brown sack. I lean to give her a kiss.

"How did you get a flat tire?" She's looking at the truck, which sits in the Judson's driveway. It sags toward the right rear where the tire has deflated. She turns down the plastic wrap on a sandwich and hands it to me.

I bite into it. Smoked turkey and Swiss with leafy green lettuce, a slice of tomato, and some kind of spicy mustard. In the past year and a half, I haven't eaten as well as I have in the last week since Sarah came to stay with me.

"Must've picked up a nail," I say, between bites. "Lee's coming about four with a spare."

I push the bill of my cap back so I can look at her. I missed her last night. It was weird, I kept rolling over in bed to reach for her. It's not possible that I'm already used to sleeping with her, but it sure seems like it. I keep feeling like I need to pinch myself, like this is all one big dream and I'll wake up any second. I take another bite of the sandwich, wash it down with Fresca. *Fresca?* Who drinks Fresca? I guess I do now.

"So?" I say. "How's Adam?" I really don't care, I just want her to talk. She seems to be struggling with something.

She sighs, pulls the second sandwich out of the bag, carefully turns down the wrapper. Everything she does is deliberate and precise. "He wants me to get all my personal crap—his words—out of the house by tomorrow. He had a fit after you called. Shoes, clothes, he even mentioned perfume bottles."

"Sorry for that." I pick a speck of something out of her hair. "I started not to call, but I really did need that saw."

She shrugs. "Something else would've set him off." She takes a chip out of the bag. "One minute he's understanding, and so sensible. The next . . . I don't know what happens. He's volatile."

"He's an alcoholic."

"Hmmm. I know that's what you believe."

"Yes, I really do."

And I thought so the whole time I was glazing the new windowpane at McIntire's house. I thought so when I was sweeping up the broken scotch bottle in the middle of Church Street. I have cleaned up after my share of alcoholics. They leave behind telltale signs. But I can see she's not ready to believe it so I change the subject.

"You want to take a look inside? It's a grand old house. They'll be gone for a few hours."

She's wearing a pink sweater and looks like cotton candy. It brings out the peaches in her cheeks. She pivots toward the front door. "I love those beveled windows."

I stand, hold out my hand to her. She takes it and I pull her up. "They left the door open in case I need to use the phone. Which as it happens, I did, to call you this morning."

We walk into the foyer. I flip on the light switch and the bangles on the chandelier prism down on us. She immediately spots the marble-top hall tree beside the front door. It has mahogany inlay and silver gargoyle coat hooks. She turns to it.

"Oh, I love this." Her hand rubs the marble. "I've wanted a hall tree for so long. It's gorgeous." She looks into the other rooms. "I feel like a prowler."

"If they were here they'd show you themselves. They're nice people."

I draw her further into the house. She stops to admire everything along the way, the china on the plate rack in the dining room, grandfather clock in the hall, Victrola in the parlor.

"I wonder if this thing actually works," she says, touching the thick black record on the turntable.

"I doubt it. Come check out the mantle." I pull her across the room to the fireplace. "It's burled walnut. See, whoever carved it left this big knot out here in front. Most carvers wouldn't do that, but I like it. Gives it character."

"I like it, too." She runs her hand along the edge of the mantle, following mine.

"Most people want things too perfect," I say.

She smiles. "I'm trying to give up on perfect."

I kiss her on the nose. She's definitely got issues going today. I'm doing my best to keep her steady. It's not easy. All I want to do is kiss her, put her arms around me, wear her like a coat.

"Look here at these." I point to the two figures carved beneath the mantle, on either side of the firebox. Egyptian nymphs hold the mantle balanced on their heads. I watch her reaction. I like showing her the details. She seems to appreciate them. She bends to touch one of the nymphs, traces its face with her finger.

"Oh, my," she says. "It's exquisite."

"Yeah, that's the right word. Exquisite. You'll never see another one exactly like it."

Before she can straighten fully, I lean in and kiss her neck. She isn't wearing perfume so her skin smells like her only.

"Did you miss me last night?" I say, when she's facing me.

"A little bit." Not exactly the answer I was hoping for. I guess she sees my disappointment and tiptoes to give me a quick kiss. "It felt strange to sleep in the guest room," she says. "I never realized you could feel the wind actually move the house in there."

It's her off-hand way of telling me where she slept, and I'm relieved to hear it. I imagined all sorts of things. I fold my arms around her. I want to make love to her, have wanted to since she stepped out of her car. I think about the lacy bras she wears, the birthmark on her neck. I ponder the idea of pulling her down on the Oriental rug under our feet. The Judsons said they'd be back about one. There's plenty of time. But I don't think she's into it.

"You really think he's an alcoholic?" she says, when I have my lips under her ear. "Problem drinker maybe, but a full-blown alcoholic?"

I feel myself sink. I back away. She watches me, waiting for me to give a comment, or my opinion, or argue with her—or hell, I don't know what she's waiting for me to say. The last thing in the world I want to do is talk about Adam Glasser.

"Lunch break's over," I say, forcing myself to sound cheerful. "I better get back to work."

I head toward the front door. Behind me, I hear her mumble something that sounds like an apology for taking so much of my time, something that doesn't mean anything to me so I don't respond. She comes out on the porch right after me, bends to pick up the trash from our sandwiches, then sends a questioning look my way. "Are you OK?"

I smile. "Are you?"

She smiles too, but it's a faltering smile. She nods, but I know she realizes something's gone wrong; I don't think she has a clue what though. She's under a lot of stress. I know I should be understanding of that and let everything be all about her needs. I don't want to throw up walls, something I've been guilty of in the past, but self-preservation keeps getting in the way. I have a feeling this whole thing might not end well for me.

"Thanks for lunch." I cup her elbow and give her a quick kiss on her forehead.

Before she's even to her car, I climb the scaffolding to the gable end of the roof. I hear her car back out of the driveway. I don't look up until she starts down the street. I'm not ready to let her know how much she means to me, especially when I haven't even figured it out myself yet. All I know is, she has altered me in some serious way. I'm feeling things I've never felt before. Odd how life can change so quick, how a person can go from satisfied with so little, to hungry for so much more.

At four o'clock Lee comes with the tire. He's been registering for spring classes at the local community college, so he's driving his parents' Impala. He has a friend with him, Chad. I've met Chad before. The two of them roll the replacement tire up the driveway toward the truck. While we're changing the flat, Lee invites me to go out with them tonight to hear a local band, some friends of theirs playing at a downtown bar.

"Maybe," I say, with a shrug.

"The boss is hanging out with a married chick now," Lee explains to Chad, but he's really talking to me. He's already warned me more than once, and does again. "No future in that, man."

"Who wants a future?" Chad says, lifting his eyebrows up and down in a leering way. They laugh like a couple of old, world-worn dudes, both of them too cool. I laugh, too, but not for the same reasons.

"If you decide to come," Lee says, once we're finished changing the tire. "They start playing at nine."

I give one wave as they reverse out of the driveway.

With the truck back in commission, I load up and go home. When I get there, I find Sarah asleep in bed. It seems to me she's sleeping an awful lot. Somewhere I heard that's a sign of depression. I would hate to think being with me depresses her. I head for the shower.

Foolishly, I thought once I got hold of her she would stop distracting me so much, but it hasn't worked out like that. When she called last night, she sounded like a stranger: "Troy, I'm staying here tonight with Adam. He's sick and I can't leave the boys." What could I say? I can't tell her what to do. All night I kept worrying, though. I figured it was over, she'd gone back to him. So this morning I decided to call. I did need the recip saw, but mostly I needed to know where I stood.

The thing is, everything I never do I've already done: Gotten in too deep, too quick, changed the way I live my life for her. She has completely consumed my brain. She's good-looking, sure. But I've been with lots of good-looking chicks before, so why is she so special? I've been asking myself that one over and over. I don't have an answer yet, except there's just something about the way she feels and moves, the way she speaks—like a river running over me. When she says my name I want to eat her up, then wrap her in a cocoon and tuck her under my arm, like some giant spider. *Man, that's weird.* I don't know what's going on with me. She's making me think some crazy shit.

Back in the bedroom, I dry off and watch her sleep. She's a calm sleeper, doesn't move around much, barely makes a sound. She looks so delicious, lying there in my bed. The need for that pinch comes over me again. I have work I need to do out in the shop. I should go pour myself into it, let her sleep for a while. Instead, I sneak in under the covers. She stirs awake when I cuddle up to her.

"Oh, hello," she says, and turns toward me. She's warm and welcoming. She's got on panties and a bra. I get those out of the way pretty easily.

ACCORDING to the portable sign in the parking lot outside The Plug Nickel, Thursday night is "Open Mike Night," which means Lee's band friends must be playing for free. The building was a railway warehouse before, and the present owners haven't put much money into renovations. Rotted holes that violate all kinds of codes pock the floor inside. Beer cases cover the real leg breakers, but then the beer cases become leg breakers stuck around in odd places. Graffiti marks the walls, most of it done by groups who have played here before. Most are unknowns, but The Fabulous Thunderbirds signed the wall near the beer bar, and just below that Stevie Ray Vaughn's name is scribbled.

Lee sees me and Sarah as soon as we come in the door. He gets up to greet us and shows us to a long bench table where Chad sits with a couple of girls. Lee introduces everyone but I immediately forget the girls' names. Both have eyes heavily outlined with black Goth makeup and New Wave haircuts. They all seem so young. Everyone is drinking beer. The music from the band is loud and clanging. I'm pretty sure I've made a mistake bringing Sarah here. The place is drafty, and the wind whips the metal walls back and forth. She keeps her coat buttoned, hands in her pockets. She doesn't look like she's having any fun at all.

I order us a beer apiece and try to make jokes in her ear about the people sitting around us. When she doesn't laugh much, I make fun of the band. They have fantasies of being bluesmen, although none of them could be more than twenty. They all wear vests and fedoras, dressed in brooding black. The bass player even has on dark shades. We listen to a couple of songs. They're not terrible but it's a good thing they're not getting paid. At one point, the lead singer forgets some of the lyrics, and boos reverberate around the room, including from Lee and his group. They all seem to be having a rip-roaring good time, laughing and rowdy. During a break in the music, I lean close to Sarah's ear.

"Do you want to go?" I ask.

She shrugs, gives me an apologetic look, nods. We stand up. I pitch some bills on the table even though I paid for our beers when they came. We didn't even finish them.

"You just got here," Lee says when I tell him we're leaving. He shakes his finger at me. His eyes are bloodshot. He leans in. "What'd I tell you about married chicks?"

I take Sarah's arm and lead her out to the parking lot. When we step into the night, a stinging wind hits us in the face. A front has blown in while we were inside, but the minute we're out of the building, she seems to relax. I want a smoke but I've quit again so it's moot.

"Sorry about that," I say. "I should've known it wouldn't be your kind of place."

She cocks her head at me. "Is it yours?"

I shrug. "I've been here before. I knew what to expect."

She says, with a sigh, "I kept thinking how Joel would have liked it. Minus the beer, of course."

"Yeah, or maybe because of the beer."

She gives me a look, then laughs. It makes me happy to see her laugh.

We walk toward her car. We came in hers so I wouldn't have to unload the truck. Parking lot has started to fill up. The wind has a chill to it. I put my arm around her waist. We sidestep a pothole in the asphalt.

"If you want to stay, you should," she says. "I can come pick you up later, or you can just drop me off and come back."

"Why would I want to do that?" I shake my head and tighten my arm around her. "I just thought maybe you'd like to get out of the house."

She loops her arm around me, and we walk like that, arm in arm. A gust of wind ripples her skirt. She laughs and twirls away from me. I love she wore a skirt and a pair of ballerina flats, little bows on the front. I steer her around another pothole as we pass a group of chattering people. A deeper pothole lurks in our path. I dance her around that one, too. We laugh at the same time. She's got me mesmerized. We're having a better time out here than when we were inside.

"They need to do something about their parking lot," she says, just as the wind takes her hair. I give her a kiss, and she kisses me back.

"Troy?" somebody says behind us. "Troy Middleton?"

I turn, still holding onto Sarah. The group we just passed have stopped halfway to the front doors. It's five women, and I think I might recognize one of them.

"It's Amy," that one says, walking closer. "Landover?" She turns to her friends. "Wait up guys, it *is* him."

Then she runs at me. Sarah dodges out of the way. I don't know whether to defend myself or what, but Amy grabs me around the neck and gives me a big sloppy kiss on the mouth. I think she must already be drunk. I haven't seen her since last summer. We only had two quick dates anyway.

She lets go of me and stands there, smiling. "Look at you," she says. Her friends join us. "I heard you finished with those ritzy people's house. And I heard you were getting a lot of work off it."

"I'm keeping busy." I try not to sound too friendly. I reach for Sarah's hand. She doesn't return my grip.

"Well, that's good." Amy gives Sarah a glance and points back at the club. The music is starting up again. It comes blaring outside. "Aren't y'all coming in?"

"We're just leaving." I turn Sarah toward the car.

Amy and her friends stay behind us for a moment longer. "Well, bye, Troy," she says, in a mocking tone. "Bye, bye Troy," the rest chime in, one at a time. They sound like The Waltons. I can't get away fast enough.

Naturally, Sarah asks, "Who was that?" as soon as we get to her car.

"Nobody. She worked at the lumber yard."

Sarah slides in behind the wheel and when I'm in, she frowns. She doesn't make a move to start the car. "Ritzy people? Was she talking about me?"

"She didn't know who you were."

"I guess not, since you didn't introduce us."

"Did you want me to? She's just a chick I hung out with for a bit. It was never anything."

As soon as it's out of my mouth, I hear how belittling it sounds—definitely not polite and gentlemanly. I laugh in an attempt to lighten the mood. She starts the car and turns to back out. There's already another car waiting to take our spot.

She glances at me. "Wasn't she a little young?"

"Like I said, it wasn't serious."

"Was it legal?" She drives out of the parking lot, hits every pothole on the way.

I let out a breath. I didn't expect this reaction from Sarah. I'm not going to squirm. Or apologize for things I did before I knew her. "Yeah. She was legal. I'm pretty sure you knew I had a history, so what's up, Sarah? You've been weird all day."

"Maybe I'm a little jealous. I don't know. That whole scene, it felt too familiar. And you saying she's *nobody*, that it wasn't serious. That was familiar, too."

"Hold it." I gesture out the windshield. "Pull over right here. Just pull up to the curb." It's not a great neighborhood. I probably should have looked around a little before I asked her to stop. She rolls up onto the curb at first, but then we jounce down. She keeps her foot pressed on the brake. "Turn off the headlights for minute."

She does. The dash lights illuminate her face. She looks gloomy, even with her face turned away from me, staring forward like she's still driving.

"I'm not Adam, OK? Would you look at me?" I say. She does, slowly. "Do I look like Adam to you?"

"Of course you don't."

"You've got a lot of baggage, I get that. So do I. But *this* . . ." I gesture at both of us, back and forth. "This is new. We're new. You and me."

"Ritzy people, though. I just don't understand why she would say that. It makes me feel like a big phony." She turns straight ahead, again, like she doesn't want to make eye contact, even in the dimness. "Adam said you set out to break up our marriage."

"Your shitty marriage," I mumble.

"He blames everything on you. He made it sound like it was all some kind of conquest for you or something."

Conquest. That word again, coming back at me all the way from Leann Hale's mouth to right now. I flinch. "He wants you to think I'm a jerk like he is." I fold my arms and stretch out my legs as much as I can in the cramped space. "Is it working? Seems like it might be working."

"No. I'm sorry for that back there. It was a kneejerk reaction, I guess." She doesn't look at me.

A car goes around us fast and rocks our car. I'm have a sudden yearning for a cigarette. My hand automatically moves to my shirt pocket. Nothing there, of course. I seem to choose the worst times to try to quit.

"I have something I need to know," I say, slowly. I don't like serious talks. It breaks the spell we've spun. My eyes slide over her profile as I reach for the key and turn off the car engine. Her foot lifts off the brake. "Why did you leave him? It doesn't seem like you really thought it through. You said I was just a symptom . . . so I guess I'm wondering how I fit in."

"I left because I'd been unfaithful, and I couldn't lie about it. It's just not in me to be dishonest." Finally, she turns to look at me. She touches my arm. "But also because I'm not ready to stop seeing you."

I look at her hand, slide my fingers underneath her fingers. "What happens when you are ready?"

"What are you asking for, some kind of commitment?"

Funny she should say that, since I'm the one who supposedly has the commitment issues. I laugh because it's hard to reveal my vulnerability. "I'm trying to assess the damage potential."

"Adam's not dangerous. He wouldn't do anything—"

"I don't give a rat's ass about Adam. In fact, for one minute I wish we could just stop talking about him." Another uneasy laugh comes from me. "I'm more concerned with you. How dangerous you are . . . for me."

The rod that's been up her spine all evening seems to release. She sits back against the seat, looking at me. I can see the sparkle of her eyes in the dash light. A gust of wind moves the car, whistles at the windows.

She says, "Are you talking about love?"

My ears ring. Like I've been shot in the head. I shrug. "It could happen."

She sits still and doesn't say anything. The ringing in my ears starts to get louder, and then she reaches out and grabs me around my neck. She comes over the console like it's no obstacle, and into my lap, pulling me to her, kissing me. I put my arms around her. It's a hot kiss and it gets hotter in a flash. In a short moment, both of us are breathing heavy, fogging up the windows. I reach under her sweater. the skin in her back feels like warm silk against my hands. She gropes at the buttons on my shirt. Her lips break away.

"Move your hand," she says, as she guides me to her breast. I put my face there. She pulls urgently at my fly. "Help me with this."

"Sarah." I still her fumbling, kiss the top of her breasts, her neck. "Let's go home." I kiss her on the mouth. "I want you in bed where I can feel you from tip to toe."

She looks me in the face, takes my head in both her hands. She gives me a last smooch on the lips before she scrambles back over the console into the driver's seat. She starts the car and shifts into drive. "I hope I don't get a speeding ticket."

IN THE MIDDLE of the night, the quiver of the mattress rouses me. No noise, just an erratic quiver, like a motor vibrating under the bed. Moonlight floods through the windows. I can see the slope of her shoulders. At first, I think maybe my eyes are playing tricks in the dark, but when I touch her, I feel the same quiver I felt in the mattress.

"Are you awake?"

She doesn't answer, so I move closer, reach over her to brush the hair from her face. I feel the wetness on her cheeks. I lie back on my pillow and stare at the silver light coming through the windows. According to the alarm clock, it's four-fifteen. She wasn't supposed to grieve. I didn't count on that.

Ma was a crier—whenever a boyfriend dumped her, whenever she couldn't pay the bills, whenever she got shit-faced drunk. By the time I was ten or eleven, tears didn't move me much anymore. But I unfold my arm and pull Sarah against me. She's reluctant at first, but finally rolls over and lays her face against my chest.

"You want to talk?" I whisper. I'm relieved when she shakes her head and presses closer. She cries quieter than any woman I've ever known, doesn't sob or sniffle. But I feel her tears wet my bare skin.

Twenty-One

The alarm clock screams and I scramble to shut it off. Sarah's side of the bed is empty. Drowsy, I sit up and grind my fists into my eyes. I smell coffee. She makes great coffee. Almost the first thing she did when she moved in was buy a coffeemaker with a timer she sets to come on earlier than the alarm clock. It's nice to have coffee brewed when I get up. It feels civilized.

I go in the washroom, douse my face and brush my teeth before I walk into the kitchen. She's rinsing glasses from last night, wiping down the counter. A clean coffee cup sits there waiting for me. I can't get used to having someone tend to me like she does. I go over to give her a morning kiss. Her eyes are puffy and hollow from all the nighttime crying. I hold her for a little while, rest my cheek on the top of her head, and look out the window over the sink. Birds are flitting around in the bare limbs. The sky is clear and blue, one of those perfect Texas winter days. I don't miss snow, and never will.

I put my nose in her hair, inhale the smell of her. "How you doing?"

After a moment, she moves out of my arms, pours coffee into

an empty cup by the coffeemaker. "Are you hungry? There's fruit and cheese, or I could fix you an egg."

I take the coffee and sit down at the table. She ghosts around the kitchen, taking out a bowl of grapes from the refrigerator, a wedge of cheddar. She gets down a plate. I sit at the table and watch her. I'm troubled by her, and confused.

"Sit down here with me, Sarah."

"I don't want to talk."

"OK, but don't we have to go after the rest of your stuff today?"

"My personal crap," she says, with sarcasm. She shakes her head. "I can take care of it."

She goes back to slicing cheese onto a plate. She puts a handful of grapes on the plate, too. Silence buzzes the air. When she says she doesn't want to talk, apparently she means *at all*.

"As it happens," I say, trying to make light. "I own a pickup that will hold a lot of personal crap. Including bottles of perfume."

I watch her for a minute more. She's wearing a clingy purple nightgown, with one of my flannel shirts over it. The house is cold. She brings the plate of cheese and grapes to the table, sets it in front of me. She stares at me like she's waiting for me to eat something. I prop my elbow on the table, put my chin in my hand, make a frown face at her for show, and reach for the back of her arm.

She draws in a deep breath, expels it in a rush. "I miss my boys," she says, and sits down hard on the chair next to me. "I shouldn't have left them there. I should have made Adam go. I miss packing their lunches, making their beds, all the things that seemed like drudgery before. I wonder what they're eating for breakfast, if they're even eating breakfast, if they made it to the school bus on time, turned in their homework on time. None of this. . . ." Her bottom lip trembles. She chokes and waves her hand in front of her face like something stinks. ". . . none of it's their fault."

I study her. I see now this is causing her grief, but the truth is, I'm relieved it isn't something else—like missing her marriage. "There's that other bedroom in there. It doesn't have much in it but we could put together some sort of room they could share."

She gives me a look like I've lost a brain cell. "I can't bring them here. That's not even an option." She lets out a hollow laugh. "You're sweet to offer but . . . no, god, no. Adam would go ballistic . . ."

"He shouldn't get to decide."

"But it's me who's having an affair."

I search her eyes for a moment. *Affair.* Is that what this is? This thing that's happening between us—happening to me? That seems like an odd word for it. All I see right now is guilt and sadness and tears. It's no way to carry on a love affair, if that's what this is. I would rather we kept it our secret, met when we could, made love all the time, sang together. Laughed together.

I push back my chair and go into the other room to take a shower. First, I pick up the phone on the bedside table and dial the Judson's number to tell them I won't make it there today. I say I'll see them on Monday.

Once I'm showered and dressed, still toweling dry my hair, I go back to the kitchen. She's still at the table. She isn't as teary but she's gloomy. I touch her shoulder.

"What needs to happen?" I drape my towel over the back of a chair. "Do you need to find your own place? So your kids can come live with you?"

"I need a job first. I don't want to ask Adam for money."

"No, don't do that." I swing the chair around and sit facing her. "Look. I want to help. Let's go get your stuff, box it up, bring it here for now, and then we'll go look for a place. Or you can go by yourself. You know what you need better than I do. I'm just here to facilitate, OK? Pay the first month's rent, or whatever is required."

"I don't want to take your money either."

"I want you in my life, but not like this. This is too hard. I know it doesn't look like it but I'm not broke, so let me help you."

"If I take money from you, it will make me feel so . . . trashy."

"So you can pay me back someday. Let's get this one thing done. So something gets accomplished, OK? We go get your things. And then you find a place of your own." I'm taking a page from Harvey's book, something similar to what he said to me when I first arrived in Rockland, broke, disoriented, confused, hopeless.

She reaches for my hand. "That's two things."

I laugh. I like seeing the smile come to her face. The truth is I just want to get past the drama. I've had enough drama to last a lifetime.

WE GET to her house around ten. The carport is empty so I back in the pickup. Her big white cat comes running out and she lifts him into her arms. While she stands there baby-talking the cat, I notice a spot under the eaves of the house that needs a second coat of paint. I don't know how I missed it before. All the trouble I had with the damned paint sprayer had me rattled, so did my preoccupation with Sarah. That imperfection is going to nag at me now. I try not to stare at it.

We go in through the back door. "I wonder if he'll let me take the bread-safe," she says, looking at the piece of furniture against the brick wall.

"You should be able to take anything you want. It's half yours."

"I'm not ready to antagonize him yet. I need to get the boys first."

"You'll get your boys. There's not a judge in this country that'll keep a mother from her kids."

Her eyebrows rise in surprise, then knit together. "I'm not ready to think about going to court either."

I find that inconceivable, also worrisome. She hasn't given any thought to custody battles or property division. That puts everything back in doubt for me. Reason tells me this situation is too big, too combustible. Odds are, I'm the one who gets burned. I've known her six weeks. Adam's got fifteen years on me, plus two kids, this big house, wads of money and material crap. If there ever was a time to bail it would be now. But she starts up the short stairway out of the kitchen and I follow after her.

We spend the next two hours packing boxes and emptying closets she claims as hers. There's one in the guest bedroom besides the one in the master, and also a cloak closet on the upper landing. She loads the boxes; I carry them down, two at a time, to the truck. Just being here in this house seems to make her happier. She finds things she wants to tell me about, and I pretend to listen, but all I really want to do is get this over with and leave. Later, when the time is right, I'll suggest she ask for the house, too —that is, when she's finally ready to see a lawyer. What she needs most is to ditch Adam. While she locks everything back down, I carry the last of the boxes out to the truck and wedge them into the pickup bed with all the others.

As I'm doing that, a car pulls to the front curb and stops. Light gray compact, chrome trim. At first, I don't pay much attention, but then recognition hits just as Carolyn Jeffrey gets out of the car. She's wearing a dress with a matching jacket, plain black pumps, a string of pearls around her neck. She looks respectable, professional, but I'm pretty sure I see trouble.

"What are *you* doing here?" she says, as she steps carefully across the sun-dappled lawn, puncturing holes in the turf with her heels. Accusation seethes in her voice, and she's loud, nearly shouting across the distance between us. So there's to be no pretense of civility.

"I could ask you the same thing." I stop arranging boxes in the truck bed. "Don't you have a job or something?"

"Adam told me Sarah was coming today. I want to talk to her. I didn't know you'd be here, too. So it's true about the two of you." She strides right up to me. "Where is she?"

"So you're hanging out with Adam all the time, now, are you?"

"What's it to you." She looks at all the boxes stacked in the truck. "I bet this is really feeding your ego, isn't it? You get to bust up a marriage *and* take home the spoils."

"We spent ten minutes together and you think you know me."

She smirks. "I know you're all bullshit. Someday she'll find out, too. Where is she?"

I shut the tailgate. "She doesn't need you harassing her right now."

But at that moment, Sarah steps out the back door. She stands at the top of the stoop and looks down at us under the carport. She has another smaller box tucked under her arms. "Carolyn?" She looks surprised. "You're off work today?"

"I came to talk to you." Carolyn turns her back to me. "In private."

"Why? What's the matter?"

Sarah sidles down the steps, watching her feet. I go retrieve the box from her, take it to the truck. There's no suitable place to stack it, so I start rearranging. It gives me something to occupy myself. I wish I could turn Carolyn around and shove her back across the lawn to her car.

"Look around you," Carolyn says, going nearer to Sarah. "Everything's the matter. Why haven't you called me? Why did you hide it from me that you were seeing . . ." She gives a dismissive wave in my direction, "*him?*"

I shake my head and keep on with the task of the boxes. Sarah glances at me. I watch her, trying to read her mind from the expression on her face. I get nothing.

"Aren't you going to answer me?" Carolyn's voice goes up a notch.

"Well, you have so many questions, I'm not sure which one to tackle first," Sarah says.

I chuckle, but I don't look up, or join in. Sarah's the main event, I'm just acting as her second right now. I start tying a rope from one side of the truck bed to the other, crisscrossing to keep the boxes from flying out on the return trip.

"You can start with why you kept it a secret. You should have told me. That day we went to his house," she points again with her stiletto fingernails, "—you should have said you two were involved."

"Well, you apparently already have all the details from Adam so I don't understand why you're here."

Another smile slides on my face. Sarah's holding her own.

Carolyn says. "Because he's really despondent. I think he's coming completely undone, I really do. This morning, when I talked to him, he sounded drunk. At ten o'clock."

"So what else is new?" I mumble. I can't hold it back, but neither of them seems to hear me.

Sarah wipes hair out of her face. "So you're talking to him every day now?"

I want to high-five her. She's had the same thoughts as me. Carolyn sure stepped in quick. I think about that godawful day at the mall, how she admitted to having a longtime crush on Adam. My suspicion seems justified.

"What about Joel and Cody? Have you stopped caring about them, too?" Carolyn's tone is judgmental, and accusing.

As soon as I hear the boys' names, my elation disappears. I can't let Carolyn take it too far in that direction. Sarah's boys are her sore spot. "Time to go," I say. "Sarah?"

"I see the boys every day after school. As soon as I get my own place, they'll move in with me." Sarah sounds touchy and defensive now. "Anyway, it's Adam who's keeping them away from me."

I take hold of Sarah's arm and steer her toward the passenger side of the truck. "Boxes are loaded, let's go." She gets in and I move around to my side. But Carolyn continues her tirade. She holds Sarah's door open.

"He won't let you have the boys as long as you're with—"

Carolyn's dirty look shoots at me again. "He'll fight you for them." Carolyn's expression and her body language changes in a flash when she sees me coming back around to Sarah's side of the pickup. My intention is to jerk the truck door out of Carolyn's grasp, but she recoils when I get closer—like she's actually afraid of me.

"Leave me alone, you asshole," she says. "You bastard, get the fuck away from me."

I slam Sarah's door, advancing toward Carolyn. She keeps shying back. "You call yourself a friend? Not one word about what Sarah might be going through. Just poor, helpless Adam. Oh, but that's right. You've always been a little bit in love with him, haven't you? How could I forget?"

"Keep away from me!" she says, and before she turns for her car, she flings one last "asshole" at me. Then she practically runs across the lawn. It's a funny sight with her heels sinking into the lawn like an aerator. I quell the desire to go after her and . . . *do what?* Shake her by the shoulders? Toss her into her car? I can visualize myself doing both those things and it makes my head hurt.

"Troy." Sarah rolls down the window on her side. "Come on, let's go."

I get back in the truck, start it, and reverse out of the driveway. Too fast. The wheels spin up gravel. *"Cherry Bomb"* is on the radio. It seems appropriate. I can see by Sarah's face the encounter upset her, too.

"What did you say to her?" she asks.

I'm still breathing hard. "She's a pain in the ass."

"She's my friend." She says it to close the subject but I'm too angry to let it pass. "Or she *was* my friend."

"I doubt that. You don't know her as well as you think you do."

"What does that mean?"

I glance at her. She's staring at me. I think about her reaction to Amy Lander at The Nickel, so I'm reluctant to mention any past encounter with Carolyn. I keep my eyes on the road ahead and drive. No need to light a match. This whole thing feels ready to blow.

For a couple more blocks I sense her eyes on me but I don't answer her. I stop at the Quik Mart for a pack of cigarettes. When I get back in the truck, she's still sitting there silent. And she stays silent for the rest of the way.

At the house, we unload the boxes and pile them in a corner of the extra bedroom. I leave her to separate out things she might need, and I head out to the shop. I need to think. It's getting too complicated and I feel the need to tend to myself right now.

I light a cigarette and sit on my stool, staring at the pegboard on the wall in front of me, trying to sort through all the noise inside my head. Part of me thinks maybe I should back off, let Sarah figure things out for herself. She's either going to want to be with me or she's not, and no amount of worrying about it will change that.

From the wall pegs, I take down two wrenches to switch out the bit on the table router. It's a two-wrench operation and I need to put in a bead bit for the work I want to do. A foot of rake molding on the Judson's house has rotted. It's an old design not available anymore so I'm going to try to recreate it from scratch. Yesterday, I cut out a piece of the old molding to use as a model. I flip on the router and let it warm up while I pencil-trace the pattern onto the end of a length of wood.

Just as I start to make my first cut I hear Harvey in my head, instructing me like he always did with tricky tasks: *Take it slow and steady, Troy-boy. Easy does it.* I pull a drag on the cigarette, then balance it on the edge of the worktable. Harvey's voice keeps talking: *Be ready to start over if you have to.* I blow out a stream of smoke, unload a dry chuckle. I think it's too late for starting over. I think I'm already sick in love.

Sarah

Twenty-Two

The only available three-bedroom apartment I find in the boys' school district is in an older complex built in the late sixties. The apartment has an awkward layout, one room opening into another. But there's a pool and a playground and one covered parking space. I ask the landlady to hold it for me while I go to the bank for money. Half the amount in the account is mine. Texas is a community property state, a fact of which Troy regularly reminds me.

I pull up to the drive-through window at the bank, drop my check in the carrier canister, and push send. Before Christmas the balance in the account was nearly ten thousand, so it's a surprise when the teller's voice comes over the intercom to tell me there aren't sufficient funds to cover my check. She sends me a paper with the balance in the account handwritten: *seven hundred dollars?* How is that even possible? If I took every cent it wouldn't cover the first and last month's rent for the apartment. So, Adam has decided to leave me cash-strapped. I feel slapped in the face by him—again. I make out the new withdrawal slip for the full balance.

The teller's voice comes over the intercom again. "I'll need Mister Glasser's signature as well as yours to close the account."

"What's the most I can take?"

"The account requires a minimum balance of two-fifty."

I decide to leave him just the minimum. *That'll show him.* When the canister comes back, there are four one hundred-dollar bills, and that won't even cover one month of rent. I pull out of the drive-through and head back to the apartment complex. I don't want to use Troy's money but Adam has left me no choice.

Inside the leasing office, I glance out the picture window at the common area in the center of the complex. From here the swimming pool looks like a blue shell embedded in the ground. I imagine it filled with cool water, lying around it in the summer on one of the loungers out there, soaking up sun while the boys dive and swim.

The apartment manager hands me a stack of papers: a floor plan, copies of the rental agreements, rules and regulations. She doesn't bother to put the pages in any order so far as I can tell, or even to tuck them inside a folder. She hands me the whole wad in a jumbled stack with a pen.

I sit down across from her desk. I don't read the fine print and I try not to think too much. I sign everywhere she draws an "X." And once I've done that, I fill out the check drawn on Troy's bank account. His small, careful signature is at the bottom. The key the apartment manager hands to me is stamped *"112."* I hope it turns out to be my lucky number.

"Welcome home," she says.

ON THE DRIVE back to Church Street, I scold myself for allowing Adam to handle all our finances, for not even taking time to ask how much we have or where he has it stashed. I remember him saying many times money in a bank is lazy money. Maybe he moved some into a CD or an investment fund I don't know about. Obviously, I should have paid better attention instead of—oh, raising kids, managing the house, cooking all the meals, scheduling doctors and dentists, teacher conferences, chauffeuring the boys to birthday parties, choir practice, summer camp, swim meets, soccer games, and volunteering at the school library, all the mundane everyday things that kept our life smooth-running. A desperate feeling creeps over me again. Am I capable enough to handle things on my own? Have I let myself get so dependent on Adam, so trapped in our marriage that I can no longer function without him?

Troy's truck is in the driveway when I get to his house. It's dreary and wet today so I hurry to the front door. My coat isn't heavy enough to keep out the brisk north wind. The cold seems to burrow deep into my bones. I wish it were spring. I think I would feel better about everything if the weather was warm and flowers were blooming.

In the kitchen, Troy stands at the stove stirring in a deep black kettle. He's already showered and changed into a clean shirt. I love how the light comes into his eyes when he sees me. After I mentioned he might look good with a beard, he grew one. It only took a few days, and I was right. He does look good. The beard tickles my neck when he hugs me hello.

"I thought a pot of razzy-dazzy stew would warm us up," he says, turning back to the stove.

"Smells good." I'm not the least bit hungry but I don't say that. I throw my coat over one of the kitchen chairs.

"So, you didn't find anything?"

"Actually, I did. I signed a lease. The apartment's nothing special, but at least it has three bedrooms. There's only one bathroom though." I shrug and take the spoon from his hand. I stir the stew. A release of garlicky, savory broth fills the room. I love that he cooks. I'm not sure he realizes what a treat that is to me. "So this is—what did you call it?"

"Razzy-dazzy. I made it up." He leans down to peck me on the lips. "When do you move?" He keeps his voice pleasant, even though I know he would like for me to stay here playing house with him. Part of me might like that, too, but Joel and Cody make it untenable. Just picking them up from school every day doesn't give me enough time with them.

"I'm thinking Saturday," I say. "I've got a million things to do before then." I lay the spoon on a saucer. "I had to use the check you gave me. As soon as I find a job—"

"Yeah, yeah. Don't worry about it."

He kneads the base of my neck. He's so accommodating, and sometimes I feel guilty because I don't think I'm giving back much. With Mom and Dad still on vacation, and Carolyn on Adam's side, Troy's the only ally I have left. I'm not sure he understands how much I need him, or how much I wish I didn't.

I lean against him. "Want to help me move?"

"Not particularly." He kisses the top of my head. "But since you're hell-bent on it—"

"I've never been hell-bent on anything." I lower the flame on the burner and rotate toward him. I smooch his lips. "How long before this razzy-dazzy is ready?"

"We've got an hour."

I take the cup towel off his shoulder and lay it on the counter. "I was hoping you'd say that."

THERE IS one secret I've kept to myself for all these years. I never have cared much for sex. For me, it was more chore than pleasure, more about generosity than desire. It seemed messy and embarrassing. I never got much out of it—except for Joel and Cody, of course. But now, I take it all back. Troy makes me feel luscious, like I'm the most beautiful, desirable woman in the world; like his only mission is to leave me thoroughly kissed, drowsy, and satiated. At thirty-six, I finally understand what the big fuss is about.

Rain peppers against the window above the bed where I luxuriate like a cat after a nap. A north wind whistles through the cracks in the sill but I stretch warm and naked, wrapped in the blanket and an oxytocin-induced afterglow. I can hear him in the kitchen, my lover, my ravisher, finishing his razzy-dazzy stew. I smile, roll the pillow, over to the cool side, and listen to him move around, setting the table, the scrape and rattle of silverware, dishes, and glasses.

Slowly, the humdrum begins to creep in, needling into my brain. Telephone company. Utility company. I should start a list: groceries, linens, a shower curtain, a bathmat, shelf paper. So much to do, and no money for simple basics.

I pull the covers around me and sit up. Impulsively, I reach for the phone on the bedside table and dial. Time to stop putting this off. The answering machine comes on and Adam picks up simultaneously. I hear his voice but I wait for the recording to shut off before I speak.

"I found an apartment today." No need to waste time on niceties. "I went to the bank for money and there wasn't much there." He doesn't respond so I continue. "Are you trying to starve me now? Is that the plan? You think if I'm destitute I'll have to come home?" *Home.* It aggravates me how I continue to think of the Queen Anne as home. I have erase that notion.

I hear him sigh. "You really think I'm a bastard, don't you? No, I'm not trying to starve you, Jesus. We—Marty and I, the company—had an interest payment come due."

"You had to dip into our personal funds for that?"

I hear him breathing, but he doesn't come back with a snide remark this time. "How much do you need?"

"I left two-fifty in the account." I feel a little humbled. I expected an argument. "I'm moving this weekend. And there's furniture I'd like from the house." His silence continues. "Like the bread-safe. And maybe the wardrobe from the bedroom."

"Take the TV in the bedroom, too. I don't ever watch it. Hell, take the bed."

I can't tell if he's being snide or benevolent. "The apartment has some furniture. I don't need the bed, but I'd like to come over on Saturday and get some other things."

"We'll be around."

"I need Troy's truck, *and* his help, so he'll be with me. I wanted to let you know beforehand so there's no surprises. We can talk when I'm there."

"What else could we possibly need to talk about, Sarah?"

"The boys. The apartment has three bedrooms. I want them to move in with me."

"Oh? So you must've found a job, too." He sounds hoarse. I can't tell if he's been drinking. I listen for ice clinking, a pop-top. There's nothing.

"I have an appointment with an employment agency Monday."

"Great! Get a job. Then we'll talk about the boys."

I feel my face flush. "Did you hear me? I'm moving out of Troy's house."

"It's a step."

"I'm their mother."

"Oh? So you've remembered. Another step."

My grip on the phone tightens. I slam down the receiver. When I look up Troy is in the doorway, holding onto the door frame. I don't know how long he's been standing there. I soften my face and smile.

"That was Adam," I say.

He lets go of the door frame and eases into the room. "Hungry?"

"I called him. He won't discuss the boys moving in with me until I get a job." I hold the blanket over my breasts.

He picks up my robe from the corner chair where I left it. "Come eat some stew." I slip out of the bed and he wraps the robe around me and holds me like that for a moment in his arms. "It's going to be all right, Sarah."

"Is it?" I turn back to face him. "You keep saying that."

"Because I believe it. This part right now—this the hard part." He reaches for my hand. "But you're brave, and smart. And you're a good mother."

"I don't feel like one." I watch him slip the wedding rings off my finger. The air goes out of my lungs.

"I had the other kind of mother. . ." He lays the rings on the bedside table, on top of a book I've been reading. ". . . and I can tell the difference. You love your boys and they know you do. That's huge."

"Thank you for that." I know he's trying to make me feel better. I rub my naked finger.

"Let's go eat before it gets cold."

I let him lead the way into the kitchen.

Twenty-Three

On the drive to my house—*or rather Adam's house, the boys' house? I don't know what to call it anymore*—on the drive there Troy chatters about the work he's doing at the Judson's house. He sounds so enthusiastic about it, the challenges it presents for him, learning how to rebuild a shell-and-double-scroll pediment, whatever that is. I wonder if he was as excited about the work at my house—*Adam's house!* I sigh.

When Troy hears the sigh, he reaches for my hand and rests it on his thigh with his larger warm hand covering mine. He knows I'm apprehensive—not about picking up things for the apartment, that doesn't bother me. It's the prospect of Troy and Adam seeing each other for the first time since the breakup. I worry Adam will make a scene. I worry how the boys will react to seeing me with another man. I suspect Troy is apprehensive too but he doesn't show it. He keeps talking about cornice returns, square cuts and plumb cuts, and I wonder if he's jabbering just to calm me down.

Adam's Jeep sits under the porte cochere. Marty's Jaguar is parked at the curb. I watch Troy's face for some reaction. The corner of his jaw ripples, minutely. "Here we are," he says, sounding like we just arrived at Disneyland.

"If he starts anything, we'll leave."

"He won't start anything. Too many witnesses." He laughs.

We walk to the back door. I knock once, then push inside. It feels unnatural to knock at my own door. "Anybody home?" I call out, though I know they're all here.

A noise comes from the second floor and Cody comes clattering down the staircase. He bounds into the kitchen, his face pink and grinning. At least somebody is happy to see me. The force of his hug nearly knocks me off balance. I laugh.

"Whoa!" I rock him back and forth. He smells like the bubblegum in his mouth. "You want to go see the new apartment later?"

He nods. "I want to get a look at that swimming pool."

Adam strolls into the kitchen. He's got a beer in his hand, of course. Marty comes right behind him, a beer in his hand, too. I'm reminded of high school boys bringing their buddies to a fight behind the stadium. Adam's smile is empty, but he shakes Troy's hand. That surprises me. So he's going to act cordial. Marty gives me a hug and a wet kiss on my cheek.

"Come in." Adam throws a nonchalant look in Troy's direction and states the obvious. "We're having a beer." I planned to have a money talk with him, but not with everybody in the room. I notice the kitchen is reasonably clean, aside from a pair of empty beer cans already in the sink.

Joel appears at the landing. His head nearly rakes the ceiling coming down. He's going to end up taller than his dad. He gives me a halfhearted hug but doesn't speak. He eyes Troy without acknowledgment. So that part's done. Everything anticlimactic.

We file awkwardly into the den. I hear Cody tell Joel about the apartment but I don't hear Joel's reply. Adam has Troy by one shoulder, telling Marty about Troy's talent with a circular saw. Then Troy says something about the house he's working on—pediments again. Everybody is acting friendly. Even if it's forced, it's a relief. I decide to postpone the money talk for another day.

"Get us some more beer," Adam says, and I think for a second he means me. I bristle but realize it's Joel who has become the step-and-fetch. He doesn't seem to mind. I follow him to the kitchen. I want to talk to him and make him talk to me. I want to hear his voice, but Cody interrupts. He pulls me by the hand toward the stairs.

"Come see my hamster," he says. "Dad brought it home yesterday."

I glance back at the men. Troy is listening to Marty describe a patio cover he wants built. Adam smiles at me as if to say it's safe for me to wander off with Cody, but the smile is hollow and worrisome.

Cody's new hamster is a cute bit of fluff inside a cage. He unrolls his head and blinks at us with big, sleepy eyes. I wonder what possessed Adam to get Cody a hamster. I feel it has something to do with the apartment, either showing me up or making it more difficult for me. The hamster seems like some kind of perverse challenge aimed directly at me.

"His name's Rufus," Cody tells me. "Dad says you probably won't let me take him to your apartment."

"Our apartment," I correct, and with that remark, I'm pretty sure I'm correct about the challenge. So we're going to play emotional ping-pong with the boys. "Of course, Rufus can come."

"Watch this. He'll take food right from your fingers." Cody sticks a sunflower seed between the cage slate. The hamster takes the seed and it disappears into his mouth. A belly laugh erupts from Cody. I can see he's completely enraptured. He gives Rufus another seed and hands me the box of hamster food. "Here, you try, Mom."

I give the hamster a seed and he takes it without touching me at all. His whiskers wiggle. His cheek pouches are beginning to fill up. I laugh. "What does Snowball think of him?"

"I have to keep my door closed now." Cody grimaces. "Let's go to your apartment?"

"Our apartment." I correct him, again. "The swimming pool

doesn't have water in it right now, but this summer—" I stand, glance at my watch. Maybe we can make a quick run over there. "Let me check with Joel, see if he wants to go, too."

From the den, Marty's booming voice comes up the stairs. So the men are still OK. I rap on Joel's door, enter when he calls out. He's sitting cross-legged in the middle of his bed. A copy of *Rolling Stone* is open in front of him. He's really starting to get wrapped up in music. Maybe he'll be a music journalist. He raises his face. He has nearly perfected the bored teenager look.

"I'm taking Cody over to see the new apartment. Do you want to go with us?"

He shrugs. "Some other time."

I smooth at the bedspread. He needs a new one. This one's starting to fray. A Madonna poster hangs on the wall above his head. She's standing hands on hips, a provocative lip-sticked pout on her mouth. I haven't seen this addition to his room and it surprises me. He seems too young for pin-ups.

"The swimming pool's not open yet but you can at least see it," I say, hoping to change his mind. "And you can pick out which room you want to be yours."

"I have my own room here." He turns a page in the magazine and keeps his focus downturned. "Are you going to make me move?"

I sit on the edge of the bed. He scoots away a few inches, as if I'm to be avoided at all cost. I reach to pat his hand. "I'd like for you to, but that's up to you."

He looks off toward the closet, anywhere but at me. He slips his hand out from under mine. "I'll stay with Dad."

I feel tears burn but blink them back. This is harder than I had hoped. "OK. Whatever you want to do."

Joel looks teary, too. He cranes his neck, blinks. His teeth grind, searching for his earlier indifference. "What did you bring *him* for?" he says, and I know *him* is Troy.

"He's helping me move." I put my hand on his shoulder. He doesn't want it there either and shrugs away.

"Is he moving into the apartment, too?"

"Of course not. He has his own house."

"Where you've been living." He says it like an accusation, not a question. I'm sure Adam has given the boys the full details.

"That's been temporary. I know you're mad at me, but nobody's perfect, honey. Not even parents. It doesn't mean I don't want to be your mom anymore, or that I don't love you."

"Don't talk to me like I'm a baby." He turns his attention back to the open magazine. Silence fills the uneasy space between us.

"OK." I stand up and tears try to come again. These are harder to fight back. "If you're sure you don't want to come take a look with us."

He ignores me and turns a magazine page. I leave the room and the instant I shut the door, Cody comes out of the bathroom. I hurry to wipe my cheeks. He doesn't seem to notice the drip spots on my blouse.

"Ready, Mom?" he says.

I nod and let him lead the way downstairs. The den is empty, and so is the place in the kitchen where the bread-safe stood. The wall looks naked. We go through the back door.

The men are strapping the bread-safe down in Troy's truck. All three of them are still acting like old buddies, chatting and joking. Troy and Adam are in the bed of the truck, one on either side of the bread-safe. It startles me for a second, seeing them together and so congenial. Marty is on the ground guiding canvas around the safe.

"Let's go, Mom," Cody says, pulling at me. Adam looks up.

"Cody wants to see the apartment," I say to him.

"Take the Jeep," Adam says. "We're a long way from being through here."

I glance at Troy. He gives an almost imperceptible nod. I'm sure nobody else but me sees it. Adam takes the keys out of his pocket and tosses them to me. I catch them and smile at him, relieved and grateful he's going to make this amenable.

It's only six miles to the apartment. Six miles there and six back. This won't take long. As usual my skill with a stick shift is lacking. Cody asks to stop at McDonald's on the way. He's hungry and wants a burger with fries. He seems excited at the adventure of apartment living. I wish I could share his excitement, but I am glad he wants to be with me.

As I show Cody though the rooms, I try not to think about Joel, or how clearly disappointed he is in me. Cody likes the twin beds in the first room and decides that one will be his. He starts planning a sleepover with Bradley Harper, and maybe some of his soccer teammates. "Maybe we can stack these two beds together to make bunk beds," he says.

"I don't think that will work, honey," I say, inspecting the posts and foot boards.

We sit at the kitchen table while he eats his hamburger. I steal a few fries. We talk about school, about me finding a job. He asks if I'm ever coming back to volunteer at the library again.

"Once I get a job I don't think I'll have time. But then you can move in here with me."

"How long will it take you to get a job? Two weeks?"

I smile, pleased with his confidence in me. "Maybe." I can type and operate a computer. Surely I can land a job quickly.

We walk out into the common area inside the apartment buildings. He looks the pool over like a property inspector, then strolls over to the playground area. I sit on one of the loungers and watch him, happy about his enthusiasm. Before we lock up the apartment, I show him the blue slimline phone Troy brought from his shop. Cody picks it up to listen. "Nothing," he says.

"It's not turned on yet. They have to flip a switch somewhere but they promised it would be this weekend. I already have the number." I tell it to him and watch him say the numbers silently, memorizing them. It pleases me.

On the way back to the house, we stop at the supermarket for more boxes. Since Adam seems in such a good mood, I hope he won't mind if I take some of the dishes and linens. Maybe he'll give up half the silverware, too. I don't want to run up his credit cards but I will if he's obstinate.

It's nearly dark when we turn the corner onto our street. My eyes linger on my grand old house up ahead. I decide I will always think of it as mine, no matter what happens. I was the one who wanted it the most. All the other houses on the block are from the same era. Except for the modern cars parked in driveways, it could be a scene from the turn of the century. In my opinion, ours is the finest of the bunch, situated the way it is on a big corner lot, with its fresh paint and new columns, lights shining through the long windows.

"Daddy rehung the porch swing," I say as I notice the outline of the swing in its old position at the end of the porch.

"We all did it last weekend. Joel and me, and Dad."

I pull the Jeep under the porte cochere beside Troy's truck. It's loaded now with the wardrobe as well as the bread-safe. The television from the bedroom is packed in also, but there's room for a few more boxes. Mentally, I calculate how many boxes will fit, and what else I might need besides linens and dishes.

The second Cody and I step in the kitchen door, loud laughter and Creedence Clearwater Revival blast us from the den. The kitchen counters are littered with empty beer cans, all of a twelve-pack and maybe more.

"How long have we been gone?" I say, more to myself than to Cody. He ignores me and races up the stairs on his way, I assume, to give Joel a review of the apartment, or to feed Rufus more sunflower seeds.

I hurry through the kitchen, peer into the dining room. Marty leans on one of the big drawing doors that separate the two rooms. His back is to me but I can hear him laughing. Once I get even with him, what I see in the den stops me cold.

Adam sits at his desk with a half dozen bottles of different liqueurs scattered in front of him. Some have spilled and ringed the bottom of two empty glasses. He pours messily into both of them. "Dance!" He shouts over the music, and that's when I see the pistol in his hand. He waves it in Troy's direction, and the three of them—especially Troy—are laughing like idiots. The sight takes my breath away.

"Dance!" Adam shouts again. Troy shuffles his feet a few times. Then they both drain the contents of the two glasses.

I grab Marty's arm. "What's going on?" I say. My eyes are glued to the pistol in Adam's hand. It's like I've barged in on some fiendish nightmare. "Sweet Hitchhiker" blares from Joel's boombox.

Marty motions with his highball glass toward Troy, who dances the same marionette jig as he did a few seconds ago. "Middleton made a bad bet. Said he could drink Adam under the table. The penalty for losing is to dance."

My hand on Marty's arm tightens. "What does the pistol have to do with it?"

"It's not loaded. Don't worry."

"That doesn't answer my question. Why does he have it?"

Marty just shrugs. "Incentive, I guess. To get him to dance."

I have never seen Troy drunk and it's not a pretty sight. His eyes are shot through with red streaks. His cheeks and nose shine, mouth slack. Neither he nor Adam seems aware of me.

"Adam!" I stride forward and turn down the volume. When Troy sees me he stops his stupid dancing. "What is going on here?"

"There she is," Adam mutters. The pistol flops to one side in his hand, as if it's too heavy to hold upright anymore. In a louder voice, meant for the men, "We ran out of beer." The three of them laugh at that.

I move toward him. "Put the gun away."

"It's not loaded," Troy says, holding onto the edge of the desk. He's sweaty. His hair hangs in his face.

I take in the array of bottles on the desk. Adam lobs the pistol absently from one hand to the other, playing with it. I glare at him. His eyes bore into me. "Don't look at me like that," he says. "I'm not half as drunk as you think I am."

Troy wobbles, wipes his hand across the end of his nose. He giggles. "I sure am."

"Put away the gun." I keep my voice steady, my eyes boring holes into Adam.

Marty comes up behind me. His hand drops on my shoulder. He moves me back a few inches. "Put down the gun, pal," he says, as if now that he sees I'm upset he intends to take charge of the situation, act as mediator.

Adam ignores him and waves the barrel of the pistol at Troy again. "When you're long gone—just a flicker in her memory—I'll still be around. You know that, don't you?" Troy holds onto the desk, a goofy smile on his face. Adam laughs. "Pour us another drink."

"Wait a minute." Marty steps toward the desk.

"This doesn't include you," Adam says, and I've never heard him speak so sharply before to Marty. Troy shakes more booze into their glasses, some from each of the assorted bottles. The color changes to a putrid green when he adds crème de menthe. Adam's laugh sounds diabolical.

"Adam." My teeth are gritted. "Stop this."

Marty steps in again. "Put away the gun, pal. It's making Sarah nervous."

Adam's eyes mock me. "Aw. Is it making Sarah nervous? I'm just showing this ol' boy here how to drink like a Texan."

Hate washes over me. I lunge across the desk for the pistol, but he raises the barrel, aims it straight at Troy, cocks his thumb like he's clicking back the hammer. "Ka-bluey," he says with a hard laugh, then he opens the desk drawer. He drops in the pistol and leers at me. "There. Does that make Sarah feel better?" His voice is simpering and mean. I breathe easier with the gun out of sight, but my heart is still pounding.

Troy grabs up one of the glasses. Green liquid sloshes all around the sides of the glass and onto his shirt. He says some garbled something, like *Salut* or *Touché*, I can't understand him, as he and Adam clink glasses. They both throw back the contents into their mouths.

Adam slams down his glass so hard I'm surprised it doesn't break. He wipes his mouth with the back of his hand. "Now, *that* was invigorating," he says, then laughs. "There's more than one way to clean out the old liquor cabinet. What do you think, Sarah? You want to try a little drinkie-winkie." He holds up his glass and shakes it at me.

Troy wobbles for a second, holding onto the edge of the desk. The stupid smile on his face goes slack, then he bolts for the front door, his hand clamped over his mouth. He barely makes it outside before I hear him retch. Marty hurries after him. I hear Marty say, "How you doing, old man?" before the front door closes.

Adam roars with laughter, propping his feet on the desk. "Stick a fork in him. He's done."

"What are you doing, Adam?" I feel the flush in my cheeks and forehead. "What is the point of this?"

"No point. Just having some fun." He sinks lower in his desk chair and links his hands behind his head. His face contorts into a sort of frowning smile. "You didn't have to bring him over here. I could've helped you load the goddammed truck."

"The goddammed truck happens to be his."

"Ah, but you wanted to flaunt him in my face. You know you did." I hear the air whistle in and out of his nostrils. "I'm not an idiot. I should've blown his fucking head off."

He stares at me. I glare back. "I'm taking the boys."

"Don't you even try."

"Give me the gun."

His eyes are stones. "Not on your life."

"I said give it to me, or I'm taking the boys."

"And I said no." He grits another cynical smile and takes his feet off the desk.

I want to slap away that smile. I lurch across the desk and grab him by his shirt with both hands. "Give me the fucking gun," I say. His eyes flicker. He's not used to me using that word. "Or I will have a restraining order put on you so fast you won't know what hit you."

We stare eye-to-eye for a moment. I can tell he wants to react, maybe get physical with me, and I know he could. He could knock me across the room if he wanted. His hands close over mine and he pulls his shirt out of my grasp. He lets go of me with a shove and laughs a mean, self-satisfied laugh. Then he tugs open the desk drawer and pulls out the pistol. For a second I think he might aim it at me, but he releases the cylinder and ejects two bullets. They fall onto the desk.

"*Now*, it's not loaded," he says, and holds the pistol toward me, handle first.

I snatch it away from him. The weight surprises me as it always does. I sweep up the two bullets and shove everything into my coat pockets. "You're out of your mind."

"Excellent observation." His eyes pierce me.

Marty comes in the front door. "I think he's going to live," he says, nodding toward outside.

Adam grunts, keeps his eyes on me. "Too bad."

I hurry out the front door. Troy sits on the top porch step with his head in his hands. I sit down beside him. Suddenly, I'm shaking all over. "Are you OK?"

He gives me a bleary sideways grin. "Snockered."

I lean down to help him to his feet, and he needs the help. He takes my arm. We don't go back inside. He can barely walk a straight line, but I get him around the house to the truck and pour him into the passenger seat. He fumbles in his pockets for his keys, laughing, finds them, and drops them between the seats before he can hand them over to me.

"Oopsy," he says, and that brings on more laughter. He slides his hand down in the crack between his seat and the console.

At least he's a funny drunk instead of a mean one. I glance back at the house. Lights are on upstairs. I pray the boys didn't see any of this, or hear the ugliness. I feel guilty for leaving without saying goodbye. For a moment, I waver over whether to try to get past Adam to get them. I visualize the fight that would occur and wonder how the boys would react to a scene like that. Especially Joel. The light in Cody's bedroom goes out. The gun in my pocket feels heavy and sags my coat to one side.

"Found them," Troy says, triumphantly. The truck keys dangle from two fingers. He drops them into my hand.

Twenty-Four

In my hurry to leave, I failed to move up the seat, and once we're on the road, I can't seem to get it to budge. I drive perched on the edge so my feet will reach the pedals. I take it slow and hope the furniture in the back doesn't shift too much.

Some time on the six-mile drive to the apartment, Troy starts to snore. Once I manage to park the pickup in front of 112, I reach across and shake his shoulder. It takes an effort to rouse him, but finally, I'm able to coax him inside. We make it to the sofa where he collapses in a heap. He mumbles something incoherent, and then I realize he's apologizing. I leave him there and hurry to the back bedroom. I take the pistol from my pocket, along with the two bullets, and lay them on top of the flimsy dresser. I stare at them, remembering the scene at the house. I tug open the middle drawer. It sticks so I have to yank hard. I shove the pistol and the bullets all the way to the back.

Out in the front room, I mull over how to get the truck unloaded with Troy passed out on the sofa. I can't leave all the furniture outside overnight, so I hurry down to the manager's apartment. At first she doesn't answer the doorbell, but when she finally does, she listens patiently to my predicament. She agrees to send a maintenance man as soon as she can raise him. She reminds me it's after hours so there will be a charge for his trouble.

While I wait by the truck, I duck inside now and then to check on Troy. He's dead to the world. Adam is right about one thing: I shouldn't have taken Troy over there. Obviously, it was a mistake to think Adam could handle it. The whole episode has shaken me. I feel fluttery like there's a vibration deep inside my body.

The maintenance man comes and we unload the furniture. The wardrobe is the heaviest and most difficult to heave. We barely get it through the front door. Even with all the noise we make Troy never stirs. A mental picture of him dancing that silly jig in front of Adam's desk keeps popping up in my brain. Each time revulsion sweeps over me. I'm not sure at which one of them —Adam or Troy. I think both of them. I pay the man forty dollars. It's all I have in my wallet.

After the maintenance man leaves, I stand just inside the front door, hands on my hips, and stare at Troy, snoring on the couch. I pull off my trench coat and spread it over him. It barely reaches his knees but it's the best I can do. I go to Cody's room and dig through the boxes for a pillow. When I come back, I slip the pillow under Troy's head.

I have never seen Adam so out of control. I remember Carolyn's words when she waylaid us outside the house the other day—*He's really despondent.* I think about the boys in the house with their despondent father. Especially Joel. How much did he see, or hear, before Cody and I got back? For the hundredth time, I relive the scene with the gun. I can't shake my discomfort at leaving the boys there. I press my fingertips against my eyelids.

I don't know what I'm doing anymore, or even what the point of anything is now. Everything has gotten so complicated and twisted, so many hurt feelings and shameful things done and said. I don't know what I thought would happen—that I could just have my secret affair and go home afterward. Or that I could leave Adam, move out, take the boys, and everybody would be happy and cooperative. How naïve to imagine it could work out so simply.

My purse and car keys lie on top of a box near the front door. I grab them and ease the front door closed behind me. As I drive back to the house, I try not to speed. The clock on the dash says *10:39*. It's Saturday night. Most likely the boys will still be up, at least Joel will be. Probably Adam as well, but I'll face him when I get there.

At first, I circle the block. Marty's car is gone and all the lights are out. The house is so dark I check the porte cochere to see if the Jeep is even there. I wouldn't put it past Adam to go off somewhere drunk and leave the boys alone.

The Jeep sits in its usual place. I pull in behind it, get out, and creep up the back porch steps. I feel like a cat burglar robbing my own house. The door is locked but I still have my key. I fumble through my ring and find it.

Joel meets me just inside the kitchen door, a baseball bat in hand, ready to swing. "Mom!" He lowers the bat. "I thought somebody was breaking in."

I turn on the laundry light. It filters through the bifolds. There's a hole at the top of the one Adam broke. That should have been a warning he was unpredictable.

"I want you and Cody to come back to the apartment with me. Get your pillow and a blanket. There's no linens yet for your beds."

He shakes his head. "I'm not going."

"Joel . . ." I take him by the shoulders. He doesn't shrug me off but he's plank-stiff. "Listen to me—"

"Take Cody if you want to, but he's already in bed. So is Dad. We're OK."

It's the most he's said to me in days. I pull him tight. He doesn't hug me back but stays still in my arms. "I love you so much," I tell him.

"We're OK, Mom," he says again. He doesn't add *without you* but I feel it's what he means. "Dad'll have a cow if either of us goes with you and he doesn't know it. Stop fighting with him. Stop bringing that man over here. Things will be OK if you just stop."

I pull back, stroke the side of his face. I kiss his cheek. He has a little fuzz there. He's blaming me for everything. That's clear enough. "Joel, honey, there's so much you don't know—"

"I don't care. I'm not leaving Dad. He needs us."

At least he walks with me out the kitchen door and stands on the back steps while I pick my way to my car. My headlights beam brilliance onto the sideyard, the birdbath, the cannas, the big burr oak. Snowball sits in the flowerbed staring at me, his eyes glowing green. I resist the urge to go scoop him up and take him with me to the apartment, a fluffy, comforting teddy bear.

Troy is still passed out when I get back, still snoring. I will away the image of Adam waving the gun, the pain on his face, the contempt in his voice: *I should've blown his fucking head off.* My mind won't shut down and doesn't until dawn when I finally drift off lying on top of the bare mattress with my flannel robe for a blanket.

THE NOISE of Troy bumping around in the bathroom—water running, toilet flushing— wakes me. I open my eyes and stare at the plain white mini-blinds over the single window. For a moment, I'm disoriented, like waking in a strange dimension, but then I hear him vomit. That terrible wounded animal, gagging, moaning sound. Last night roars back and hits me. I feel nauseated, too, and depressed and pained, like my heart isn't working right.

I rise. I've still got on my clothes from last night. I go to the bathroom door and press my ear there. I hear him clear his throat and run more water. I tap two fingers and speak against the door. "Is there anything I can do for you?"

The door opens. I step back. He's using his shirt as a towel to wipe his face. "You can chain me to a post and whip me bloody."

I wince at that image. "Would that help?"

He shakes his head and follows me to the bedroom. He sinks onto the bare mattress. I sit on the edge of the bed, facing my reflection in the dresser mirror: puffy bags under my eyes, stricken face—I don't look so great myself. I long for a cup of coffee, but there's no coffee or coffeemaker. I focus on his reflection in the mirror. He lies flat on his back, staring up at the ceiling.

"How did all that happen yesterday?" I ask. "Everything seemed fine when I left."

He lets out a sigh. "I guess he wanted to humiliate me. Worked, too. I feel plenty humiliated."

I pivot on the bed so I'm looking directly at him. "A drinking contest? What were you thinking? Adam's an old pro."

"I know." He rolls to his back, wads his shirt under his head. "It got uncomfortable after you left. He started to get hostile. So I thought maybe if I had a drink with him—"

"Hostile?"

"Yeah. Making remarks. I overheard him say to Marty . . . something like, 'See if swinging dick wants a beer.' That kind of moronic stuff." He lifts his hand and lays it on my knee. It feels heavy, hot. An image of him doing that idiot dance rushes to my mind. I wish I could let it go.

"So he got out his gun, and you just let him point it at you?"

"By then I was pretty wasted. You saw the swill we were drinking. And I knew it wasn't loaded."

"How did you know that?"

"He just wanted to show it to me."

"For what reason?"

"I don't have any idea, Sarah. I can tell you're disgusted with me. I don't blame you. I'm disgusted with me, too."

"Did he *tell* you the gun wasn't loaded?"

He raises to his elbow. Alarm creases his forehead. "It wasn't, was it?"

I yank open the dresser drawer. The bullets roll like marbles. I take them out and toss them beside him on the bed. He picks up one, holds it lengthwise between his thumb and finger. He digs the other one out from under his ribs, holds that one up too. He inspects them in the muted sunlight through the window.

"These came out of that pistol?" He sits up slowly.

"I got it away from him at least." I show him the pistol in the drawer, too, take the bullets from his hand and shove it all back in the drawer. "I can't believe you would drink with him. You've said yourself a dozen times he's an alcoholic."

I move to the window, twist open the mini blind. Dust falls on the windowsill. I should be cleaning the apartment, getting ready to move in, not having this conversation. Outside, frost is on the ground and the sky is a perfect blue.

"I'm sorry," he says, quietly.

"I feel sleazy." My breath fogs the pane of glass. "Like I'm living in some trashy B movie. You could have stayed sober. Ignored his childish remarks until I got back. Joel was there. He probably heard the whole thing."

A moment passes. Silence. Then the mattress springs squeak.

"So it's my fault." He sounds gloomy. "You're the one who left me there with him, but it's my fault."

"You made the decision to drink with him."

"OK. I see." His voice takes an edge I've never heard. "He points a loaded gun at me but it's my fault, and he gets a pass?"

I glance at him in the dresser mirror. He's shrugging into his wet shirt. "This is not about Adam," I say.

"The hell it's not. First he breaks my window. Then he waves a loaded gun in my face, and you're not even planning to see a lawyer? I love you, but I can't take this shit." I turn from the window. He's buttoning his shirt. His hands shake. "I get it you're having a hard time, Sarah, and I've tried to be sympathetic. But I can't work. I can't think about anything else. And this is all just too messed up." He raises his eyes. "I can't do it anymore."

I reach out but he moves away. "What are you saying?"

He shakes his head, his mouth a grim line. "I'm saying make a decision. One way or the other." He gives me a penetrating look and heads out of the room.

Stunned, I stand there paralyzed and watch him go. In a minute the front door slams. I jump. The thin walls of the apartment rattle. I rush to the living room, start to pull the door open and run after him, but something stops me.

I move aside the drapes and look through the window as he goes to his truck. He doesn't lift his face. His collar is bunched the wrong way inside the neck of his shirt. Buttons aren't even done all the way. He throws in his jacket first, then sidles in after it. He looks desolate, and I caused that. He said he loves me and I've made him miserable. I reach for the door, grab the knob. But again, I hesitate.

Maybe he *should* get away from me, for his own sake. All I seem able to do is upend the lives of the people around me: Troy, Adam, the boys, even Carolyn. Because I'm needy and suspicious and self-centered and discontent. And now here I am in this dreary apartment, watching out the window as Troy drives out of the parking lot . . . maybe out of my life.

THE MORNING TURNS OFF GORGEOUS. If the grass wasn't brown and the trees bare, it might be mistaken for an early spring day instead of mid-January. I don't even need a coat when I step out of the apartment. There are groceries to buy, a kitchen to stock, and bed linens to find. If I keep active I can fend off the depression that threatens to engulf me.

Just as I'm about to get in my car, I notice the Jeep across the lot, backed in next to the privacy fence surrounding the complex. Adam leans on the steering wheel, arms folded, watching me through the windshield. For a moment, I pretend I don't see him, but there will be no more pretending. That's over.

I hook my purse over my shoulder and stride toward him. He rolls down the window and sits back against the seat. His eyes stay on me until I'm alongside the Jeep. "Hey, good looking," he mumbles, something he used to say to me years ago.

"Are you stalking me?"

He squints one eye up at me. "Cody told me how to get here."

"So why didn't you come up to the door and knock?"

"He couldn't remember the apartment number. I thought I would just wait till you came outside." His hand runs around the steering wheel. "I'm here to apologize."

"How long have you been sitting here?"

He aims his eyes straight ahead. "Long enough to see Middleton leave. He didn't look too good."

"So then you *did* know which apartment was mine."

He shrugs. "I figured you'd come out sooner or later."

I stare off into the distance at the entrance to the parking lot, the busy road beyond. Cars go flashing by. It's the same method he used in college, popping up from behind bushes as I walked by, standing outside my classroom smiling through the small glass inset in the door. Why do I feel so conflicted? I shouldn't even be speaking to him after last night.

"How do *you* feel this morning?" I ask.

"Fine physically, if that's what you mean. Otherwise crappy."

I go to the other side of the Jeep and get in. I hold my purse on my lap. "Adam . . ." I shake my head at him. "Why do you do it? Get so drunk and then do things you have to apologize for the next day?"

He waves me off. "Yeah, yeah."

"I'm serious. What's going on with you?"

"You knew I drank when we met. I brushed my teeth with vodka back then."

"It's different now. You're not in college."

He studies the apartment building in front of us, then glances at me. His eyes are clear but as sad as I can ever remember. "It's not in me to share you. I get so goddamned angry just thinking about you with that guy."

"You scared me last night."

"I scared me, too. I wanted to kill him, I really did." He lays his arm across the back of the seat. His hand touches my hair. "What did you do with the gun?"

"Got rid of it." I shrug out of his reach. "What have you done with all our money?"

He sighs and shakes his head. "I asked you how much you need."

"You really expect me to beg you for every cent? You wanted me out of Troy's house. Well, now I'm out but I can't live on air."

"So what do you want? An allowance?"

"I hate the sound of that word."

"Jesus Christ, Sarah. What do you want me to call it? A stipend. Like you're my intern?"

"Stipend is good. I want enough to live on until I can find my way. I quit Balcor because you wanted me to. You wanted me home with the boys, remember?"

"I still want that. I don't understand the end game here. Is it a divorce? Is that what you want?"

I look at him. His eyes are on me, too. Those sky-blue eyes I used to get lost in. I think it was his eyes I fell for first. "I don't think we can fix what's broken."

I glance at my car sitting across the parking lot under the 112 carport. I suddenly feel such a terrible sadness, but I don't want to cry. Not here. Not in front of him.

He moves and the Jeep rocks. He folds his arms and stares out the window on his side for a long moment. "Where were you going just now?"

"I have a list of things I need for the apartment."

"How were you planning to pay for it?" he asks, and I hear a note of merriment. My face whips toward him. His grin dissolves. "Oh Christ, you were going to use plastic. Please, don't." This surprises me. It's as if he read my mind. He reaches for his sunglasses on the dash. "Got that list with you?"

I pat my purse. "Of course."

"OK." He cranks the ignition and pulls the Jeep forward. "Where to first?"

WE SPEND the afternoon buying things for my apartment. Adam pays for everything with cash. He even talks me into things I hadn't planned on, like a satiny down comforter that I would never have chosen—too frilly. Too girly. It's as if he has conceded defeat, or is telling me he won't fight with me anymore. There are still things to be discussed—the boys especially—but I don't want to spoil this unexpected peace.

We have lunch at an Italian place, and we don't talk about the present situation. Instead, we joke about the people around us, make up stories about them the way we did when we were first married, before our lives got bogged down with routine and bills and responsibilities. It's been years—I can't even remember the last time—since we went shopping together. Somehow it feels like the most natural thing to be here with him. Once or twice, I almost slip my hand inside of his before I catch myself.

When we get back to the apartment, he helps me carry everything inside. We manhandle the wardrobe into the bedroom, and the bread-safe into the tiny kitchen. It takes up most of the room in there but I know I'll like having it here, with my grandmother's teapot on the shelf. We hang the shower curtain together and fix the bed with the new sheets and lacy comforter.

"It's not a bad place, Sarah," he says, watching me put shams on the pillows.

"I think it'll be all right. It's close to the schools."

He leans in the doorjamb. "Joel's not coming."

I nod, and swallow a lump in my throat. "He told me that, too."

"Give him time. I think he'll come around to the idea."

How I wish Adam could always be like this—sober and unselfish. My heart wells up. He sees it and holds out his arms. I go into them, and wind my arms around him, too. I hear the air moving in and out of his lungs. He presses my face to his shoulder.

"We've done this all wrong," he says, rubbing my back. "You should be at the house, and I should be moving in here. Do you love him, Sarah?"

Of course, I know who he means. I think about earlier this morning, as I watched Troy leave, my heart breaking in two. I move out of Adam's embrace. "Why do you have to keep asking me that question?"

"Because as soon as you say you love him I know I'll have to let you go."

"You have to let me go. We can't patch this up. Too much has happened now."

"We can try. You can still come home." He moves my hair away and when I look up, he kisses my lips. I accept the kiss but cut it off when he tries to make it more.

"Thank you for today." I keep my distance. I don't want him to try for a repeat of the kiss. He does anyway, grabbing at me.

"Come on, baby. I've missed you so much."

I shrug him off but he keeps pulling, pawing at me. Finally, I shove him away. "Stop it, Adam."

He staggers back. "So you'll give it to that fucking bastard but not to your own husband?"

"We've had a nice day. Why does it have to end ugly?"

He starts to say something else, even jabs a finger in my face, but stops short. When he turns and leaves the kitchen, he's burning red. I don't follow him to the front door, but I do run to lock it after he's gone. I lean my back against the door and take in a deep breath. Now is not the time to fall apart. I've got an apartment to finish. I go to the bedroom, change out of my skirt and into a pair of old jeans and a T-shirt.

By late evening, the apartment has begun to take shape. I need more pictures on the walls, and knick-knacks to sit around.

But I have bread and eggs, milk, shampoo, and a coffeemaker. I have a few dishes, a few pans, and I can make myself a rudimentary meal if I want.

All afternoon, especially after Adam leaves and by contrast, Troy dominates my thoughts—how caring he's been to me, understanding and patient through my tearful nights and indecision. Now, he's had enough, given me an ultimatum. But also, he said he loves me. It must have taken courage for him to say it out loud like that, even though he mixed it in with a lot of other words. I stare out the window over the sink, watching daylight fade into a smear of red, purple, pink, and yellow.

I reach for the blue phone from Troy's shop, the phone he scrubbed clean before he presented it to me. I put it to my ear. It still smells like Lysol. I've checked a dozen times today, recalling the assurance the phone man gave me that service would be turned on over the weekend. This time a dial tone hums happily in my ear.

On the third ring Troy answers. The sound of his voice brings an automatic smile. "I wonder if you can help me?" I say, in a teasing but formal voice. "I'm looking for a crafty carpenter to put a drawer in an antique bread-safe. You wouldn't happen to know of anyone with a talent for something like that, would you?"

"Sarah?" I've come to adore the weird way my name rolls from his mouth, the whisper of an *a* at the end.

"I picked up the phone and like magic, I got a dial tone." I wait for a response. Silence. "Are you still unhappy with me?"

"A little."

"Well, that's an improvement." I listen. I can hear he's still there, but he doesn't say anything else. "I haven't considered your feelings. Or how you've been affected by my big mess. And I'm sorry for that, Troy. I really am."

Another long silence comes, then, "Mess? What big mess?"

I laugh, loud and suddenly, and as soon as I do I find I can breathe again. Maybe I haven't lost him. I hear him chuckle and the sound warms me from the inside. "Don't give up on me yet."

His next silence doesn't last as long. "Are you in the mood for chili?"

"I'm always in the mood for chili." I'm smiling, happy to have his voice in my ear. "Would that be Maine chili, or Illinois chili?"

"I was going for Texas chili. But you'll have to be the judge."

I turn and the cord wraps around me. I lean against the kitchen counter. "In that case, should I bring crackers or cornbread?"

"Whichever one's quickest."

I open the overhead cabinet and take down a brand-new box of saltines. "See you in ten minutes."

I LET myself in with my key. The smell of chili meat, onions, peppers, and spices greets me. I throw my coat across the couch. I set my purse there, too. Propped against the wall behind the blue easy chair is a stack of yard signs lying on their side. I set the crackers on the chair and crane my head sideways to read the top sign:

MIDDLETON CONSTRUCTION. Free Estimates. No Job Too Small.

He comes out of the kitchen, a cup towel draped over his shoulder. I look up. The sight of him brings a big smile to my face. "You got your signs."

He moves forward, wiping his hand on the cup towel. "They were on the porch when I got here. Guess they came yesterday."

"Turned out nice."

"Yeah? What about the color? School bus yellow."

"It'll attract attention," I say, as he comes behind me and twines his arms around my waist. I lean back against him, letting the feel of his body sink into my bones. "People will notice it when they drive by."

"I got four. I figured if I ever have a really big job, four will be plenty."

"For now anyway." I close my eyes and he sways me just the

slightest bit, side to side. It's restful and sweet. I could stand for hours inside the warmth of his arms. "Did you mean to say you love me or did that just slip out?"

He kisses me above my ear. "Slipped out."

I pivot in his arms. His eyes find mine. "Because we hardly know each other."

"I know enough."

I touch his jaw, trace the outline of his mouth. "This week, while I'm looking for a job, I'm going to find a lawyer, too. You're right, it's time."

He leans down to kiss me.

Adam

Twenty-Five

Cody is upstairs packing. He's filled every box I brought home for him, plus multiple grocery sacks, a laundry basket, and anything else that will hold his things. While I fry burgers, he brings down a shoebox full of Star Wars figures and dumps them in the trashcan.

"I'm too old for these," he says when he sees I'm watching. He turns and heads back up the stairs.

I leave the burgers cooking and go inspect the plastic figures in the trashcan—men, helmets, guns, sabers, a robot or two. I pick up one for a closer look. It's Chewbacca—with a grimace of determination on his face. The green army men I played with had barely recognizable features. No detachable guns or light sabers, just WWII soldiers with platform feet. I drop Chewbacca back in the trash and flip the burgers in the skillet.

Down comes Cody again. This time he trashes books. Hardback books that came in the mail every few weeks for years. Sarah was always a strong believer in storybooks and reading to young kids to broaden their minds. She says it builds their curiosity and their ability to listen—which is why she so easily landed the job at the city library this week. I don't think she'll make enough to pay her bills, but she seems proud of herself.

"Cody!" I holler after him, as he gallops back up the stairs. "This is good stuff you're throwing out!"

"I'm too old for it," he yells back.

I plan to pretend I'm rooting for Sarah to succeed on her own, but the truth is I hope she fails with this misguided independence she thinks she wants. She complained the whole time she worked at Balcor about all the office politics, unfair promotions, unequal pay. I think she's forgotten that. I think she's forgotten a lot of things.

Joel slinks down to the kitchen. He reminds me of a panther the way he skulks around with his broody eyes. He inspects the hamburgers.

"Finished your homework?" I keep it pleasant. I never know what mood to expect from him. At least he's coming out of his room more. That's got to be a positive.

A loud *wham!* from overhead shakes the walls. Joel peers up at the ceiling. "What's with the kid?"

"You mean your brother?" I bite my lip to keep from smiling. Ever since Joel decided to stay with me and not go with Sarah, it's been like we're co-conspirators. "He's packing."

"He's driving me nuts," Joel says.

I tear a paper towel off the roll and spread it on a paper plate. We don't use the stoneware anymore. Nobody wants to load and unload the dishwasher. Soon we will switch to plastic forks and knives. They're on my grocery list.

Cody bounds back down the stairs, a herd of elephants on the wooden steps. He goes to the trashcan, pulls off the lid, and starts stirring around inside it. One by one, the Star Wars figures come back out. He wipes each one with a cup towel. Apparently, he's changed his mind about being too old. He ducks into the pantry and comes out with a sack, starts scooping the action figures into it. He looks at me and smiles his munchkin smile. He holds up the sack. "Think these will be all right packed like this?"

"Sure, buddy." I smile back at him. I really want to go over and lift him in my arms like when he was a baby, and blow a raspberry on his belly. Time goes by too damned fast.

Joel sniffs the meat. If he *were* a panther, his whiskers would be twitching. "Are these ready?"

Just as I'm scooping the burgers from the skillet, the telephone rings. I give Joel the spatula to finish. On the third ring, I reach the den phone. I wipe my greasy hands on my jeans and pick up the receiver.

"Hi, whatcha doing?" It's Carolyn with her daily check-in. I don't think she realizes she's starting to annoy me.

"Cooking supper. We're about to sit down."

"What happened with the bank?" she says, wasting no time on small talk. "Did they call the note?"

"We'll know something tomorrow. I guess we'll have to hold our breath till then."

"Is this a bad night to drop in on you?"

The idea of her coming over surprises me. We've had a couple more lunch dates, but no house visits. "Sarah's picking up Cody at seven."

"So he's really going? I still can't believe she would split them up."

I turn my back to the kitchen in case the boys are in there listening. "Well, she wants both of them. As well as the house. I got served with papers today."

"Oh no, Adam . . . she wants the house, too?" She sounds as surprised as I felt when the constable came by my office today. "God, this is all happening so fast."

"I don't think it's hit me yet."

"Is nine too early for me to come?"

"Make it nine-thirty. Who's a good divorce lawyer, Carolyn? Do you know anybody?"

"Let me ask around."

I hang up as Joel steps into the den. "Can we eat now?" he says.

"Get everything on the table," I say, my hand still on the telephone.

I contemplate calling Sarah about the papers she wants me to sign. She'll be here in an hour but I don't want a scene in front of the boys. I haven't really had the chance to think everything over. There's just too much right now. My brain feels fried.

The prism paperweight Joel gave me for some long-ago birthday or Father's Day makes a reflection on the legal paper lying under my elbows:

IN THE MATTER OF THE MARRIAGE OF
SARAH GLASSER AND ADAM GLASSER.
ORIGINAL PETITION FOR DIVORCE.

I pick up the paperweight. It feels solid and cool in my hand. I catch the light with it, steer it up the wall, around the ceiling, before I aim it again at the paper in front of me. The diamond pattern dances on the words:

The marriage has become insupportable because of discord . . . conflict of personalities . . . destroys the marriage relationship . . . prevents any reasonable expectation of reconciliation . . .

My apartment on Duval Street was four blocks from campus. We could have walked to our classes, but we never did. We drove my Mustang back and forth, hunter/gatherers stalking a parking place, sometimes finding one nearly four blocks from classes anyway, but we were too busy in love to care, singing with the radio. *"Baby, I'm-a want you . . ."*

The Duval apartment was a two-room dump, furnished, all bills paid, seventy-five a month. But the day Sarah moved in, she brought something to the place that was missing before—some unnamable something that made the paint on the walls seem brighter and the ugly gray linoleum on the floor shine. I didn't think much about it then, but I remember it now—that tight, crazy, knotted-up feeling I got just looking at her clothes hanging in my closet. But how do you keep that giddy feeling when you know a person too well? How do you hold onto the magic? It's so ephemeral, like holding onto glitter.

The boys are in the kitchen, squabbling over mustard and ketchup, complaining we don't have buns and they'll have to eat their burgers on—*God forbid*—sandwich bread. They file into the dining room with their paper plates. They sit down and immediately start kicking each other under the table. *Brothers.*

"Cut it out, you two," I say, and slip the papers into the lap drawer. I stand up from the desk and go fix my own hamburger on homey bread.

WHEN SARAH ARRIVES, I'd already cleaned up the kitchen, which mostly consists of throwing paper plates away and wiping down the stove. She comes in the back door, looking beautiful, hair tied back in a ponytail, cheeks glowing pink from the blustery wind outside. I want to be angry at her but instead the sight of her breaks my heart.

"Smells like hamburgers in here," she says.

"Boys got to eat." I motion toward the pile of boxes and bags against the brick wall where the bread-safe used to stand. "He's been packing since he got home from school."

She looks startled. "I hope I can fit all that in my car."

"I told him we'd bring the hamster over this weekend."

She sneers at me. "Gee, thanks."

Cody comes banging down the stairs. "All right, Mom! Let's load up."

She laughs and squeezes him in a hug. I see the glance she gives toward the stairs, waiting for Joel to come down, too. He surely knows she's here, but he doesn't show himself. He's not through punishing her yet.

She holds Cody at arm's length. "I left the car open. Why

don't you take some of those bags out there, and let me talk to your dad for a second."

He goes to grab up some bags, too many. I hold the door for him to hobble through with his big load. "Watch your step." He won't make it to the car with half that.

I turn back to Sarah. She opens her mouth to speak, but I go first because I know what she's going to say. "I got the papers but I haven't had a chance to go through them, yet."

"You know I'm willing to compromise."

"On everything but another chance."

She ignores me and glances again in the direction of the stairs. "Is Joel in his room? I'm going up to say hello."

"You'll be disappointed," I say, but she continues up the stairs. Cody comes back inside the door, red in the face, excited. "Come on, hotshot, I'll help with these boxes."

We fill our arms. I take the heavier ones. We file out through the door. At the car, he says, "I'll see you this weekend, Dad."

"I know, buddy. I'm just across town."

He grabs me in a bear hug.

After they've gone I stop ignoring the six-pack in the refrigerator. I crack one open and go sit in front of the TV in the den. Joel doesn't come down and I know I should go up to check on him, maybe console him if he needs consoling. It's so hard to figure out what he's thinking about these days. Truth is, I need some consoling myself. I can't remember when I felt so downhearted, no reason to get out of bed in the mornings. The company is going down the drain. Sarah wants a divorce. I'll likely have to move out of this house, give up on a custody battle. And according to the papers, she expects me to somehow pay for everything. I thought things got easier once you hit forty. So far it shows no sign of letting up.

At ten till ten, Carolyn taps on the back door. I'm nearly

through with the six-pack. Joel has retired to his room. We have a deal. He goes to his room by ten and lights out at ten thirty. It's still a school night.

As soon as I open the door, she rushes into my arms. Her perfume almost knocks me over. " Oh Adam, I just don't know what to say. Divorce . . ."

I hold back a sneeze as I lead her through to the den. I pick up the remote and turn down the volume on the TV but leave it on for background noise. She sits on the couch and eyes the beer bottle sweating on the coaster.

"I'd offer you one," I say, "but there's only the one left and I kind of need it."

"I don't drink beer. You should know that."

"Well, there's nothing else. Sorry, no wine." *Or grass,* I nearly add but don't.

She picks up her purse and starts fishing inside it. "I made a couple of calls after we talked. I have the names of two lawyers here." Her hair is up in one of those French braids and she actually looks better with her hair back. Sexy collarbones. She finds what she's looking for and drags out a piece of paper from her purse. "I can't vouch for either of these, but they did come recommended." She holds out the paper. I don't reach for it, but I do sit down on the couch beside her. "Well, you can look later." She puts the sheet on the coffee table beside my beer.

"I'd rather talk about almost anything else."

"Cody's gone?" She glances around like she expects him to pop out of hiding.

I nod, reach for the beer, take a swig. "Little guy seemed so happy about it. I think Joel misses her, too; he's just too proud to show it."

"And he thinks he needs to take care of you."

I breathe a laugh. "Probably." I gaze at her. She's easy on the eyes and takes pains to always look beautiful. Her blouse is unbuttoned down to her cleavage. I try not to stare at that but I notice.

A whole lot more about the night I went to her apartment has come back to me. It's blurry but I've decided we must have had sex. There was a lot of kissing and flirty conversation at that joint, and I have a sense we showered together. We've never discussed it again but she's taken ownership of me since Sarah left, calling to check on me all the time, taking my side in every situation. It feels odd and unworkable, but part of me needs the doting. I try to take it easy around her; however, this house call feels like a new direction.

Her eyes linger on me for a moment, and I definitely sense a change. "Are you going to fight for the house?"

"It was always more her place anyway."

"So you're just going to give her everything she wants . . . when she's the one who's at fault?"

"Well, it's the boys' home, too." I fold my arms across my chest and study her while her eyes sweep around the room, not landing on anything for long, casing the place—the eyes of a squatter. Something about how she's acting makes me wary. "So? What's up?" I say. "Why did you come all the way from Austin on a Wednesday night?"

She shrugs. "I thought you might need to talk to somebody after getting served with papers."

"You knew about the papers?"

"You told me." She gives me a toothy smile.

"Yeah, after you said you were coming over. Have you got something diabolical up your sleeve?"

"Diabolical?"

"That smile on your face."

"I don't even know what you're talking about half the time, Adam." She reaches over and lays her hand on my thigh. "I just want to help you through all this."

I look at the rings on her fingers, her long manicured nails. She gives me a little squeeze and there's something so familiar about it, something that tweaks more from my memory. I smile at her and lift her hand off my leg.

"Hey Carolyn," I say, starting in. "Question . . . did you come onto me that night? Because I've got to say, I can't see me initiating a shower. That seems pretty far from something I'd do."

"Oh, so you remember the shower?" There's a tone in her voice I don't recognize. "I thought it might help sober you up. You know, black coffee. Cold shower."

"Yeah? What was on your mind when you got in with me? Was that to help sober me up, too?" I'm not comfortable with the conversation but it's time to get it out in the open. I'm tired of evading the subject.

"What are you asking me?" She lifts one leg up on the couch and turns fully toward me. It seems designed to be provocative, and it works. "If I forced you to fuck me?"

I wince at the word. I don't know why. It's not like I don't use it myself, but it sounds vulgar coming from her mouth. I think she means for it, too. I remember water from the showerhead drowning me, her nipples, and a whole lot of soap. "I can't figure out what started it. I just wanted to talk to you about Sarah."

"Neither one of us was much concerned with Sarah. You don't remember making out on my couch? You were already hard when I got in the shower with you, so I don't think you can accuse me of seducing you. Some guys can't get it up when they're drinking."

"Yeah, OK." I've heard enough, but I still don't remember how it got started. I have a mental picture of her bending over the tile bench in her shower. I feel queasy. The back of my neck is on fire.

"I saw a movie once about a man who commits murder during a blackout . . ." Her hand ventures onto my thigh again. " . . . but I didn't know you could forget—"

I bolt off the couch. "Jesus Christ, Carolyn, I already feel like a jackass. What are you doing?"

"What am I doing?"

"Yes, what did you really come all the way here for? I don't think it was to give me the names of a couple of lawyers."

She sits in the center of the couch with a pout on her face, looking away from me, at the rocking chair with one of Sarah's crocheted Afghans flung across it. "I had news I wanted to share," she says. "But now I'm not sure I want to anymore."

"News?"

She grabs up her purse, fumbles around inside it, and comes out with a Ziplock. There's a swizzle stick thing in there with something like a Bic pen cap. She opens the bag.

"It's one of those new test kits," she explains. "It says on the box it's ninety-nine percent accurate, but I've made a doctor's appointment to confirm it."

The hair on my arms starts to stand on end. "What the hell are you talking about?"

"This at-home pregnancy test. If you take off the cap you'll see it's positive."

She forces the Ziplock into my hands. I push it away. It drops onto the cushion beside her. "Come on. You're not trying to say I caused that."

"I'm not trying to *say* anything except I seem to be pregnant. Like I said, I've made an appointment with a doctor. Want to go with me?"

"I want you to stop hustling me."

"That hurts my feelings, Adam." Her mouth turns down at the corners. "I came all the way over here to tell you because it's probably yours. And now that you've remembered, you know it's possible . . . especially since I haven't had a period since that night."

"Jesus, don't you use birth control?" My voice croaks.

"I'll admit I am kind of scattered when it comes to my periods, not always so regular. But the pill gives me migraines. So no, I don't take it. And the answer to your other question is also no. I did not come onto you. It was you who started groping me so don't act all innocent. I knew you were wasted. I don't think I have ever seen you so wasted. And I kept telling you to go home to Sarah. And you kept saying you didn't want her anymore. That you didn't love her. And you kept touching me. You know, my arms and neck. My thighs."

I have an urge to cover my ears. I don't want to know any of this after all.

She continues, "I tried to stop you. That's why I made coffee and started you a shower." She gives me a helpless look. "But you were so funny, and oh my, so drunk, and you kept on kissing me, and . . . well . . . I gave in. Because I had been wanting you, too . . . for a long time. And I thought nobody would have to know except you and me . . . well, just me, as it turns out since you couldn't remember anything."

I lean forward to rest my elbows on my knees. I clasp my forehead. My face is on fire. I stare at the floor between my feet, and all the air goes out of me. I think about that night, really concentrate: the shower stall, Carolyn in there, lots of water raining down. I think about later: Driving home. Guilt coming in the door with me. Passing by the oven light, shining so wistfully, letting me know Sarah had saved my supper. Trudging up the stairs, waking her. I was going to tell her. I was going to confess everything. I remembered it, or enough of it, that night. It was fuzzy, boozy, but I knew what I had done. Did I will myself to forget, to blank it out, to hide it even from myself, because I didn't want to take responsibility for my actions? Because I didn't want to admit to Sarah that I messed up again, that I failed her . . . easier to tell her I didn't love her anymore . . . *that* was easier . . . because it was her best friend this time. What a stupid, stupid mistake.

Carolyn sits on the edge of the couch, waiting for me to say something. She seems teary and I feel like a thug. I think about what she must have gone through, too, with all this—betraying her best friend, then betraying herself, feeling her body change, and wondering what to do.

"What about the sleazy bastard?" Our code name for Middleton. "Are you going to tell him, too?"

She shrugs. "It did occur to me to accuse him. Mess up their little love affair. Except I had already missed by the time I met Troy. Besides, he used condoms."

I feel myself swirling and sinking like somebody just pulled the plug. I force myself to give her a resigned smile. "You don't look pregnant."

"My clothes are tight." She smiles, too, and her cheek dimples.

"When is your appointment?"

She looks hopeful. I notice her white-knuckled grip on the edge of the couch cushion. "Two-thirty. Friday afternoon."

I nod. "I should be finished with the bank meeting by then."

She turns her face away, but I see a slight quiver of her chin. When she turns back to me, though, there are no tears. She reaches for my hand and I give it. She squeezes. I squeeze back.

Sarah

Twenty-Six

My new job isn't much different from the volunteer job at the school library, except there will be a check at the end of the week. And Cody and I did all right this morning sharing one bathroom. We had to sift through some of the boxes in his room for clothes, but I got him fed and to school on time. Next week I'll check on the school bus schedule.

He's supposed to be sorting out his room while I stow away the groceries we bought this afternoon, however, he keeps getting distracted. A little while ago I caught him standing on a chair pawing around on the high shelf inside the coat closet. He found an unpacked box up there and thought it might contain his missing books. It was a box I brought days ago, full of framed family photos: last year's school pictures of him and Joel, my mom and dad taken by a cruise ship photographer. I set it down on the floor in the living room.

"If you want any of these for your room, take them," I say. "We'll get Troy to help us hang them when he gets here."

"Are we going to McDonald's again tonight? I'm hungry."

The McDonald's is so close, and we stopped there again last night. Cody loves a Happy Meal, so I'm afraid this might become a continuous battle. "Troy's bringing Popeyes chicken, remember?" I say. "Now get back to putting up your clothes."

"I'd rather have McDonald's." He follows me into his room. "Hey! You think Troy can stack these bunk beds in here?" He flops down on the one he slept in last night.

"Hay is for horses." I take hold of one of the posts on the footboard. "These are not bunk beds, sweetie. They're twin beds. They won't stack like bunk beds. See, there's no connectors on this post."

"Well, maybe Troy can figure out how to do it. And make a ladder, too, like Bradley Harper's, that slides along the top rail. That'd be really cool."

I shake my head at him. "I don't think that's going to happen. Now, get back to unloading these boxes and putting away your clothes."

I leave him in his room and return to the kitchen. I'm trying to make space for all the groceries we just bought, but it's a jumbled mess, cereal shoved in, peanut butter. I'll never find anything. I miss my big walk-in pantry.

During the past two weeks since I've been here, Troy has spent the night six times, helping me get organized, moving furniture around, making love in my bedroom, and once on the couch. I'm going to miss that, too. Last time he was here he put in that drawer on the bread-safe. I love it—seems like it should have always been there. The drawer glides as slick as glass and holds my placemats and napkins.

I hear something fall in the other room. I holler out, "Cody? What are you doing?" I lean to glance down the hall and see a pile of folded towels strewn on the floor. He's trying to gather them up, but keeps dropping them, and most have come unfolded. I go to help.

"What happened? What were you doing in the linen cabinet?" I scoop up a few towels and refold them on my knee.

"I need someplace to put my toothbrush." He pushes another

bundle of towels at me. I've brought over too many. Just like in the kitchen, the linen cabinet is stuffed too full.

"Put your toothbrush by the sink. There's a holder."

"Yours is already in there."

"I don't have cooties, Cody Glasser."

He takes his Batman toothbrush into the bathroom while I rearrange the towels. "This place is too little," he grumbles.

"We'll make it work." I try to sound confident.

He's right, though. The apartment is small, a lot smaller than it seemed when I leased it. And all the boxes and detritus sitting around make it feel more crowded. Cody's room is in complete disarray. I think he's overwhelmed by it. The only things he's done are arrange his Star Wars figures on the windowsill and throw a few clothes into his top drawer.

"Think we can bring Snowball to live here?" he says.

"I don't know, sweetie, there would be a pet deposit. Don't you think he'll be OK with Dad and Joel?"

"He likes me better than he does Joel."

"Remember, though, Dad's bringing Rufus this weekend. Now, go do some more unpacking and I'll come help you when I'm through in the kitchen."

The phone rings. I race for it, thinking it's probably Troy to say he's on the way. I expected him a half hour ago. Instead, it's Adam.

"I got the papers signed and back to your lawyer today," he tells me. His voice sounds peculiar.

I'm almost shocked he signed without a fuss. I expected arguments, a settlement. I stretch the phone cord out and unload a loaf of bread from the grocery sack. "That was fast."

"Well, you should have the house. You always liked it more than I did."

"You used to like it."

"I think I'm moving back to the city. Get closer to everything, the office . . ."

"Really?" This surprises me. I twirl the long cord around my hand, and for a moment, I feel sad thinking of Adam back in the city rat race. But the elation of moving back into my house overrides. My big beautiful, homey old house. I almost cover the mouthpiece and holler at Cody to stop unpacking. I sit down on one of the kitchen chairs. "Will you rent an apartment, or buy a place?"

"I haven't gotten that far with my plans, yet." I hear him take a deep breath. There comes a silence I don't try to fill. Then he says, "Listen, Sarah, there's something I need to tell you. You're going to find out eventually so I thought I should be the one—"

"Is Joel all right?"

"Joel's fine You might want to sit down for this."

"I'm sitting." My mind races. Adrenaline begins to pump.

"It's Carolyn." He lets out a strangled laugh. "Let's see, how do I want to say this—"

And it suddenly dawns on me what he's about to tell me. It literally seers up from where it's been lying dormant all these months. I know everything, have known. It's like one of those moments of clarity you read about. Discovery of the germ; the bacteria that started it all.

"You got her pregnant," I say, and silence answers.

He exhales. "My God, how did you guess that so easily?"

I snort, and without realizing it, I'm on my feet, standing at the sink, peering out the window at the building behind ours, the row of air conditioner units, and the water hydrant with a snake-green garden hose attached.

"Because I know you" My voice is harsh. "And I know her. She wants a baby more than anything, and you can't keep your trousers zipped." I hear Cody moving around the apartment. I glance and don't see him. I realize I'm barely breathing. I gasp.

"She's due in July," Adam says. "She saw a doctor today. We went together."

"That was big of you." My mind does the math, counting back from July. I land on October. A spasm jolts through me. It takes me sideways and I feel like I might hyperventilate. So I was right all along, and they both lied to me. But Adam, especially, made me feel crazy, jealous and belittled.

"Sarah," he says, in his oh-so-sincere voice. I've heard that voice many times. It's the way he talks to clients. "I could give you the truth but you wouldn't believe it anyway."

"So don't bother."

"I've always loved you. The best way I could. And I always will."

What am I supposed to say to that? Good to know? Congratulations? I have no words. "Bye, Adam. I have a million things to do." I don't wait for him to reply. I hang up.

For a moment, I stand quietly, letting it all sink in. I expect fury or at the least indignation. I brace for it. But instead, it's as if a big dark shroud falls off me. I almost think I should be able to see it swirling around my feet like Peter Pan's shadow. My eyes land on the bread-safe, Granny Mabrey's teapot, spring flowers embossed on its side, and the turned-wood knob on the new drawer. I think about moving it back where it belongs, against the brick wall in my kitchen in *my* Queen Anne across town. My breath begins to regulate.

I lift the phone from the hook. What does it say that Troy is the first person I want to call? What does it say that I can hardly wait for him to walk in the front door? I want to find out if he's on the way. I start to dial, and that's when I hear the thing no mother ever wants to hear. A gunshot, like a cannon, explodes in the small apartment, followed instantly by the smashing of glass. It reverberates inside my head and blows out my ears. Terror follows.

"Cody!!" I tear down the short hall.

He's standing in my room, in front of the open dresser drawer, holding Adam's pistol. The lamp on the bedside table is shattered all over the corner of the room. There's a hole in the wall, too. I take it in—all of it—in a flash, as he turns to me, tearful, fear bright on his face. He holds the gun out to me.

The second shot deafens me. I lurch toward him but my legs

crumple under me. I fall against the bedroom door which ricochets into the closet door. The gun falls from Cody's hand. It bounces on the carpet. I lunge for it, but my leg is heavy. Then he's right in my face, crying, hands on both my cheeks. His nose is running. His voice sounds like he's in a well.

"Mama! Mommy! Did it shoot you? Did it? Mommy! Did it?!"

That's when I look down and watch the red flower bloom on the leg of my jeans. I press at it with my hand, but the flower keeps blooming, growing, then seeping hot onto the carpet.

"Get a towel, Cody."

"Mommy! Mama! I didn't mean to. I didn't think it had bullets. Mommy!" He's hysterical.

"Listen to me." My voice is drifting, ears ringing. "Get a towel. Call nine-one-one. Say Forest Glen Apartments. Number one-twelve." He gets to his feet. I hear him crying, running. "Cody!" I want him to come back and repeat it all to me, but the burning begins to build. My leg is on fire from the inside out.

From way off, there comes banging, and a distant echoing voice: "Miz Glasser!" That's when I start to shake, can't stop. Even my teeth clatter.

Troy

Twenty-Seven

Sarah's car sits parked in her spot, but nobody answers the door. I balance the box of chicken in my left arm and fish my keyring out of my pocket. I find the one to her apartment, splotch of blue paint on the bow of a Kwikset. A few days ago I blew a puff of graphite into the keyhole so now the key turns easily. Lights are on throughout the apartment. I call out but get no reply. I make it as far as Cody's bedroom when I see the tumble of towels on the floor in the hallway and know something's wrong. Behind me, somebody knocks on the door. It's the landlady. She stands outside, squinting through the porch light at me, clutching at the buttons on her blouse.

"Mister Glasser?" she says.

"Middleton," I correct and open the door wider.

"The neighbor heard the shots. I came as quick as I could. The little boy let me in. Poor thing was crying so hard."

"Shots?" My heart starts pumping. Immediately I think of Adam. He was served yesterday with divorce papers. That cowardly son of a bitch. If he's hurt her—

"Your wife. I'm sorry, they took her in an ambulance. The boy went, too." The woman clutches at her blouse. Her hand trembles. "I'm not sure which hospital they went to. The police came, but they left pretty quick. Nothing like this has ever happened here before."

I stop listening to her. She doesn't know anything. I shove the box of chicken into her hands. She takes it and keeps blabbing as I lock up the apartment. Seven steps and I'm back in my truck. I pull out onto the road, leaving the landlady standing there, probably still blabbing, the Popeyes Chicken box in her hands.

The first place I go to is the Glasser house. If that SOB is there, I think I might kill him. *Sarah shot?* I imagine Adam on the run, police searching everywhere. The divorce papers drove him batshit crazy, he came over here to argue and ended up shooting her. All I know is they better catch him before I do.

The Glasser house is dark inside and out. The Jeep isn't in the carport. I don't bother to stop. My mind races ahead, dreaming up another scenario. *Sarah? Shot!* My brain won't connect with that reality. It sounds like a foreign language.

I drive straight to the hospital, park, and race through the Emergency Room doors. People look at me like I'm deranged but they move out of my way. The woman at the window is no help. She tells me to try admissions at the front of the hospital. I smash my fist down on the ledge outside her window.

"No! *You* try admissions." I point at her keyboard. "She was brought in by ambulance. Sarah Glasser. Punch it in."

"Sir, I have to ask you to tone it down. Or I'll be forced to call security."

I mumble an apology and she begins to peck away on a keyboard. I can't stand still. I shift from foot to foot. "Your relationship?" she says without looking up. "How are you related to the patient?"

"She's . . ." Geez, what do I say? *She's my everything.* Too dramatic, even if it feels true. "She's my . . . my girlfriend," I say finally, thinking how insignificant that sounds. "I went to her apartment. They said an ambulance had taken her with a gunshot wound."

A man in white—a doctor? intern?—walks behind the

woman. He stops when he hears me and stoops to gaze at me through the window. "She was brought here, yes," he says. "Accidental gunshot. We sent her to a trauma hospital."

Accidental. "It was an accident?"

"The boy, I think. They weren't here for long."

He gives directions to the Austin trauma hospital. I rush through the doors the same way I came in. I squeal out of the parking lot and soon merge onto the interstate heading north. I keep a lookout for highway patrol because I am speeding way over the limit, way over what the old pickup will endure for long. Thirty minutes to Austin. Even at eighty, it takes thirty never-ending minutes.

As soon as I find a parking place, I run to the ER door. Once inside, I glance around for Trauma. I can't find a sign pointing anywhere. Someone on the hospital staff directs me toward the ICU. "There's a waiting area, there," the woman says. I'm already past her before she finishes the sentence.

The waiting room is a gang of blue plastic chairs lined up facing each other across a hallway. I spot Adam in one with both boys on either side of him. He looks as shabby as I have ever seen him in gray sweatpants, ragged HOOK 'EM HORNS sweatshirt, and gym shoes. My instinct is to charge for him, but Cody leans against him dead asleep.

Joel, in the next chair, half rises with a ferocious scowl. "What are *you* doing here?"

"Joel." Adam tugs the boy back down. To me, he says, "You got my message." He sounds relieved.

My fists relax. "What message?"

"I called to let you know what happened. Have a seat. We're waiting to hear something."

I remain standing. "I didn't get any message. What happened?"

Adam looks down at Cody asleep against him, then lowers his voice. "Cody was fooling around with the thirty-eight."

"Geez." I sink onto a chair across the hallway from them. I

remember that gun in Sarah's drawer, the loose bullets. The sick feeling starts in my gut.

"It went off." Adam looks at the boy. "He says it fired on its own. I don't know. It hit her in the thigh."

My hand goes automatically to the pack of cigarettes in my pocket then remember I'm in a hospital. No smoking signs everywhere. "Oh geez," I mumble.

"Is that all you can say?" Joel pipes in.

"Joel," Adam says. "Watch your mouth."

"Why is he here?" Joel doesn't look at me.

"Because I called him to come, that's why," Adam answers, even though that isn't why I'm here at all. That call, if he really made it, will be on my answering machine.

"Why, Dad?" Joel says. "Why did you—"

A nurse walks by, and we all look up. She smiles at us, makes eye contact, then goes on by. The place smells like Pine-Sol.

"Cody rode with her in the ambulance," Adam says.

"I heard." I imagine how scary that ambulance ride would have been.

"Stupid kid," Joel spits out. "He's such a dumb stupid kid." Adam nudges him for quiet. Joel folds his arms across his chest, clearly disgusted with everything that's going on right now. "If she doesn't make it—" he mutters.

"She's going to make it," Adam says. "Now zip it, OK?"

"I talked to the landlady," I interject. "She's the one who told me." Adam nods and looks at me questioningly. It feels weird to be sitting here talking in a civilized way with him, and with Sarah's boys present. It's too intimate, too buddy-buddy, especially after my last encounter with Adam. "She said a neighbor heard the shots. Said the police came."

"They came here, too. I guess the hospital has to report gunshots. For a minute I thought they were going to take me in for the pistol being loaded and *unsecured* as they said. I couldn't get anything coherent out of Cody," Adam says. "He was too rattled."

I stare at Cody and remember playing video games with him in the mall. Ten million thoughts race through my head. *Hit her in the thigh*—where there are arteries and bone and nerves, the potential for so much damage. An image of Adam brandishing that pistol at me comes to my mind—and me hopping around like a moron. Sarah brought the damned thing to her apartment to keep it away from her drunken husband. And Cody, he's almost the biggest victim, caught up in this rotten mess. I'm sick, just sick of it all, as sick of it as Joel with all that hate in his eyes aimed at me.

"Christ," I mumble. My elbows rest on my knees. I stare at the tile floor.

"The hospital called me," Adam says. "I'm still listed as next of kin. They had Cody. He was babbling. I think he thought he had killed her."

I shake my head. "God, I hate guns," I say to the floor, to myself, to the world.

"What's that?" Adam says.

"I said I hate guns." I say it louder and raise my head to look at him. He's watching me, too. "Look at the carelessness—I mean, your boy—Cody there—he's going to have to live the rest of his life with that scene in his head, playing over and over, the day he shot his mom. And all because of what? Some macho bullshit?"

"*I* didn't pull the trigger," Adam says, defensively.

"You might as well have. We're supposed to be grown-ups. We can't go around throwing bottles or rocks. Or breaking windows or waving a loaded pistol at each other. Christ!"

"Are you blaming me? I called you to come here, remember that, pal? I could have left you out. And now you're shaming me in front of my boys."

"That's what you should have done, Dad," Joel says. "You should have left him out."

It all reminds me too much of my own childhood, watching a train of men coming in and out, one after the other, hollering and fighting; me sleeping with a wooden rolling pin under my bed, head wrapped in my pillow to block out the cackling laughter from the other room, music turned up too loud; the smell of whiskey in the morning, smashed cigars in ashtrays, sink full of sour dishes, the seediness, and the confusion it caused me. It took me years and I thought I was over it, but I feel nauseated just sitting here with Joel staring at me like I'm scum.

"You had to humiliate me, didn't you?" I say to Adam. "Try to scare me off with your gun." I hear myself talking and I don't know where it's coming from—somewhere deep, where it's been bubbling for a while. "If not for that whole thing she wouldn't have had the gun in her apartment. Has that set in, yet?"

"You goddammed asshole. If it's anybody's fault it's yours for tearing my home apart."

"No, I think you did that pretty well on your own."

Adam comes up off the chair and I can see he's fighting mad. "You sleazy bastard," he says and lunges at me. I spring to my feet, dodge away from him. He swings with everything he's got and I duck the punch. When I come up it's with a right to his solar plexus. It deflates him. So I add a left to his kidney to sit him down. Another lesson from Harvey and growing up in South Peoria. It works. Adam bends over, sinks. I steer him backward onto the chair I just occupied.

"Stop it, you piece of shit!" Joel spits out the words as he comes headfirst at me. I don't expect it. He rams into me pretty hard. I grasp him by the shoulders and hold him back as gently as I can. I see his tears and have the urge to hug him. I know exactly how he feels.

"I'm sorry," I say to him.

"Joel," Adam grunts. He sounds done in. The gut punch. I felt it in my shoulder. Adam's outstretched fingers wave Joel in. The other hand holds onto his side.

I let go of Joel. He collapses next to his dad, misery on his face. The commotion has wakened Cody. I glance down the corridor. Nurses and janitors and all sorts of other hospital workers go back and forth on their busy errands. Nobody seems aware we exist, let alone that we just came to blows down here.

"I guess maybe I had that coming," Adam says to me.

"*Dad.*" Joel hides his face in his hands. Adam puts his arm around him. Cody sits up, clearly excited by what he just missed. I feel bad for both the boys. They can't help it their dad's a jerk.

"Truce?" Adam sticks out his hand at me. I hesitate, not sure whether to trust him. I want to slap back his hand, but finally, I grasp it. We shake.

"What does truce mean?" Cody asks. "Will somebody tell me what's going on?"

Adam keeps his gaze on me but he's answering Cody. "It means surrender, buddy. Sometimes you got to know when it's time to give up."

A door halfway down the corridor opens, and a woman doctor walks through reading the clipboard in her hand. She looks up at the group of us standing there. She gives us a wooden smile. "Are you Sarah Glasser's family?"

All four of us come to attention. She quickly scans us. I wonder what she makes of us all. *Family?* That's a stretch.

"She's awake and stable," the doctor says. "We're going to keep her in ICU tonight. Then if all goes well, we'll move her to a room tomorrow. The trajectory was fairly clean, severed a tendon so she'll be on crutches for a bit. X-ray shows some very small bone fragments, but she's awake and stable." I let out my breath. Seems like all of us do it at the same time. The doctor says, "She's sleepy but she can have one visitor at a time."

"Can she have two?" I ask, quickly. "Just this first time. Both these guys really need to see their mom." I point at the top of Cody and Joel's heads.

The doctor smiles. "Well . . . I suppose we can make an exception. This once." The doctor gathers the boys ahead of her and herds them through the metal doors.

After they've gone, Adam turns to me. "That was decent of you."

"I just needed to know she's all right. I'll come back in the morning."

"No," Adam says. "I think she'll want to see you before then." He presses his hand against his side. "God, I hope you didn't crack my damned rib. That's a mean left." He winces, sounds embarrassed, gives a little laugh. "Look, I'm ready to end this war. I signed the divorce papers. She's all yours."

Something skips in my chest. I stand straighter. "She doesn't belong to anybody but herself."

"Well, yeah, sure. Still, I'm glad you'll be there to take care of her." A smile stays fixed on his face. We study each other. I don't know what I feel—too much. I'm almost numb. "I just have one request," he adds. "Don't move into my house until the divorce is final. It's going to be hard enough on the boys for a while."

"I don't have plans for that. I have a house." I try to sound solemn but inside I'm rejoicing. She's free, or soon will be. It's over, and I'm not the loser this time. I almost smile, but not at Adam. It's going to be a while before I can bring myself to go that far.

Sarah

Twenty-Eight

The boys walk into the ICU room together. I'm so happy to see them I hold out both arms, despite all the hospital paraphernalia I'm hooked up to. Cody rushes tearfully into my arms first. He buries his head in my shoulder.

"Mama, I'm sorry. I didn't mean to—"

"Shh, honey. Hush, it's OK. They said I'm going to be OK." I rub at his arm. "Good thing you're not a crack shot, though."

He raises his head an inch to laugh, then goes back to sniffling. "Does it hurt?"

"Not one bit." Thanks to the good medicine flowing into me. I hold out my other arm to Joel who eases up on the left side of my bed—a glorified gurney. I reach for him, too.

"Eww, gross. What's that?" He points to the needle taped onto my wrist.

"Just an IV. It doesn't hurt either. They give me medicine through that." Cody continues to lie against me and I pet him. I reach again for Joel's hand.

"That builder guy just punched out Dad," Joel says in a spiky voice. His face looks tear-streaked. Cody mumbles something I can't make out.

I glance through the glass door at the nurses' station, straining as if I can see out to the waiting room. "What happened?"

"Dad took a swing, and your boyfriend punched him out. Yeah, right outside in the waiting room."

"Joel." I squeeze his hand and look right into his eyes. "His name is Troy. I know you know that. Get used to it."

"I like Troy," Cody says. "He talks funny, but he's nice."

"Don't you even care he was beating up Dad?" Joel says. "Right in the hospital?"

"Dad's not beat up," Cody says. "He was sitting in the chair a second ago. They shook hands."

"Oh lord." My eyes close, imagining it.

"Well, I'm on Dad's side," Joel says.

"I'm on Dad's side, too, but I like Troy. He's going to make me bunk beds."

"Are you and Dad getting divorced?" Joel asks, pointblank.

"Yes. I'm not going to lie to you, honey, yes, we are." I let go of his hand. It's obviously what he wants. He's been trying to move away from me for the last minute or two.

"It's because of that builder—" Joel stops when I raise my finger. I wag it and frown. "Troy!" He nearly spits out the word.

Cody finds that hilarious and starts to laugh. "He doesn't even want to say his name." Cody has crawled onto the gurney and sits on the edge.

"Shut up, turd," Joel says.

"Language!" I'm already getting tired. They're both too hyper.

"Dad says turd isn't a cuss word," Cody says.

"Well, I say it is." I ruffle Cody's head.

"Are you getting married?" Joel says, softly. "You and—" He thumbs over his shoulder toward the door.

"Troy?" I say the name for him since it seems to be so difficult for him. "The only certain thing is I'm moving back into the house with you two, and your dad is moving out. When I leave here, I'll be going home."

"What?" Cody's brow furrows into a deep frown. He gives me an incredulous look. "Oh, man! Does this mean no swimming pool this summer?"

I touch his cheek. "Sorry, sweetie. Life doesn't get any easier."

A nurse comes in and tells the boys it's time to go. They give me kisses before they leave. When they're gone, I have little wet spots from their lips on my cheeks. I don't wipe them off. When the nurse comes back, she pushes something into my IV. It takes about three seconds for the warmth of it to flow through me, and that's the last thing I remember.

I SLEEP AND SLEEP—AND sleep. I have no idea how long I'm out. It seems like an eternity. I can't keep my eyes open for longer than a few blinks before I drift off again. My dreams are erratic and plentiful. There's a large, painful bandage wrapped around my leg. It tries to pull me awake when I shift positions, but it never succeeds for long. Now and then, I hear an external voice or some odd noise. Mostly, I am deep in a nothingness fog due to the beautiful IV. I'm certain I snore.

When, finally, I do begin to awaken I find myself in a large hospital room with a wallpaper border around the ceiling. It's a blurred pattern of mixed shades of pink, blue, and turquoise. I wonder how long I've been out, how many hours or maybe days. Feels like weeks. I remember dreaming I was having a big steak. I'm so thirsty my lips feel like they will tear if I press them together.

Gradually, my eyes begin to focus. I dream I see my mother standing next to my bed. A hallucination, remnants of my drug-induced sleep. "Aren't you in Europe?" I say to the hologram beside my bed. My tongue sticks.

A cool hand takes hold of mine. A straw pushes between my lips. I suck and cold water floods my mouth. *Manna.*

"Fourteen hours ago I was, yes. I was in Amsterdam," the

hologram says. "You should go there one day, Sarah, you'll love it. Probably won't happen until the boys are grown. The world opens for empty nesters."

My eyes blink. Mother's face hovers over me. "Are you real?"

"Of course. Do you want some ice?"

I nod. She puts a sliver of ice between my lips. I suck it into my mouth. *Divine.* "I hope you didn't come back because of me." My voice flutters.

"Our trip was winding down anyway. We were both ready to get back to the States." She sounds like a world traveler now, simply saying *The States.* She takes my hand. "Dad said he'll see you this evening. He's unpacking. Adam is bringing the boys this afternoon." Her hand squeezes mine. I squeeze back.

"What day is it?"

"Sunday. It's almost noon. You've had a very long, Rip Van Winkle nap." She gives me a little smile and studies my face. "Tell me, darling, who is Troy Middleton? He seems quite pleasant but he's become a fixture out there in the waiting room."

I manage to smile back at her without cracking my dry lips. "He's in love with me."

"Oh? How nice to have an admirer," she says. "Well, it's clear he won't leave. Should I feed him?"

"He probably wouldn't turn it down." My smile expands. "By the way, I'm in love with him, too."

"How inconvenient for you." She pats my hand. I see she's still in traveling clothes. I know because she would never be caught in a turtleneck with threads of gray showing in her hair unless she came straight from the airport. "Poor Adam. I'm sure he's unhappy. So much seems to have happened since we left."

"You would never believe it."

She smooths my hair back from my forehead. I smell *Joy* on her wrist. I wish I could rise up and kiss her cheek, but I have absolutely no energy. I'm so relieved she's here.

"Adam's been a good provider," she says, "but he's always

been too taken with himself to make much of a husband. I'm not surprised you moved on to someone more devoted to you."

I picture Troy out in the waiting room, sitting patiently, wanting a smoke but not leaving to have one. That Olivia Newton John song from *Grease* starts playing in my head: "*Hopelessly devoted to you.* . . . . . ."

"Mother, please, go tell him I want to see him now."

"I'm sure that will do him a world of good." She reaches for her purse, starts rummaging through it. "Let's comb your hair first." She pulls out one of those fold-up travel brush/comb combinations. It doesn't look as if it's ever been used. She unfolds it and starts to fix my hair. "And how about some lip balm?" She unrolls a tube of Chapstick and dabs some on my mouth. "It's OK. We have the same germs." She leans down and plants a kiss on my forehead.

I laugh. "I might've believed that when I was a child."

"Look." She holds her hair back from her ears. Diamond studs decorate her lobes. And they are far from tiny. "Pierced ears."

"Beautiful." I reach to squeeze her hand again. "I'm so happy to see you. Now, please, go get Troy for me."

She brushes my cheek with the back of her knuckles, lingers, then hurries from the room. After she's gone I glance around, up at the machine blipping my vital signs, down at my right leg hooked over a foam bolster.

The next moment, there's Troy, peering around the corner first, then smiling as he eases into the room. He's wearing a black and white striped shirt, his best colors, and no cap. He reaches the side of the bed and sandwiches my hand in his warm ones.

"You look better," he says.

"You saw me before?"

He nods. "While you were beauty sleeping."

"I seriously doubt it was beautiful." I squeeze his hand. "I hear you've been moping around the waiting room."

"I wouldn't say moping." He smiles. I feel his eyes search my face. "Your mom's funny. I see where you get it."

"I'm not funny. Come closer." He slides the chair over, and I reach to touch his face. "I heard you punched out Adam."

"That's an exaggeration. Who said that?"

"The boys. The first night I was here. Whenever that was, I've lost track."

"Friday night." He shrugs. "I was a little hot-wired."

I try to sit up more. He reaches to help me and adjusts my pillow behind my back. "I'm sure he deserved it. I kind of wish I had seen it."

I lace my fingers in between his. I can tell he hasn't slept in a while. He looks tired. He's obviously been here at the hospital fretting over me although he won't admit it. Mother's right. Adam never needed me. Not the way Troy does.

My heart feels full to bursting. "You weren't counting on all this when you gave me that Christmas kiss, were you?"

"You mean the kiss you gave me?" He lets out a little laugh and brings my fingers to his lips.

"Did Adam tell you he's going to be a father again?" I watch Troy's expression. He only blinks but keeps his smile. "Carolyn. Apparently she's three months along. And apparently it's Adam's."

Troy shakes his head. "I didn't know."

"But you don't seem surprised."

"I'm more concerned about you."

He leans down and kisses me on the lips. I can only imagine what my mouth must taste like. I put my arms—even the one with the IV—around him. He rests his head against my chest, almost like he's listening to my heartbeat. I pet his hair. It's soft, shiny, and too long. I suddenly feel emotional and a little weepy.

"When I get out of here I'm giving you a haircut," I say.

"Good, that'll save me a few bucks."

I run my finger along his jaw. His beard is soft, too. "I love you."

He raises his head and our eyes lock. "Did that just slip out accidentally?"

I nod. "Accidentally on purpose."

He puts my hand to his lips, smiles, leans forward, and kisses me on my mouth and on my forehead, then goes back to just holding my hand to his lips. His smile is so broad I almost laugh.

"What? No snappy come back?" I say.

He shakes his head. "I think I'm speechless." And then he just sits there beside the bed, holding my hand and smiling at me.

Epilogue

THREE YEARS LATER

Rose Grace was born early on a Tuesday morning, March 21, 1992, just before sunrise. Because of that sunrise, Troy immediately nicknamed her Rosie. I was determined to stick to the agreed-upon Gracie, but by that evening, Rosie had already caught on with her two big brothers. Even Dad betrayed me and joined with the other male members of the family. Mother refused both nicknames, calling her Rose Grace, the whole mouthful, defying us all.

At six pounds, six ounces, Gracie's full name—Rose Grace Middleton—was bigger than she was. I was relieved she was small; it made for an easy birth, which I deserved after the ungodly months spent in bed with my feet up to stave off miscarriage. During those weeks, Mother scolded me, "Of course, you're having a difficult pregnancy, Sarah, you're forty years old. In my day women knew better than to give birth at forty."

"Thirty-nine if you don't mind," I retorted.

"Tomato, to-mah-toe," Mother said, but I knew she was delighted with this unexpected gift—this only granddaughter.

Troy gave Gracie her first bath, minutes after she was born, with an OB nurse supervising. Cody filmed it through the nursery window with a camcorder small enough to fit in one hand. Joel put music to it— "Splish Splash" of course—so I could watch later. The smile on Troy's face in the video is indescribable—pure, beautiful joy. He looks like a giant holding a tiny doll baby. Every time I watch it I laugh.

Congratulations flooded in from everywhere: aunts and uncles I hadn't seen in years, even Troy's mom sent a note, as did his sister who recently moved to Dallas. Flowers came from Mother and Dad, of course, and surprisingly a potted plant from Marty and Laura. A silver cup engraved with Gracie's name and birth date came from Unified Builders, an organization we joined after we sold our first spec house with Mother and Dad as our investors. They both have faith in Troy.

Middleton Custom Homes got half a dozen contracts after that first house. We're still working through them. Troy draws up preliminary plans himself before he gets with an architect. He inspects all the lumber, and although he subcontracts most of the work, he still does a lot of it himself, laying a floor, or building a bookcase—or shaping a mantle. I pick out the paint colors and other fixtures like tile, carpet, countertops, appliances. So we have, as it turns out, built a house together. More than one, and I love it. And he loves having me involved. So far no tree house, but never say never.

Once Gracie gets a little older, I'll take her with me to the job sites. For now, I'll just hold down the home office, which happens to be the room that used to be the front parlor, with the stained glass in the window. We've gradually been overflowing into the den, too. Most of the time nowadays I keep the big, double drawing doors between the den and the dining room shut. Clients enter the grand old Queen Anne via the front door. The family still uses the back, as always.

Our wedding took place under the porte cochere, which Mother decorated with so many stargazers we all sneezed for days afterward. I wanted to wait until at least a year after the divorce was final, but we only made it six months. Troy was in a hurry and harassed me daily. He looked beautiful with a tie on, in a gray sportscoat. I put a silver stud in his ear, the first time I had seen him with an earring. He looks sexy with it, and clients don't seem to notice.

My second wedding was a lot less spectacular than my first. But it's sweeter and more special when it's your true soulmate. Mother and Dad kept the boys while we went on a quick three-day honeymoon. Troy wanted to show me Rockland. We got there just after the peak leaf-peeper weekend, already cold enough for jackets as we sat on our hotel balcony watching the harbor ferry come and go in Penobscot Bay.

At the end of May, Joel graduates from high school. He's already been accepted at UT Austin, so at least he'll be nearby. He's more interested in music than ever, and even plays in a band on the weekends. He traded the saxophone for an electric guitar. And he has a new girlfriend every other week.

No surprise, Cody shows no interest in hunting now. He says he's sworn off guns forever. The scar on my right thigh looks like an inverted pyramid, but there are no lingering effects, except for an occasional twinge when it rains. Even though he pretends to be too big for them, he still sleeps in the bunk beds Troy eventually built for him. Those two are great pals, hanging out on weekends to check progress on job sites.

As far as Adam, the last time I saw him was at Oliver's funeral two years ago. Adam was grief-stricken. Maureen was cool but cordial. Adam's brother Brent didn't seem to remember who I was, although he did recall his nephews. Since then, I only hear about Adam from the boys. He lives in a high-rise apartment in downtown Austin. Joel will move in there once college classes start in September. Adam is always on time with support payments. The boys say he doesn't drink anymore and I hope for his sake that's true. He works for a new wealth management firm, one with a long name I can't keep straight. So far, he hasn't remarried but he does have another son, Dylan Jeffrey Glasser, who lives in Nacogdoches with his mother. Odds are, the boy is spoiled rotten.

So many twists and turns this path of life takes us, going off in one direction, doubling back sometimes, before heading off again —like a pretzel. I never dreamed I would get divorced, and remarried, or that I would love my second husband even deeper than my first—or that I would end up with a third child, a girl for the heart. Sometimes I think about that turning point, leaving my first marriage unfinished, finding Troy in such unlikely circumstances, a moth to a flame. If one little thing had happened differently or not happened at all . . . if he hadn't come to Texas when he did . . . if he hadn't sold his car so he could apprentice with Harvey in Maine . . . if I hadn't wanted to leave the city and live in an old house that needed renovations, if . . . if . . . if. . . . It was as if some primeval force guided me through the turmoil and out the other side to the place where my heart and soul now reside. A force of nature perhaps. Or maybe fate. Who knows? Life's a crapshoot, as my husband would say.

THE END